KU-799-592

Jackie Collins is the author of twenty-two international, provocative and controversial bestsellers. She lives in Beverly Hills, California.

Praise for DEADLY EMBRACE

'Jackie Collins' novels are addictive. Lord, the woman can tell a story. A rollicking tale that grabs you by the throat and takes off . . . Come on Jackie, get on with it and write the next one. I want another fix' DAILY EXPRESS

'Fans will love the latest Collins' HEAT

'Jackie is still the queen of sexy stories. Perfect' OK!

'This book has everything – a restaurant hold-up, unfaithful wives, movie stars, sex and murder' NEW YORK POST

'The unstoppable Ms Collins is back . . . raunchy, racy and fun!' B MAGAZINE

'Vintage Collins filled with sex, seduction and suspense' NEW WOMAN

'The godmother of glam/vamp fiction returns with a campy prequel/sequel to *Lethal Seduction* . . . Collins knows no limits – in salacious prose or sales. Expect *Deadly Embrace* to sizzle on bestseller lists' PUBLISHERS WEEKLY

Books by Jackie Collins

THE SANTANGELO NOVELS

Dangerous Kiss
Vendetta: Lucky's Revenge
Lady Boss
Lucky
Chances

Also by Jackie Collins

Hollywood Wives – The New Generation
Lethal Seduction
Thrill!
L.A. Connections – Power, Obsession, Murder,
Revenge
Hollywood Kids
American Star
Rock Star
Hollywood Husbands
Lovers & Gamblers
Hollywood Wives
The World Is Full Of Divorced Women
The Love Killers
Sinners
The Bitch
The Stud
The World is Full Of Married Men

Jackie Collins

Deadly Embrace

POCKET
BOOKS

LONDON • SYDNEY • NEW YORK • TOKYO • SINGAPORE • TORONTO

First published in Great Britain by Simon & Schuster UK Ltd, 2002
This edition published by Pocket Books, 2003
An imprint of Simon & Schuster UK Ltd
A Viacom Company

1 3 5 7 9 10 8 6 4 2

Simon & Schuster UK Ltd
Africa House
64–78 Kingsway
London WC2B 6AH

www.simonsays.co.uk

Simon & Schuster Australia
Sydney

A CIP catalogue record for this book is available from
the British Library

ISBN 0-7434-0406-8

Typeset by SX Composing DTP, Rayleigh, Essex
Printed and bound in Great Britain by
Bookmarque Ltd, Croydon, Surrey

This book is dedicated to everyone who lost their lives in the American tragedies of 11 September 2001. And to the incredible bravery and tenacity of the firemen, policemen and emergency workers, who toiled way and above the call of duty.

New York, Washington and in the skies.
Heroes and heroines every one.

Chapter One

Tuesday, 10 July 2001, Los Angeles

The American Airlines plane from New York was three hours late arriving in L.A., and Madison Castelli was not pleased. She'd planned on going straight to her best friend Natalie De Barge's house. However, Natalie had informed her they were meeting her brother, Cole, in a restaurant at eight, and since the plane was so late, Madison decided she'd better go directly to Mario's – a small Italian restaurant on Beverly Boulevard.

'I'll see you there,' she said, speaking to Natalie on her cellphone as she strode through the airport.

She was looking forward to getting together with her friends. The truth was that she couldn't wait to hash out the ruins of her life. Over the last few days everything had fallen to pieces. Her father, Michael, had been accused of a double murder. His estranged wife, Stella (Madison's step-mother) and Stella's live-in lover, had been shot execution-style. Now there was a warrant out for Michael's arrest, and he'd mysteriously managed to vanish.

As if that weren't enough to worry about, her boyfriend, Jake, was also on the missing list. Her wonderful, sexy, smart Jake – an ace photographer who'd been covering a drug cartel in Colombia with a couple of colleagues – had not been heard from in ten days, which was pretty damn worrying. Kidnapping was rife in Colombia, and so was murder.

All of this was on her mind as she collected her luggage, hailed a cab, and headed for the restaurant. This visit west was exactly what she needed to get her head straight. A few days of hanging with her friends doing nothing was her plan. No work. No hassles. And then she'd fly back to New York refreshed and ready to deal with anything.

Cole was already at the restaurant when she arrived. A personal trainer, Cole was an extremely good-looking, tall black man in his twenties, with a well-toned powerful physique and a killer smile. He was also gay, and proud of it.

They kissed and hugged. 'You're lookin' hot, babe,' Cole said, checking her out.

'Not me,' she said ruefully. 'And *you're* sounding very L.A.'

'Could be 'cause I live here,' he said, escorting her to their table in the corner.

'So *that's* how the men in L.A. speak to their women,' she teased.

'No,' he said, grinning. 'That's how *I* speak to the guys – keeps 'em comin', if you get my meaning.'

'You'll have to teach me,' she said, sitting down.

Madison was, at thirty, a striking-looking woman: tall and slender with full breasts, a small waist, and exceptionally long legs. She usually attempted to play down her good looks, but her green, almond-shaped eyes, sharply defined cheekbones, full seductive lips, and clouds of black hair marked her as a beauty. A very smart beauty, because she was a well-respected journalist, who specialized in insightful profiles of the rich, famous and powerful. She worked for a magazine called *Manhattan Style*, she'd recently had a book about relationships published, and she was currently working on an investigative piece about old, notorious New York crime families. Over the last year she'd discovered that her father's past wasn't exactly the way it seemed. In fact, she wasn't sure she knew him at all. She'd decided that if she wanted to find out the real truth, she had to dig for it.

'Where's Natalie?' she asked, glancing at her watch.

'Late as usual,' Cole responded. 'What else is new?'

'I miss her,' Madison said wistfully.

'She misses you, too. It's a real shame you don't live in the same city. Think of the trouble you two could get into.'

'How's her radio show going?'

'It's a big deal. She loves puttin' her voice out there. You know our Natalie – gets off on the attention.'

Minutes later, Natalie rushed in, looking glowingly pretty as usual. She was short and sassy with a curvaceous body and luscious lips. 'Sorry, sorry, sorry!' she exclaimed, grabbing Madison in a bear hug. 'Gettin' out of the studio was a total nightmare. Wow!' she added, flopping into a chair. '*I* need a drink.'

'Me, too,' Madison agreed, signalling to a waiter.

He came over. He was slight of build and very Italian-looking, with shaggy black hair and an appealing accent.

'Wine,' Natalie said. 'I'm desperate.'

'Red or white, Signora?'

'House red for everyone.'

'Good idea,' Madison said.

The waiter hurried off.

'Hmmm . . .' Natalie said, to his retreating back. 'Nice booty.'

'Yeah, *I* noticed that,' Cole said. 'Wonder what team he plays on.'

'Mine!' claimed Natalie. 'I can always tell.'

'I wouldn't be too sure,' Cole said, grinning.

'You two!' Madison exclaimed. 'Nobody's safe around either of you.'

'That's not true,' Natalie objected. 'Old people, and anyone under fifteen.'

'Shocking!' Madison scolded.

'No, merely *honest*,' Natalie said.

Suddenly their attention was taken by a huge commotion at the front desk.

'What the hell is goin' on?' Natalie said, peering over.

'Dunno,' Cole replied.

And then the unthinkable happened. Three men burst into the centre of the restaurant brandishing guns. 'Dontcha move, assholes, or I'll blow your mothafuckin' heads off.' The chilling words, yelled by a ski-masked male holding an Uzi machine-gun, immediately silenced the busy restaurant.

Madison stared at them in disbelief. It had been a tough week, and now *this*. No *way*, this couldn't possibly be happening.

But it was: Mario's was under siege and they were right in the middle of it as the three armed bandits, dressed all in black with face- and head-covering knitted ski masks, commandeered the room, blocking the exit and the entrance to the kitchen.

'Jesus *Christ*!' Cole muttered, while Natalie sat perfectly still, frozen with fear.

Madison knew why. Ten years ago when they were college roommates, Natalie had experienced a traumatic gang rape. She'd got over it and gone on to succeed in her profession as a celebrity interviewer – but this random hold-up had put her into shock.

'Stay cool, both of you,' Cole warned. He was ready to deal with anything, although even *he* knew it wasn't smart to argue with a gun.

Automatically Madison leaned over to comfort Natalie, murmuring, 'I don't believe this,' as she pushed back her long dark hair, her green eyes darting round the room, her journalist's mind taking in every detail.

'You'd better believe it,' Cole said in a low voice. 'This is L.A. Shit happens.'

'Shut the fuck up!' yelled the leader, the one with the Uzi. He was nervous and jumpy, moving round on the balls of his sneaker-clad feet like a stoned runner at the end of a particularly invigorating race. Madison noticed his eyes staring at them through the slits in his mask. They were angry eyes filled with undisguised hate. She reckoned he was young, probably still in his teens.

Young, agitated and pissed-off at the world. Just what they needed.

'Empty your fuckin' purses, take off your jewellery, an' do it now!' he screamed.

A second bandit, armed with a handgun and a crumpled black garbage bag, began running from table to table collecting money, wallets, watches, rings, cellphones, anything of value, while the third masked man herded the kitchen staff into the centre of the room.

Madison willed herself to remain calm, but her heart was already pounding. She had no desire to be a victim, she was in the mood to do something, *anything* – not just sit there and hand over her stuff like an obedient sheep.

The elderly woman at the table next to them was attempting to remove her pearl necklace. Her hands were shaking so much that she couldn't quite manage it. The younger woman with her leaned over and tried to help.

Whack! The bandit collecting the loot hit the younger woman in the face with the butt of his pistol. She slumped over, blood pumping from a vicious cut to her temple.

'Oh, my God!' gasped the elderly woman. 'What have you done to my daughter?'

Madison couldn't help herself, it was an unprovoked act of violence and she wasn't about to stand for it. 'Coward,' she hissed at the ski-masked robber. 'Big man with a gun in your hand.'

'Don't go there,' Cole managed, his voice an urgent command. 'Stay cool – stay quiet.'

Too late, the guy turned on Madison, waving his gun recklessly in her face. 'Keep outta my business, ho, an' gimme your watch.' He jerked his gun towards Natalie. 'You too.'

Natalie was still frozen to the spot, her brown eyes wide with fear.

'Give him your watch, Nat,' Madison urged, in what she hoped was a calm and steady voice.

Natalie didn't move.

'Come on, sweetie, do it,' Madison cajoled.

Natalie still didn't move.

Without warning, the gunman grabbed Natalie's arm and tore the gold Cartier watch off her wrist.

Natalie screamed, a loud, piercing scream that almost drowned out the sound of police sirens in the distance.

'Motha*fucker*!' yelled the leader, turning on Cole, eyes glinting dangerously through the slits in his mask. 'Which one a you shit-ass fucks called the cops?'

'Hey, man,' Cole said evenly. 'Don't look at *me*.'

As he spoke, the burly-looking man at the next table made his move, suddenly producing a pistol from under his jacket and aiming it at the ringleader.

'Drop your weapon,' the man commanded, in a salty voice. 'Give it up now before you get into even more trouble.'

For a second, Madison thought the ringleader was about to comply and instruct the other two to do the same. But no – even though the lights of police cars now flashed outside the shuttered front windows, he was not prepared to give up. 'Drop *your* fuckin' weapon,' he sneered. 'Or you got any fuckin' idea what *I'm* gonna do?'

The burly man stood his ground. He was a retired detective ready to make his final stab at being a hero, and no punk with a gun was about to stop him. 'Listen, sonny, don't be dumb—' he began, in a patronizing tone with the slightest hint of an Irish accent.

The word 'dumb' triggered immediate action from the gunman, who let loose with a sudden burst of gunfire. Everyone screamed. The burly man fell to the ground, a look of complete surprise on his face.

'Who the fuck's dumb now?' sneered the leader, waving the Uzi threateningly round the room. 'Not *me*!'

Then he began yelling at his two cohorts to lock the doors and get everyone into the centre of the restaurant.

'Christ!' Cole muttered. 'We're screwed.'

And Madison had a gut feeling he was right.

Tuesday, 10 July 2001, Las Vegas

Vincent Castle watched his pretty wife, Jenna, through hooded eyes. Jenna wasn't merely pretty, she was a true peach, with soft-as-satin skin, natural honey blonde shoulder-length hair, wide-apart pale blue eyes, real breasts and extraordinarily long legs.

Vincent was no slouch in the looks department himself: six feet three inches tall, with dark curly hair, intense black eyes, a straight nose, dimpled chin and worked-out body. Women creamed themselves over Vincent Castle. Not only was he a partner in the extremely successful Castle Hotel and Casino, he was also hot, and rich, and still only thirty-six. But unfortunately for the women who continually circled this fine prospect, he was married to the delectable Jenna.

And even more of an obstacle, he was faithful.

Of course, they had not been married a year yet, so there was still time.

'Jenna seems happy tonight,' the woman sitting next to Vincent on the red-leather booth said, in a sly, seductive voice, placing an elegant hand on his thigh. Her name was Jolie Sanchez, and she was the wife of Vincent's business partner and childhood friend, Nando. Jolie was also a beauty. In her early thirties she had cat-like, amber eyes, turned-down sensual lips and long, raven hair.

Vincent knew that if he wanted to, he could avail himself of everything she had to offer.

He didn't, because other men's wives were not his style, and he would certainly never go near his partner's. Besides, Nando – who was half Colombian and half French – had an out-of-control temper. He'd once cut off the ear of a rival he believed had screwed him in a deal. Unfortunately, the man had almost bled to death, causing Nando to think three times before losing his violent temper again.

'She admires movie stars,' Vincent said, casually shifting his leg so that Jolie was forced to move her hand.

'Ah, but no movie star is as gorgeous as her husband,' Jolie murmured, flattering him, which was her way.

Vincent gave a thin smile, keeping his rising anger under control. Jenna was disrespecting him the way she was draping herself all over Andy Dale, a one-hit movie wonder with lank, dirty-blond hair and a boyish grin. Andy Dale was in town for the big fight taking place the following night. He was accompanied by Anais, a surly black super-model who was quite obviously coked out of her head and couldn't care less *who* he came on to. Nando had invited them for dinner and then promptly left, making the excuse that he had a business meeting.

Lately Vincent was beginning to wonder if he'd made a wrong move in marrying Jenna. She was a very young twenty-two year old, and surprisingly inexperienced. Unlike him. He'd covered the waterfront, exactly the way his father, Michael, had taught him to. At the age of seventeen, Michael had set him up with a twenty-year-old call-girl in a suite at the MGM Grand for twenty-four hours, all expenses paid. What a deal! What a dad!

The young girl had taught him everything he was

supposed to know about pleasing a woman, and although at the time he had not appreciated sticking his tongue between her legs and eating her out, he'd soon learned how much girls got off on it.

'Good looks are not what's gonna get you places,' his father had lectured him. 'You have to be the fastest an' the smartest in business, *and* you gotta know how to treat a woman in bed. That way you'll have the world by the balls. Believe me, son, *that's* what makes a man.'

Michael Castelli was a man who did indeed have the world by the balls. Vincent looked up to him – in spite of the fact that Michael had never married Dani, Vincent's mom.

Vincent had not yet heard about the arrest warrant and his father's disappearance. He was hardly in contact with his half-sister, Madison, whom he'd only met once, several months ago under strained circumstances. Michael had called him up and said he needed a favour. Naturally Vincent had obliged.

Some favour. Madison had been locked up in a Vegas hotel room with a girlfriend, Jamie, and the dead body of a billionaire's son. Jamie had apparently screwed the poor guy into an early grave. It was Vincent's task to dispose of the body discreetly. Which he did. No questions asked.

It galled him that Madison had had no clue about Michael's other family. How come *he'd* been told the truth, and yet *she'd* led some kind of sheltered life believing she was an only child?

Well, she wasn't. There was him and his younger sister, Sofia. And if Madison thought she was any better than them, she was very much mistaken.

'Oooh, *stop*!' Jenna squealed, smooth cheeks flushed as she playfully pushed Andy Dale away.

'What's going on?' Vincent asked, keeping his slow-burning temper under control.

'Andy's trying to see if I'm ticklish,' Jenna giggled.

'Bet you are!' Andy said, lunging once again, his groping hands brushing up against her perky breasts.

Vincent stood up. 'Andy,' he said pleasantly, 'got something to show you.'

'What?' Andy questioned. He was young, famous and full of himself. He was a fucking *movie star*, for crissakes. He could have anything or anyone he wanted.

'You'll like it,' Vincent promised, with a thin smile.

'*Not*,' Jolie murmured under her breath.

Andy stood up. He was five feet eight, thanks to cleverly concealed lifts in his custom-made shoes – without them he barely grazed five-six. 'Where we goin'?' he asked, following Vincent out of the plush restaurant into the packed casino.

'There's something in my office that might interest you,' Vincent said evenly.

'If I can snort it or fuck it, I'm your man,' Andy chortled.

Cretin, Vincent thought. *Two more movies and you're over.*

Tuesday, 10 July 2001, Marbella, Spain

Sofia Castle was a wild one. Tall, tanned, lean and street-smart, she had no idea what she wanted to do with her life. A school drop-out at fifteen, she'd rejected the very thought of college, and for three years had backpacked her way round the world with two girlfriends and a gay guy. One by one they'd all got into trouble. First, one of her girlfriends was arrested in Thailand for smuggling drugs. A year later, in Hawaii, her other girlfriend ran off with a married surfer she'd known for only five days. And Jace, her gay friend, managed to get himself beaten up wherever they went.

'Like – what the hell do you *do?*' she'd demanded of him.

'Nothing,' he'd answered primly. 'Except be myself.'

Which was too gay for most people.

So eventually Sofia had ended up alone, apart from a series of transient boyfriends.

In spite of being by herself, Sofia had no desire to go home to Las Vegas, where her big brother Vincent bossed the crap out of her, and her mom was always trying to tell her what to do. Yes, the gambling capital had lost its appeal long ago, so instead of heading home, she'd moved on to Marbella and landed a job as a roving photographer covering the nightclub scene during the tourist season.

At eighteen Sofia was a free spirit, and nobody could stop her. Not her mother – who, God knew, had tried. Nor Vincent – with whom she enjoyed a love/hate relationship. And certainly not her father, Michael – a man she resented big-time because he'd never been around when she'd needed him.

Sofia was her own person. Only tonight she wasn't so sure. Tonight she was trapped in a penthouse apartment with two drugged-out Spanish playboys who were old (at least forty) and very horny.

Earlier she'd hooked up with a group of people at one of the clubs and thought they were fun. Never one to turn down free champagne and plenty of grass, she'd gone with the group to the penthouse, and suddenly everyone else seemed to have vanished, leaving her stuck with two horny old men.

'Gotta go,' she announced nonchalantly.

'No!' horny Spaniard number one said. His name was Paco and he had slit eyes and slicked-back boot-polish brown hair.

'You stay with us,' horny Spaniard number two said, making kissing noises with his lips. He was a thin man in an off-white seersucker suit and shiny two-tone patent leather shoes. He smelt of lavender.

Stoned as she was, Sofia knew it was time to get out. She also suspected that they'd locked the front door, which was *not* a good sign.

'Sorry, guys,' she said, heading for the door and trying the handle. Yes, it was locked. Damn! 'My old man's a cop,' she said sharply, furious that she'd got caught in such a stupid situation. 'So we don't want any trouble, do we? You'd better let me out. And I do mean *now*.'

'No, no – you come here, *cara*,' Paco crooned, coming after her and pawing her bare shoulder with his sweaty palm. 'We show you sexy time.'

'No, *thanks*,' she said, twisting away from him. 'And open this *fucking* door before I kick it in.'

The men exchanged conspiratorial looks, then Paco grabbed her, while the other man moved in.

Sofia experienced a shiver of fear for the first time in her young life. She knew she was in trouble, and it wasn't a feeling she appreciated.

Tuesday, 10 July 2001, Las Vegas

My daughter is in trouble. The thought kept running through Dani Castle's mind. She'd awoken that morning after experiencing a vivid nightmare about Sofia, and hadn't been able to stop thinking about her since. Now it was night-time, and she was having dinner with the man she *should* have married, but even so, she couldn't concentrate: her mind was elsewhere.

Dean King, a distinguished-looking man in his sixties, tall and barrel-chested, with a thick head of silver hair, had never failed her, never let her down. However, in spite of their long relationship, she still lived with the hope that one day Michael would marry her and legalize their union.

Michael Castelli. The love of her life.

The father of her two children, Vincent and Sofia. She loved him. She always would.

Dani, at fifty-three, was a beautiful woman, tall and naturally blonde, with smooth skin, ocean-blue eyes and a showgirl's body. Once a headline performer in Vegas, she now organized the occasional PR event at her son's hotel. She was very proud of Vincent, he'd done so well – with only a small amount of help from his dad.

Yes, Vincent could certainly take care of himself; it was Sofia she was worried about.

Both of her children bore a strong resemblance to Michael. They had inherited his deep olive skin and jet black hair. And Sofia had definitely inherited his wild streak. One memorable day, after a big fight with her dad, she'd dropped out of school and taken off, leaving only a short note.

Fifteen years old and she was gone. The only contact Dani had had with her since then was the occasional phone call or postcard.

There was nothing she could do about it. Sofia possessed a will of steel, exactly like Michael, who had not seemed at all concerned by his daughter's taking off. 'The kid can look after herself,' he'd assured her. 'You gotta stop worrying.'

Easy for *him* to say.

Sometimes Dani thought the only offspring he *really* cared about was Madison, his daughter from another woman.

'What are you thinking?' Dean asked, leaning across the table and attempting to take her hand.

She pulled back; Dean's devotion was endless, maybe rejection *did* make the heart grow fonder. It certainly did in his case.

Dean lived in Houston. He owned oil wells, and was extremely rich and quite powerful in his own way.

So why didn't you marry him, Dani?

Because I never loved him.

'I'm thinking about Sofia.' She sighed, sipping her wine. 'I worry about her so much. I wish I could see her.'

Dean studied her face. 'Have you heard from her lately?' he asked.

'A few weeks ago. She's in Spain somewhere, she never says exactly where.'

'I've told you many times,' he said. 'If you want me to, I can hire people who'll find her and bring her home.'

'No.' She shook her head. 'Sofia will come back when she's ready.'

'Then you've got to stop worrying.'

God! He sounded like Michael!

'I have an early meeting,' she said, placing her napkin on the table and pushing back her chair.

'Does this mean dinner is over?' he asked, raising a quizzical eyebrow.

'You don't mind, do you?'

'Would it matter if I did?' he said, thinking that this woman drove him insane – she always had. The problem was that he couldn't stop being crazy about her. Two marriages to other women along the way had done nothing to extinguish the flame.

'Of course it would,' she lied, trying to figure out why she kept Dean in the wings.

'Well . . .' he said hesitantly '. . . I can postpone leaving and stay another day.'

It won't do you any good, she wanted to say, but she didn't. Dean lived to please her, and she lived to please Michael, whom she hadn't heard from in months. She wondered where he was and what he was doing.

She refused to call him. She had her pride.

Thirty-six years ago, at the age of seventeen, she'd given birth to his only son, and then eighteen years later, a daughter. He'd never married her, and yet there was no way she could ever stop loving him.

Yes, it's true, she thought ruefully. Rejection *does* make the heart grow fonder.

Tuesday, 10 July 2001, New York

I'm running, Michael Castelli thought. *I'm running like a rat being chased through the sewers, and I hate myself for doing this.*

But I have no choice.

I have no fucking choice.

His past had finally caught up with him, and it was either run and discover the truth, or rot in some lousy jail.

Michael knew that if he was ever incarcerated again, he would not survive.

And in Michael's world, survival was the name of the game.

Chapter Two

Michael: 1945

Anna Maria was a pretty girl. Dark-haired, with a heart-shaped face, she spoke only a small amount of English. Her husband, Vinny Castellino, had tried to teach her with not much success. He didn't mind: as far as he was concerned, Anna Maria could do no wrong. So what if she couldn't speak the language? He was there to look after her *and* the baby she was carrying.

Vinny was the proudest man on the block. He couldn't take his eyes off his wife. Such a little girl. Such a big belly.

He'd run into Anna Maria at the end of the war outside Naples. She was frightened and lonely – most of her family had perished and she was by herself. Vinny had befriended her, gifted her with chocolates and nylons, slept with her, and promised to keep in touch.

Then he'd returned to his steady girlfriend in America, and tried to forget about the young Italian girl with the big soulful eyes and voluptuous body. His girlfriend, Mamie, a flashy blonde hairdresser who lived near him in Queens, was immediately suspicious. 'You do anything you shouldn't while you was overseas?' she demanded, while treating him to a vigorous blow-job in the back of her cousin's beat-up old Pontiac.

'Course not,' he answered guiltily.

'You *sure*?' Mamie persisted.

'I'm sure,' he lied.

'You'd better not have,' she threatened, 'or I'll have your balls for earrings!'

Mamie had a colourful way of putting things.

Vinny was used to it.

'Oh, yeah – YEAH!' he yelled, reaching a satisfying climax.

The truth was, he couldn't get Anna Maria out of his head. She lingered in his thoughts, and as the weeks passed he knew he had to see her again in spite of Mamie's threats of bodily harm if he so much as looked at another woman. Mamie was marriage-minded. If he wasn't careful she'd have him marching down the aisle before he knew it.

A few months later, he still couldn't forget Anna Maria, so he informed Lani, his mother, a big-boned woman of Sicilian descent, that he was returning to Italy.

'Why you wanna do that?' Lani asked, her large, workworn hands on her ample hips. 'Europe ain't safe yet. The war's only just over with.'

'I havta go, Ma,' he explained. 'There's someone I gotta see again. It's kinda fate.'

'Fate my big fat ass,' Lani exclaimed, rolling her eyes. 'You got a girl there, aintcha?'

'No, Ma,' he protested.

'Ha! Liar!' Lani snorted, wiping her hands on her apron. 'How ya gonna pay for a ticket to Italy?'

'You'll lend me the money,' he said confidently.

And Lani did, because Vincenzio was an only child, and since his dad had passed away several years ago, she had given him more or less anything he wanted. Besides, she longed to see the back of Mamie – a feeling she'd had ever since she'd first set eyes on the blowsy blonde with the loud mouth who was certainly not good enough for her precious son. Maybe this was a convenient way of breaking them up.

So Vinny flew to Italy with his mother's blessing, and immediately reconnected with Anna Maria, who was thrilled to see him again.

Several weeks later, much to Lani's surprise, he returned home with a pregnant wife – a seventeen-year-old Italian girl who spoke barely a word of English.

At first Lani was deeply disappointed that her son had got married without her being there, but the fact that he'd found himself a girl from the old country did a lot to help her get over her initial disappointment – although it struck her that it would have been nice if Anna Maria could have waited to get herself knocked up.

Still . . . they were married, Mamie was definitely out of the picture, and Lani decided to make the best of it.

She soon fell in love with Anna Maria – everyone did. The girl had a sweetness and a vulnerability about her that were quite irresistible.

When Vinny's dad had passed on (Lani called it a heart attack – the truth was that he'd had too many beers, fallen into a drunken stupor, hit his head on a shelf, and never recovered), Lani had taken over his business, the convenience store on the corner. She ran the place herself, ordering the stock, balancing the books, and taking care of everything else that needed doing. Most often she served customers in the shop, although she employed a man called Ernie, who was way into his sixties and whom Lani considered useless.

Shortly after Vinny returned to America with his bride, Lani put them both to work. After all, they were living with her, it was only fair. She arranged for Ernie to take care of the store in the mornings, Anna Maria was allotted afternoons, and Vinny got the late shift.

'But, Ma,' Vinny objected at first, 'shouldn't I be gettin'' into business for myself? I got a wife now, an' a family on the way.'

'This *is* your business,' Lani pointed out. 'When I'm gone, the store'll be all yours, so you'd better take damn good care of it.'

Vinny loved his mom; however, he couldn't wait for the day when it *was* all his. Not that he wished her any harm, she was the best, and the good thing was that she and Anna Maria had bonded in a way he could only have dreamed of.

Early February the weather was cold and stormy. Anna Maria was huge, the birth of their baby only weeks away. Still she insisted on working at the shop, trudging through the snow and rain, always making sure she was there on time, refusing to let her mother-in-law down. Things were tough all over, and Anna Maria knew she was a very lucky girl indeed. She didn't take anything for granted. Besides, hard work was not foreign to her. Before meeting Vinny she'd worked as a maid in a hotel filled with Germans, and struggled to get enough to eat. She'd been raped twice, beaten up a few times, and in spite of her delicate appearance she'd learned to look out for herself. Then Vinny had come along and rescued her, and she would do anything for him. She adored her husband. To her he was the American dream personified. Tall, handsome, kind. What more could any girl ask for?

Weekends Ernie didn't work, so on this particular Saturday morning in February, Anna Maria was on her own. She had trouble turning the key in the rusty padlock affixed to the back door. Her fingers were swollen and she felt a touch nauseous. She'd promised Vinny that this would be the last weekend she'd work before the baby came. Lani had already spoken to Ernie about taking over her hours and he'd agreed.

The shop smelt of stale beer mixed with the faint aroma

of rancid cheese. There was a bar next door and the stale beer smell always seemed to hang in the air.

Anna Maria shivered. It was too cold to open the back window to get rid of the offending smell, so she rubbed her hands together for warmth, switched on the lights, set up the cash register, opened the front entrance, and waited for the first customers.

There were quite a few regulars, and Anna Maria had quickly learned their names. Mr Rustino, who always bought two loaves of bread and a dozen eggs. Mrs Bellimore, who requested three small bottles of club soda, then went down the block to the liquor store for a quart of gin – as if the liquor were an afterthought. The widow, Sylvana, who never purchased anything, but enjoyed gossiping.

The customers loved Anna Maria. They all asked after her health, patted her belly and inquired when the baby was coming. Even though the entire neighbourhood knew exactly when it was due, they asked anyway, happy to spend time with the sweet young Italian girl who reminded them of their roots.

As the day progressed, the sky grew dark and snow began to fall. Anna Maria busied herself cleaning up the back of the shop, making sure everything was in its place.

At a few minutes past two, a buxom blonde girl burst into the shop, accompanied by two unruly young men. None of them looked familiar, but Anna Maria smiled politely and asked if she could help them.

The blonde's heavily mascaraed eyes raked Anna Maria from head to toe. 'So *you're* the foreign tramp who tricked my Vinny into marrying you,' she sneered. 'You're not so pretty, an' fat as a sow.'

'Excuse me?' Anna Maria ventured, sensing trouble. 'My English – it is not so good.'

'I *bet* it's not,' Mamie said derisively, tossing back her dyed hair.

Anna Maria turned her attention to the two young men, who were roaming round the shop acting suspiciously as they checked everything out. One of them was flicking through the magazines, bending the pages. The other was playing with a stack of cans, almost knocking them over.

'Please. Can I help you?' she asked, emerging from behind the counter.

'Yeah, honey,' Mamie drawled. 'You can gimme back the boyfriend you stole from me. Although, on second thought, I wouldn't take the jerk back if you wrapped the dumb creep in dollar bills an' had him delivered to my door.' She roared with laughter at her own humour. 'C'mon, boys,' she said, going towards the exit. 'This place stinks of wops. I gotta smell me some clean air.'

The three of them departed, leaving Anna Maria with an uneasy feeling.

Later that day, when Vinny arrived to take over, she'd forgotten about the trio. Vinny kissed and hugged her, told her she was the prettiest girl in the world, and warned her to be careful on the short walk home because the sidewalks were slippery and a storm was on the way.

'Maybe I should lock up an' walk you home,' he suggested. 'There's nobody out anyway.'

'No.' She shook her head. 'I'll be fine.'

'You sure?'

'Yes, Vinny.'

He hugged her again, nuzzling his chin against her cheek.

She loved the feel of his strong arms round her, especially when the baby was kicking in her belly and she knew that he could feel it too. Secretly she wished for a boy. Life – the way she'd experienced it – was too tough for girls.

Half-way home she remembered the flashy blonde and her two low-life companions. There was something about them she didn't trust, especially since the girl had mentioned Vinny by name. She recalled that when she'd first started working at the shop, Lani had warned her to report anything suspicious. Well, they were definitely suspicious, and now she felt that she should have alerted Vinny.

In spite of the icy sidewalks and bitter cold, she decided to go back and tell her husband of the incident. As she turned round to retrace her steps, the baby suddenly kicked. Placing her hands on her stomach, she murmured, with a smile on her lips, 'My *bambino*. My *piccolo bambino*.'

Thunder rumbled in the distance as she neared the shop. The street was dark and deserted: most people were aware of the upcoming storm and had retreated to their homes.

Standing outside, blocking the entrance to the shop, was the blonde from earlier, a scarf tied round her brassy hair. She looked startled when she spotted Anna Maria.

'Excuse me, please,' Anna Maria said, attempting to squeeze past her.

'Not so fast, honey,' Mamie said.

'Please move. I wish to go inside,' Anna Maria said, frowning.

'I don't think so,' Mamie snapped, an arrogant tilt to her pointed chin.

'Oh, yes, I think so,' Anna Maria said, asserting herself. And with that she pushed past the blonde and entered the shop.

The sight that greeted her caused her to gasp in horror. Vinny was trapped behind the counter with his arms in the air. One of the blonde's companions from earlier had a gun in his face, while the other man was busy ransacking the cash register.

'*Bastardo!*' Anna Maria screamed, fury overtaking her as every bad memory of the violence she'd experienced in her past came rushing back. '*Bastardo! Bastardo!*' she repeated, before throwing herself at the man with the gun, arms flailing wildly, her pretty face contorted with fury.

'No!' Vinny yelled, frantically trying to stop her. 'No, sweetheart! *No!*'

He was too late. The man holding the gun reacted fast, pointing his weapon at her, shouting a rough 'Get off me, you crazy bitch!'

But still she attacked him, even though her heart was pounding out of control, and the baby was kicking in her stomach.

Vinny jumped into the fray, more concerned with saving his wife than his own safety.

Then it happened. One gunshot. Two. Three.

And the men grabbed the money and ran.

New York Times
10 February 1945

> *A baby boy was safely delivered by doctors on Saturday night, after the mother of the infant, Anna Maria Castellino, was fatally shot earlier in the evening during a store robbery. Her husband, Vincenzio 'Vinny' Castellino, was also shot and is currently undergoing an operation to remove a bullet lodged in his spine. The shooting took place at Lani's, a convenience store in Queens. The police are looking for two male suspects who robbed the store and escaped on foot with a blonde female accomplice.*
>
> *The baby boy, born several weeks premature, weighed four pounds three ounces, and is reported to be in stable condition.*

And so Vincenzio Michael Castellino entered the world.

It was quite an entrance.

Chapter Three

Dani: 1948

Dashell Livingston had three wives, even though in the state of Nevada it was not exactly legal. Dashell didn't care: he called himself a hovering Mormon and boasted to whoever would listen that it was a man's right to have as many wives as he chose. Dashell had fathered seven children, all girls, which didn't bother him because he reasoned that girls would take care of him in his old age. Girls were useful – they would never run off and desert him.

Dashell, a big man in his late fifties, with a weatherworn face and a mane of white hair cascading down to his shoulders, was a degenerate gambler. In between raising horses on his run-down ranch several miles outside Las Vegas, he would make occasional forays to the Vegas strip and score enough money to support himself and his ever-growing family for the next few months. While there, he would visit the local whorehouse and avail himself of a girl or two. Dashell had a voracious sexual appetite.

Dashell's number one wife was Olive. Almost forty, she was the mother of four of his children and quite the controller. If Dashell wasn't giving orders, *she* was.

Wife number two was Mona, a small, slight woman with

a permanently frightened expression. Mona had produced three children for her big bear of a husband.

And lastly there was Olive's cousin Lucy, who at twenty-one was the youngest of the three women, and also the prettiest, with long, corn-coloured hair and bright blue eyes. Lucy had come to live on the ranch after a bad marriage to a man who abused her verbally and beat her on a daily basis. By the time she arrived, she was fragile and exhausted.

Dashell and his two wives had offered comfort and a place to stay, and although she had not found Dashell physically attractive, she soon realized that with him she'd at least be safe.

Shortly after becoming wife number three, Lucy found herself pregnant with her first child. Regrettably, because once she discovered her condition, everyone's attitude immediately changed. Dashell became cold and distant, Olive, bossy and demanding – forcing her to do more than her share of the household chores – and Mona, who had never welcomed her into the family, chose to ignore her.

Lucy soon realized that joining Dashell's extended family might have been a big mistake.

But once in, there was no out. She had no money, no means of leaving the ranch, which was located in the middle of nowhere. *And* she was pregnant.

Dashell, Lucy soon discovered, did not believe in doctors. 'Greedy bastards. All they're after is a man's money,' he complained, in his gruff voice. 'Round here we take care of our own.'

Lucy could not believe he had no intention of taking her to see a doctor, even though she begged him to do so.

'No!' he said sternly. 'An' stop naggin' me, woman.'

Lucy attempted to elicit help from Dashell's two other wives.

'What makes you any different from us?' Olive demanded, an unsympathetic curl to her thin lips.

'I . . . I just thought—'

'Well, *don't* think,' Olive snapped, while Mona looked on. 'You'll be fine. Dashell takes care of delivering our babies round here. He's done it seven times already.'

When Lucy finally went into labour, it was in the middle of the night. With no nurses or a doctor to guide her through the pregnancy, she had no idea what to expect when her waters broke.

The lack of knowledge threw her into a panic. And when her contractions started, she began wailing aloud in pain, waking Mona, who slept in the same room along with Emily, her youngest child.

Mona sat up in bed. 'Be quiet!' she commanded. 'Stop that horrible noise. You'll wake the dead.'

'I . . . I think my baby's coming,' Lucy stammered, frightened and confused.

'You can't have it now,' Mona said, as if her very words would stop the baby from entering the world. 'Dashell's gone into town. He won't be back till morning.'

'Then you must get me to a doctor,' Lucy gasped, as another contraction swept over her with an intensity the like of which she'd never felt before. She screamed, feeling as if her whole body was being torn apart.

'Can't,' Mona said flatly. 'Dashell took the truck.'

Olive came bustling into the room, tying her bathrobe, a grim expression on her plain face. 'Bite on this,' she said matter-of-factly, thrusting one of Dashell's leather belts at her young cousin. 'And, for the love of God, stay quiet, you're frightening the children.'

'Please . . .' Lucy whispered, unbearable pain sweeping over her. 'You . . . you have to get me to a doctor.'

'You'll be fine,' Olive said, stripping off the bedcovers while Mona shepherded little Emily from the room. 'You're

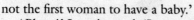

not the first woman to have a baby.'

'*Please!*' Lucy begged. 'I . . . need . . . a doctor!'

'Open your legs an' push,' Olive said sternly. 'And stop making such a godawful fuss.'

Baby Dani was born twenty-five minutes later.

Her mother bled to death.

Chapter Four

Michael: 1960

'How old are you?' the girl asked.

She was nineteen, Michael knew that for a fact. Nineteen, with big breasts, teased black hair, and the faint shadow of a moustache. Her name was Polly, and she lived a few blocks away. He'd made it his business to find out everything he could about her because he thought she was the sexiest woman he'd ever seen.

'Eighteen,' he lied. Actually he was fifteen, but he looked much older and was confident that he could get away with the lie.

'Yeah?' she said, not quite convinced.

'Yeah,' he confirmed, blinking rapidly – long, thick eyelashes curling over deep green eyes.

'Hmm . . .' Polly said, checking him out with an appraising stare. He might not be eighteen, but he was certainly the best-looking hunk of flesh *she'd* ever encountered. Her sometime boyfriend Cyril didn't come close.

'So you're really eighteen, then?' she said, convincing herself.

'Sure,' he answered confidently, adding a cocky 'Why? You think I look older?'

They were standing on the street corner outside her

girlfriend Sandi's apartment. Sandi had thrown herself a birthday party. Michael had heard about it and promptly crashed. Nobody had questioned his presence, so after a while he'd started making a move towards Polly. When she left the party he was right behind her.

The sound of Elvis Presley singing 'Are You Lonesome Tonight' came drifting down from Sandi's apartment – maybe it was a sign.

'So . . .' he ventured '. . . wanna get an ice cream?'

'Ice cream!' she snorted derisively, turning up her nose. '*You're* not eighteen.'

Actions spoke louder than words. Grabbing her by the arm, he pinned her up against the side of the building and began kissing her – shoving his tongue down her throat.

She started to push him off.

He wasn't giving up so easily. Working on instinct, he went quickly for her big breasts, fingering her nipples the way he'd seen some ugly guy do it in a porno movie he'd watched with a bunch of his pals.

Bingo! She stopped struggling and gave a little moan.

He felt an erection grow in his pants, and prayed to God that tonight he'd have somewhere to put it. Somewhere, anywhere – he was tired of his hand, and Grandma Lani lurking outside the bathroom door, yelling, 'What're you doin' in there? It better not be anythin' dirty or I'll smack you silly.'

He pressed his body against Polly's, making sure she could feel his excitement. At the same time he kept up the hand action on her big breasts while wondering if he should manoeuvre his other hand under her sweater, or was it too soon?

By this time she was kissing him back with a great deal of wet tongue *and* plenty of enthusiasm. This was a good sign.

Deciding he had nothing to lose, he slid his hand under

her sweater, pushed up her bra, and grabbed a handful of soft, warm flesh.

'Cut it out!' she giggled, surfacing for air. 'We're on the street, anybody can see.'

'No, they can't.'

'Yes, they *can*.'

'Let's go somewhere else.' He gulped, hoping he wasn't about to come in his underwear.

'Like *where*, Mr Smarty Pants?' she asked, pulling her sweater down and recovering her composure.

'How about a hotel?' he suggested.

'What kind of a girl do you think I am?' she said indignantly.

A girl I'm gonna fuck, he thought, *or die trying*.

She threw him another look. He was so damn handsome. And hot. And big where it mattered. All the things that Cyril was not.

'You got money for a hotel?' she asked. ''Cause I live with my parents, which means we can't go there.'

'I got money,' he boasted, trying to control his excitement at what might lie ahead.

'Then what're we waiting for?' she asked, slipping her arm through his.

Holy cow! He was finally about to get laid. He couldn't believe it. The furthest he'd got before was with a girl at school, Tina, and although Tina was pretty and popular, she was not into experimenting. The most he'd ever got out of her was a few French kisses and a quick feel of her breasts – which were no way as large as Polly's, and always fully covered.

'Sex is for marriage,' Tina had often told him, her pretty face deadly serious. 'We have to wait.'

Like he was ready for marriage. No way. Besides, he was fed up with waiting. He knew what he wanted, and if he didn't get it soon he'd go crazy.

He was fifteen. He was a man. He *needed* sex.

One day he'd attempted to raise the subject of sex with his dad who, unfortunately, was confined to a wheelchair. Vinny had stared at him for a few silent minutes before shaking his head in a gloomy way. 'Stay away from falling in love,' he'd warned. 'It only leads to heartbreak.'

Michael knew that his dad was bitter, although it was hard to ignore that Vinny never had a good word to say about anyone or anything. He sat in his wheelchair, either at home or in the store, and rarely spoke. If he wasn't at the shop, he was stuck in front of the TV – his favourite place.

What kind of a life is that? Michael thought. Certainly not the kind of life *he* wanted.

He'd never known Anna Maria, his mother, although he certainly knew what she'd looked like. There was a big picture of her in the centre of the mantelpiece, surrounded by candles. Every Sunday at six o'clock his dad lit the candles and said a prayer.

Lani had explained to him that some bad men had shot his mom, and that he'd been born a short time after she died. When he'd first heard the story it hadn't meant much to him, but as he grew older he started thinking about it more and more. Instead of having loving parents, like Tina, he was stuck with a grandmother who barely had time for anything except work and a dad who was trapped in a wheelchair. It made him think about his mom, and how different things might have been if she'd lived.

It had been occurring to him more and more lately that he wanted to know how the crime had happened, so one day he'd taken himself to the police station and asked if they could look up the case and give him some more information.

The detective in charge was a jovial fellow who knew Lani, so he'd obliged and retrieved the file. 'Not much to tell, except that they never caught the perpetrators,' he'd said. 'Sorry, son.'

'Did anyone find out who they were?' Michael had asked.

'Nope.' The detective had shaken his head. ''Fraid the case is closed.'

It seemed strange to him that in a neighbourhood where everyone knew everyone else's business, nobody had any clue who'd shot his mother, crippled his father and robbed the store.

Polly clung to his arm as they walked along the street. She smelt sort of flowery. He wondered what she'd smell like when he got her clothes off.

He had a plan; it wasn't as if he'd pulled the idea of a hotel out of the air. His best friend, Max, had a night job working as an assistant porter at a small fleabag hotel. Max often boasted that if he ever needed a room it could be arranged.

Okay, Michael thought. *Let's see if he's full of crap.*

The hotel was dark and dismal-looking, the pungent aroma of cooked cabbage lingering in the air. Holding tightly on to Polly, Michael marched up to the small scratched reception desk, where a bespectacled old man sat leafing through a well-thumbed girlie magazine.

My luck, Michael thought. *This has gotta be the one night Max isn't working.*

Just as he was swallowing his disappointment, Max came walking in, carrying two mugs of steaming hot coffee. Max, who was no slouch in the 'getting it' department, took one look and handed the old man one of the mugs. 'Here you go, Burt,' he said cheerfully. 'Take a break. You look like you could use it.'

'Don't mind if I do,' Burt said, getting up and shuffling into a back room.

'Hey,' Michael said to his friend.

'Hey,' Max responded, fighting to keep the knowing look off his face. Their eyes met, acknowledging the situation.

'I'd, uh . . . like a room,' Michael said, attempting to sound worldly.

'Sure,' Max said. He picked up a stained and torn reservation book and stared at the blank pages. 'Got a nice one on the first floor, number eight.' He reached back to one of the slots behind him. 'Here's the key,' he said, handing it to Michael while giving Polly a furtive once-over.

She stared at him defiantly, daring him to say something.

Michael took her hand and led her to the stairs.

'You didn't tell me you had a friend who worked in a hotel,' she said accusingly. 'No wonder you were so anxious.'

'Not that I come here often,' he explained, with a sheepish grin.

'Often enough to know what you're doing, I hope,' she said, deciding that if she was going to cheat on Cyril, she might as well make sure it was worthwhile.

'I can find my way round,' he boasted.

'I'm sure you can,' she replied flirtatiously.

The room – painted a dull green – was small and depressing. In the centre was a narrow bed covered with a patchwork bedspread that had seen better days. A small window overlooked nothing.

'Hmmm . . .' Polly said, glancing round. 'Not exactly the Plaza, is it?'

'Didn't know you were here for the fancy trimmings,' Michael said, burning up with anticipation.

'Ha! Let's see what kind of fancy trimmings *you've* got,' she said, licking her lips in a very suggestive way.

He was breathing fast. This was quite an experience. He had a girl, his fantasy girl, right in front of him in a hotel room with a bed. And now it occurred to him that he wasn't *exactly* sure what he was supposed to do. Yes, he knew he had to touch her tits. Yes, he knew he had to kiss her in a passionate way. But what did he do after that? Just shove it in? Was that what she expected?

It would have been nice if his dad had given him some guidelines. His pals at school weren't much help either. Virgins, every one, much as they claimed otherwise. He was the first one doing the dirty deed and he couldn't wait.

Polly sashayed into the tiny bathroom. 'I'll be right out,' she called, shutting the door behind her.

He hurriedly pulled the bedspread off the bed. A roach ran across the once-white sheets. He hit it with his shoe and flipped the body behind a chair. Girls didn't like crawly things, he knew that.

Should he take his pants off, or keep 'em on? That was the burning question. He decided to keep them on.

When Polly emerged a few minutes later she'd removed her sweater, but she still had on her knee-high white boots, fake leather mini-skirt, and a white bra. 'So,' she said, facing him, a challenging look in her eyes, 'you gonna fly me to the moon, or what?'

He grabbed her with a show of strength and began kissing her again, pushing his tongue round her teeth, kneading her breasts, reaching for the clip at the back of her bra, struggling to get it off.

Impatiently, she helped him. The bra came off and her breasts tumbled out, big and round, with enormous nipples.

Jeez! Once again, he almost came in his pants.

Somehow he managed to maintain control, and by the time the two of them fell back on the bed, he'd decided he was going to try to savour every moment of this fantastic new experience, make it last as long as he could. Which, the way he was going, was not about to be too long.

*

'Where you bin?' Grandmother Lani demanded the moment Michael walked through the door. She was always questioning him, criticizing his friends and trying to find out what he was up to. She drove him nuts.

'What?' he mumbled, hardly in the mood for conversation. He had one goal, and that was to make it to the safety of his room, where he could relive the whole incredible experience with Polly, and maybe jerk off, because he was already horny again.

'I *said* where you bin, young man?' Lani repeated, folding her arms across her chest.

He wondered if she suspected he'd just got laid. Grandma Lani was very intuitive.

Vinny, glued to the TV watching *The Andy Griffith Show*, didn't bother looking up.

'I was, uh . . . out with some pals,' Michael said.

'Those boys you hang round with are nothing but trouble,' Lani complained. 'You should spend more time at home with us.'

Sure, he thought. *That'd be a laugh a minute*.

'Anyway,' she continued, 'some girl dropped by with cookies for you. Seemed sweet enough.'

'Who was she?'

'I think her name was Tina.'

'Oh, yeah,' he said, suddenly remembering that he'd promised to call her and hadn't. She'd probably come snooping round to see what he was up to – girls were like that, always wanting to know everything. 'She ask where I was?'

'She did,' Lani said. 'Only I couldn't tell her, could I? 'Cause you don't tell me anything, do you?'

'I was with the guys,' he said, repeating himself. 'Y'know, Max an' Charlie.'

'Those two louts,' Lani said, her voice full of disapproval. 'I hope you weren't smoking.'

'Who, me?' he said innocently.

'All boys smoke,' Lani grumbled. 'Don't think I don't know what you get up to, young man. And you'd better not let me catch you. Smokin's a filthy habit. I *hate* filthy habits.'

I know that, he thought, attempting to slide out of the room.

'Don't you want your cookies?' she asked, coming after him.

He mumbled a quick 'No.'

'And you'd better not forget, you're working in the store tomorrow.'

'How many times I got t'tell you?' Vinny said, dragging his eyes away from the TV. 'Michael does *not* work at the store on Saturdays.'

'That's ridiculous!' Lani snorted. 'It's just a superstition on your part.'

'No, it's *not*,' he said, turning to his son. 'You hear me, Michael? You will *not* work there on a Saturday. Don't listen to her.'

'God help me!' Lani sighed, throwing her hands in the air. 'Somebody save me from these two impossible men.'

''S all right, Grams,' Michael said, trying to placate her. 'I'll do whatever you want.'

'No, you *won't*,' Vinny interrupted fiercely. 'You do not go near that place on a Saturday as a sign of respect for your dead mother. You understand me?'

'Yes, yes,' Lani said irritably. 'He understands. I'll get extra help if you force me to. Things are bad enough, but what do you care if I have to pay for another pair of hands?'

'Do that,' Vinny said, returning his attention to the TV.

Michael escaped to his bedroom and slammed the door. The room was small, but at least it was all his. On the wall he had a large, blow-up poster of Wilt Chamberlain tacked up next to a glamorous picture of Elizabeth Taylor lounging on a leopard-print couch in a sexy white swimsuit.

Tonight he didn't need the inspiration of Elizabeth. Tonight he would sleep like the man he now was.

Chapter Five

Dani: 1961

The day she got her period, Dani knew she had to escape from the godawful place she called home. At thirteen she was still a child, although physically she looked like a young woman, with her blossoming body, gossamer yellow hair, clear blue eyes and fine features.

'Can't wait for this one t'be of an age,' her daddy often said, to anyone who'd listen. 'She's as ripe as a peach ready for the pickin'.'

'You'd better watch out,' Emily, one of her older half-sisters warned her. 'Soon's he knows you're bleedin', he'll be at you.'

'No,' Dani said defiantly. 'I won't let him.'

'Try stoppin' him,' Emily said. 'He'll force you, exactly the same as he did me.'

Little did Emily know that Dashell had already molested Dani. When she was younger he'd sometimes take her into his bedroom, lock the door, and make her touch him. 'When you're a big girl we'll do a lot more than this,' he'd promised, with an evil chuckle.

'You mean y-you've slept with him?' Dani stammered, keeping her secret to herself.

'Wasn't *my* choice,' Emily said, turning up her nose at the memory. 'He's a pig.'

'That's horrible! Disgusting!' Dani said, shuddering.

'It'll be your turn next,' Emily warned.

Emily was short, with light brown frizzy hair, a compact body, and big breasts. She was seventeen and quite smart. Dani worshipped her and followed her around whenever she could.

Although over seventy, Dashell took advantage of all the female members of his family. Since Lucy's unfortunate death (they'd buried her in the back garden and told Dani when she was old enough that Olive was her mother) he'd taken on two more wives. One was an ex-prostitute, the other a teenage runaway. Between them they'd given him five more children.

Dashell ruled his large household like the Pasha he imagined himself to be. All seven of the older girls had to sleep with him whenever he summoned them, and so did his four wives. Recently two of his daughters had become pregnant by him. He called it 'the grand circle of life'.

Dani dreaded the day when he would come after her. Emily was right, she knew it would be soon.

'If you don't want him on top of you, you'd better run,' Emily said. 'God! I wish I had.'

'Run where?' she asked.

'Anywhere – as long as it's away from here.'

'Will you come with me?'

'I might,' Emily answered mysteriously. 'The thing is, if we get caught he'll beat the bejesus out of us. That man is full of vengeance – he don't care what he does.'

Emily knew things the others didn't on account of the fact that she'd palled up with Sam Froog, a cocky young man with bright red hair who occasionally worked part-time at the ranch and had eyes for her. She liked him too. He smuggled her books and magazines, and from them she learned plenty about the outside world, information she sometimes shared with Dani.

Sam rode in on his motorcycle for a few days every month. He'd sat next to Dashell at the roulette table in Vegas, and the old man had offered him good money to come out to the ranch and help him. Mostly he took care of the horses, cleaning their stalls, grooming them, and stocking up on feed.

'Your old man's a perv,' he told Emily one day when they were getting more than friendly in the back of the barn.

'What's *that* mean?' she asked, picking straw out of her hair.

'He's screwin' all these women. Whaddaya think that makes him?'

'A pig!' Emily said.

'A perv,' Sam said.

And then they began necking again.

Soon, Sam began telling her all kinds of stories about Las Vegas and life outside the ranch. Emily couldn't believe how exciting it all sounded.

'Y'know, there *is* a better way of living out there,' she confided to Dani, passing on her knowledge. 'I've been thinking that maybe we *should* go find it. We've got nothing to lose.'

'Yes,' Dani said, nodding fervently. 'I want to get away from here more than anything!'

So they made their plans, eliciting the help of Sam, who was sure he could squeeze them both on the back of his motorcycle as long as they were really serious about splitting.

'If I help you, I can't ever come back here,' he said. 'The old geezer pays me plenty, so I'll be losin' out.'

'Think of it this way,' Emily said persuasively. 'You'll be *rescuing* Dani *and* me. That makes you a real hero.'

'It does?' Sam said, liking the hero idea.

'Oh, yes,' Emily said encouragingly, giving him a quick peck on the cheek.

'It's not like he knows where I live or anything,' Sam mused. 'He only comes t'town every coupla months – so he'll never track us. We'll see *him* before he sees *us*.'

'Then you'll take us?' Emily asked.

'Why not?' Sam said, imagining himself as a kind of Superman figure. 'I'll help you.'

'We'll pay you back,' Emily promised.

'You bet you will!' he joked.

Two days later they took off in the middle of the night while everyone was sleeping. Sam wheeled his motorcycle a good distance from the property before he dared start it.

'Don't worry about waking him,' Emily said, climbing on the back and helping Dani aboard. 'He sleeps like the dead, snores so loud he wouldn't hear a bear fart if it was standing next to him.'

'I know, but the old guy's some kinda wacko,' Sam said, experiencing second thoughts. 'We don't want him catching us.'

'He won't,' Emily assured him.

'I could give him up to the cops, you know,' Sam said. 'Havin' all those wives – it's gotta be against the law.'

'Really?' Dani said, thinking how satisfying it would be to see Dashell led off in handcuffs.

'Oh, yeah,' Sam said confidently. 'An' how about none of you goin' t'school? *That's* not legal for sure.'

'*I* taught Dani to read and write,' Emily said proudly. 'She learned good.'

Dani's heart was fluttering at the thought of this new adventure. All she'd ever known was the ranch, and Olive forcing her to work. Every day she'd had to feed the animals, clean the house, do the cooking, washing, sewing and scrubbing. Her workload was endless.

She clung on to Emily, her arms round her sister's waist, hoping and praying that they'd make a clean getaway and Dashell wouldn't come after them.

As they neared the bright lights of Vegas she went into shock. 'It's – it's like a fairyland,' she gasped, darting her head this way and that.

'Just you wait,' Sam said, chuckling. 'You got the good stuff to come.'

'I do?'

'Bet on it.'

And sure enough, the moment they hit the Strip she could barely speak. 'Oh, my Lord!' she exclaimed. 'Look at all these people.'

After driving up and down a couple of times, they stopped at a coffee shop, where Sam bought them all hamburgers, milkshakes and big slices of apple pie.

'What'm I gonna do with you two now I got you here?' he said, realizing that he might have made a rash move.

'You can let us sleep on your floor for a couple of days,' Emily suggested. 'I promise we'll stay out of your way.'

'It's not like I got a palace or anything,' Sam explained. 'It's only one bedroom, so that means we'll all havta sleep in together.'

Emily giggled and gave him a knowing look. 'Sounds like fun to me.'

'Yeah, but not with your sister watching.'

'Dani won't watch,' Emily promised. 'She'll curl up in a corner and go to sleep.'

'Honestly,' Dani agreed, wolfing down her pie. 'I'll make sure I don't bother you.'

'Tomorrow we'll both go out and find jobs, then we'll look for somewhere to live,' Emily said. 'You won't be sorry you brought us here.'

'You can't get a job unless you got a social-security card,' Sam pointed out.

'What's that?' Dani asked.

'Somethin' you gotta have.'

'How do we get one?' Emily wanted to know.

'Well,' Sam hesitated for a moment. 'I know a man who knows someone who might be able to fix it. Don't suppose you got birth certificates?'

'No,' Emily said. 'We're lucky to have clothes.'

Ten days later Sam came up with two fake social-security cards.

'You're the best!' Emily squealed, kissing him soundly on the lips.

'Thanks,' he said, looking embarrassed. 'Now you *really* owe me.'

'I don't mind that,' Emily said, with a half-smile.

'You're so nice,' Dani added shyly. 'God will reward you for being so nice.'

'Don't go spouting all that God crap,' Emily said crossly, glaring at her younger sister. 'We're not at the ranch now, so drop it.'

'Sorry,' Dani muttered.

'That's how he kept us in line,' Emily continued. 'Threatening us, telling us that everything was God's will. It's *not* God's will that he was poking us.'

'That's incest, y'know,' Sam said knowledgeably.

'What does incest mean?' Dani asked.

'Go to the library and find out,' Sam said.

'What's a library?'

'Oh, my!' Emily exclaimed, exasperated. 'I thought I taught you stuff like that.'

'Not well enough,' Sam said, chuckling.

Armed with her forged social-security card, Dani passed as seventeen, and got a job working as a maid at one of the big hotels. Emily scored a job as a waitress at the same hotel. With their combined wages they were able to move out of Sam's room and rent a tiny apartment, although Emily spent most of her spare time over at Sam's.

When Dani wasn't working she visited the public library, soaking up information. Being ignorant was not a good thing. She was thirsty for knowledge and determined to get it.

Unaware of her tender age, but well aware of her beauty, men began coming on to her.

She shuddered at the thought of being with a man. Dashell, her illustrious father, had put her off men forever.

Many nights she lay in bed experiencing nightmares about the things he'd made her do when she was younger. *Touch this, stroke that, lick this.*

His vile words and actions remained her secret.

She willed herself to put the disturbing memories out of her mind, but there were times when the nightmares were too vivid to disappear.

Now she was a little girl in a big city, and at last she was learning how to survive.

Chapter Six

Tuesday, 10 July 2001, Los Angeles

Never let 'em see you sweat, Madison thought, recalling the line from a stupid TV commercial. For a moment she almost smiled. Then she realized what a potentially dangerous situation she was caught in, and that a man had just been shot.

The gunman had herded everyone to the side of the room near the kitchen, and now they were taking stock of one another as the man continued to wave his weapon in the air. There were about twenty-five people in all. The oldest was the woman who'd been sitting next to them, and the youngest seemed to be a skinny teenage girl with freckles, who looked like she was about to burst into tears. And who could blame her if she did?

Madison glanced across the room at the burly man who'd been shot. He was lying on the ground quite still. 'Do you think he's dead?' she whispered to Cole, dreading the answer.

'Who knows?' he said, shrugging.

'Can't we do something ... maybe try to stop the bleeding?'

'Are *you* gonna get up and go over there?'

t

'No, but perhaps I can ask one of the gunmen to help him.'

'Yeah,' he said sarcastically. 'I'm sure they're ready to do that.'

Realizing that Cole was probably right, she tried to imagine how Jake would handle a situation like this. Hmm . . . knowing Jake, he'd probably whip out his camera and start photographing everyone.

Damn! She wished he was here with her. And then she began wondering if he was all right and when she'd see him again. Jake was a very special man; she couldn't bear the thought of losing him. He was also very smart, and if he was in trouble in Colombia, there was nobody better at talking himself out of a bad situation.

'You okay, kid?' Cole asked.

'I'm okay,' she murmured, thinking how when she and Natalie had been in college, Cole was just a punk teenager up to no good, and now he was calling her kid. Strange how things changed. 'It's your sister I'm worried about.'

They both glanced at Natalie, who still seemed to be in a catatonic state, which was so unlike her: Natalie was the one who usually couldn't stop talking. Reaching over, Madison squeezed her arm. 'We'll get through this,' she whispered. 'You do know that.'

Silently Natalie nodded.

'Shut *the fuck* up!' the gunman yelled. 'No talkin'. Down on the floor, all of you. Down! Down!'

Madison sank to the floor with the rest of them. She was writing the story in her mind, aware that once they got out of this mess, it was important to remember every detail.

'It's gettin' hot in here,' Cole muttered, sweat beading his forehead. 'They must've turned the air-conditioning off.'

'Who'd do that?' Madison asked, slipping off her jacket.

'The cops. They've probably got this place surrounded.'

'So we're hostages?'

'Well, *yeah*,' Cole said, shooting her a look as if he couldn't believe she'd said something so stupid.

'I know I sound dumb, but shouldn't someone be trying to communicate with these guys?'

'They will,' Cole said grimly.

'Anyway,' she whispered, 'why would the cops turn the air off?'

''Cause they want to make it as uncomfortable as possible.'

'That's comforting to know.'

'It's not such a great plan.'

'How's that?'

''Cause it'll mean these guys'll have to take their masks off, an' it's better if we can't identify 'em.'

'I guess I should applaud you on your great choice of restaurants,' she whispered, attempting to lighten the situation.

'Hey – I figured you'd had a boring time in New York, so I thought I'd make this evenin' fly.'

'I'M NOT SAYIN' IT AGAIN!' the gunman screamed. 'SHUT THE FUCK *UP*.'

The older woman raised her hand as if she was in class. 'I have to go to the bathroom,' she said, in a quavery voice.

'Piss your pants, lady,' the gunman growled, ''cause you ain't goin' nowhere.'

Then, to everyone's relief, they heard a voice on a loudspeaker coming from outside. 'Put down your weapons, walk out and nobody gets hurt. Do you hear me? Hands in the air and come out.'

'Mothafuckers!' muttered the gunman. 'They got shit for brains if they think I'm doin' that.'

No, Madison wanted to say. *You're the one with shit for brains.*

But for once she kept quiet. She knew it was the only way to get through this.

*

'What is it you wanted to show me?' Andy Dale mumbled, already bored as he slouched round Vincent's expensively appointed office.

Vincent sat behind his impressive mahogany desk and stared at the short, insignificant movie star. 'My books, my pictures, my objects,' he said, gesturing.

'Yeah, well, does one of your *objects* have some coke sittin' in it?' Andy asked, with a maniacal little laugh. ''Cause if it doesn't, you lost me.'

'Why do you do drugs?' Vincent asked, levelling the actor with a cold stare.

'Why *d'you* get up in the morning?' Andy Dale retorted, slumping into a leather chair.

'Here's what I have to tell you,' Vincent said, in a low, even tone. 'You put your hands on my wife one more time, and I'll break your chicken neck. Do you understand?'

'You talking to *me?*' Andy Dale said, startled, because *nobody* spoke to him that way.

'I don't see anyone else in here,' Vincent said mildly.

Andy Dale narrowed his eyes. 'You got any fuckin' idea who I am?'

'More important,' Vincent replied coldly, 'do you know who *I* am?'

'What?' Andy Dale said, nose twitching, face blank.

'Look in the mirror and who do *you* see?' Vincent said. 'Because I'll tell you who *I* see when I look at you. A moronic, coked-out movie star who thinks he owns the world. Only *I'm* here to tell you that you don't.'

'What the fuck *is* this shit?' Andy Dale spluttered.

'I'm making it real for you, Andy,' Vincent said. 'I couldn't give a damn *how* many people worship your skinny ass. My *wife* is not one of them, and if you touch her again, it'll be a move you'll live to regret.'

'Are you *threatening* me?' Andy Dale asked, outraged.

'No,' Vincent said calmly. 'Simply telling you the way it is.'

'An' I'm telling *you*, asshole,' Andy Dale retorted, leaping to his feet, 'that when my manager an' my agent hear about this, they'll bust your freakin' nuts.'

'How old are you?' Vincent asked.

'Old enough to do what the fuck I want,' Andy Dale replied belligerently.

'Nobody does what they want,' Vincent said. 'There are always compromises.' He rose from behind his desk. 'Now, you're coming back to the table with me like a good boy, and when you get there you'll behave yourself. Because if you don't . . .' His words trailed off, the threat implicit.

'Whaddaya think this is, a freakin' Pacino *movie?*' Andy Dale exploded, red in the face.

'Care to test me?' Vincent said, heading for the door. 'Go ahead. Only you'd better believe me, Andy, one more hand on my wife and we'll see whose balls get crushed.'

'Where have you been?' Jenna asked, directing her question to Andy Dale, *not* her husband, which was a big mistake on her part.

Ignoring her, Andy clicked his fingers at his exotic model girlfriend, who was sipping an apple martini and wondering who a girl had to fuck to get out of there.

'Up!' Andy Dale said, glaring at her, his voice tense.

'What?' Anais said blankly.

'We're going.'

'Where?'

'For *crissakes!*'

Getting the hint, she slid from the booth, flashing plenty of well-toned, chocolate-hued thigh in the process, plus a whisper of well-trimmed pubic hair because wearing panties was *so* out.

'Why are you leaving?' Jenna asked, her voice a plaintive whine.

Anais shrugged. Andy Dale glowered. Jolie gave a knowing smile – *she* knew why they were leaving: Vincent had no doubt given the studly movie star the 'hands off my wife' speech.

'They have some place to go,' Vincent said brusquely, sitting down next to Jenna.

'Where?' Jenna persisted, her pretty face pouting with disappointment.

'Do you care?' Vincent said, fixing her with a steely look.

She opened her mouth to say something, thought better of it, and shut up. Vincent was in one of his moods.

Andy Dale stormed off, girlfriend in tow.

'Nice work, Vincent,' Jolie murmured, caressing the stem of her champagne glass with elegant hands. 'I'd bet money on you any day.'

'Where does Nando *find* these punks?' Vincent asked, shaking his head. 'And not only does he find 'em, he dumps them on me.'

'Jenna didn't seem to have any complaints,' Jolie said, stirring the pot.

'Jenna's too young for her own good.'

Meanwhile, Jenna had transferred into sulky mode, and was tapping her freshly manicured nails on the table, preparing to throw a fit. She didn't know what Vincent had said to Andy Dale, but whatever it was, it hadn't been good. After all, what harm was there in talking to a movie star? How many times did she have *that* kind of opportunity?

Damn Vincent and his jealous streak. She wasn't his possession, she was his wife – big difference. And Jolie was so annoying, with her smug smile and knowing expressions. Jolie was simply jealous because Andy Dale hadn't come on to *her*.

'I'm going to the ladies' room,' Jenna announced, getting up.

'Don't be long,' Vincent said.

'Want to come with me?' she responded, in a challenging tone.

'Y'know, sweetheart, a smart mouth doesn't suit you,' he answered, thinking it was about time he knocked his wife up, got her good and pregnant so she'd stop this nonsense.

'So . . .' Jolie said, once Jenna was out of sight '. . . what *did* you say to him?'

Vincent shrugged.

'Having movie stars round is good for business,' Jolie remarked. 'Nando won't be pleased if you've frightened Mr Dale all the way to another casino.'

'Perhaps if your husband had joined us, this wouldn't've happened,' he said, ordering a Scotch on the rocks. 'Where is Nando anyway?'

'He had a business meeting,' Jolie said, wondering if Nando had told her the truth. Perhaps 'business meeting' was a euphemism for assignation. Vegas was crammed with beautiful, ambitious, *easy* women. She should know, she used to be one of them. And Nando was a big catch.

'Business, huh?' Vincent said, and their eyes met for a long moment.

'Oh dear,' Jolie sighed, trying to decide if Vincent was in on Nando's infidelities. 'Sometimes I think I chose the wrong partner.'

'Now, don't start,' Vincent said, fully aware of how Jolie felt about him.

'Start what?' she asked innocently, reaching for a cigarette.

Growing up with a brother eighteen years older had *some* advantages. Sofia remembered Vincent teaching her self-defence when she was a lanky eleven year old.

'Gotta kick 'em in the balls an' gouge their face with your nails,' he'd informed her. 'An' don't screw round. Be forceful.'

'Where *are* their balls?' she'd asked, with a puzzled expression, as if she didn't know.

'Here,' he'd said, pointing between his legs.

Quick as a flash she'd kicked him hard. He'd roared in pain, and as soon as he'd recovered, he'd chased her round the house yelling that she'd ruined him for ever.

When he finally caught her, they'd rolled on the floor and he'd tickled her until she'd screamed for him to stop.

She'd never had to use the 'kick 'em in the balls and gouge their face' form of self-defence, but tonight was obviously the night.

Paco had a hard-on, she could feel it digging into her thigh as he pawed at her breasts. The other one was shrugging off his white jacket and unzipping his pants, preparing for action.

Yeah, Sofia thought, remembering her big brother's advice, *like you've got no chance, morons. One way or another I am out of here.*

The front door might be locked, but the double glass doors leading to the roof terrace were wide open – she knew that, because earlier they'd all been drinking out there. And, as far as she could recall, the terrace overlooked a swimming-pool.

There was no way she was going to allow herself to be sexually abused or, even worse, raped by these two jerks. It was unthinkable. She was Sofia Castle, she could look after herself. She always had.

As Paco lunged once more, she brought her knee up, jamming it into his balls. Surprised, he gave a yelp of pain. She followed up with a swift kick in the same direction.

Startled, the other man leaped forward. Without taking a beat she raked her nails down his cheek, drawing blood, and then for good measure, kicked him too.

'*Bitch*!' he shouted. 'American *bitch*!'

She was already running across the room, dashing out on to the terrace.

The penthouse was on the eighth floor. As she reached the edge and glanced over, the pool seemed further away than she'd thought. *You can do it*, she told herself. *You can do it. Anything's better than being trapped in this apartment with these two losers.*

She could still hear the groans of the one she'd kicked in the balls. The other man was already chasing her out to the terrace.

What did she have to lose by jumping?

Only my life, she thought grimly.

Kicking off her shoes, she climbed on to the edge of the terrace railing, gauged the distance, held her breath and jumped, propelling herself as far forward as she could.

As she flew through the air a hundred thoughts raced through her head – the main ones being – *Am I going to make it? Or will I be crushed to death on the concrete below?*

Oh, God! she prayed. *If I ever needed Your help – it's now.*

Dean escorted Dani to the downstairs lobby of her apartment building. She said good night to him with a chaste kiss on his cheek.

'I suppose this means that you don't want me to come up?' he said ruefully.

'Not tonight,' she said, always leaving a small amount of hope lingering in the air. 'When will you be coming back?'

'When would you *like* me to come back?'

'Call me,' she said.

'That's all I ever do.' He sighed, and left.

Her son, Vincent, had bought her a lavish apartment in a security building ten minutes away from the Strip. It had all the modern amenities – a gym, sauna, swimming-pool, restaurant. If she wanted to, she could live in great luxury and do nothing. Only she preferred to work at a job she was good at, and putting together important PR events at her son's hotel casino appealed to her.

The three-bedroom apartment she owned was on the twelfth floor. She'd wanted an apartment large enough to accommodate grandchildren – if Vincent ever decided to procreate. The girl he'd married, Jenna, was hardly her favourite. Jenna was a pretty baby blonde with a spectacular body and absolutely no brains. Jenna was not smart enough for Vincent.

Unfortunately he'd married looks instead of brains. Wasn't that the problem with most men?

She felt bad about dumping Dean tonight; he'd obviously expected more than just her company over dinner. The problem was that she had too much on her mind, and wasn't in the mood to listen to Dean's never-ending declarations of love.

She got out of the elevator and put the key into the door of her apartment and stepped inside the cool marble foyer. As she reached for the light switch, someone grabbed her from behind.

Fear coursed through her veins.

She opened her mouth to scream, but nothing came out.

Chapter Seven

Michael: 1962

The day after his sixteenth birthday, Michael dropped out of school and to the envy of his friends began working full-time at the store.

'How come *you* get all the luck?' Max demanded.

''Cause he's a pretty boy,' Charlie snickered. 'An' his grandma lets him do anythin' he wants.'

'Screw both of you,' Michael countered. 'I'm a workin' man now, so you losers better watch it.'

'Yeah, yeah,' Max and Charlie said, in mocking unison. 'We're *scared*!'

The three of them were best friends – they'd grown up together. Charlie, the son of a cop, was big and burly with a solid Irish face and Elvis sideburns. Max was shorter and wiry-looking, with crooked front teeth, a friendly smile and floppy brown hair. Michael was simply dead-on handsome.

When Vinny found out that his son had dropped out of school, he was angry, but since he'd also left school at an early age there was nothing much he could do about it, especially as Grandmother Lani welcomed the full-time help. As she got older she was gradually slowing down, and having her grandson in the store was a big asset.

By the time Michael was seventeen he was almost totally

in charge. He was smart and savvy, knew what he was doing, and the customers liked him – especially when he let them run up tabs, helping them out when things were tough.

Before long he figured out a way to make extra money because business was *not* booming, and he soon realized he had to do *something*. So, after a while he began making side deals that Lani knew nothing about. For instance, she'd always refused to sell cigarettes in the store, which he thought was plain stupid. 'This is the sixties, Grams,' he'd informed her, on countless occasions. 'People smoke, you gotta sell 'em what they want.'

Eventually she'd agreed, and he'd cut a deal with an acquaintance who was able to deliver cartons of cigarettes that happened to have fallen off the back of a truck. He bought them for cash, then sold them in the shop at the going price, making a healthy profit, which he put back into the business. Another acquaintance supplied him with jars of coffee, and sometimes he'd score a whole truckload of canned goods that had never quite made it to their intended destination.

Grandma Lani didn't notice what was going on, and since he was now in charge of the books, it made things easy. Her arthritis was so bad that she could barely use her hands, plus she was becoming vague and distracted. She was still smart enough to appreciate her grandson's active interest in the store, because Vinny certainly didn't give a damn.

Michael didn't consider what he was doing illegal, it was merely good business. Still, he made sure not to confide in Max or Charlie, because he was well aware that neither of them would approve. They came from families who *cared* about what *they* got up to.

He got a kick out of being in charge, and since he looked much older than his age, nobody questioned his authority.

His sex life was also going well. Shortly after dropping out of school, he'd broken up with Tina. She'd found out about Polly and confronted him. He'd admitted that, yes, he *was* seeing someone else, and then, as gently as he could, he'd suggested it was best they stop seeing each other.

She'd screamed, sulked, and several weeks later taken up with Max – who couldn't believe his luck because Tina *was* the prettiest girl in school. Also the most virtuous. No sex before marriage – Michael could vouch for *that*. Perhaps if she'd been a little more forthcoming in that department, they might have stayed together.

Max had asked him if he minded. 'Go ahead,' he'd said magnanimously.

Privately he considered it a revenge move on Tina's part. She couldn't have him, so she'd go with his best friend to try to make him jealous.

Newsflash. It wasn't working.

He met regularly with Polly. Even though she was almost twenty-one and he was only seventeen, they spent many a sweaty night in the back of the local movie-house where he found he was able to perform some of his best work.

Sometimes Polly's girlfriend, Sandi, lent them her apartment. Those were the best nights. And there was always the hotel, although Max no longer worked there so paying for a room wasn't something he wanted to do too often.

Polly freely admitted that she still saw her steady boyfriend, Cyril, which didn't bother Michael at all. They both knew they were in it for the sex – and as long as the sex was hot, why should it concern him?

Things were pretty good all round. He worked hard, hung out with his friends, and Polly was there whenever he needed sex – which was most of the time. He certainly had nothing to complain about.

One day two men sauntered into the shop. The shortest man put up the closed sign and hovered by the door, while the other came over to Michael, leaned his elbows on the counter and said, 'Hey, you. Hear you're runnin' plenty of business here.'

'Maybe,' Michael said, recognizing the man as a known wise-guy.

'It's your lucky day,' the man said, scratching his chin, "cause I'm here to make things run even smoother.'

'How's that?'

'How's that?' the man repeated. 'Well, sonny, you'll pay us a little somethin' every week, and for that you ain't gonna be bothered.'

'Bothered by what?' he asked.

'Don't act dumb,' the man said irritably. 'You know who I'm representin' here.'

It occurred to Michael that he could stand up to them – until he remembered what had happened to several other store owners in the area who had resisted paying protection. He thought about the smashed windows in the bar next door. The fire in the dry-cleaner's. And old Mr Cartwright from the pawn-shop getting beaten up. The rumour on the street was that all the stores were now paying.

'I guess we can work something out,' he said slowly.

'Smart,' the man said, picking up a pack of cigarettes from the counter and breaking the seal. 'My boss likes smart ones who don't give him no trouble.'

'Who's your boss?' he asked, although he was pretty sure he already knew.

'Ain't *that* a stupid question,' the man said, shaking out a cigarette.

'Vito Giovanni,' Michael blurted out. 'An' I'd like to meet him.'

'A punk like you?' the man said, snorting his amusement. 'Forget it.'

But he didn't forget it, and a few weeks later when he and Polly were snogging in the back of the movie house, he was excited to observe the entrance of Vito Giovanni, surrounded by several henchmen and his brassy blonde wife.

He quickly shoved Polly's hand out of his crotch. 'Quit it,' he said tersely.

'What's the matter?' she asked, quite put out.

'You see that guy sittin' over there?' he said, leaning forward to get a better look. 'That's Mr Big.'

'Mr *Big*?' she sneered. 'What does *that* mean?'

'He's the man who runs this neighbourhood.'

'What is he? The mayor or something?'

'No,' Michael said impatiently. 'He's Vito Giovanni.'

At last she got it. 'The Mob guy?' she asked curiously, her interest piqued.

'Not so much a Mob guy as a man who does things his way,' Michael explained.

'And what way is *that*?' she asked, tilting her head.

'Any way he wants.'

The movie playing was *The Birdman of Alcatraz*, starring Burt Lancaster. Suddenly he'd lost all interest in seeing it. All he could think about was that sitting a few rows in front of him was Vito Giovanni, and he was desperate to meet him. Ever since he was a kid he'd heard stories about the man who ruled the neighbourhood. Vito Giovanni was rich. He was powerful. He was everything Michael aspired to be.

The movie started and Polly obviously expected the usual goings-on in the back row, but he wasn't in the mood to touch her: he had more important things on his mind.

'What's with you?' she asked, after a few minutes.

'I wanna *see* this movie,' he lied. 'Do you mind if I concentrate for once?'

'*Sorry*,' she drawled sarcastically. 'Didn't know we came to the flicks to actually *see* the film.'

'Thought you liked Burt Lancaster.'

'Wouldn't kick him out of bed,' she admitted, with a sly giggle.

As soon as the movie finished, Michael was on his feet, standing in the aisle just as Vito Giovanni and his entourage were about to pass.

'Excuse me, Mr Giovanni,' he said, blocking the way of the short, heavy-set man who was famous for favouring cashmere overcoats and flowing white silk scarves.

'Out the way, punk,' one of his bodyguards said, shoving him aside.

'All I wanted t'do was meet him,' Michael said indignantly, almost losing his balance.

'Get lost,' the henchman growled, as the group moved on.

The following day Mrs Giovanni walked into the shop. Michael recognized her immediately. She looked like an overblown Hollywood starlet, with her teased blonde hair and enormous bosom. She was wearing a skin-tight white dress, and was accompanied by her Cousin Roy, who stood outside the shop smoking a cigarette.

She sauntered over to Michael and came right to the point. 'You Vinny Castellino's kid?'

'Uh . . . that's right,' he said, trying not to stare at her big breasts.

'What didya wanna talk to my husband about?'

'I pay him protection,' Michael said, startled by her visit, 'so I kinda figured we should meet.'

She threw back her head and roared with laughter. 'You're a ballsy little one, aintcha?'

'Not so little,' he answered boldly.

'You look like Vinny,' she said, squinting at him through heavily mascaraed eyes. '*And* you got a mouth, which is more than I can say for him.'

'Where *d'you* know my dad from?' he asked, quite

shocked that she'd mentioned Vinny by name.

'It was a long time ago,' she said, thoroughly checking him out. 'How old're you anyway?'

'Twenty.'

She gave a derisive laugh. 'No way, sonny.'

'Nineteen,' he lied.

'Try *seventeen*,' she said, tapping her long red nails on the counter. 'Am I right?'

'Maybe,' he answered cagily.

'Yeah, I'm right,' she said, very sure of herself.

'How well didya know my dad?'

'Well enough,' she replied, with a secretive wink. 'If you get my drift.'

'An' my mom, didya know her too?'

'Oh – *her*,' she said, dismissively. 'Wasn't good enough for your old man. He dragged her over from Italy on account of the fact that he knocked her up. I guess *you* was the bun in her hot little oven.'

Michael stared at her, trying to decide what to make of this flashy blonde woman with her huge breasts and disrespectful attitude.

'Okay, kiddo,' she said, smoothing down her short skirt. 'Why don't you come see Mr Giovanni tomorrow, two o'clock? I'll make sure he gives you the time of day. Oh, yeah,' she added, turning on her way out, 'an' you can tell Vinny that Mamie says hello.'

'Mamie?'

'That's my name, honeybunch.'

'I'll tell him.'

'Sorry he's stuck in a wheelchair,' she said, hesitating for a moment. 'Only that's what you get when you choose the wrong path, ain't it?'

'Huh?'

'No big deal,' she said. 'Vinny's the loser. *I'm* the winner.'

'My dad's not a loser,' Michael said, quickly defending Vinny, because family was family and he didn't want to come across as disloyal.

'Have it your way,' she said, pausing to lick her jammy lips. 'I'll see you tomorrow. An' you'd better not be late. I got no patience, sonny.'

Then she was gone.

Michael was excited, he couldn't wait to question his dad. How come Vinny had never mentioned he knew the wife of the most important and powerful man in the neighbourhood? Even cooler than that, he now had an appointment to meet with Vito Giovanni, and who knew what *that* would lead to?

Vinny was watching *Ben Casey* on TV when Michael finally got home. Grandma Lani was sitting in an armchair, fast asleep, her head lolling to one side.

He circled his dad. 'Who's Mamie?' he demanded, tapping him on the shoulder.

'What?' Vinny said, looking up and frowning.

'Mamie. Mrs Giovanni,' he said impatiently. 'She claims she knows you. Says she even knew Mom.'

'What're you doin', mixing with people like that?' Vinny demanded, his face reddening.

'People like *what*, Dad?'

'The dregs of the earth. Gangsters. Cowards,' Vinny said fiercely.

'Where d'you know her from anyway?'

'Never you mind,' Vinny said, increasing the volume on the TV.

Grandma Lani awoke with a start. 'What's happenin'?' she croaked. 'Did I cook dinner yet?'

'Who's Mamie, Grams?' Michael asked.

'Oh, *her*,' Grandma Lani said crossly. 'Don't tell me *she's* comin' around again, tryin' t'get her hands on my Vincenzio. Somebody should tell her it's too late. He's a married man now, and,' she added, lowering her voice to a conspiratorial whisper, 'his wife is pregnant.'

Soon they would have to consider putting Grandma Lani in a home.

He could see he was getting nowhere with either of them, and since he had a date with Polly, and tonight they were borrowing Sandi's apartment, he didn't plan on being late.

He ran upstairs, took a quick shower, and changed his clothes.

By the time he left the house he still had no clue what connection Mrs Giovanni had to his dad, although if there was any truth in what Lani said, it seemed as if Mamie Giovanni could have been an old girlfriend.

The thought blew his mind. Sex and Vinny did not go together. *Especially* sex with a woman like Mamie. As far as he was concerned, his dad was some crusty old guy confined to a wheelchair; it was hard to imagine him any other way.

Polly was waiting at her girlfriend's apartment. 'You're late,' she said crisply.

'I'm here,' he said, looking forward to losing himself in the sheer voluptuousness of her warm flesh.

'We've got two hours,' she said, unzipping her skirt and stepping out of it.

'Keep your stockings on,' he said, as she dropped her pink lace panties.

'Kinky!' she exclaimed, leaving her flesh-coloured garter-belt and tan nylons in place.

He was immediately hard. She had that effect on him – although at his age a stone statue would have had that effect on him.

'How about dancin' for me tonight?' he suggested, sitting on the edge of Sandi's pull-out bed, which Polly had thoughtfully covered with a large terry-cloth towel.

'Don't be daft.' She giggled, reaching up to pull her sweater over her head.

'C'mon,' he coaxed. 'It'll be a kick.'

'There's no music,' she protested.

'I'll hum.'

'Okay,' she said, quite liking the idea.

He started humming 'Tossin' and Turnin''. Polly began gyrating in front of him, swivelling her hips like a professional.

He was mesmerized by her thick triangle of black pubic hair outlined by the garter-belt, and found himself getting even more turned on.

Polly was attempting a few stripper moves, thrusting her crotch at him, then drawing back.

He grabbed a tuft of overgrown pubic hair and pulled her down on the bed beside him.

'Ouch! That hurt!' she complained. But as soon as he jammed his hand between her legs, he could feel that she was as turned on as he was.

Frantically he pulled off his pants and underwear. Then he spreadeagled her, ready for action.

'Give it to me, Mike, give it to me good,' she moaned, as he plunged inside her.

She was so hot and ready that he thought he might come immediately.

She wrapped her legs round his waist and began making loud noises.

He manipulated her legs until her ankles were firmly clasped at the back of his neck.

Holy shit! Six solid thrusts and he *was* coming. The best one yet. Jeez! It seemed to last forever.

As soon as he was finished, he rolled off and let out a victory yell.

'Pretty good, huh?' she said, licking her lips.

'Freakin' *fantastic*!'

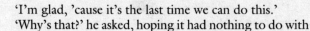

'I'm glad, 'cause it's the last time we can do this.'

'Why's that?' he asked, hoping it had nothing to do with his performance.

She sat up in bed, casually reaching for her bra. 'Cyril and I are gettin' hitched,' she announced matter-of-factly. 'So . . . I hate to tell you this, Mike, but I'm afraid it's goodbye.'

Chapter Eight

Dani: 1964

'You're a very pretty girl,' Mr Lomas said.

'Thanks,' Dani replied, lowering her blue eyes so she wouldn't have to look at his smarmy face.

Mr Lomas was the floor manager at the Estradido Hotel, where Dani worked as a maid. Nobody had any idea how young she was, which suited her because she was well aware that if her employers discovered the truth she'd be out of a job.

'Yes,' Mr Lomas said, repeating himself. 'Very pretty.'

Dani managed to stay silent. It was not like she hadn't heard it a hundred times before. Men were always coming on to her, invariably handing out the same old lines.

So far she'd been able to repel what she considered their crass advances, although recently Emily had given her a lecture. 'You're gonna be sixteen any day soon,' Emily had said, in full big-sister mode. 'Isn't it about time you got yourself a boyfriend? You can't spend *all* your time stuck in the library.'

'I *like* the library,' Dani had answered stubbornly. 'I enjoy finding out about stuff I never had a chance to learn.'

Emily had rolled her eyes. Dani was such a sweetheart, it would be nice to see her out having fun instead of spending all her spare time locked away reading books.

Emily and Sam were married now. They lived together in his apartment, while Dani stayed put in the small place she and Emily had shared. She could just about afford it, although Sam kept on telling her it would be smarter to get herself a roommate and split costs.

The good news was that, as far as they knew, Dashell had never come searching for either of the girls. Sam always kept a sharp lookout and had not spotted him. 'It's like he knows you could nail him for all the bad things he's done,' Sam reasoned. 'He probably feels safer at the ranch an' don't dare come to town.'

'I'm sorry for the other kids we left behind,' Dani said wistfully. 'At least *we* got to escape, thanks to you.'

'And *I* got me a wife,' Sam boasted, with a broad grin. 'The best girl in the whole world.'

Emily giggled. They truly were a happy couple. Emily now worked as a waitress at the Stardust Hotel, and Sam was a parking valet at the Desert Inn. They were both into their jobs and loved living in Vegas. In their spare time they managed to see most of the shows, getting in on their employee discount. Sometimes Dani went with them, not often, because she was more interested in educating herself.

'I was thinking,' said Mr Lomas, a skinny man with sparse brown hair combed carefully over his forehead, and thick, bushy eyebrows – hardly a prime candidate to date the delectable Dani.

'Yes, sir?'

'I was thinking that you and I should go out and, uh . . . celebrate,' he said, stroking his chin.

'I'm sorry, Mr Lomas,' she answered carefully. 'But what exactly would we be celebrating?'

'You've worked here a while now,' Mr Lomas continued, clearing his throat. 'I never see you with a boyfriend, an' since today is your birthday – I saw it on your job

application – *somebody* should take you out to celebrate.'
He smiled, revealing tobacco-stained teeth. 'I know a nice
motel near here where they serve a fine dinner.'

Yes, she thought to herself. *And I'm sure there's a fine
room with a fine bed right next door to the fine dining room.*

Dani was no longer the naïve young girl who'd arrived
in the city three years previously. She'd learned plenty along
the way, and it seemed to her that staying away from men
was the wisest path to take.

'That's very generous of you, Mr Lomas,' she said
politely. 'Only it's not such a good idea.'

'Why?' he asked, a nerve twitching on the left-hand side
of his narrow face.

'Because you have a wife.'

'I'm not asking you to marry me, dear,' he sneered,
refusing to accept defeat gracefully. 'I'm merely inviting
you for a spot of dinner.'

'I understand, Mr Lomas,' she replied, wishing he'd
leave her alone. 'And perhaps if your wife were to join
us . . .'

'Forget I asked,' he said, marching off in a huff.

Fiona, one of the floor maids who'd been standing
nearby, quietly applauded. '*You* told him,' she said. 'Mind
you, he might've given you a raise.'

'Who wants a raise if *that's* the way I have to get it?'
Dani said scornfully.

'Dead right,' Fiona said. 'That man is a big old *married*
lech. The worst kind.'

'He sure is,' Dani agreed.

'Y'know,' Fiona continued, 'my boyfriend has some
really nice friends. So . . . if you *do* want to go out and
celebrate . . . ?'

Dani shook her head, thinking that was the last thing
she wanted. 'No, thanks,' she said quickly.

'Why?'

'I'm not interested.'

'In *what?*'

'Getting involved with anyone.'

'One date's hardly gettin' involved.' Fiona sniffed.

'Besides,' Dani added, taking the edge off, 'my sister's throwing me a party.'

'Nice,' Fiona said snippily. 'Thanks for the invite.'

'Not a *big* party,' Dani added hurriedly. 'Actually it's only me, my sister and her husband.'

'Sounds like a laugh a minute.'

She couldn't care less what Fiona thought: it was *her* birthday and she would celebrate it any way she chose. Besides, Sam and Emily were the only two people she cared about.

By the time she finished work and got over to their apartment, it was past seven. Emily had promised to cook, and she was looking forward to her sister's delicious roast chicken and home-style potatoes – Emily's speciality.

Sam answered the door looking agitated. 'Where *is* she?' he asked, peering past her.

'Who?' Dani asked, disappointed because there was no smell of cooking in the air.

'Emily.'

'How would I know?' she answered, shrugging off her knitted jacket. 'I thought she'd be here.'

'So did I,' Sam said. 'But, as you can see, she's not.'

'Then where is she?'

'*I'm* asking *you*,' he said, exasperated.

'Haven't seen her. I came straight from work.'

'Damn!' Sam said, frowning. 'She was due home three hours ago.'

'Did you call the restaurant?'

'Yeah.'

'What did they say?'

'That she signed off her shift at four o'clock.'

'Maybe she went shopping.'

'She did all her shopping yesterday. The food's in the kitchen, waitin' for her to cook.' He ran his hand through his tousled red hair. 'It's not like Emily to screw round.'

'Do you think something might have happened to her?' Dani asked tentatively.

'Dunno,' he said, grabbing his jacket. 'I'm gonna run over to the hotel, see if she's there.'

'I'll come with you.'

The restaurant at the hotel where Emily worked had no news of her. She'd signed off at four o'clock, exactly as the manager had informed Sam over the phone.

'Is there anyone here who was workin' with her today?' he asked.

'I think Sharon's still round,' the manager said.

'Can I talk to her?'

'Wait in the back. I'll see if I can find her. No need to disturb the customers.'

'You got it,' Sam said.

He and Dani made their way to a small stockroom at the rear of the restaurant and waited.

Five minutes later Sharon appeared. 'What's up, Sam?' she asked.

'What's up is Emily ain't come home,' he said agitatedly. 'Did she say anythin' about where she was goin' after work?'

'No,' Sharon replied. 'She told me she'd see me tomorrow, that was it.'

'Maybe we should check the hospitals,' Dani suggested, joining in.

'I'm sure she'll turn up,' Sharon said cheerfully. 'You know Emily. Miss Reliable.'

'Yes,' Dani agreed, trying to stay positive.

Six hours later, after checking the hospital emergency rooms, Dani and Sam were sitting in the police station attempting to file a missing persons report.

'We don't consider anyone missing until they've been gone for twenty-four hours,' said the desk cop, a big man with weary eyes and plenty of attitude.

'She *is* missing,' Sam said forcefully. 'She should've been home by four thirty. It's now one in the morning.'

'Sorry,' the cop said. 'There's nothing we can do.'

'Goddamn it!' Sam yelled, banging his fist on the desk. 'You gotta do *somethin*'.'

'Can't,' the cop said. 'Come back when it's been twenty-four hours.'

Muttering under his breath, Sam strode from the station, Dani right behind him. She'd never seen him so angry.

'I'm gettin' on my bike an' searchin' the Strip,' he decided. 'Y' know, check out every hotel, motel, casino. She's gotta be *somewhere*.'

'I'm sure she's all right,' Dani reassured him.

But deep down she had a gut-wrenching feeling that they'd never see Emily again.

Chapter Nine

Michael: 1964

'I'm comin' to your grandma's funeral,' Mamie Giovanni announced, as she flounced round the store picking out canned goods and tossing them into a basket carried by one of her husband's henchmen, who trailed behind her.

'You don't have to do that,' Michael answered, surprised that she'd suggested it.

'Yes, I do,' Mamie insisted. 'I knew her, I should be there.'

'That's real nice of you, Mrs G.'

'Nice, schmice,' she said, with a casual shrug. 'It's the least I can do.'

Grandmother Lani had passed away in the middle of the night. She wasn't alone: Michael had hired a nurse to sit with her. Unfortunately the nurse had fallen asleep, failing to notice that her patient had died until early morning. Then the woman had panicked and run round the house yelling hysterically that it wasn't her fault.

Filled with guilt that he hadn't been with his grandma at her passing, Michael had immediately called the doctor, who came over and later issued a death certificate. It was all very depressing.

He wasn't sad that Grandma Lani had died. At the end she was senile and in pain, so it was almost a relief to see an end to her suffering. He'd miss her though, she'd always treated him well.

Vinny didn't seem too upset. 'She's better off where she is,' he'd said, staring at a rerun of *I Love Lucy*. 'This is a shitty world. Now at least she can have some peace.'

Michael was glad he didn't share the same attitude. He had no desire to follow his dad into a life of doom and gloom. He wanted more, he wanted everything he could get. In fact, he wouldn't mind being like Vittorio Giovanni, a man who had respect and money. Everybody talked about Vito being a gangster, but he'd seen no signs of it. As far as he could tell, Vito Giovanni was a smart businessman who did things his way.

Two years ago, Mamie had kept her promise and introduced him to her husband. She'd told Vito she'd known Michael since he was a kid, and that they should be good to him. To please his wife, Vito had put various small jobs his way – such as occasionally delivering a package or storing stuff at his shop.

'I gotta say I like ya, kid,' Vito had told him, after a few months. 'You're smart – you'll do okay 's long as you don't fuck up.'

'Fuck what up?' Michael had asked.

'Anything,' Vito had said, and roared with laughter.

'Don't expect my husband to come to the funeral,' Mamie said, as she roamed round the shop in her usual outfit of high heels, tight skirt and low-cut sweater.

'Didn't think he would,' Michael answered.

'You'll ride in the car with me,' she added, tossing two cans of tomato sauce into her basket.

'Can't,' he said, going behind the counter. 'Gotta go with my dad.'

'Hmm,' she mused, walking over and leaning on the

counter, revealing quite a bit of deep cleavage. 'It'll be somethin' seein' Vinny again.' She paused, licking her over-glossed lips. 'He ever talk about me?'

'Uh . . . I never heard him say anythin',' Michael replied, trying to avert his eyes from her generous bosom.

'Does he know you've been doing things for my husband?'

'No,' Michael said quickly. 'An' I'd sooner you didn't tell him.'

'Yeah, yeah,' she agreed, sucking on her lower lip. 'Knowing Vinny, he wouldn't approve.'

Just how well *did* she know Vinny? Whenever he pushed for details, she changed the subject, and every time he asked Vinny, all he got was a blank stare.

Now that Grandmother Lani had passed on, Michael started wondering who she'd left the shop and the house to – him or Vinny? It didn't make any difference – they'd be his eventually. He'd been running the shop by himself for the last year. Vinny rarely bothered coming in, and even if he did, he didn't know shit about anything.

Lately Michael had found that women were tripping over themselves to get near him, which was okay because Polly was long gone. She'd married Cyril and moved out to the boondocks. No big loss. Even Mamie Giovanni occasionally threw out a hint that she might be interested – not that he'd ever think of going anywhere near her. First of all she was twenty years older than he was, and second, she was married to a man he wouldn't dare cross.

Still . . . he'd noticed that flirting put him in good stead with women. They got off on being told how pretty they looked, or how nice they smelt. He wasn't stupid: he realized that his exceptional good looks gave him plenty of advantages.

He'd made a one-night-a-week deal with the local motel, and every Friday he took a different female there.

Sex was his way of relaxing, getting his rocks off, which put him in a good mood for the rest of the week. None of his 'dates' meant anything to him – they were all inter-changeable. Women were easy, and in a way that took away the thrill.

The Giovannis treated him like family, inviting him over to their house on holidays and special occasions. He was closer to Vito than he was to his own dad.

He'd found out from one of Vito's henchmen that Mamie couldn't have children. She'd given birth once and the baby – a boy – was stillborn. After that it was a no-go situation. In his mind he began imagining that he was the son they'd never had.

On the day of the funeral, Vinny was in a worse mood than usual. He wheeled himself into the kitchen, scowling with anger. 'Do I gotta go?' he demanded, glaring at his son.

'It's your mom,' Michael pointed out, feeling as if *he* were the adult in the relationship. 'You havta show respect, Dad. It's only right.'

He didn't mention that Mamie Giovanni would be there. Truth was, he was interested in seeing how Vinny would react when he saw her.

'Shit!' Vinny muttered, slamming his coffee mug on to the table.

The neighbourhood turned out for the funeral. Grandma Lani had been quite a force in her day and everyone had liked her.

The simple ceremony took place in the local church. Afterwards, a small procession of people trooped out to the burial ground to witness the coffin being lowered into the ground.

Pushing his dad's wheelchair, Michael glanced round hoping to spot Mamie, who so far had not put in an appearance.

He couldn't see her, so he decided she probably hadn't meant it when she'd said she'd be there. Why would she want to come to his grandma's funeral anyway?

As the priest chanted a prayer over Lani's coffin, Michael stared straight ahead, thinking that things would be different now. He'd be in total control, with nobody to answer to.

His friend Max suddenly nudged him. 'Take a look at *that*,' Max muttered.

He took a look.

Mamie Giovanni was tottering across the grass clad in a skin-tight red suit cinched in at the waist, a revealing black blouse, and four-inch hooker heels. Her dyed blonde hair was teased high on her head, and she was heavily made up. Her Cousin Roy was with her. She hovered at the edge of the crowd, standing out like a beacon in a sea of sombre black.

Max stifled a laugh.

'Shut the fuck up,' Michael whispered, sneaking a quick glance at his dad, who didn't appear to have noticed her arrival.

Later, everyone came back to the house. Some of the women in the neighbourhood had organized a spread of cold cuts, salads, and baked goods. As they all sat round eating and talking, there was quite a festive atmosphere. After a short interval, several of the women trooped up to Grandma Lani's bedroom and began rifling through her clothes.

Michael stayed close to Max, Tina and Charlie. Max and Tina were still together in spite of Tina's no-sex edict. They seemed like the perfect couple. Tina broke his balls, and Max enjoyed every moment. She treated Michael with a mixture of coolness and contempt – still smarting because he'd dumped her. He suspected she was dying to break up the close friendship he shared with Max, only she had no chance. He and Max were tight, lifetime best pals, and no girl could come between them.

Picking at the food, he kept an eye out for Mamie, wondering if she'd turn up at the house.

Across the room, trapped in his wheelchair, Vinny couldn't wait for them all to leave so he could get back to his TV. He hated the house being filled with people disturbing his routine. In fact, he hated the house, period.

He hadn't told Michael, but his plan was to sell the business, then the house, and move to Florida where he'd get himself a place on the beach and a big TV. They could all go screw themselves, he didn't care. Michael was nineteen, he could fend for himself. The boy was big enough and handsome enough. And he was able to *walk*, for crissakes. Up until now Michael had had it too easy; it would do him good to be out on his own without his grandma fussing round him.

Sometimes, when Vinny looked at his son, he saw himself at the same age, when he'd *had* a future. Anna Maria's murder and getting shot in the robbery had destroyed not only his legs but his spirit too. As far as he was concerned everything had ended that fateful day. Now he didn't care about anything.

Michael spotted Mamie the moment she walked into the house. She was hard to miss in her tight red suit and teased blonde hair. People stared and gossiped.

Mamie couldn't care less; as Vito Giovanni's wife she was used to it.

She headed straight for Michael. 'Take me to see Vinny,' she commanded.

He jumped up and obliged. Behind him he heard Tina say, 'Who's *that*? What a *tramp*!'

He led Mamie across the crowded room until they reached Vinny. 'Hey, Dad,' he said. 'Got a friend of yours here – she'd like to say hello.'

'Who?' Vinny said, shifting in his wheelchair.

'Mamie Giovanni.'

And to Vinny's surprise, there she was, Mamie, his old girlfriend, standing in front of him, just as big and brassy and blonde as ever.

'Hiya, big boy,' she drawled. 'Long time no see.'

'Mamie,' he said, utterly shocked.

'Remember me?' she said, flashing him a big smile. 'I'm the girl you dumped for that piece a trash you dragged back from Italy.'

'Don't talk about my wife like that,' he muttered, his face twisting with fury.

'Oh, *so* sorry,' Mamie said sarcastically. 'Have we made her into a *madonna* now she's gone?'

'Why don't you get outta my sight?' he said, livid that she could be so disrespectful.

'Didn't want you worryin' about me, Vinny,' she said, savouring every moment. 'Y'see, I did okay for myself. Married the most important guy in the neighbourhood. Vito Giovanni, I'm sure you know who he is.'

'Did you *hear* me?' Vinny shouted, blinking rapidly. 'Get the hell outta my house!'

There was a hush in the room as everyone strained to see what was going on.

'Dad!' Michael interjected.

'And you,' Vinny said, glaring up at his son, 'what kind of fool are you, bringin' her here?'

'She, uh . . . wanted to pay her respects to Grandma,' Michael mumbled, shocked at the way things were going.

'Respect, my ass,' Vinny said harshly. 'Lani couldn't stand the sight of her, and she knows it. The bitch came here to gloat 'cause I'm in a fucking wheelchair.' His voice rose. 'Now get her *out*!'

Michael had never seen his father display so much emotion, and now the entire room was watching. 'Uh . . .

Mrs G,' he said, quickly grabbing her arm, 'I think we gotta leave. I'll, uh, walk you outside.'

But Mamie wasn't going anywhere until she'd finished having her say. Shaking Michael's hand off her arm, she leaned over Vinny's wheelchair. 'Still the same old Vinny,' she taunted. 'Funny, I don't remember you telling me to get out when I was sucking your *little dick*!' And with those final words she stood up straight and flounced her way to the front door.

'Jeez,' Michael said, running after her while everyone in the room stared at them. 'Why'd you havta say that? This is my grandma's *funeral*.'

'Why'd I say it, sonny?' she said, exiting the house and standing on the sidewalk. ''Cause it's true. Before the *Eye*talian came along, *I* was your dad's girlfriend.'

'I didn't know that,' he said. 'You never told me.'

'We was gonna get married,' she continued. 'Only Miss *Italy* got herself knocked up, an' *forced* him to dump me. So don't go off on me if I'm mad.'

'You shoulda told me about you an' my dad. I shoulda known.'

'Aw, shit, it's old news. Anyway, don't start feelin' sorry for *me* – I did a lot better than Vinny Castellino.'

This new information was confusing. Mamie and his dad. A couple. It didn't seem possible, and yet she wouldn't make it up.

'Uh . . . Mrs G, you shouldn't talk about my mom that way,' he ventured.

'Why not?' she said defiantly. 'It's the goddamn truth. *You* didn't know her, Mikey, but believe me, she *was* a tramp. She tricked Vinny into marryin' her.'

'Don't *say* that.'

'*Everyone* knows about the way she carried on behind Vinny's back,' Mamie said, her eyes narrowing vindictively. 'The story goes that *she* set up the robbery with a boyfriend she had on the side, an' it backfired on her. So here's the truth – *she's* the one responsible for Vinny bein' in a wheelchair. You can blame *her.*'

'I . . . I can't believe that.'

'Well, it's true. Beats me why your dad didn't fill you in.'

'I gotta go,' he said, trying to keep a check on his emotions. Mamie seemed so secure in her knowledge, and yet Vinny hadn't told him shit about any of it.

'Sorry I hadda be the one t'tell you the truth,' Mamie said, reaching up to touch his cheek with her long painted nails. 'Y'know, I'm very fond of you, Mikey, an' I hate to see you hurt, only it's better you know, isn't it?'

Why? he wanted to yell. *Why would I want to know that my mom was a tramp who set my dad up?*

But he didn't say a word. Instead he turned and walked off down the street, leaving Mamie standing there.

He couldn't go back inside. As far as he was concerned, the funeral was now over.

Chapter Ten

Dani: 1964

Dani was right about never seeing Emily again. They searched for months, failing to come up with any leads. Sam even took a trip out to the ranch to find out if Dashell had abducted her. Dani wanted to go with him, only Sam didn't think it was a wise idea, and rightly so, because what he discovered when he got there shocked him. The ranch was abandoned, everyone gone, the place in complete disarray as if they'd left in a mighty big hurry. Even the horses were gone.

'What do you think happened?' Dani asked, when he got back and told her what he'd found.

He was as puzzled as she was. 'Dunno,' he said. 'All I can say is it was dead creepy out there. I'm glad you weren't with me.'

'Should we tell the police?' she ventured, her active mind imagining all kinds of terrible things.

'Tell 'em *what?*' he said irritably. 'They're not interested in findin' out shit. Emily's just another missing person to them.'

And, as usual, he turned to the bottle – his one solace since Emily's disappearance.

Dani couldn't stop him drinking, although she tried. He

refused to listen to her, preferring to wallow in his own misery. The problem was that he seemed content to stay there, which meant that she had to spend all her spare time looking after him, making sure he got to his job on time, cooking him meals, cleaning his apartment and washing his clothes. He wasn't an abusive drunk, he merely became maudlin, talking about Emily non-stop.

Eventually he got fired from his job, and after that his drinking *really* escalated. Dani didn't know what to do. Fortunately, she still had her job, and since she was rarely at her small apartment, she gave it up, saving on the rent, because now she had to support both of them. She slept on the couch at Sam's place, while he stayed in the bedroom. She didn't mind. Sam had saved her from a life of purgatory, and now it was her turn to save him.

One day she decided it was time to go through Emily's things, pack them up, and get them out of Sam's sight. She'd noticed that at night he kept on picking up one of Emily's sweaters or her old robe, holding it close to his face and rocking back and forth. It simply wasn't healthy, so after work Dani purchased a large travelling bag, brought it back to the apartment, and began filling it with Emily's things.

'What're you doing?' he demanded, attempting to stop her.

'Emily's not coming back,' she said, determinedly shoving him away as she continued packing.

'Yes, she *is*. I know she is,' he argued. 'She wouldn't leave me like this. Not my Emily.'

Dani shook her head. 'I don't think she's coming back, Sam.' His miserable expression forced her to add, 'But you know what? We'll keep her stuff. I'll put everything in the bag and store it in a closet. How's that?'

'Do whatever you want,' he said, giving up and reaching for the bottle.

In the bottom bureau drawer, hidden under a pile of underclothes, she discovered a journal. Scrawled across the front of the book were the words: PRIVATE – DO NOT OPEN.

Her heart started pounding. Could this book contain a clue to Emily's disappearance?

She agonized over whether she should read it or not. Was it right to read someone else's journal? Yes, if that person was your missing sister it certainly was.

The following day she took the journal to work. She didn't tell Sam, in case there was something in it he shouldn't see.

On her break, she sat in the tiny dinette where the maids spent their time off, and began reading. She soon discovered that the journal was not about days and weeks and months, it was a rambling continuation of random thoughts. Mostly Emily wrote about Sam. How much she loved him, how good he was to her, and how happy she was that he'd rescued her and Dani from the ranch.

Dani turned to the most recent entry, hoping for a clue.

Dani will be sixteen tomorrow, and I'm so proud of her. She works hard and still finds time to study. One day she'll make something of herself. On her birthday I've decided to tell her the truth; it's only fair she knows Olive is not her mom, that her real mom, Lucy, died giving birth to her. Dashell was a heartless bastard – he buried Lucy in the back garden. No service, nothing. When Dani hears the truth, I think she'll want to go back to the ranch and search for her mom's grave. If it was me, I'd want to give my mom a proper burial. Trouble is, I'm frightened to go there. I'm sure Dani will be too. Got to go now and do the shopping for tomorrow so I can cook Little Sis her favourite meal. Sam and Dani are my life. I love them both so much. I'd do anything for them.

Emily's words ended there.

Dani closed the journal, tears streaming down her cheeks. She was full of mixed feelings. It wasn't as if Olive had ever been a true mother to her, but to suddenly discover that her true mom had died giving her life was a terrible shock.

When she got home that evening, Sam was huddled in his favourite chair, gazing at a picture of Emily he kept in a tarnished silver frame.

She decided not to tell him what she'd found out; the important thing was to get him sober.

She went over to him and put her arm round his shoulders. 'You've got to stop doing this,' she said quietly.

'Stop doing what?' he responded belligerently.

'Stop mourning Emily. She's gone, and we have to start afresh.'

'How d'you suggest we do that?' he asked, slurring his words.

'First we've got to get you better,' she said. 'There's an organization I found out about at work called Alcoholics Anonymous. If you'll go to a meeting, I'm sure they'll be able to help you.'

'Why would I go?' he said blankly. 'I've nothing to live for.'

'You've got me, haven't you?' she answered softly.

'You? You're just a kid.'

'I'm sixteen,' she said earnestly. 'I've been working for the last three years, so I'm certainly not a kid.'

'Yes, you are,' he mumbled.

'Please,' she begged. 'Do it for me. And if not for me, for Emily. She loved you so much, and seeing you like this would break her heart.'

'Okay, okay, I'll think about it,' he said reluctantly.

She kissed him on the cheek. 'Thank you.'

*

'Excuse me!' Dani gasped, blushing a bright red.

It wasn't the first time she'd walked in on a hotel guest in the buff. But this was different, this was two women making out in the shower of penthouse number one, a suite reserved for the hotel's directors and high rollers when they were in town.

'I'm s-so s-sorry,' she stammered, hurriedly backing out of the bathroom, quite shocked.

It wasn't *her* fault she'd interrupted them. There'd been NO DO NOT DISTURB sign on the door. If people wanted privacy they should at least activate the security lock.

'Wait!' one of the women called out.

Dani paused outside the bathroom door, wondering if she was about to get fired.

After a few moments the woman emerged, wrapped in a fluffy white towel. She was in her forties, with dyed blonde hair and trampy features. The towel ended at the top of her thighs and her legs were sturdy and pale. She didn't seem at all embarrassed.

'You!' she said to Dani. 'You didn't see nothin', right?'

'N-no, ma'am,' Dani replied, still stammering.

'Course you didn't,' the woman said, picking up her alligator purse from a table beside the large double bed. 'Nothin' you would ever wanna repeat to anyone, right?'

'Absolutely not,' Dani assured her, attempting to recover her composure, although she was still shocked. Two women together. It wasn't normal.

'Here,' the woman said, fishing three ten-dollar bills from her wallet and thrusting them at her. 'Thirty bucks for you.'

'It's – it's not necessary,' she said, refusing to accept the money.

'Yeah, it is,' the woman said, pressing the bills into her hand. 'I'm here for a week, an' I require personal maid service, so, honey, you're it.'

'I am?' she gulped.

'Yeah. I'll call the hotel manager an' fix it. My husband does business with this hotel, so they're inclined to give me anythin' I ask for. An' personal maid service is the order of the day.' A ribald chuckle. 'Only don't get no fancy ideas. My old man arrives tomorra, an' just 'cause *I* indulge myself don't mean *he* can. So keep your pretty little paws to yourself, your mouth tightly closed, an' everythin' will be hunky-dory.'

Dani was speechless.

'We're in business,' the woman said, hitching up her towel, which was in danger of falling. 'I got two suitcases need unpacking. Get everythin' pressed, an' book me a hairdresser to come up to the suite. Oh, yeah, an' have Room Service deliver ice, two bottles of their best champagne, an' a tray of goodies to snack on.' She clapped her hands. 'Get goin', sweetie. I need my blue silk dress ready to wear tonight, an' make sure there's not a crease in sight.'

'I have other rooms to clean,' Dani said, completely awed by this forceful woman.

'Are you *listenin'* t'me?' the woman said, her voice rising. 'One phone call an' you're all mine. I'm makin' that call now.'

'Yes, *ma'am*.'

'Call me Mrs Giovanni. I don't dig that ma'am crap.'

'Yes, Mrs Giovanni.'

Mamie grinned. '*That's* more like it.'

Mrs Giovanni did as she promised, called the hotel management and arranged for Dani to work as her personal maid now and whenever she was in residence.

Soon Dani began looking forward to her visits: it was certainly better than having to clean a series of anonymous hotel rooms while fending off various male guests' advances.

Mrs Giovanni was quite a woman. Loud-mouthed and demanding, she drank a lot, and spent money like it was going out of style. Her female lovers came and went, a new one every trip.

'Our secret,' she informed Dani, after several vodkas and a lengthy session with a zaftig Latina singer. 'You keep your mouth shut, an' one of these days I might do somethin' nice for you.'

A couple of months and three visits later she took a long, appraising look at Dani and said, 'Y'know what, cutie? You're too pretty to be a maid. How about I get you into the chorus of the show downstairs?'

'Excuse me?' Dani said, busy unpacking a shopping bag full of cashmere sweaters that Mamie had recently purchased.

'You're wasted here, even *I* gotta admit that.'

'I am?'

'Dunno why I'm helpin' you when I should be lockin' you away in a room so my old man don't get a peep at you. Not that he can get it up any more. I'm gonna introduce you to Lou, the guy who runs the show downstairs. Do you dance?'

'Uh . . . no.'

'That's okay, you'll learn.'

'I'm not sure I can, Mrs Giovanni.'

'Oh, for God's sake,' Mamie snapped. 'We're talkin' opportunity here. I'm givin' you a chance, so for crissakes, take it. That's unless you'd prefer slavin' away as a maid all your life?'

'I . . . I'd be happy trying something new,' Dani said hesitantly.

'You got a boyfriend?'

'No.'

'Who's that kid I see picking you up in the back?'

'That's Sam, my sister's husband.'

'Uh-huh. Well, okay, I'll call Lou, get you in to see him tomorrow.'

Lou had taken one look at her and told her that if she could dance he'd hire her.

'I can't,' she admitted.

'Then take a class,' he said, thinking that with looks like hers, who needed talent?

Willing to learn, she threw herself into dance class and soon excelled. When she came back to see Lou, he was duly impressed. 'You're hired, honey,' he told her. 'A coupla weeks' rehearsal an' you're out there.'

Sam was not happy about her joining the chorus line at the Estradido Hotel. 'You was better off doin' your other job,' he complained.

'I'm making more money now,' she reasoned. 'That's good for both of us, isn't it?'

'I suppose so,' he conceded, still not pleased.

He'd been going to AA meetings for several months, and they seemed to be helping him. He'd quit drinking, and after a few months of sobriety he'd even managed to get his old job back.

The two of them lived like brother and sister, with only Emily in common. They talked about her often, both determined they would never forget her.

But Emily was *all* they had in common, and Dani knew that soon she would have to think about moving on.

Chapter Eleven

Tuesday, 10 July 2001

The heat in the restaurant was becoming intense. Madison could feel trickles of sweat making their way down her back. She was concerned for the man who'd been shot. As far as she could see he wasn't moving, merely lying across the restaurant in a pool of his own blood.

What if he was dead? She shuddered at the thought.

Hunched on the floor, her arm firmly round Natalie's shoulders, she glanced at Cole, who was over by the kitchen with the other men. The thug with the Uzi had separated them – men on one side, women on the other.

Although there were three bandits altogether, Madison kept her eye on the ringleader: *he* was the one to watch, *he* was the one who made all the decisions and told everyone to shut up – including his two cohorts.

The negotiator's voice on the loudspeaker had made a couple more requests for them to come out quietly.

Yeah, as if they would.

Finally, the phone rang. She sighed with relief because, hopefully, proper negotiations would now start and soon they'd all be free.

Bandit number one – as she'd christened him in her

mind – walked over to the ringing phone and snatched it up. 'Nobody's comin' out,' he yelled into the receiver, the Uzi swinging from one hand. 'Nobody. An' we got plenty hostages here. So get your fuckin' shit tight, an' start listenin'.'

She couldn't hear the negotiator's reply, but it obviously didn't please bandit number one, who slammed the phone down, screaming, 'Fuck you!' He whirled round and faced the female hostages, glaring at them, his eyes narrow slits through his ski mask.

'Screaming won't do you any good,' Madison said, speaking up and surprising herself.

'What didya say?' he shouted, eyeballing her.

'I said screaming isn't going to do any good,' she repeated, keeping her tone low and even, as if talking to a recalcitrant child. 'If you want action, then you must negotiate properly, tell them exactly what your requests are.'

'Lady,' he said harshly, 'you sure got a lotta balls.'

'Why?' she said boldly. 'Because I'm trying to tell you the best way to get out of this mess?'

'What're you?' he spat in disgust. 'A lawyer or somethin'?'

'No,' she answered calmly. 'I'm a journalist. And . . . if you'd like, I could write your story. I'm certain you've got an excellent reason for doing this.'

'Shut the fuck up along with the rest of 'em,' he said, continuing to glare at her.

'You're the man with the gun,' she said. 'Which puts *you* in charge. I suggest that when they call again, you tell them what you want, and that you'll release the hostages when you get it.'

He didn't say anything. Instead he summoned his two accomplices and huddled in a corner conferring with them.

Three dumb boys, Madison thought. *Three dumb boys*

who've screwed up a robbery and don't know what to do next.

Across the room, Cole shook his head at her as if to say, 'What the hell are you interfering for? Do as he says and keep quiet.'

She'd had enough of being quiet, she was entitled to speak. As far as she could remember, forging some kind of a bond with hostage takers was the right move. What was the worst he could do? Shoot her?

'How're you doing?' she whispered to Natalie.

'This isn't my idea of the perfect evening,' Natalie replied, trying desperately to pull herself together. 'I'm scared, Maddy. I'd like to wake up and discover this was all a bad dream.'

'At least you're talking now.'

'That's 'cause of you,' Natalie said, attempting a weak smile. 'He's right, girl – you got more balls than any of 'em.'

'My father told me that once,' Madison said, laughing wryly. 'I think he was hinting I took after him.'

'You probably do. Anyway, you make *me* feel safe.'

'That's the main thing,' Madison said, sounding braver than she felt as she checked out the other female hostages clustered together on the floor, most of them shell-shocked like Natalie.

'Stay cool everyone,' she warned in a low voice. 'If nobody makes any rash moves, we'll get out of this alive.'

'Who elected *you* President?' snapped a short redhead in a tight blue dress. 'That low-life took my seventy-five-thousand-dollar Harry Winston engagement ring, and I want it back.'

'What's more important, your life or a stupid piece of jewellery?' Madison asked sharply.

'Jump off your white horse and get real,' the redhead said, in a strident voice. 'The cops'll bust these guys, so *you* should stay out of it.'

'I should, huh?' Madison said, temper rising.

'Yeah,' the girl said. 'Sorry to be the one to tell you, but this isn't a story opportunity.'

Before Madison could reply, the phone rang again. The gunman zigzagged over and snatched it up. 'You wanna talk?' he said loudly. 'Then listen good. Get me a black van with a full tank. Park it in the alley with no cops round – no fuckin' sharp shooters. We'll be gettin' in the van with hostages. When I'm sure there's no one followin', an' no helicopters trackin' us, we'll release 'em. You don't – an' I'll be wastin' one hostage every fifteen minutes. I'm givin' you twenty minutes, then I start shootin'.'

'Twenty minutes doesn't give them enough time,' Madison said, her throat dry. 'You've got to make it an hour.'

Christ! Was *she* now in cahoots with the gunman? This was insane.

'Fuck you!' he said, and walked away.

The truth was that his words chilled her. He'd probably already killed once. What difference did it make if he shot them all?

By the time Nando turned up at the dinner in Vegas, the atmosphere at the table was strained. Jenna was sulking. Vincent was pissed. And Jolie wanted to know exactly where he'd been.

'Hey,' Nando said, waving his arms expansively in the air as he faced up to his wife, 'you know I don't like bein' questioned. I told you I had a business meeting and that's what it was, strictly business.'

Nando was a wiry-looking man a few months younger than Vincent. Not conventionally handsome, he had his own particular style that appealed to both men and women. Ballsy and full of testosterone, he was Vincent's partner and best friend. They'd grown up together and had much in common. Women loved Nando, a fact that was not lost on his beautiful wife.

Jolie narrowed her amber eyes. She didn't trust her husband. On the other hand, whatever *he* did, she could do too. And she was quite prepared to do it with Vincent, if only he was ready to play.

Which he wasn't.

Too bad.

'How's my favourite beauty?' Nando asked, swooping down to kiss Jenna.

'About time you showed up,' Vincent said, wondering, like Jolie, if Nando was playing on the side.

'Where's Andy?' Nando asked, checking out the table.

'He had to go.'

'Vincent frightened him off,' Jolie said.

'Shit!' Nando said, sliding into the booth beside her. 'I got people wanna invest in a movie for him.'

'I'm sure he *really* needs your investors,' Jolie murmured drily.

'Do me a favour,' Vincent said, frowning. 'Don't invite your assholes to dinner then do a no-show. The prick was all over Jenna. He's lucky he *walked* out of here.'

'Jesus, Vin,' Nando said, clicking his fingers for the waiter then ordering another bottle of champagne. 'You think everyone's got the hots for your wife. She's hot, but trust me – Andy Dale has women fallin' over themselves to get near him. He doesn't need to hit on Jenna.'

'Keep him away from me *and* Jenna,' Vincent warned.

'Yeah, yeah,' Nando said, taking no notice.

'Nobody needs to keep anyone away from me,' Jenna said, speaking up, her voice a girlish squeak. 'Andy wasn't doing *anything*. I'm, like, *so* humiliated that Vincent imagined he was.'

'Hey,' Nando said, with a rakish grin, 'marry an

irresistible woman an' you're gonna have guys hittin' on her. It comes with the territory. *I* should know,' he added, placing his arm round Jolie's smooth bare shoulders. 'Look at the beauty *I* got.'

A guilt hug, Jolie thought. *He's screwing someone else, the bastard*.

'So,' Nando continued, 'we all gonna sit here with long faces, or we gonna have ourselves a good time?'

'A good time, please,' Jenna said, cheering up. She liked Nando: he always put a smile on her face.

'That's my girl,' Nando said, winking at her. 'Now why don't you an' Jolie go powder your noses or whatever you girls do when you spend three hours in the head? Vin and I got somethin' to discuss.'

'What would *that* be?' Jolie asked. Nando silenced her with a look. 'Okay, okay, we're going,' she said, getting up hastily. 'C'mon, Jenna.'

'I just went,' Jenna complained.

'C'*mon*,' Jolie repeated. 'The guys need private time. Maybe we'll hit a few slot machines instead of the ladies' room. Got any change?'

'You know I don't like you to play,' Nando said, the smile slipping from his face.

'Big deal!' Jolie said. 'Slot machines. I can *really* break the bank, can't I?'

Nando threw her another look.

Jenna got up from the table. 'I hope you're planning to apologize to Andy Dale,' she said stiffly, directing her words to her husband. 'I have no idea what you said to him, but whatever it was, he didn't look happy when he came back. You embarrassed me.'

'*I* embarrassed *you*?' Vincent said incredulously.

'Yes,' Jenna said, slightly unsure of herself.

'Baby,' Vincent said, shaking his head, 'if you think *that* was an embarrassment, you ain't seen nothin' yet.'

'I don't like it when you speak to me like that,' she complained.

'You'd better go, before I say something I might regret,' Vincent said, waving her away with a dismissive gesture.

Jenna's blue eyes filled with tears. Sometimes she didn't understand her husband one little bit. He wasn't her boss, and it was about time he stopped treating her like an employee.

The two women left.

'What's on your mind?' Vincent asked, turning to his partner.

Nando picked up his champagne glass and took a long swig. 'Got a proposition.'

'Yeah?'

'We've always been partners an' shit,' Nando continued, 'so I didn't wanna do something without givin' you a chance to get in on the action.'

'What action?'

'I got a couple of acquaintances who own the Manray strip joint. You know the place I mean?'

'Yes, it's a real sleazy dive.'

'Sure it is,' Nando agreed. 'Half the girls are hookin' on the side, an' the rest are busy doin' drugs. Only *we* got an opportunity to buy it, make it a classy operation – y'know, put in a hot restaurant, top-of-the-line girls. Vegas is changing, Vin. For the last ten years it's been all about family. Now fuck family, it's back to the basics. Girls an' gamblin'. Whaddaya think?'

'Who owns the place?'

'Leroy Fortuno and Darren Simmons.'

'Jesus, Nando,' Vincent said in disgust. 'Those guys are bad news. We run a clean operation. Why ruin our reputation?'

'I'm talkin' plenty cash,' Nando said persuasively. 'The Manray could be a money-making machine.'

'Hookers and drugs,' Vincent said, shaking his head. 'Not my scene.'

'Like we don't have hookers workin' the hotel an' casino now?' Nando questioned.

'Every place does. The difference is they're on their own – we're not taking a cut.'

'Hey, Vin,' Nando said restlessly, 'I'm not plannin' on blowin' this deal. You don't wanna come in, I'll partner with them.'

'Does Jolie know about it?'

'You think I tell my *wife* about business? I'm not *completely* loco.' He laughed his crazy laugh. 'Women got a purpose in life – an' it sure as hell ain't business.'

As Jolie and Jenna headed for the ladies' room, they had to pass through the casino.

Jolie nudged Jenna. 'Look who's over there,' she said, purposely causing trouble.

'Who?'

'Your boyfriend, Andy Dale.'

'Don't *say* that!' Jenna said, blushing. 'He's *not* my boyfriend.'

'Just *f*-ing with you,' Jolie answered with a secretive smile.

'Anyway,' Jenna asked, trying to sound casual, 'where is he?'

'At one of the blackjack tables.'

'Oh, goodness!' Jenna exclaimed excitedly, unable to help herself. 'Perhaps I should go over and apologize.'

'For *what*?' Jolie asked, amazed at Jenna's level of complete naïveté.

'For whatever my husband said to frighten him off.'

'You *were* flirting,' Jolie pointed out.

'I was not,' Jenna objected.

'Looked like it to me.'

'I think I will go over,' Jenna decided. 'I should tell him that Vincent didn't mean it.'

'Whatever,' Jolie said casually. 'Only remember, if Vincent finds out, you will be in deep trouble.'

'You wouldn't tell him, would you?'

'Why would I?'

'Because you two are old friends,' Jenna said quickly. 'You knew him before I did.'

'I won't tell him, okay?' Jolie said impatiently. 'Go over there if you must, only try not to make a fool of yourself.'

'Where will you be?'

'In the ladies' room having a smoke,' Jolie replied. 'And don't keep me waiting too long. It wouldn't be wise for me to go back to the table without you.'

Jenna nodded and, face flushed with anticipation, she set off to apologize to Andy Dale.

'Don't hurt me,' Dani gasped. 'Please don't hurt me, I'll do whatever you say.'

Her heart was thundering in her chest as the intruder held her from behind. He was strong and tall – she could feel the power in his arms.

Without saying a word his hands dropped to her breasts.

Oh, God! Was he going to rape her? Was this what it was about?

Why hadn't she invited Dean up to her apartment? If he had been with her this would never have happened.

The intruder flicked open the front clasp of her bra, releasing her large breasts.

The tips of his fingers began caressing her nipples.

To her horror, she felt herself becoming aroused. His left hand stayed on her breasts, while his other hand reached down and started pulling up her skirt.

'No!' she said sharply. 'Please! No!'

'Why not?' he said. 'You told me you'd do whatever I said.'

'Michael!' she exclaimed, recognizing his voice and spinning round to face him. 'You *bastard*! How *dare* you scare me?'

'I wanted to see if you'd fight back,' he said, laughing.

'You're not funny,' she said, reaching for the light switch. 'I could've had a heart attack.'

'Who, you?' he said, still laughing. 'You're strong as a horse.'

'I can't believe you did that to me,' she said, fastening her bra.

'And I can't believe *you* were out on another date with Mr Perfect. Doesn't that jerk ever give up?'

'Just because you've hated Dean for years, there's no need to be rude. If *you* wanted to run my life, you should've married me.'

'If I'd married you, we wouldn't still be having sex, would we?'

'We're *not* having sex.'

'Says who?' he said, coming after her.

'What are you doing here?' she asked, pushing him away. 'I don't hear from you in months, and all of a sudden you appear in the middle of the night to scare me.'

'I'm here. Isn't that enough?'

'No. You treat me like crap, Michael, then you expect me to fall gratefully into your arms like you're God's gift.'

'It seems to work for us, doesn't it?' he said, walking into the living room. 'How many years is it now?'

'Long enough for me to know better,' she said, wishing he didn't look so damn good.

'Want a drink?' he asked, strolling over to the bar.

'Help yourself,' she said sarcastically, taking another long look at him. Yes, he was still the most handsome man she'd ever set eyes on. His dark hair was only slightly flecked with grey, he was in excellent shape, and he'd always been a great dresser. Tall, dark, and handsome. Her weakness.

He fixed himself a hefty Scotch on the rocks. 'Sure I can't make you something, baby?'

'I'm not your baby,' she said stiffly.

'You've *always* been my baby,' he answered. 'You're the only one who's been there for me through everything.'

'Y'know, Michael, you use me,' she complained.

'What?' he said, frowning.

'The only time you come here is when you need something. The rest of the time I'm by myself.'

'That's bull—'

'No!' she interrupted. 'It's fact. And another thing, the moment I start a relationship, back you come to ruin everything.'

'Don't mean to.'

'Yes, you *do*.'

'It's a little late for regrets, isn't it?'

'Not at all,' she said heatedly. 'I've a lot of good years left.'

'Sure you do, sweetheart,' he said, soothing her anger. 'You're still an extremely beautiful woman.'

Determined not to fall for his flattery as she usually did, she thrust out her jaw. 'I repeat, *why* are you here?'

'You want the truth, or how about I make something up?'

'The truth would be nice for a change.'

'Okay, you asked for it,' he said, gulping down his drink. 'There's a warrant out for my arrest.'

'You're kidding!'

'Wish I was.'

'For *what*?'

'Here's the deal,' he said slowly. 'I'm being accused of shooting Stella and her boyfriend.'

She stared at him for a long time. She'd heard so many stories about Michael and Stella. Quite frankly, she didn't know what to believe. 'Did you?' she asked at last, her throat quite dry at the thought.

'What do *you* think?' he answered.

'I think you're a man who's capable of anything.'

'I didn't do it, Dani, okay?' he said sharply. 'You can take my word on it.'

'Have you seen a lawyer?'

'Lawyers,' he said, his voice filled with contempt. 'Show me a lawyer an' I'll show you a guy who sits in a fancy office runnin' up big bills while screwing his secretary *and* his clients.'

'You're very cynical, Michael.'

'No shit.'

'So,' she said, sighing, 'what you're telling me is that there's a warrant out for your arrest, and that you're a fugitive. Right?'

He nodded.

'And since you're here, in my apartment, doesn't that make *me* an accessory?'

'I guess so,' he agreed, nodding again.

'And I'm supposed to protect you?'

'That's about it.'

'Oh, gee, thanks,' she said fiercely. 'I don't get you as a husband, but I *do* get you as a fugitive.'

'What's with this marriage crap?' he said irritably. 'You and me, sweetheart, we've had a longer relationship than any dumb marriage.'

Suddenly she'd had enough of him. Once again he was coming to her because he was in trouble, and it simply wasn't fair. 'Screw you, Michael,' she said, turning away so he couldn't see how much he affected her.

'That's exactly what I had in mind,' he said, moving in her direction.

'Of course you did.' She gave up.

And as he came towards her, she knew there was no way she could resist him.

Michael was an addiction – one she'd never been able to overcome.

Time stood still for Sofia as she flew through the air, waiting to see whether she hit water or concrete.

Holy shit! she thought. *What a way to die. Escaping from two horny old Spaniards. This isn't the way it's supposed to be.*

If I make it, she promised herself, *I'm going home. Enough of this crap!*

Then she hit water, and the relief was overwhelming.

She felt herself sinking, sinking, sinking . . .

Was she about to crack the bottom of the pool? Smash her skull? How far did she have to go before she started coming up?

Oh, man! This was like *so* insane.

Then suddenly she was surfacing, gasping and spluttering for air, her lungs filled with water.

I made it, I made it, she thought triumphantly, splashing to the side of the pool and hauling herself out on to the cold concrete, where she collapsed.

Holy shit, I made it! I made it!

She lay on the ground for a moment, gathering her strength. Then she rolled over and glanced up.

Paco was leaning over the terrace, a look of amazement on his face.

'Screw you, asshole!' she yelled. 'I'm calling the freaking cops. And if *they* won't do anything, I'll get my father, and he'll beat the crap out of you. You *bastards*!'

She wondered if he understood her. Probably not. The jerk didn't speak English.

What was she supposed to do now? Walk home? Her

purse with everything in it – including her passport and money – was still in the penthouse.

She remembered seeing a hall porter when she'd entered the building, so as soon as she felt she could stand, she got up and made her way round to the front of the building and into the lobby.

The concierge stared at her in alarm as she marched up to the front of the reception desk.

She knew she must be a strange sight, dripping wet with an angry gleam in her eyes. 'Go to the penthouse,' she commanded, 'and get my purse. If the assholes in the apartment won't give it to you, tell 'em I'm calling the police.'

'*Qué*?' the man said, twitching nervously.

'Penthouse. My purse,' she repeated. 'You go get it.'

He still didn't understand her.

She began shivering uncontrollably. She might be half drowned and unable to speak the language, but she was mad as hell, and if this suckface didn't move soon, she was about to start screaming and *really* cause a riot.

'Do it!' she yelled. 'Do it *now!*'

Chapter Twelve

Michael: 1964

'Who's that girl?' Michael asked, his gaze following the willowy blonde with the knock-out body high-kicking at the end of the chorus line.

Manny Spiven didn't even bother looking. 'Just another Vegas cooze,' he chortled, amused by his own choice of words.

Michael shot him a look. He didn't like Manny, but business was business, and since he was now working full-time for Vito Giovanni, he had to deal with him.

This was his third trip to Vegas in so many weeks. He was kind of getting off on being Vito's trusted courier – because basically that was his job, hand-delivering packages. He didn't know what was in them, although he suspected it was money, and that was okay – there was nothing wrong with shifting cash from state to state.

Things had changed considerably in the last few months. Vinny selling the shop and the house had been a big blow. 'You gotta get out on your own now,' Vinny had informed him. 'Your grandma spoiled you, made you soft, it's time you toughened up.' Shortly after that charming speech he'd handed his son three hundred bucks and run off to Florida with all the money from the sales.

At first Michael couldn't believe it: Grandma Lani would turn in her grave and then some. She'd never imagined Vinny would sell everything and leave him out in the cold with only three hundred lousy bucks. She'd wanted *him* to have the shop *and* the house, not Vinny.

Fortunately, he'd stashed away some of his profits from the last couple of years – it wasn't much, but it was sure better than nothing.

Max had come through for him, persuading his mom to let him stay at their house for a few days while he found somewhere to live. He had no clue what he would do next. Three hundred bucks plus his savings was not about to take him very far.

Then Mamie Giovanni had invited him over for dinner – mainly to inform him that Vinny was a no-good bastard, always had been, and she wasn't surprised that he'd behaved like a selfish, greedy prick.

A week later Vito had summoned him back to the house and suggested he work for him full-time.

'Doin' what?' he'd asked suspiciously.

'Anythin' I want,' Vito had replied, with a crafty laugh.

'I ain't gonna be one of your bodyguards,' he'd said boldly. 'Not my style.'

Once more Vito had laughed. 'A punk like you, forget it. I got other things in mind for you.'

When he'd told Max about his new job, his friend had recoiled in horror. 'He's a freakin' *gangster*, Mike. Whaddaya wanna get involved with him for?'

''Cause I need t'make money.'

'You gotta consider the consequences.'

Screw the consequences. He'd needed a job, and Vito was the only one offering.

A week later, he was on a plane to Las Vegas – a place he'd only ever seen in movies.

Vegas blew him away: the long parade of neon lights and

the huge gambling palaces, not to mention the unbelievably gorgeous showgirls and dancers, vast hotels and lavish shows.

Manny Spiven was his contact at the Estradido Hotel where Vito conducted business. They hated each other on sight. Manny was short and overweight with greasy brown hair, pockmarked skin, alarmingly large ears, and a permanent limp. The limp was Manny's claim to fame. The rumour was that he'd got shot in the thigh protecting Philippe Estradido, the hotel owner, from a Mob hit. Manny had been a parking valet at the time. After that, his fortunes had taken a turn for the better, and now he worked full-time for Mr Estradido doing this and that.

At twenty-one Manny was a couple of years older than Michael, and he used his seniority like a sword, claiming that *he* knew everything and Michael knew nothing.

'If you know so much,' Michael said, shifting his attention from the delectable blonde dancing at the end of the chorus line to Manny, 'what's in the packages we exchange?'

Manny's small squinty eyes darted this way and that, fearful of being overheard. 'You shittin' me?' he spluttered.

'No,' Michael said, wondering if Manny actually knew.

'That's not the kinda question you're supposed to ask.'

'Do you know or not?'

'Fuck *you*,' Manny mumbled. 'Wouldn't tell ya if I did.'

'So you don't know.'

'Fuck you,' Manny repeated, scowling.

They were sitting at a front table in the Starburst Lounge, watching the lacklustre show, which consisted of a tired black singer, a not very funny comedian, and a chorus line of hard-faced, over-made-up women – with the exception of the blonde on the end, who was something else. He might only be nineteen but Michael had an eye for picking the best, and this one was a peach.

He'd only got laid once in Vegas, and that was on his first trip. It had turned out to be an unfortunate experience: the girl had given him a dose of the crabs, and the subsequent itch in his crotch had driven him crazy until he'd got some foul-smelling cream from the pharmacist, which he'd had to plaster all over his pubes. After that particular incident, he'd decided that all the girls in Vegas were probably crawling with sexual diseases. Too much action, too many players. Besides, who needed them? He had enough girls in New York to keep him busy for the next five years.

Although he had to admit, the blonde in the chorus could make him change his mind. She was so pretty and fresh-looking, totally unlike the others in the line.

Manny claimed to know every dancer, cigarette girl and waitress in Vegas. This, of course, was a lie. If they *did* know him, they ran when they saw him coming. Whereas Michael could strike up a conversation with any one of them. Women were always willing to talk to him, he had the knack. Plus he'd been extremely blessed in the looks department, and it didn't hurt that he also possessed the gift of charm.

He'd seen photos of his dad before he got shot: Vinny had been handsome too. Mamie had obviously thought so.

When the show finished, he informed Manny he was tired and planning to hit the sack early.

'Aintcha comin' t'play craps?' Manny asked, not particularly caring one way or the other.

'Naw, my boss don't want me gambling while I'm here. This trip is strictly business.'

'Aw, screw business,' Manny said, picking his nose. 'Lose a few hundred, win a few – what's the difference?'

'The difference is he don't want me doin' it.'

Truth was that he suspected Vito couldn't care less *what* he did as long as he made a safe delivery and collection.

Manny shrugged and muttered something about 'no balls' under his breath. Then they swapped packages, and Manny signed the check and slouched off into the night. Michael circumvented the busy casino, making his way round to the stage door, where he knew the dancers would eventually exit.

He hadn't decided what he'd say to her, he only knew that *something* would occur to him when she emerged.

Lighting a cigarette, he paced around impatiently, thinking that maybe he'd go with the well-used line of 'Don't I know you? And if not, I'm sure I know your sister, 'cause you look exactly like her.' It was a dumb line that always worked.

Ten minutes later, out came the pretty blonde with another girl. Her friend had long brown hair, big tits and a pronounced overbite.

He hung back, watching her for a moment. Out of costume she was even prettier than he'd thought and very young.

Too young?

Naw, exactly right.

The two girls stood outside chatting animatedly, then just as he decided it was time to make his move, a redheaded guy on a motorcycle zoomed up, and the blonde waved to her girlfriend, climbed on the back of the bike, and took off.

'Shit!' he mumbled under his breath. How was *that* for bad timing?

The girl with the long brown hair and the big tits was still standing there.

Without taking a beat he approached her. 'Uh . . . excuse me, Miss,' he said politely. 'Wasn't that Sarah who just left on the bike?'

'Who?' she said, looking him over and liking what she saw.

'Sarah . . . She's a girl I know from New York.'

'You must mean Dani.'

'Really?' he said, sounding surprised. 'She's the image of Sarah. Maybe they're sisters.'

'Could be.'

'You wouldn't have her phone number, would you?'

'Oh, c'*mon*,' she said, laughing. 'Like I'm gonna give *you* her phone number.'

'Why not?'

'Some strange guy on the make. You *gotta* be kidding.'

He gave her the innocent stare, the one that always scored him points. 'Don't I look like I deserve it?'

'No,' she said, shaking her head, long brown hair swirling round her shoulders.

'Yes, I do,' he said, turning on the charm. 'You know I do.'

She couldn't help giggling. He had her.

'So who was the guy on the bike?' he asked, making it casual.

'Dani lives with him,' the girl said. 'Which means *you*'re outta luck.' She paused for a moment, then added, 'But *I'm* free.'

'And very pretty too,' he said. 'Problem is I got an early flight outta here tomorrow. You know how it is.'

'Not really,' she said, batting her eyelashes.

'Havta get back to New York. Business, y'know.'

'Shame,' she said, giving him a why-don't-you-stay look.

'Yeah,' he agreed. 'I'll be here again soon.'

'Drop by and see me,' she said, with the appropriate amount of interest. 'My name's Angela. We can hook up.'

He wondered if he should seize the opportunity with Angela, who was definitely hot to tango. Then he decided against it.

Dani. That was the name that lingered.

On his next trip he was determined to meet her.

'How was Vegas?' Mamie asked, a cigarette dangling from her scarlet lips, a glass of vodka balanced in one hand. She was lolling on the couch in the Giovanni living room, wearing a leather skirt that was way too short, a flimsy transparent blouse and red slingbacks.

She must be almost fifty for crissakes, Michael thought. *Why can't she dress her age?*

'It's a fantastic place,' he replied. 'Only I gotta say, it ain't New York.'

'What about the girlies?' Mamie inquired, blowing a stream of smoke in his direction.

'Not bad,' he answered, in a noncommittal tone.

'How come you ain't got yourself a steady?' she wanted to know. 'You're big enough an' handsome enough.'

'Why buy the cow when you can get the milk for free?' he said, quoting his grandma.

His reply made her shriek with laughter. '*That's* my stud,' she said with a saucy wink. 'You wouldn't want some whining little tootsie hangin' on to your coat-tails, would you, now?'

'No,' he agreed. 'I wouldn't want that.'

He wished Vito would put in an appearance so he could give him his package and get the hell out. Good as she'd been to him, there were times when Mamie made him uncomfortable, and this was one of them.

'So tell me, Mikey,' she asked, dragging deeply on her cigarette, 'do the girlies you sleep with got any clue what they're doin' in the sack?'

He couldn't believe she was asking such a personal question. 'Huh?' he mumbled, hoping she'd get off the subject.

'You know what I mean,' she said, crossing her legs. 'Do they give you a *really* good time, or are they only in it for themselves?'

'Mrs G—' he began.

'Don't "Mrs G" me,' she interrupted. 'It's about time you called me Mamie. And you know exactly what I'm gettin' at.' She paused for a moment – then, 'Do they suck you off the way you like it? Or is it amateur night?'

'Jeez!'

'Oh, for crissakes, quit the shy act,' she said, stubbing out her cigarette. 'It don't suit you.'

'Thanks!'

'Do you make 'em come?' she asked, leaning forward, a gleam in her heavily mascaraed eyes. 'I bet you're a pistol between the sheets.'

He was saved by the appearance of Vito, who entered the room in a hurry – short and stout, puffing on a cigar, clad in a dark green velvet smoking jacket, green pants, and black patent leather shoes. Vito considered himself an arbiter of fashion.

'You got it, kid?' he asked, wheezing and coughing his way across the room.

'Sure have, Mr G.'

'Good, good,' he said, waving his cigar in the air. 'Gimme, gimme.'

Vito had a habit of repeating words, as if saying it once wasn't enough.

Michael handed over the large manilla envelope he was carrying and waited for his payment, which was always in cash. Vito was never without a thick stack of bills carried somewhere on his person.

Vito groped in his pocket, and produced the usual wad. 'Any problems?' he asked.

'Nope,' Michael replied, thinking, *How could there be problems with such a simple job?*

'You sure?'

'Yeah, I'm sure.'

'Hi, honey,' Mamie crooned, waving a beringed hand at

her husband. 'While you're handin' out money, how about li'l old me?'

'Whaddaya doin' drinkin' so early?' Vito growled, throwing her a disapproving look.

'Just bein' social,' she replied.

'Social, my ass,' Vito muttered. 'You're turnin' inta a lush.'

'Honey!'

Ignoring her, he turned back to Michael. 'Gotta feelin' you should start carryin' a piece,' he said.

'Huh?'

'A piece. A gun. Bang-bang. You understand what I'm sayin'?'

Michael frowned. Carrying a gun was not on the agenda of things he thought he should do. 'Well, uh . . .'

'You ever shot a gun?'

'No, Mr G.'

'You'd better learn. I'll set you up with someone who'll teach ya.'

'D'you really think—'

'Ya work for *me* now, kid,' Vito interrupted. 'These are tough times, ya gotta be prepared for anythin', an' I do mean *anythin'*. Get it?'

He got it.

Chapter Thirteen

Dani: 1964

When Dani was a few weeks shy of her seventeenth birthday, she realized that continuing to depend on Sam's companionship was not healthy for either of them. They both had to move on.

The big problem was that every time she mentioned moving out, Sam broke down in tears, which made her feel totally guilty.

Angela, her friend in the chorus line, counselled her. 'Sam's not *your* responsibility,' Angela said. 'He expects you to do everything for him, and that's crazy. It's not like he's your *boyfriend* or anything, is it?'

'No,' she answered hesitantly.

'Then you gotta dump him,' Angela said, a decisive tilt to her chin. '*I* need a new roommate, and you're *it*.'

Angela's motives were obviously selfish, but all the same, Dani knew she was right. Continuing to live with Sam was not a good idea, and even though they weren't girlfriend/boyfriend, he was horribly possessive. Every day he insisted on taking her to work on his motorcycle, and every evening he was waiting outside the stage door to bring her home. She couldn't do anything without him questioning her, and she was beginning to feel stifled. As

Angela had pointed out, it wasn't as if he was her boyfriend, and although she'd made it her business to steer clear of men, she'd decided it might be interesting at least to *try* going out on a date. All the other girls in the chorus talked about men constantly – it was their obsession. After a while she had felt totally left out.

Most days she practised conversations in her head about how she would inform Sam of her imminent departure.

Oh, hi, Sam. I think it's better for both of us if I move out. That way, we can have a more normal relationship.

Hmm . . .

Y'know, Sam, isn't it about time you started seeing other girls? After all, Emily's never coming back.

No, not so good. Any mention of Emily and he'd go berserk.

Reluctantly she decided the truth was best: *Sam, I'm leaving. It's the right thing to do.*

Still, she couldn't bring herself to tell him, it was too awkward. Emily's disappearance was exceptionally sad for both of them, and because he'd loved her so very much, even more difficult for Sam to bear.

The chorus line at the Estradido Hotel was by no means the classiest line in town. The hotel itself was hardly on the same level as the big hotels such as the Stardust, the Sands and the Desert Inn. The Estradido was Mob-owned, and everyone knew it. Low-level gamblers came there and lost their money. This suited Philippe Estradido fine. All he wanted was their money; he didn't need movie stars and moguls hanging out.

Dani was by far the most beautiful girl in the chorus. This didn't make her particularly popular with the other women, who were mostly veterans, apart from Angela, who was young enough not to feel threatened.

'Here's what you need,' Angela informed her one night, as they sat in front of their communal dressing-table mirror preparing for the evening show. 'A handsome stud who'll sweep out the cobwebs and wake you up. My God, sweetie, if you don't do something soon, you'll end up an old maid.'

Angela had no idea that Dani was still only sixteen: like everyone else, Angela was under the impression she was almost twenty.

'Actually,' Angela continued, 'a guy stopped by the stage door the other night who'd be perfect for you.' She paused for a moment. 'Course, I kinda went for him myself, but if he comes back I'll be generous and let *you* have first shot.'

'Who was he?' Dani asked curiously, not at all sure that she wanted first shot.

'Gorgeous!' Angela exclaimed, applying thick black fake eyelashes with a practised hand. 'That's all you need to know.'

'I'm not sure I'm ready,' Dani began.

'Oh, *please*,' Angela said, spidery eyelashes firmly in place. 'I'm sick of hearing you say that.'

'Sorry,' she murmured.

'Now,' Angela said, reviewing her reflection. 'When are you telling Sam you're sharing my apartment? 'Cause if you don't do it soon, I gotta get someone else.'

'This week,' she said quickly.

'Promise?' Angela said, reaching for her scanty costume.

'Yes, I promise,' Dani said, deciding that she'd tell Sam soon.

A few days later, she cooked Sam his favourite meal. They sat at the kitchen table eating chicken and french fries, while Frank Sinatra serenaded them on the stereo. After a while she broached the subject. 'Sam, I'm, uh . . . moving out,' she ventured.

He pretended he hadn't heard her.

'Are you listening to me? I'm leaving,' she repeated. 'Angela needs a roommate, and I've decided it's a good idea for me to move in with her.'

'What?' he said, crinkling his forehead.

'I'm sharing an apartment with Angela,' she said, speaking fast. 'I mean, you and I – we'll still be friends and everything, and I'll see you all the time, but we've both got to get out and meet other people.'

'Why?' he said, putting down his fork.

'Because right now we depend on each other too much.'

He stared at her for a few moments. 'Is this how you want to treat me?' he said at last. 'By telling me that you're leaving me by myself?'

'Of course not,' she said patiently. 'It's just that I feel it'll be better this way.'

'No, Dani,' he said fiercely, 'it won't. You're too young to be on your own. It's my job to make sure you don't get into trouble.'

'I keep on telling you, Sam,' she said, quite exasperated, 'I might be young in years, but I do know what's going on. I can look after myself.'

'Emily thought *she* could look after herself, and look what happened to her,' he pointed out. 'You *need* my protection.'

'We don't *know* what happened to her, do we?' Dani said.

'She could be anywhere,' he answered, grim-faced. 'She could've been white-slaved and taken off to . . . I dunno – one of those countries where they keep girls in brothels. Do you even know what a brothel is?'

'Yes.'

'Is that what you want for yourself?' he said sternly. 'Somebody to stick a needle in your arm, smuggle you on to a boat, and take you off to a foreign country?'

'What're you *talking* about?'

'That's probably what happened to Emily,' he said dourly.

'Look, Sam,' she said, determined not to weaken, 'I love you very much. You rescued me, and I'll never forget it. Now I have to go.'

'No, you *don't*,' he said stubbornly. ''Cause if you do, I'll tell them how old you are, an' you'll lose your job.'

'I'm almost seventeen, Sam,' she said, upset by his weak attempt at blackmail. 'I can work then.'

'Yes, but they'll realize you've been lying to them all this time so they'll fire you anyway.'

'Please don't threaten me,' she said, close to tears. 'I want us to stay friends.'

He pushed his plate away and stood up. 'And what if *I* want more than that?'

'Excuse me?' she said, startled.

'What if *I* want to be more than friends?' he demanded. 'Don't you think you owe me that?'

She tried to pretend she didn't understand what he was getting at, but she understood only too well, and it made her cringe. Sam was Emily's husband, and she had never thought of him in a physical way.

'I'll be moving next week,' she said, starting to stack the dishes.

'You can't do this to me,' he said plaintively.

'I'm not doing anything to you,' she said, wishing he would stop making her feel so guilty.

'Yes, you are.'

She took a long, deep breath and uttered her final words on the subject. 'Next Monday, Sam. You'll just have to accept it.'

A week later she moved.

'So you're actually doing this?' he said, fixing her with a malevolent glare as she carried her two suitcases to the front door.

'I told you I was.'

'I don't believe it,' he muttered.

116

'It'll work out fine,' she assured him. 'I'll probably spend more time over here than at my place.'

'Don't bother,' he said sulkily.

Angela's apartment was on the fifth floor of a smart building complex. Dani was impressed and also a little surprised that Angela could afford such a nice place. They'd discussed how much rent she'd contribute, but as soon as she saw the apartment, she knew it couldn't possibly be enough.

'Don't worry about it,' Angela said airily, when Dani brought up the subject. 'One of my boyfriends owns the building. He gave me a sweet deal.'

Angela had plenty of boyfriends, but, as far as Dani could tell, none of them meant much to her. 'Horny guys are a dime a dozen,' Angela explained. 'Use 'em for what you can get out of the poor bastards, then move on.'

'I'd like to find someone special,' Dani said wistfully, remembering what Sam and Emily had once shared.

'Dream on!' Angela exclaimed. 'Guys are only after one thing. An' once they get it, they are *history*.'

'Surely there's some nice ones out there?'

'You are *so* naïve,' Angela said scornfully. 'I bet you've never even slept with a guy, have you?'

Dani shook her head.

'Ha! You must be the only twenty-year-old virgin in Vegas.'

For a moment Dani was tempted to tell her how old she really was, then decided against it. Angela might not want her as a roommate if she revealed the truth.

Two nights later Angela informed her they were going out on a double date.

'We are?' Dani said, wide-eyed at the thought.

'Two hot guys, it'll be a blast,' Angela assured her.

For almost four years Dani had been repelling all

advances; now Angela was expecting her to go out with a stranger on a blind date. It didn't make sense, and yet she feared coming across as a bad sport. Besides, she'd made up her mind to discover what all the fuss was about concerning the male sex.

Angela lent her a sexy gold lamé top and jangly rhinestone earrings. 'Be nice to the guy,' Angela instructed. 'Tell him he's a stud an' shit like that. They get off on flattery.'

'I don't even know him,' Dani demurred.

'You will!' Angela said, with a coarse giggle.

Dani's half of the double date was short and overweight, with greasy hair and the biggest sticking-out ears she'd ever seen. His name was Manny Spiven, and the moment he opened his mouth she knew she'd made a big mistake agreeing to accompany Angela on this adventure.

Henry, the guy with Angela, was scrawny, with lank blond hair and tinted aviator glasses perched on the end of his long, pointed nose.

'Henry's training to be a dealer,' Angela boasted. 'That's a pretty important job.'

'Don't make *that* my claim to fame,' Henry objected, winking knowingly. 'I got other assets, y' know.'

'Oh, yes,' Angela said with a low, sexy chuckle. 'And *I'm* lookin' forward to seeing them!'

'*That* can definitely be arranged,' Henry said before switching his attention to Dani. 'So how long *you* bin' in town, cupcake?' he asked.

'Long enough to know it's safer to avoid you,' Angela said, giggling.

'Why?' he said proudly. 'You think I got me a reputation?'

'You *know* you have,' Angela retorted, which pleased Henry no end.

Manny decided it was time to join in the conversation.

'How ya doin'?' he said, leering at Dani. 'Feelin' good? 'Cause I'm feelin' *real* good. We're gonna rip the town tonight, little lady. You an' me, Dani an' Manny – some combination!'

Trapped, Dani thought. *I'm trapped. Why did I allow myself to get in this position?*

Because I wanted to please Angela. I wanted to show her that I'm not some naive girl who doesn't know how to behave.

'Where are we having dinner?' Angela asked, clinging to Henry's arm.

'Wherever you want, doll,' he replied.

Not to be left out, Manny grabbed Dani's arm. 'I could go for a big juicy steak,' he announced. 'Me an' my girl, we're gonna need all the strength we can get, don't we, babe?'

As the evening progressed, Dani decided that things were going rapidly from bad to worse. First there was the dinner, when Manny proceeded to display the table manners of an ape, chewing on his steak like a food-deprived caveman. This was followed by a long gambling session on the slot machines at the Sands. When Manny and Henry were finally through, they suggested a stroll round the large outdoor pool, whereupon Manny grabbed her in a tight embrace, his pudgy hands roaming all over her breasts.

'Get *off* me,' she said, shoving him away.

'Don't gimme that hard-to-get crap,' he sneered. 'You *know* you want me.'

'Oh, *please*,' she said heatedly. 'I never did and I never will.'

He did not appreciate her reply. 'Who the *hell* d'you think you are?' he said angrily. 'Some dumb hoofer in a bad show. You're *lucky* t'be out with a guy like me, an' dontcha forget it.'

Henry and Angela had walked ahead of them and were

now standing by the deserted outdoor bar, locked in a deep French kiss. Obviously it was no use trying to attract their attention.

'I'm leaving,' Dani said, attempting to remain calm.

'Not until you've paid for dinner,' Manny said, scowling. '*I* ain't gettin' stuck with *your* part of the check. Fact is, you *owe* me.'

'Ex*cuse* me?' she said, outraged.

'You heard,' he said, grabbing her again.

'Take . . . your . . . hands *off* me,' she said, struggling out of his grasp.

'What is it with you good-lookin' broads?' he snarled. 'You're all the same – think we should treat you like fuckin' princesses.'

'How much *was* dinner?' she asked, desperately trying to control a flood of tears.

'What?' he snapped.

'Here,' she said, groping blindly in her purse and shoving a bunch of dollar bills at him. 'Take this – and do me a favour. Forget we ever met.' And with that she was on her way.

'Hoity-toity *bitch*!' he yelled after her. 'You'll get yours.'

She didn't look back.

Chapter Fourteen

Michael: 1964

In New York things were heating up. Vito Giovanni suddenly found himself in the headlines. The Feds, who'd been tracking his activities for quite a while, had decided to go after him on a tax-evasion charge and it was infuriating him.

His high-powered lawyers assured him the Feds had no case, but in the meantime the newspapers latched on to him. They began calling him all kinds of names, and dogging his movements. Every time he left his house there was a bunch of photographers gathered outside pushing and shoving to get the best shot.

Mamie loved the attention. 'Makes me feel like a movie star,' she exclaimed, trying on yet another recently purchased expensive outfit.

'Don't,' Vito informed her, his face grim. 'In my business the trick is to stay *outta* the newspapers.'

'But, honey,' she answered playfully, 'we're *famous*.'

'Fuck that famous shit,' he growled. 'Who needs the attention?'

Meanwhile, Michael was learning how to use a gun. Vito had arranged for a tall, brooding man, known as the Chronicle, to teach him. The two of them drove out to a shooting range three mornings a week, where the Chronicle instructed him on every aspect of handling and shooting guns.

'It's like I'm gettin' me a crash course,' Michael boasted to Max when he picked him up from his job. Max, who was currently selling women's shoes in a discount store on Seventh Avenue, threw him a disapproving look.

'How come you wanna learn to shoot?' he asked, scratching his head.

'Gotta know how to protect myself,' Michael explained, as they set off down the street.

'From *what?*'

'You never know,' Michael answered, with a casual shrug.

'Yeah,' Max said, quite exasperated. 'I guess ya gotta protect yourself from all those low-lifes you hang out with.'

Max was always carrying on about Michael's connection to the Giovanni family. It pissed him off. So far his so-called connection had made him nothing but money. 'You're beginning to sound like my grandma,' he remarked.

'Thanks a lot!'

'Don't mention it.'

They continued on down the street, both busy with their own thoughts.

Why am *I learning to shoot?* Michael thought. *It is kind of a crazy thing to do, an' the Chronicle is a total freak with his flat dead eyes and creepy attitude. But, hey, if Mr G wants me to learn, I gotta go along with it. He's the boss.*

Max was thinking about other things. He had something to tell Michael, and he wanted to get it over with as soon as possible before Michael heard it from someone else.

'Uh . . . I got news,' he ventured at last.

'Yeah?' Michael said, waving at a girl he knew.

Max hesitated a moment: he wasn't sure what kind of reaction he was about to get. 'Tina an' me,' he finally

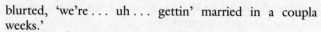

blurted, 'we're . . . uh . . . gettin' married in a coupla weeks.'

Michael stopped short. '*Whaaat?*'

'You heard,' Max said quickly. 'An' I'd like you t'be my best man.'

'Aw, c'*mon*,' Michael said disbelievingly. 'You only just got engaged.'

'We've decided we don't wanna wait.'

'You're nuts,' Michael snapped. 'There's no way you can afford to get hitched.'

'I can do it,' Max answered stubbornly.

'Jeez!' Michael said, in disgust. 'You're not even twenty yet, you work in some lousy women's shoe store, an' you still live at home. What've *you* got to offer a girl like Tina?'

'I don't suppose you've ever heard of bein' in love,' Max said, defending his decision. 'I'm not like you, Mr Fuck 'Em an' Leave 'Em. *I*'m different.'

'Yeah,' Michael said flatly. 'You're different all right. *You*'re a jerk.'

'Better than bein' some gangster's boy,' Max shot back.

'Who're you calling a gangster's boy?' Michael demanded, putting up his fists.

'You're so far up Giovanni's ass you got a brown nose,' Max responded.

They started getting into a fake fight, fists flying, a scenario they'd been playing out since they were kids.

Passers-by stared. They didn't care: it was all about cutting loose.

After a few minutes Michael got bored. 'Let's go grab a burger,' he suggested. 'I got a hot date later, so I'm gonna need all the energy I can get.'

'You an' your hot dates,' Max scoffed. 'Dontcha ever plan on settlin' with the right girl?'

'Why would I do that when I got pussy comin' out my ears?'

Max shook his head. 'You should hook up with a girl like Tina. She's the greatest.'

'I did. Remember?'

Max preferred to forget that Michael had once dated his future wife. It wasn't something he cared to think about.

'So,' Michael asked, purposely needling his friend, 'she puttin' out yet?'

'Like I'd tell *you*.'

'How come?'

'Can it, Mike. We're talkin' about the girl I'm gonna marry.'

'Oh, *now* I get it,' Michael said, with a knowing grin. 'You knocked her up, right?'

'No freakin' way,' Max said, his face reddening.

'Okay, okay,' Michael said, starting to laugh. 'Hey, remember the time you was workin' at that fleabag hotel, an' I came in with Polly? You was *green* with envy.'

'I was?'

'Bet your ass you was.'

'What happened to her?'

'Married some jerk an' went to live in the suburbs. She's probably a fat old bag with a houseful of screamin' kids by now.'

'It was only a coupla years ago,' Max pointed out.

'Those kinda women, they go downhill fast,' Michael said, turning into one of their regular hamburger joints. He winked at the girl behind the counter and ordered his usual – a double cheeseburger with everything on it. Max went for a grilled ham sandwich.

'So . . . you're gettin' married,' Michael said, as they sat at the counter, waiting for their food.

'Yup,' Max said sheepishly. 'Guess I am.'

'Jerk!'

'Asshole!'

'I've been thinking,' Michael said, on a sudden impulse,

'how about I treat you to a plane ticket to Vegas an' we celebrate your bachelor night there?'

'Why d'you keep on goin' to Las Vegas?' Max asked, swigging a Coke.

'Business.'

'Business my ass.'

'No, really,' Michael insisted. 'I gotta take care of stuff for Mr G.'

'What kinda stuff?'

'Don't worry, it's legit.'

'Says you.'

'You wanna come or not? My treat all the way.'

'Vegas,' Max said, deeply tempted. 'Tina'll kill me.'

'Run it by her,' Michael said, as the girl behind the counter slid their orders in front of them. 'Maybe she wants her own night out with her friends.'

'You think?' Max said hesitantly.

'Yeah,' Michael said, reaching for the ketchup. 'I'm sure she does.'

'Maybe . . .'

'Look, you're comin'. I don't want no argument.'

Later, Michael hooked up with his hot date, an Asian waitress with a penchant for gymnastics.

She arrived at his small, one-room apartment carrying cartons of take-out food and an insatiable sexual appetite. They fucked, then ate, three times in a row. She was so agile that she managed to tire *him* out, and that was some feat.

Eventually she went home. He liked a girl who knew when it was time to leave. Clingy females were not for him: he appreciated his freedom too much.

Now that he'd invited Max to Vegas he had to figure out a way to mention it to Mr G. Then he decided no way was the best way. Since he was paying for his friend to make the trip, there was no reason he had to tell.

A week later he picked Max up in a cab and they headed for the airport.

Max was excited. 'I didn't tell Tina where we're goin',' he confessed. 'She thinks we're on our way to Atlantic City.'

'Atlantic City?' Michael said, raising a quizzical eyebrow.

'Yeah, an' let me tell you, she wasn't too happy about *that*.'

'How come?'

'Considers you a bad influence.'

'Jeez!' Michael exclaimed. 'She got you by the short and curlies already?'

'It's not like that,' Max said quickly. 'It's just that I don't want her feelin' left out. She'd *kill* t'go to Vegas.'

'She would?' Michael said, not convinced. When *he*'d been dating Tina she'd never wanted to go anywhere.

'Yeah, she's into all those Rat Pack movies, so I couldn't let her know I was goin' without her – right? An' who knows? Maybe I'll get to take her one of these days.'

'On *your* salary? Forget it.'

'I ain't *always* gonna be workin' in a shoe store,' Max responded indignantly.

'I should ask Mr G to hire you. That way you can make some real money.'

'I wouldn't work for that scumbag.'

'You wouldn't, huh?'

'No way.'

'He's sure bin good to *me*.'

'Read the papers. *Mr* Giovanni is bein' accused of all kinda shit.'

Michael knew exactly what Mr G was being accused of – extortion, blackmail, loan-sharking, even murder. None of it had been proven, so he chose to ignore it.

'Aw, c'mon,' he said. 'You don't believe that crap they write, do you?'

Max thought it prudent to drop the subject; pissing Michael off was not a good idea – especially since he was paying for the trip.

By the time they arrived in Vegas it was late afternoon. Michael swaggered off the plane feeling quite proud that he was about to show his friend the sights. 'I got a room at the Estradido Hotel,' he announced, showing off. 'You'll bunk in with me. An' if you score a little honey to have fun with before Tina cuts off your nuts, I'll hang out in the casino till you're finished.'

'I'm not *lookin'* t'get laid,' Max objected.

'You're not, huh?' Michael said, poking him in the ribs. 'Wait till you get a load of the girls in Vegas. Not only will you wanna get laid but, believe me, you'll be *beggin'* t'spend the rest of your sorry days here.'

'Not me,' Max said firmly.

Michael grinned. 'We'll see.'

Vito Giovanni's right-hand man, Tommaso, had issued explicit instructions about how Michael was supposed to handle delivery and collection of all packages. The package on this trip was bigger than usual, so instead of carrying it on his person, he'd had to stuff it into a nylon carry-on bag. 'Do *not* let it outta your possession,' Tommaso had warned. 'Not until you make the switch.' Boldly, Michael had inquired what was in it. 'Ask Mr Giovanni,' was Tommaso's cryptic reply.

Yeah. Sure. Like he'd dare to do that.

The routine was always the same. Meet Manny Spiven for a drink and dinner, spend a few hours with him, make the switch, and be on the early-morning plane back to New York.

Michael failed to understand why he was supposed to spend time with Manny. It was dumb, but Tommaso had assured him it was necessary.

This time he'd make the exchange and split. Manny wouldn't care: their dislike of each other was mutual. That way he could spend the evening showing Max the town, and nobody would be any the wiser.

After checking in, he got the usual message to meet Manny outside the entrance to the Starburst Lounge at eight.

Crap! Now they'd get stuck with the jerk. And what was he supposed to do with the nylon bag? Lug it round with him all night?

'We gotta go meet this guy,' he explained to Max. 'It won't take long.'

'What guy?'

'Relax. You'll have a few drinks, eat good, see a show . . .'

'I wanna gamble,' Max announced.

'How much you got to lose?'

'Who said anythin' about losin'?' Max joked.

'Shit!' Michael said. 'Amateur gamblers are what this town was built on.'

'Lead me to the tables,' Max said confidently. 'I'm gonna bust the bank!'

By the time they met up with Manny Spiven, Max had lost every dime he'd had with him and was in a miserable mood. 'Told you,' Michael couldn't help saying. 'Gambling's a mug's game.'

'You gotta lend me fifty bucks,' Max begged. 'You gotta do this for me.'

'Uh-uh.'

'Then what chance I got of gettin' even?'

'No chance,' Michael said grimly.

'Aw, give the poor bastard fifty bucks,' Manny said as Max went off to the men's room.

Michael shot him a look. He didn't need Manny Spiven's advice: *he* knew what was good for Max, and there was no way the idiot could afford to lose one more dollar.

'He's through,' Michael said. 'This'll teach him a lesson.'

'Who is he anyway?' Manny asked.

'A friend.'

'Mr G know he's with you?'

'Sure,' Michael lied.

'That's funny. Mr G usually likes t'keep things tight.' Manny slurped his drink. 'I heard that when his old lady was makin' the Vegas run she wasn't allowed no company.'

'Mrs Giovanni used to do this?' Michael asked, surprised.

'Sometimes. Only she didn't meet with me. She dealt with Mr Estradido.' Manny lowered his voice. 'Rumour is she was into Dyke City.'

'What?' Michael said blankly.

'Dyke City. Suckin' pussy.' Manny pulled a face as if to say, *How stupid can you get?* 'Gettin' it on with snatch, for crissakes.'

Shocked as he was, Michael didn't let on. He kept his expression blank while wondering if Manny Spiven was lying. Mamie Giovanni a lesbo? If Mr G ever found out he'd go ape-shit.

As soon as Max came back from the men's room they headed into the lounge, in time for the start of the show. Manny knew the *maître d'*, so they always got a front table, and Michael never had to show his fake ID, which he carried on him at all times just in case.

He ordered a beer. So did Max, who was still busy bemoaning his losses.

'Snap outta it,' Michael said in a low voice. 'You gonna enjoy yourself or what?'

'Lend me the fifty an' I'll enjoy myself,' Max muttered. 'I gotta get even.'

'No freakin' chance,' Michael answered, figuring he was doing him a favour.

Then the music started, and on came the girls clad in their scanty, gold-fringed toy-soldier outfits, boobs and legs out front.

Michael immediately spotted the one he liked. Dani, that was her name. Dani with the long blonde hair, blue eyes and dazzling smile. Not to mention a body to die for.

Manny leaned over. 'Y' see the cooze with the big tits?' he said, leering and pointing at Dani. 'I had her, an' she ain't so hot.'

'What?' Michael said, frowning.

'You heard,' Manny responded. 'She fucks like a dead fish an' smells like one too.' He guffawed, rubbing his hands together.

'No shit,' Michael said, his expression impassive.

'I've had 'em all,' Manny boasted. 'An' this one was a real dud.'

Michael stared straight ahead, refusing to give Manny the pleasure of questioning him about the girl. She'd fucked Manny Spiven. End of story. He wouldn't go near her with somebody else's cock.

'Fifty,' Max pleaded in his ear. 'Fifty lousy bucks. You gotta do this for me, Mike. I gotta get even or Tina'll kill me!'

Angrily Michael reached into his pocket. 'Take the lousy money,' he said, thrusting some bills at Max. 'An' when you blow this, don't come runnin' back for more.'

Max grabbed it and took off.

Michael shook his head in disgust. This wasn't turning out to be the evening he'd planned.

Chapter Fifteen

Dani: 1964

'Guess who's sitting at one of the front tables,' Angela said, as they changed costumes.

Dani already knew. She'd spotted Manny Spiven the moment she'd hit the stage for their first routine, and it had taken all her willpower to block out his offensive presence.

'Manny,' Angela continued. '*And* he's with that cute guy I told you about, the one from New York.'

Who cares? Dani wanted to say. *Manny Spiven is a rude, horrible disgusting pig.*

'Want me to set you up?' Angela asked, adjusting her feathered headdress.

'No thanks,' she answered coolly. *I wouldn't go out with one of Manny Spiven's friends if he was the last man standing.*

'Then *I'll* bag him,' Angela said, quite happy at the thought. 'I'm not letting *this* one slip away.'

As far as Dani was concerned, Angela could do what she liked.

Unfazed by her complaints about Manny, Angela had tried to fix her up on several more blind dates, all of which she'd declined. It seemed that Angela had an endless supply of men and, unfortunately, most nights she brought one back to the apartment. Lying in bed at night, Dani could hear the vigorous sounds of Angela's lovemaking coming from the next room. Had she made a mistake moving in with Angela? Sam might have been right – maybe she *wasn't* ready to be out on her own.

One morning she'd noticed money on the kitchen table. When Angela emerged from her bedroom, wrapping a satin robe round her, she'd asked her where it had come from.

'That's from Petey,' Angela had answered casually. 'He told me to buy myself a present. What a guy!'

Dani was naïve, but not *that* naïve. Was her roommate getting paid for sex? Everything seemed to indicate that she was.

'I still don't understand what Manny did that was so terrible,' Angela said, leaning into the dressing-room mirror and adding more blush to her already over-rouged cheeks. 'He's a man, honey, they're *all* horny. What's the big deal about that?'

'I told you,' Dani answered patiently. 'He grabbed me, then yelled all sorts of rude insults when I pushed him off.'

'The guy's feelings were probably hurt,' Angela said. 'Y'see,' she added knowledgeably, 'you gotta baby 'em. Deep down they're all little boys.'

'I don't have to baby anyone.'

'You sure babied that Sam guy,' Angela remarked. 'By the way, he called this morning.'

'He did?' Dani said. 'You never mentioned it.'

She hadn't heard from Sam in over two weeks. She'd been wondering where he was and why he hadn't called. She really wanted to see him: he was her safe zone – always there to protect her.

'Sorry,' Angela said, pushing up her cleavage.

'Show time,' yelled the stage manager. 'Get your asses on stage, ladies.'

No time to call Sam back now, he'd have to wait.

'Don't forget to take a peek at the cute guy,' Angela reminded her, as they lined up at the side of the stage. 'And remember, you blew it, so now he's all mine.'

In the next number some of the girls were topless. Dani had elected not to go that route, although she was certainly tall enough and the director had urged her to do it, claiming she would make more money that way.

'I prefer to stay dressed,' she'd insisted.

'Hey, babe, your call,' he'd replied. 'Although what difference it makes beats me – you can see everything you got as it is.'

This was not exactly true. Minuscule as her costume was, it still covered certain body parts that she didn't care to put on view.

Angela was contemplating going topless. 'I gotta get a tit job first,' she'd said. 'My boobs ain't what they used to be.'

'You'd actually do that?' Dani had asked, shocked at the thought of parading half naked in front of hundreds of strangers every week.

'Yeah, maybe. I got me a surgeon friend who promised he'd do it for nothing, only I gotta do *him* a small favour in exchange.' She'd winked. 'Know what I mean?'

Unfortunately, Dani was beginning to realize *exactly* what she meant.

The girls hit the stage to the sound of Sinatra singing 'Come Fly With Me' – a perennial favourite.

Dani managed scrupulously to ignore Manny, who appeared to be leering up at her. However, she couldn't help taking a quick peek at the guy with him. Angela was right: he was exceptionally good-looking, young, dark, and extremely handsome.

He caught her looking and averted his eyes. No sign of interest there, which was fine with her. Angela could have him, she couldn't care less.

By the time they finished their third number she was tired and her feet hurt. Two shows a night was tough and she couldn't wait to get home.

As soon as they hit the dressing room, Angela was on the move. 'I gotta get going,' she said, grabbing her street clothes and dressing hurriedly. 'I'm saying hello to Manny and then he'll have to introduce me to the stud. Who knows what'll happen then?'

Dani knew exactly what would happen then.

Idly she wondered if Angela would get paid for it, although Manny's friend hardly looked the type who'd have to pay. He was too movie-star handsome – girls were probably tripping over themselves to get near him.

'See you at home, sweetie,' Angela called, racing from the dressing room.

'She's *such* a whore,' remarked Ellen, one of the dancers, a flat-faced, thirtyish redhead.

'What?' Dani said.

'I repeat, she's such a whore,' Ellen said, carefully peeling off her black fishnet stockings. 'I can't imagine why you hang round with her.'

'I don't,' Dani said flatly. 'I share her apartment. And you shouldn't call people names.'

'Doesn't do much for your reputation, dear,' Ellen remarked, wriggling her toes. 'You seem like a *nice* girl.'

I am a nice girl, she wanted to yell. *I'm a nice girl caught in a difficult situation.*

But she didn't say a word.

After she'd changed out of her costume, she called Sam from a pay phone. He wasn't home.

She couldn't help wondering if he'd found himself a girlfriend. Part of her hoped that he had, because he deserved to be happy. On the other hand, she wished that he hadn't, because even though she no longer lived in his apartment, it was comforting to know that she was the most important person in his life. Like her, he had no other family.

Once she got home it was nice and quiet. When Angela was around, everything always seemed chaotic. She enjoyed having the apartment to herself: it was cool and tidy.

After fixing herself a can of Campbell's vegetable soup, she curled up on the couch and watched half an hour of TV before taking a shower and climbing into bed.

An hour later she was awoken by loud music, 'Baby Love' by the Supremes, followed by Dean Martin crooning 'Everybody Loves Somebody', and then the Beatles 'A Hard Day's Night'. Willing herself not to listen, she finally fell back to sleep, ignoring the noises now coming from Angela's bedroom.

In the morning she woke early, jumped out of bed, and wandered into the kitchen, where she opened the fridge, poured herself a glass of apple juice and was just popping a piece of bread into the toaster when a male voice said, 'Uh, 'scuse me.'

She spun round, cheeks flushing, well aware that the baby-doll nightie she had on was totally transparent.

The guy who'd been sitting with Manny Spiven stood there, the handsome one from the previous night.

'Who are *you?*' she blurted, crossing her arms across her chest, soon realizing that it didn't do much to cover her lower half.

'Uh . . . name's Michael. I'm a friend of Angela's.'

Sure. I heard you moaning and groaning last night. Did you have to pay?

'You startled me,' she said accusingly, backing towards the door.

His dark eyes were all over her. 'Bein' startled suits you,' he said.

Michael. Nice name. He does *look like a movie star.*

She hesitated for a moment before taking flight,

running past him to the sanctuary of her bedroom, where she grabbed her robe and quickly put it on, belting it tightly.

'Your toast's burnin',' he called from the kitchen. 'Want me to pop it out?'

Summoning all the dignity she could muster, she returned to the kitchen, where he was now pouring himself a cup of instant coffee. He'd placed her toast on a plate.

'Thank you,' she managed.

'Coffee?' he offered.

This was supposed to be *her* kitchen, and he was taking over like he owned it. He had some nerve. 'No,' she said stiffly.

'Sorry about walkin' in on you,' he said, sitting down at the kitchen table. 'I was lookin' for Max, an' the front door was open.' He chuckled. 'Guess they must've been in a hurry.'

'Max?' she asked, frowning.

'My pal. He, uh, came home with Angela last night. Now I gotta get him to the airport or we'll miss our flight.'

'I thought *you* were with Angela,' she blurted.

'Naw, not me,' he said, sipping his coffee and thinking she looked even prettier without all that heavy makeup plastered over her face.

'So you simply walked in here this morning?'

'I shoulda rung the bell, right?' he said sheepishly. 'Only, like I said, the door was open, an' I didn't know anyone else lived here.'

'*I* live here,' she said lamely. 'Angela and me, we're roommates.'

'Oh, yeah,' he said, nodding. 'I know who you are, you're a girlfriend of Manny Spiven's.'

'I am *not*,' she said indignantly. 'I *hate* that rude pig.'

'You do?' he said, surprised.

'Yes, I do. I had the horrible experience of going on a

blind date with him once. The pig tried to jump me, and when I didn't respond, he shouted all kinds of insults at me.'

'That's not the way *he* tells it.'

'Ex*cuse* me?' she said, furious that there was a Manny Spiven version of their one unmemorable date.

'Did you know that he goes round sayin' that he's . . . uh . . . got it on with you?'

'*What*?!' she exclaimed, blushing a deep red. 'That's absolutely *untrue*.'

'Guess he was makin' up stories.'

She was so humiliated. How dare Manny Spiven make up lies about her? 'I *told* you he was a pig,' she said fiercely. 'A lying pig!'

Michael grinned. He should have known Manny was full of crap.

'Anyway,' she said vehemently, 'maybe *you* should teach him some manners – he's *your* friend.'

'No,' Michael corrected. 'Business associate. Sure as hell not friend.'

'I thought . . .' she said tentatively.

'Manny's an asshole,' he said, reaching for an apple and taking a bite. 'Seems like you found that out for yourself.'

'At least we agree on that.'

'So,' he said, 'now that we've straightened Manny out . . . it's nice to finally meet you.'

'Finally?' she said, big blue eyes meeting his.

'I've been watchin' you for a while,' he said, mentally kicking himself for blowing the opportunity of getting together with her the previous night.

'You have?' she said, surprised and quite flattered.

'Saw you a few weeks back, only just when I was about to make my move you ran off with some guy on a motorcycle.'

'My sister's husband,' she said quickly.

'Glad to hear he doesn't belong to you.'

'What?' she murmured breathlessly.

'That he's not your guy,' he repeated, giving her a direct stare that made her go weak at the knees.

Before she could answer, Max staggered into the kitchen bleary-eyed and bare-chested, clad only in his crumpled boxer shorts, his hair standing on end as if he'd just put his finger into an electric socket.

'Jeez!' Michael exclaimed, controlling his laughter. 'You look like crap!'

'Water,' Max gasped. 'I need water.'

'It's the desert air,' Michael deadpanned to Dani. 'New Yorkers – they can't take it.'

'You're from New York?' she asked.

'Yup,' he said, standing up. 'An' we're supposed t'be on a plane any minute.'

'Oh,' she said, strangely disappointed.

'But I'll be back,' he said cheerfully. 'Soon. An' next time we won't let Manny Spiven come between us.' He winked at her. 'Will we?'

'No,' she said, and for the first time in her short life she felt a stirring within her that made her want to grab this man and hold on to him forever.

Chapter Sixteen

'F uck!' the gunman exploded, punching a hole in the wall, his rage and frustration quite apparent. Almost an hour had passed and nothing was happening. Every communication had promised that a van was on its way. So far no van.

'You!' he yelled, pointing at Madison. 'Get over here.'

She felt a coldness in the pit of her stomach. Was he about to make good on his threat and start shooting the hostages? Was she to be the first victim?

Bravely she stood up and walked over to him.

He thrust the phone at her. 'Tell 'em five more minutes or someone fuckin' dies.'

She took the phone and began speaking. The negotiator on the other end sounded like an idiot.

'They mean business,' she said urgently. 'Where's the van? Why isn't it here yet?'

'How many of them are in there?' the negotiator asked, his voice cold and impersonal. 'Are they all armed?'

'Yes,' she answered quickly. 'Three minutes is good.'

'Try to keep everyone calm,' he said. 'I'm used to these situations. We're working on getting you all out safely.'

Was he kidding? They were locked up with armed men

who were threatening to kill them, and he was telling her to keep everyone calm. This was insane.

'What's with the three minutes?' the gunman snapped.

'They're trying to get a van here.'

'You're comin' with,' he decided.

Cole was on his feet in a flash. 'You can't take her without me,' he said urgently.

The gunman looked him over. 'You her old man?'

'Yes,' Cole lied.

'Get the fuck over by the door. An' you,' he said, waving his weapon at the short redhead in the tight blue dress, 'you get over there, too.'

'I want my ring back,' the redhead whined. 'It's my engagement ring.'

He ignored her, picking out three more hostages to go wait by the door.

Please, God, Madison prayed. *Let them send a van soon. Because if they don't, somebody's going to die.*

Jolie was on her third cigarette when she realized that Jenna had been missing for far too long. This was not good, and she wasn't about to hang round in the ladies' room all night waiting for her. Impatiently she stubbed out her cigarette and re-entered the casino. The room was still packed with people gambling their lives away. As she walked through the throngs, she glanced over at the blackjack table where she'd first spotted Andy Dale. He was no longer there, and Jenna was nowhere in sight.

Oh, shit! It wasn't *her* fault – all she'd done was point him out, *and* she'd told Jenna to hurry back. Too bad if the ditz couldn't follow instructions.

'Where's my wife?' Vincent demanded as soon as she returned to the table.

'Playing the slots, I think,' Jolie murmured vaguely, sliding into the booth.

'Jenna doesn't play,' Vincent said. 'You're the one who's into that.'

'And *I* didn't feel like it tonight,' she answered coolly.

'You left her in the casino by herself?'

'I'm not her keeper, Vincent.'

He glared at her, his eyes hard.

'Maybe she bumped into a friend,' Nando offered.

'If she bumped into a friend, she'd bring whoever it was to the table,' Vincent said, getting up. 'I'll be back.'

Nando shrugged. 'Whatever,' he mumbled, not happy about his partner's reaction to the deal he'd suggested. What was so terrible about hookers and drugs? They were a Vegas tradition. Besides, everyone else made money with them. Why shouldn't they? Vincent could be so uptight.

As soon as Vincent was out of earshot, Nando turned to his wife. 'So where is she?' he asked.

Jolie picked up her champagne glass and took a sip. 'She spotted Andy Dale and went running over to him. I couldn't stop her.'

'Damn! Vin's gonna beat the shit out of him,' Nando warned. 'The kid makes a living with his face. How's he gonna look with a broken jaw and nose and three black eyes?'

'*Three* black eyes?' Jolie said, laughing.

'You know what I mean,' Nando said irritably.

Jolie tapped her long, silver-painted nails on the table. 'Why are *you* in a bad mood?' she asked.

''Cause Vincent drives me loco,' Nando replied. 'Could be our partnership has gone on long enough.'

'That's ridiculous,' Jolie scoffed. 'You love each other. You're as close as brothers.'

'Yeah,' Nando said grimly. 'An' sometimes one brother's gotta move outta the house before they slit each other's throats.'

*

After a lot of screaming and shouting, Sofia was getting nowhere with the concierge, who was now threatening to call the police.

'Call 'em!' she yelled directly into his face. 'I *want* you to. I'm *begging* you to.'

At which point a man appeared in the lobby – a tall, well-dressed man in an expensive suit who spoke both English and Spanish.

'Is there a problem?' he asked, with only the slightest of accents.

'You bet your ass there's a problem,' Sofia said, her voice rising.

'Please explain. Perhaps I can be of assistance.'

So she told him her story and, without hesitation, he immediately took command of the situation. He removed his jacket and draped it round her shoulders while urging her to calm down.

'I nearly *killed* myself escaping from those two assholes upstairs,' she spluttered. 'Tell this moron to come with me so I can collect my purse without getting attacked again.'

Calmly the man explained things to the concierge, who reluctantly agreed to accompany Sofia upstairs. 'Will you come too?' she asked the tall stranger. 'I need protection.'

'If you think it's necessary.'

'Oh, yes, I *do*.'

The three of them got into the elevator and rode upstairs in silence. When they reached the penthouse, Sofia began hammering on the door with her fists.

Eventually Paco opened the door, security chain firmly in place.

'You fucks are lucky I'm not *suing* your asses,' she yelled. 'I had to jump out the fucking *window* to get away from you two *perverts*. How do you think *that* will look in court?'

Paco responded in Spanish, gesticulating wildly. She didn't understand a word he was saying.

'Where is your purse?' the man from the lobby asked.

'In there,' she said, pointing past Paco into the living room.

The man spoke to Paco in Spanish. Whatever he said was obviously effective, because before she knew it, the other would-be rapist appeared at the door with her purse, shoved it through the crack and slammed the door shut.

'What did you say to them?' she asked. 'Did you tell them they're a couple of sick fucks who deserve to have their *dicks* cut off?'

'What language!' the tall man said, taking her arm and guiding her back to the elevator.

'*You* try jumping out of a window and staying calm,' she fumed. 'I'm lucky I didn't *kill* myself.'

The elevator reached the lobby and they all stepped out. The concierge practically ran back to the reception desk, anxious to be rid of them.

'Do you have somewhere to stay?' the man asked.

'Of course I do,' she said scornfully. 'God! Morons like that should be locked up.'

'Perhaps I can drive you to your home.'

'That's okay,' she said, handing him back his jacket. 'I'll call a cab.'

'Haven't you had enough drama for one night?'

'Hmm,' she said reluctantly. 'If you're sure you won't attack me in the car, 'cause you can see what happens to people who get on my bad side.'

'Yes, I can see that,' he said, slightly amused.

'Who are you, anyway?' she asked.

'Gianni,' he replied. 'Gianni Ruspeli.'

'Oh, God! You're that famous Italian dress-designing guy,' she said. 'The one who makes those cool jeans. I *thought* you looked familiar.'

He laughed drily. 'We prefer to call it couture. And the jeans are merely a lucrative amusement.'

'Okay, couture. Whatever *that* means.'

'And you are . . . ?'

'Sofia.'

'Ah . . . Sofia. A beautiful name for a wild beauty.'

'I'm not wild and I'm not a beauty. I'm merely pissed off.'

'Then being pissed off, my dear, agrees with you.'

He slipped the concierge some money and they stepped outside. Parked kerbside was a gleaming black Bentley. A uniformed driver stood at attention, holding the door open for them.

'You'll hate me, 'cause I'm about to drip all over your upholstery,' she said, climbing gingerly into the car.

'Lucky upholstery,' he murmured, getting in beside her.

'Wow! A guy who doesn't go ape-shit over his wheels. *That*'s a first.' She settled back into the luxurious leather and wondered if she was making another mistake. Maybe this dude was a better-class pervert in an expensive suit.

'Have you ever done any modelling, Sofia?' he asked.

'Oh, please!' she said, immediately suspicious. 'Now I gotta listen to your smooth lines. I *knew* this was a mistake.'

'You have a very exotic young look. You might be the perfect model for my new jeans.'

'Here comes the bullshit.' She sighed, rolling back her eyes. 'You'll give me a lift if I come back to your apartment and audition my bare body – is *that* the deal?'

'Not at all,' he said casually. 'Besides, Sofia, you are too young for me. I prefer my women to be at least *slightly* sophisticated.'

'Ha! That's a new one.'

'Why don't I give you my card?' he suggested. 'The next time you are in Rome, you can call me.'

'I'm not exactly on my way to Rome.'

'Then maybe you should consider it.'

'Why?'

'Because, my dear, it is quite obvious you have nothing to lose.'

Going to bed with Michael was as good as the first time, and Dani clearly remembered the first time, even though it was over thirty years ago. He'd been so handsome, she'd been so naïve. And a virgin. He'd treated her like a princess, and for one memorable night she'd been in heaven.

'Why are you here?' she murmured as they lay in her king-sized bed after making long leisurely love. 'Can't you get out of my life permanently and leave me alone?'

'We have children together, Dani,' he said quietly. 'Even if we didn't, I'd still want to be with you.'

'If you'd *really* wanted to be with me,' she said accusingly, 'you would never have married Stella.'

'I married Stella because *you* rejected me – and in a way she reminded me of you.'

'That's comforting.'

'Only physically. Stella had none of your sweetness, which is why I've always come back to you.'

'No, Michael.' Dani sighed. 'The only time you come back to me is when you're in trouble.'

'Not true,' he said, reaching for a cigarette.

'True,' she said, propping a couple of pillows beneath her head. 'Now, tell me, Michael, what are you planning to do about your present situation?'

'I have enemies,' he said mysteriously. 'They've tried for a long time to bring me down.'

'Why would anybody want to murder Stella and her boyfriend, then make it look as if *you* did it?'

'People do things for many reasons. Revenge is one of them.'

'Who wants revenge on you?'

'It's better you don't know.' A beat. 'And, Dani, you have to be more careful.'

'Me?'

'If their thirst for revenge is strong enough to murder Stella and her boyfriend, then I have to wonder if you're safe. Or even Madison and Sofia.'

'My God, Michael,' she said, alarmed, 'what are you saying?'

'Where *is* Sofia?'

'Still in Europe. I can't get her to come home.'

'I need her here, Dani.'

'Then *you* find her. She's a free spirit – just like you. Totally different from Madison.'

'Madison's the smart one,' he said. 'Did I mention that she met Vincent?'

'When?' Dani asked, startled.

'A few months ago.'

'How did they meet?'

'Madison was in Vegas, she needed a favour, and, uh . . . Vincent was able to take care of it.'

'What kind of a favour?'

'Nothing you want to know about.'

'Why didn't Vincent tell me?'

'That's between him and you.'

'Oh, God, Michael, you're too complicated for me to keep up with. I only know you shouldn't involve Vincent.'

'He's a big boy.'

'Did you tell Madison that he's her half-brother?'

'All she had t'do was take a look at him an' she figured it out.'

'Was she upset?'

'Who knows?' he said, inhaling deeply. 'The last time I spoke to her she was in New York. When Sofia gets home, I think they should meet.'

'There's no need for Sofia to know you had another family that you cared more about.'

'Not true, Dani. I love all my children equally.'

'*You* might think so, but Madison grew up with you; Vincent and Sofia didn't. If Sofia felt you'd been there for her, she might not have run off to Europe.'

'So you're blaming me?'

'It would have been nice if they'd seen more of you.'

'I did my best, Dani.'

'Have you ever thought that your best might not have been good enough?'

'Oh, for God's sake,' he said angrily. 'Don't give me more problems.'

'Fine,' she said, equally angry. 'I'll keep quiet. I always have.'

Vincent strode through the casino, his eyes scanning every table. Eventually he stopped to talk to one of his pit bosses. 'You know the actor, Andy Dale?' he asked brusquely.

'Sure, Mr Castle.'

'What table was he playing at?'

'Blackjack number three.'

'Did my wife happen to join him?'

'Yes, sir. They left together.'

'Find out what suite he's in.'

'Certainly, Mr Castle.'

A few minutes later, armed with a pass-key, Vincent was in the private elevator to the penthouse suites.

How stupid could Jenna be? He'd married her because she was young and innocent. Not a tramp like so many of the girls who soon became corrupted by the Vegas lifestyle.

Was she *really* foolish enough to betray him?

No. He didn't think so.

The elevator came to a stop at the penthouse floor. He could hear loud music, ice clinking in glasses, and the sound of laughter.

The elevator doors opened directly into the living room

of penthouse number two. He knew the set-up well, he'd helped design it.

The centrepiece of the living room featured a large, round, green marble Jacuzzi. Vincent had ordered the marble from Italy. He remembered the day it had arrived and how pleased he and Nando had been.

Sitting in the Jacuzzi was Andy Dale, with Anais lounging naked along the side, her glistening body on full display.

Jenna was also in the Jacuzzi, next to Andy, her perky pink breasts quite visible in the bubbling water. Jenna. His wife.

Vincent was filled with rage. A red mist began forming in front of his eyes.

'Hey, man,' Andy said, totally stoned, 'why don't you drop your pants an' join us?'

Four minutes passed and still no van. Five minutes, six minutes, seven minutes.

The gunman was not patient. He was hot, agitated, and so pissed off he could barely think straight. He lifted the Uzi, brandishing it round the room. The only satisfaction he got was from the frantic screams of the terrified hostages.

'I warned 'em!' he yelled, throwing down the Uzi near his feet. 'Nobody can say I didn't warn the mothafuckers.'

Then, before anyone could stop him, he lunged at the short redhead, grabbing her round the neck, pulling her back, and twisting hard until she was unable to move. All she could do was let out a strangled scream.

Madison felt sick. Violence was about to take place, and she was powerless to stop it.

She glanced over at Cole, who seemed ready to make a move. Then she began edging forward, desperately hoping she might be able to talk some sense into the young gunman.

She was too late. Grabbing a pistol from his belt, he let out a crazed yell and shot the redhead in the head.

Blood splattered everywhere.

And then there was silence.

Chapter Seventeen

Michael: 1965

Michael had taken to spending more and more time in the company of Vito Giovanni. Mr G had added him to the payroll, so now he was official. It wasn't as if he was his bodyguard or anything, it was simply that Mr G liked having him around. And Michael got off on the reflected notoriety of being perceived as somebody Mr G had regard for.

'Ya always gotta carry a piece,' Vito informed him. 'For your own personal protection.'

'I don't need no personal protection,' Michael objected.

'When ya work for me, ya need it,' Vito insisted. So he carried a piece. And the truth was it made him feel important, gave him a feeling of power that was quite addictive.

Mamie resented Michael's new-found closeness with her husband. 'You got no time for me any more,' she complained. 'Too busy with Mr so-called Big.'

Max also resented it, claiming that Michael was selling his soul to the devil and that Vito Giovanni was an evil man who had no regard for anything other than getting rich and stepping all over the less fortunate.

Michael had laughed in his face and told him that he

could probably score him a job if he wanted it. Max declined the offer.

Max's big night in Vegas had turned out to be a memorable one. First, he'd lost all his money at the crap table. Then, with Michael's fifty bucks, he'd won it all back, and to celebrate he'd got good and drunk on shots of tequila, which he'd insisted on buying for everyone in sight until he ran out of money. Then Angela had arrived at their table, and he'd gone after her big-time, even though she was obviously hot for Michael, who'd ignored her.

Since then, Max had been filled with guilt about cheating on Tina. He'd made Michael promise faithfully that he'd never tell her.

'I don't get why you're makin' such a big deal out of it,' Michael had said. 'It's not like you was already *married* or anything. It was your last fling, for Crissake.'

'It was my last fling all right,' Max had responded miserably, ''cause if Tina ever finds out, she'll never marry me.'

But marry him she did, blissfully unaware of his infidelity.

They were married at the local church, with Michael as best man.

At the reception, after several glasses of champagne, Tina whispered seductively in Michael's ear, 'It could've been you, you know.'

Yes. He knew.

Women. They were not to be trusted.

Except Dani. He had a strong feeling that she was the one, and he couldn't wait to get back to Vegas so that he could see her again.

A week later he got his wish. Mr G entrusted him with another large package and off he went.

Upon arrival in Vegas he realized that he didn't have Dani's number, but at least he knew where she lived, so he wasted no time getting a cab from the airport straight to her apartment. She'd be surprised to see him, although he hoped she'd be pleased, too.

Angela answered the door. 'You!' she exclaimed, tossing back her long brown hair. 'I *knew* you'd be next in line.'

So there was a line. Nice.

'Uh . . . I'm lookin' for Dani,' he said.

'You are?'

'Max sends you his best.'

'Max who?' she said blankly.

Max had confided that Angela had requested money. 'Told her I didn't have any, an' she screwed me anyway.'

'Remember Max? My pal.'

'Oh, *that* cheapskate,' she said, scowling. 'He owes me money.'

'For what?'

'A present.'

'Guess it must've been your birthday, huh?'

'Funny.'

It was obvious she was not about to invite him in, and standing on the doorstep was hardly what he had in mind. 'So . . . uh, tell me, does Dani know you charge?' he asked, making an attempt to throw her off-balance.

'What?' she said, biting her lower lip.

'Does she know?' he repeated.

'Getting an occasional present is *not* charging,' she said, her voice rising.

'Is Dani around?'

'No,' she said spitefully.

'Where can I find her?'

'Dani's not for you.'

'That's for her to decide.'

'*I'm* deciding for her.'

'You are?'

'Yes. You'll mess with her mind. You good-looking ones are all the same, too full of yourselves for your own good.'

Impasse. They stared each other down.

Who does this cow think she is? Michael thought.

Who does this stud think he is? Angela thought.

And then Dani emerged from her bedroom, where she'd been taking a nap. As soon as she saw Michael, her face lit up.

'Hey,' he said, delighted to see her.

'Hey,' she responded, with a shy smile.

'I would've called, only I forgot to get your number.'

'That's okay,' she said, lowering her blue eyes in a way he found quite irresistible.

'You're sure?'

'Oh, yes,' she murmured, finally meeting his gaze.

'Holy cow!' Angela exclaimed. 'Why don't you two get a room?'

'Shut *up*,' Dani said, embarrassed.

'Uh . . . maybe we should take a walk,' Michael suggested.

'Yeah,' Angela drawled sarcastically. 'Walk her all the way to your *bed*.'

'Sorry about Angela,' Dani said, as soon as they got outside. 'She doesn't mean any harm. That's just her way.'

'How well d'you know her?'

'Well enough to share her apartment.'

He wondered if he should mention that Angela was probably a part-time hooker, then decided against it. He didn't care to talk about Angela: it was Dani he was interested in.

They took a cab to the Sands Hotel, where they strolled round the grounds checking out the sights. Dani admired the statues and the fountains – even though she probably saw them every day. She was excited, like a little kid, which he found most appealing.

Eventually they made their way back over to the Estradido coffee shop.

Sitting opposite her, Michael found himself doing all the talking, telling her about New York and his life there, even confiding about Vinny and Grandma Lani – things he never spoke about.

She listened intently, big blue eyes fixed on his.

'What about you?' he asked, after a while. 'How did *you* get to Vegas?'

'On a motorcycle,' she said, thinking he'd never believe her story and, anyway, she wasn't quite ready to tell it to him.

He laughed. 'Sounds like a trip.'

'Oh, it was.'

'I bet.'

She could have sat with him for ever, listening to his stories, staring at his handsome face. However, she knew she had to be at work soon, and the company manager didn't like it when any of the girls turned up late. Sometimes he even went so far as to dock their pay.

'What time is it?' she asked anxiously.

'Why? You gotta be somewhere?'

'The first show is in an hour. I'm supposed to be backstage.'

'Yeah,' he said lazily, ''cause the show is crap without you.'

'Don't say that,' she answered modestly.

'I'm sayin' it. You're the only one worth watchin'.'

Then he leaned across the table and began kissing her. She found herself responding with a passion she'd never felt before. 'Come on,' he said, helping her up. And without any more conversation they left the coffee shop.

'I gotta get somethin' from my room,' he said, holding her hand and leading her towards the elevator.

Obediently she went with him, although she knew it was time to go backstage and get ready for her show.

The moment they entered his room he began kissing

her again. She kissed him back, revelling in the moment, breathless with the anticipation of what might happen next.

He didn't stop kissing her until she was filled with heat and desire. For the first time she realized what all the fuss was about. She felt quite giddy.

Within moments he began undressing her – first removing her blouse, then her bra. She gasped as he touched her breasts, thrusting them towards him, shivering with ecstasy at his touch. Then he pulled off her skirt and panties, and without inhibitions she opened herself up to him.

He marvelled at her beauty as he manoeuvred himself on top of her.

It was then he discovered she was a virgin. 'Jeez! You should've told me,' he said, rapidly moving off her.

'No, no,' she said, pulling him back. 'I want you to make love to me, Michael.'

For a moment he hesitated. Then he thought, What the hell? She wanted him to – so why not?

Handling her gently, he began moving at a very slow pace, doing nothing to alarm her.

When she bled, he comforted her, cradling her in his arms until she felt secure, fondling her breasts, making her cry aloud with pleasure. Then he started going down on her while she covered her face with a pillow, trying desperately to stifle her screams of pure pleasure.

They made love for a long while, until eventually they were both exhausted, and fell into a warm and satisfying sleep.

A little later on they woke up.

'Hungry?' he asked, stroking her hair.

'Starving!' she replied, feeling as if she were floating on clouds. He ordered from Room Service, and when the food arrived he fed her shrimp and french fries, ice cream and strawberries.

Finally they fell asleep again in each other's arms.

In the morning, Michael awoke first. It occurred to him that he had not contacted Manny to exchange packages, he had missed his morning flight back to New York, and Dani had missed both shows the previous night. Talk about fucking up. But who cared? It had been worth it.

Dani was still asleep, golden hair spread across the pillow, smooth cheeks flushed with satisfaction, breasts exposed.

He couldn't resist reaching over and touching her nipples, causing her to stir slightly.

He was immediately erect, only he didn't want to force himself upon her. After all, last night had been her first time and maybe she was sore down there.

'Dani,' he whispered, 'we gotta get up.'

She rolled over into his arms, slowly opening her eyes.

No hiding his erection now, it was digging into her stomach.

'Hello, sleepyhead,' he greeted her. 'We've blown everything – including my flight this morning.'

She reached up, gently touching his cheek. 'You can't go,' she murmured. 'I won't let you.'

'You won't, huh?'

'Never.'

And then, in a perfectly natural way, she was guiding his erection to the right place, and taking him on another heavenly trip.

Ten minutes later the phone rang.

It was Tommaso calling from New York. 'What kind of shit are you pulling?' Tommaso demanded, in a cold, flat voice. 'You didn't make the delivery last night an', believe me, that ain't good. You're also not on the flight you're supposed to be on. Mr Giovanni is pissed.'

'Jeez!' Michael said, thinking fast. 'I musta passed out. I gotta fever – don't remember a thing.'

'A fever, huh?' Tommaso said disbelievingly.

'Temperature. Stomach-ache. Dunno what it is.'

'Listen carefully, punk. Meet Manny, do the exchange, then get on a fuckin' plane an' get your dumb ass back here pronto. You got it?'

'I got it.'

He put down the receiver, aware for the first time that he was no longer his own man. He worked for Vito Giovanni, and because he did, he'd better be prepared to jump. It was quite a revelation.

The phone call had broken the spell. Now reality was staring him in the face. 'I gotta get goin',' he told her.

'When will you be back?' she asked.

A good question. He hoped he hadn't blown his Vegas run. 'Soon,' he promised.

'I'll miss you, Michael,' she whispered.

'Not as much as I'll miss you,' he responded, hurriedly getting dressed.

'Michael?' she murmured, watching him closely.

'Yeah,' he said, buttoning his shirt.

'Last night was so special.'

'I know.'

'I hope I didn't disappoint you.'

'Disappoint me? Are you kiddin'?' He grabbed his jacket and bent to kiss her.

She clung on to him for a moment. 'Michael,' she whispered softly.

'What, sweetheart?'

'I love you.'

New York was cold and gloomy, and Mr G was angry. 'You pull a stunt like that again an' you're out,' he raged.

'It wasn't a stunt, I was sick,' Michael explained.

'Sick my ass,' Vito exploded, red in the face. 'You was probably gettin' your cock sucked by one of them Vegas whores.'

'That's not—'

'Shut the fuck up. Pussy is pussy, an' work *always* comes first. Dontcha forget it. An' dontcha *ever* lie to me again.'

Why was Mr G making such a big deal out of it? What was in the packages he carried back and forth anyway? And what did it matter if he was a day late delivering?

He decided to ask Mamie. She knew everything, and sometimes she didn't mind sharing, especially when she was mad at Vito – something that seemed to be happening more and more frequently.

He caught her when she was on her way back from the beauty parlour.

'What do *you* want?' she asked, waving freshly lacquered scarlet nails in his face.

'Haven't seen you lately,' he said. 'Thought I'd drop by an' say hello.'

'You did, did you?' she said, staring at him suspiciously.

'Yeah,' he said, putting on the charm. 'An' I brought you a box of chocolates, your favourite kind.'

'How transparent can you get?' Mamie said, grabbing the box anyway. 'The big man's mad at you, so you come whining to me. What's the matter, Mikey?' she taunted. 'Frightened he's gonna throw you back on the street where you belong?'

'It's not like that,' he objected.

'Sure it is,' she sneered. 'So what *were* you doin' in Vegas that was more important than your job?'

'How many times I gotta say it? I was sick.'

'Yeah, honey, an' *I'm* Doris Day!'

Wrong time to start asking questions. He decided the next package he carried, he'd take a peek and find out for himself.

Unfortunately his next trip was a long time coming. Vito put Mamie back on the Vegas run, and relegated Michael to driving duties, which didn't thrill him.

'Ya wanna be my right hand one day, then ya gotta do everythin',' Vito informed him. 'Somma this, somma that. What's the harm?'

'I liked takin' care of the Vegas run.'

'Sure you did,' Vito replied, blowing cigar smoke in his face. 'Who wouldn't?'

'When can I do it again?'

'When *I* say so.'

Vito Giovanni was not a man to be argued with.

Michael decided to hold off phoning Dani until he was sure about when he'd be returning to Vegas. She was such a sweet kid, and it was obvious she cared, so he didn't want to give her false hope that he'd be back soon, especially as he had no idea what day or week or even month it would be.

Even though he didn't call her, he thought about her a lot. In fact, he found himself thinking about her all the time. She was special. The most special girl he'd ever met. And although he wanted to take it further, the truth was that he was scared of getting too involved. He'd taken her virginity. She'd said she loved him. Jeez! If he wasn't careful he'd be doing the Max thing and asking her to marry him! And that was crazy time. He was only nineteen, too young to stay with one woman when there was a lifetime of pussy out there.

And yet . . . he still couldn't stop thinking about her.

When his Asian girlfriend turned up unexpectedly, he sent her home because he wasn't in the mood. That was a first.

'I met this girl,' he confided to Max.

'Ha!' Max whooped, getting it immediately. 'You finally got hooked!'

'Not me.'

'Yeah, *you*.'

'I'm not interested in seein' other girls right now. I'm not even interested in gettin' laid.'

''Cause you're hooked.'

'I think about her a lot.'

'Sure you do.'

'What I gotta do to forget her?'

'Nothin',' Max said, with a fiendish grin. 'Your goose is good 'n cooked. Join the freakin' club.'

A week later Tommaso asked him if he'd ever driven a truck.

'I guess I can do it,' he said.

'Good,' Tommaso said. 'Tonight – ten p.m. Mr Giovanni wants you back of Alissio's. Roy'll pick you up an' take you to the place.'

'What place?'

'You'll find out.'

He didn't like the sound of it. Roy was a dour older man with ferret features and slight lisp, who did the occasional job for Mr G. He was also Mamie's cousin.

'You gotta tell me more,' Michael insisted.

'I don't gotta tell you nothin',' Tommaso said. 'You work for Mr Giovanni, you do what Mr Giovanni wants. *Capisce*?'

Ever since his Vegas screw-up things hadn't been the same. Even Mamie had cooled towards him. Now he was treated as if he was just another goon, and he didn't like it. He'd do the truck thing, then he planned on having it out with Mr Giovanni. He wasn't an errand boy – he was better than that.

Roy turned up late in a brown Ford.

'Where's the truck?' Michael asked.

'Jump in, pretty boy,' Roy said. 'I'm takin' ya to it.'

An hour later they were way out in the country and still driving.

'Where the fuck are we?' Michael demanded.

'Mr Giovanni wants t'see if ya got stones,' Roy said,

pulling the Ford over to the side of the deserted road.

'Huh?'

'Get out,' Roy said, consulting his watch. 'There'll be a truck comin' by here in approximately ten minutes. One driver. Big cargo of booze. You hijack the mothafucker, drive it to Arnie's garage in Queens, a job well done.'

'You *gotta* be shittin' me?'

'Nope,' Roy said, handing him a slip of paper. 'Here's the address of Arnie's. They're expecting you. Now get out.'

Reluctantly Michael got out. 'And what'm I supposed to do with the driver of the truck?'

Roy leaned over and slammed the passenger door closed. 'That's your problem, pretty boy. See ya round.'

And he drove off, leaving Michael standing in the middle of nowhere.

Chapter Eighteen

Dani: 1965

'I'm pregnant,' Dani said, her eyes filling with tears.

'Why are you telling *me*?' Angela said brusquely, not exactly full of sympathy. 'Why aren't you telling the stupid dick who knocked you up?'

'Because . . . because . . . after that one night I never heard from him again.' A lone tear slid down her cheek. Michael had taken her virginity and never so much as sent her a flower. Maybe she'd been reading too many romance novels, but surely he should at least have called her?

'Men!' Angela snapped. 'They're all the same. Selfish users.'

'There must be *some* nice ones.'

'You gotta be joking,' Angela said, with a brittle laugh. 'They're all rats, and now we've got to track *your* rat down.'

'Why?' Dani asked, alarmed.

'So the bastard can pay for the abortion.'

'I . . . I don't want an abortion.'

'Get real, kiddo,' Angela said briskly. 'It's your only answer, unless you want to have the kid an' sell it. Believe me,' she mused, her expression turning thoughtful, 'that's not such a bad idea – some rich couple would pay plenty for a kid that looks like you.'

Dani stared at her in horror. 'I can't believe you said that.'

'Why? It's the truth. And you'd better face up to it. *You* can't afford to have a baby.'

'Who said I can't?'

'You *know* it's true. You got no savings, nothing. And as soon as your belly starts to show, you'll have to give up work. Then what?'

'I'll find a different job,' she said quickly. 'One where it doesn't matter what I look like.'

'This is Vegas, hon. Wherever you go, it'll matter.'

Unfortunately, Dani realized, Angela was right. The workforce in Vegas consisted of girls who looked good. Being pregnant and landing a high-paying job was a no-go situation.

'I suppose the daddy is Mr Handsome,' Angela said scornfully. 'I coulda told you that one was no good. I bet the bastard didn't even wear a rubber, did he?'

'It – it was my first time,' Dani confessed. 'I didn't think I could get pregnant.'

'Ha!' Angela snorted. 'Whoever told you that is a big fat liar!'

'Michael didn't say that,' she whispered.

'What *did* Mr Handsome tell you?' Angela demanded.

'That he'd be back soon.'

'And that was *how* long ago?'

'Seven weeks.'

'Typical!' Angela exclaimed, full of disgust. 'One dip in the honeypot an' they run for the hills. Y'see, I know what they're like, so *I* make sure they pay.'

'That's what prostitutes do,' Dani muttered.

'And what do you think opening your legs is all about? Get real, sweetie. It's all one great big barter system, and the smart ones end up getting paid – not pregnant.'

'He seemed so . . . so wonderful,' Dani said sadly.

'When they're tracking pussy, they *all* seem wonderful.'

'You're so cynical, Angela.'

'Yeah. I'm cynical and *you're* pregnant. So tell me – who's got the right take on it?'

Dani sighed. She wished she had Emily to talk to. Emily would know what she should do, because Emily was the only living person who'd ever cared about her and, of course, Sam, whom she hadn't heard from in weeks. She'd tried calling him on several occasions, but he was never home.

She decided that after the show tonight she'd go to his apartment and wait outside until he appeared.

Sure, her inner voice whispered, *because you need his help.*

No, I don't. I can manage without anyone's help.

If only she could get over a broken heart. Because that's how Michael had left her – pregnant with a broken heart.

Dani waited outside Sam's house for over two hours before he appeared. She was sitting on the ground, her back against the door when he finally showed up.

He was drunk and not alone. He was accompanied by a short, bleached-blonde with black roots and wide hips.

'Who's this? Your wife?' the woman cackled.

Dani stood up. 'Sam,' she said, 'I've tried calling you back, you never answer your phone. Are you all right?'

'Jeez, honey,' the woman said, throwing her arms round his shoulders. 'It's two in the morning. Whyn't you go home? This one is *taken.*'

Staggering slightly, Sam began groping for his keys. 'Whatcha doing here, Dani?' he asked, slurring his words.

'I wanted to see you,' she said.

'Get lost,' the woman interrupted. 'Him an' me – we got business to conduct.'

'Yeah, yeah, go home,' Sam said, waving his hands in the air.

'You mean me?' Dani asked.

'No, I mean *her*,' he said.

'And how'm I supposed to get home?' the woman shrieked, furious at the way things were turning out.

'Give her some money,' Dani said quickly.

'Yeah, yeah,' Sam said, pulling out his wallet. 'Money.'

Dani took his wallet from him, extracted ten dollars and handed it to the woman, who rewarded her with an angry glare.

'You know,' Dani scolded, helping Sam inside, 'you shouldn't be drinking.'

'I know,' he said miserably. 'I got nothin' else t'do.'

'Sam,' she said earnestly, 'I've been thinking.'

''Bout what?'

'Maybe you were right. Maybe I *should* be here looking after you.'

'You moved out on me, Dani,' he said accusingly. 'Dumped me flat.'

'I didn't *dump* you. I simply didn't think it was healthy for us to live together.' She hesitated a moment before continuing. 'When I see you like this, I realize you *do* need someone to look after you, and . . . perhaps that someone should be me.'

'Really?' he said hopefully.

'We shouldn't talk now,' she said. 'I'll come back in the morning when you're sober. We'll go out for breakfast.'

'Sure,' he mumbled, as she helped him into the bedroom and got him on to the bed, where she proceeded to take off his shoes and socks and loosen his pants.

Within minutes he was snoring loudly.

Was she being unfair? Was she running back to Sam because she was pregnant and she wanted *him* to look after *her*? Or was it the other way round? Would she have come back if things had worked out with Michael?

Probably not.

Angela was right about men. They were only after one thing. And when they got it, they took off.

Sam was different. Maybe she could have a life with him.

It was worth a try.

Two weeks later Dani and Sam were married in one of the local wedding chapels. She'd wanted to tell him about the baby, but Angela had persuaded her not to.

'It wouldn't be fair to him,' Angela had reasoned. 'Marry the guy, sleep with him, let him think the kid's his. *That*'s what's fair.'

'No, *that*'s deceitful,' she'd answered.

'It's not,' Angela had argued. 'It's simply smart business. And good for the kid, too. You want the tyke growing up not knowing who its father is? And Sam won't care as much about the baby if he doesn't think it's his.'

She hadn't thought about marrying Sam, but when she'd got him sober and he'd asked her, it had suddenly seemed like the answer to all her problems.

It was quite apparent she'd never see Michael again. He'd used her as a one-night stand, another conquest – of which he'd probably had many. Her feelings towards him hardened every day.

On their wedding night she and Sam lay together in bed half dressed. Nothing happened. Dani knew that she'd better persuade him to make love to her as soon as possible; the only problem was that she was just as wary of physical contact as he was.

However, they *were* married, the union had to be consummated. And soon.

The following night after cleaning her teeth and brushing her hair, she threw all modesty aside, abandoned her nightdress and walked into the bedroom, naked.

It didn't take long for Sam to respond. He pushed her down on the bed and jumped aboard fast, climaxing almost immediately. Then he beamed and said, 'That was fantastic, wasn't it?'

The experience was nothing like it had been with Michael. It was all over in five minutes and meant nothing.

She nodded, swallowing a lump in her throat, fully aware that it hadn't been fantastic at all.

She waited four weeks and then informed him she was pregnant.

Sam was ecstatic.

And she was filled with a horrible, nagging guilt that refused to go away.

Chapter Nineteen

Michael: 1970

I0 February 1970 was Michael's twenty-fifth birthday, a memorable day for him because for the last five years he'd been incarcerated, locked up in a stinking hellhole of a jail. And today he was finally getting out.

He had no doubt that he'd been set up, and once out, he was determined to find out why.

He suspected the culprit was Tommaso in cahoots with Mamie's loser cousin Roy. Neither of the men had ever liked him. The feeling was mutual. He'd never trusted Tommaso, and Roy was a sleazy whiner who only had a job because he happened to be related to Mamie.

At the time of his arrest, Vito Giovanni had sent a lawyer to see him. The lawyer had informed him that Mr Giovanni had no knowledge of the liquor-truck hijacking.

'He's *gotta* know about it,' Michael had insisted. 'He's the one who ordered me to do it.'

'Mr Giovanni has no idea what you're talking about. So for your own good, when we get into court I suggest you *do not* mention Mr Giovanni's name in connection with this crime.'

'What freakin' *crime?*' he'd protested. 'I didn't touch the driver. All I did was stop the truck, told the guy to get out an' start walking. The jerk didn't even put up a fight.'

'You waved a gun in his face, didn't you?'

'Yeah,' he'd admitted.

'The DA will call that armed robbery and attempted murder. Not to mention carrying an unregistered weapon.'

'You gotta straighten this out,' he'd said, panicking. 'I didn't *do* nothin'.'

'You hijacked a truck at gunpoint.'

'For five minutes. I wasn't a mile down the road before the cops pulled me over.' He'd taken a long beat. 'Can I get bail?'

He'd got bail all right, but it was too high for any of his friends to put up. Max immediately contacted Vinny who, in true fatherly fashion, said he wasn't at all surprised and flatly refused to help. Since Mr Giovanni was not forthcoming either, Michael was forced to stay in jail until the hearing.

After a short trial, the judge sentenced him to eight years.

One bad move and he was fucked. It didn't seem real, but unfortunately it was.

Prison was worse than he'd imagined. He tried to keep to himself, which was not easy. Regarded as new blood, it wasn't long before he was targeted by some of the more hardened inmates. Whenever they came after him, he fought back, soon gaining a reputation as a tough guy, with several scars to prove it.

Survival meant staying strong, so every day he worked out in the yard. It wasn't long before he palled up with Gus, a fellow prisoner doing time for extortion. Gus was a friendly guy who talked a lot. On the outside he worked for Dante Lucchese, and he was currently finishing up a five-year sentence.

'When ya get out, ya gotta look me up,' Gus said, a couple of days before his release.

'I will,' Michael promised.

For the first two years he worked in the kitchen and the laundry, until eventually he scored a better gig in the prison library, where he found himself working alongside Karl Edgington, a man who'd got himself locked away for embezzling two million dollars from the Wall Street firm he'd worked for. Karl was a strange one: well educated and quiet, he talked constantly about his two cats and his priceless stamp collection. The other inmates had labelled him a wacko and left him alone. But Michael thought Karl was an interesting man, and extremely knowledgeable regarding money and the stock market. He began picking his brain, getting an education about the financial world. It was a fascinating subject, and one that Karl was only too willing to talk about.

'I got a few thousand put away,' Michael confided one day. 'What d'you think I should do with it?'

'Do what I tell you, and I can make you a lot of money,' Karl said.

'Yeah?' Michael said, apprehensive. 'An' why would I trust *you*?'

Karl shrugged. 'Sometimes taking a chance is the only way to go.'

'Would you be able to double my money?'

'I'll do a lot better than that.'

'Yeah, what?'

'Can you keep your silence and follow instructions when you're released?'

'Sure.'

'Good. Because I have a proposition that will benefit us both.'

'What would that be?'

'Something mutually advantageous.'

'So spill.'

'I'll give you a number to call. When you're out, you'll

contact this number and we'll take it from there.'

He wasn't sure whether he trusted Karl or not, but he wrote down the number and stashed it in a safe place.

Sometimes, late at night when he wasn't able to sleep, his thoughts turned to Dani. He had an urge to write to her, but what good would that do? He was a convicted felon, and as such he should do her a favour and stay away. Dani was an unforgettable memory of better times – and that's the way it had to be.

The only person who came to see him in prison was Max. Good old Max. Married man, best friend and staunch supporter, Max never missed a visit.

On the day of his release, Max was waiting for him outside the prison. He was driving a second-hand Ford Mustang and looking very pleased with himself in his Paisley shirt, bell-bottom pants, a shaggy duffel coat and Beatles-style haircut.

'What the fuck happened to *you?*' Michael said, choking back laughter. 'That's some pansy outfit.'

'Screw you,' Max retaliated. 'It's the fashion.'

'Fashion, *shit!*' Michael said, taking a deep breath of cold, fresh air. He was free. What a feeling!

'Forget about the outfit,' Max said, clapping his friend on the back. 'How about the wheels?'

'Not bad,' Michael said, circling the Mustang before climbing into the passenger seat. 'Things must be goin' your way.'

'They are,' Max said enthusiastically. 'Tina's dad made me a partner in his car dealership, which means that one of these days *I'll* be takin' over.'

'Cushy deal.'

'Now listen t'me,' Max said sternly. 'You gotta stay away from those low-lifes you was mixin' with before you got locked away. Look what happened to you. If you hang out with them, it'll happen again.'

'Yeah, yeah,' Michael said, hardly in the mood for a lecture.

'You'll stay with us,' Max continued, revving the engine. 'Tina's makin' up the couch for you.'

'Wait a minute,' he said. 'I haven't got out of jail to sleep on your freakin' couch.'

'You've done it before, an' you'll do it again,' Max said, driving like an old fart, with both hands on the wheel. 'Y'know, till you get yourself settled.'

'Maybe for a night or two,' Michael said, suddenly aware that he had nowhere else to go. 'Hey,' he added, 'this piece of tin got any juice under the hood?'

'You prick!' Max said, putting his foot down. ''Course it does.'

Max had turned into a family man. He and Tina had two children, four-year-old Harry, named after Tina's father, and Susie, aged three. With the help of Tina's dad, they'd purchased a small house in the old neighbourhood.

Proudly Max drove Michael there, and parked outside, showing off the tiny patch of grass in the small front yard, which was blanketed in snow and ice.

Tina came to the door and greeted Michael with an awkward embrace. Then she proceeded to tell Max off about tracking snow into the house. It was glaringly obvious that she ruled the household, and wanted everyone to know it.

Michael noticed that, although she was still very pretty, she'd definitely put on a few pounds. It didn't matter, because she smelt delicious and felt even better. He'd almost forgotten what it was like to be close to a female. Had to do something about *that*.

'What are your plans?' Tina asked, linking her arm through his.

'Dunno,' he answered vaguely. 'Haven't thought about it.'

'Sure,' Max said, joining in. 'Shut away for five years and you haven't thought about what you're gonna do the moment you get out.' A dirty laugh. 'I know what *I'd* do.'

'Max,' Tina said, in a bossy voice, 'make Michael feel at home – ask him if he wants a drink.'

'He's not a freakin' *guest*,' Max said. 'He's my best pal. I got no need to *ask* him, he knows he can help himself to anythin' he wants.'

Tina shot her husband a vengeful look. She didn't appreciate the way he was speaking to her, especially in front of her former big crush.

'Where are the kids?' Michael asked, tripping over a toy truck sitting in the centre of the floor. 'I wanna meet 'em.'

'Max thought it would be a good idea if they spent the night at my mom's,' Tina said, 'so you can kind of get used to being out . . . Oops!' she exclaimed, clapping a hand over her mouth. 'Is that okay for me to say?'

'Sure,' he answered easily. 'I'm not sensitive.'

'What *was* it like being locked away all that time?' she asked, her eyes wide with curiosity. 'Was it the same as prison in the movies?'

'Don't ask questions like that,' Max snapped. 'He don't wanna talk about prison.'

'That's okay,' Michael said. 'It's not something I'd recommend.'

'I'm dying to know,' Tina said. 'Why *did* you hold up that truck and threaten the driver with a gun? I mean, it was kind of a stupid thing to do, wasn't it?'

'Yeah, Tina,' he said ruefully. 'I guess I learned me a lesson.'

And the lesson was that the next time he got involved in something that wasn't legal, he'd check out his associates and make sure they weren't selling him out.

'Good,' she said, playing wife-of-the-best-friend. 'Now – I've been thinking about your future. You've got to be more like Max. We'll find you a nice girl, get you married, you'll have a couple of kids, and settle down to a proper life.'

Yeah, he thought. *And get myself nagged to death.*

Max went into the kitchen, opened the fridge and removed a couple of cans of beer.

Michael followed him in. 'I guess bein' in the joint is one way of gettin' out of Vietnam,' he remarked. 'How come *you* didn't get your sorry ass drafted?'

'On account of my asthma,' Max replied, handing him a beer. 'Didya hear about Charlie?'

'No, what happened to him?'

'Did a tour of duty an' got his leg shot off. Now he's on disability. Poor bastard can't find a job. He's livin' at home, boozin' plenty. It ain't a happy situation.'

'I'd like to see him.'

'We will.'

'At least *you*'re doing well,' Michael said, taking a swig of cold beer.

'Not bad,' Max answered modestly. 'I got my own house, a car, two kids an' Tina. She's the best.'

'You're a lucky man.'

'You can say that again!'

Tina cooked pasta for dinner. They ate it in front of the TV off plastic plates. Max seemed to have caught Vinny's disease – TV eyeballs. First he watched *The Johnny Cash Show*, then *Rowan & Martin's Laugh-In*, followed by *Gunsmoke*.

After a while Tina got bored and went off to gossip on the phone.

Michael noticed that during the course of his TV viewing Max managed to consume three more beers and two full bags of potato chips.

'Workin' on your gut, huh?' he joked, noticing that it wasn't only Tina who'd put on weight.

'Yeah, well,' Max said sheepishly, patting his expanding stomach. 'That's what married life does to you. No point in stayin' in shape when you got it right there waitin' in the bedroom.' He winked. 'That's gotta be your next move, huh? Five years without pussy – jeez! How'd you manage?'

'You don't wanna know.'

'Plannin' on callin' any of your old girlfriends?'

'Naw.'

'Hey,' Max said enthusiastically, 'maybe tomorrow night you an' me can go out – like old times. Tina won't mind.'

'Tina won't mind what?' she asked, entering the room.

'Uh . . . you wouldn't mind me takin' my old buddy out tomorrow night?'

'I'll come too,' she said, gathering up empty beer cans and depositing them in the kitchen.

'It's not that kinda night out,' Max yelled, grimacing at Michael.

'Then I *do* mind,' she said, coming back into the room. 'I don't want you hanging around any of those sleazy strip joints.'

'Wasn't what we had in mind, hon,' Max said innocently. 'Just, y' know, drinkin', catchin' up on old times.'

'Fine,' she said sharply. 'If you're doing that, then I'll go out with the girls.'

This got his attention. Max was very possessive of Tina. 'You know I don't want you doing that,' he said, scowling.

'Too bad,' she answered tartly.

And they started to bicker.

Christ! Michael thought. *Is this how I'm spending my first night of freedom in five years? Watching these two go at it?*

'I'm kinda beat,' he said, interrupting them. 'I wouldn't mind gettin' a night's sleep.'

'Oh, sorry,' Tina said, immediately contrite. 'I'll fix you up a bed.'

She fetched pillows and a blanket and made up the couch, then she and Max said good night, went upstairs and left him to it.

He tossed and turned restlessly, listening to Tina and Max continue their argument, their loud voices drifting downstairs.

It was a strange feeling not being locked into a cell and having the lights go out at a certain time. If he wanted to, he could get up and walk the streets, do anything he liked. He was free.

The problem was that there was only one thing on his mind, and that was to find out who'd set him up.

Tomorrow, that was exactly what he planned on doing.

'Mikey!' Mamie exclaimed. 'I don't believe it!'

'Believe it,' he said. 'An' quit callin' me Mikey.'

They were standing outside the Giovanni house. There was fresh snow on the sidewalk and it was freezing cold. Mamie had just emerged and was on her way to a chauffeur-driven gold Cadillac standing kerbside. She was enveloped in a big fur coat, and as usual her face was caked with an excess of makeup. Mamie Giovanni was beginning to show her age.

A young bodyguard stepped forward. 'Everythin' all right, Mrs Giovanni?' he asked, glaring at Michael.

'Yes, Mo,' she said, waving him away, her beringed fingers catching the morning light. 'Well, well, well,' she said admiringly, checking Michael out. '*You* sure grew up, didn't you?'

'It's amazing what five years in the joint will do,' he said caustically. 'Oh, yeah – an' thanks for all the visits, it meant a lot.'

'I don't do prisons,' she said, patting her beehive hairdo. 'You here to see Vito?'

'That's the idea.'

'I'm sure you've got an appointment?'

'Do I need one?'

'Yes, dear, you do,' she said, moving towards her car.

The young bodyguard threw him a surly look and opened the door for her.

She climbed in, flashing a great deal of thigh. 'See you round, Mikey,' she said. 'Gotta run.'

He watched her car drive off. It was quite obvious that Mamie Giovanni was no longer a fan.

As soon as her car was out of sight, he approached the house and rang the doorbell.

Another unfamiliar face answered the door. 'Yeah?' the guy said, peering at him suspiciously. He was a goon who looked like he was carrying a piece.

'I'm, uh, here t'see Mr Giovanni. Name's Michael Castellino.'

'Wait,' the guy said, shutting the door in his face. The man returned a few minutes later. 'Mr Giovanni's in a meeting. He said t'ask you what it's about.'

Christ! When the Giovannis closed a door, they really closed it hard.

'Personal,' Michael said.

'So write him a freakin' letter,' the goon said, and once more slammed the door shut.

What was going on here? Once he'd been next in line to be Vito's new right hand, now he was out in the cold, an ex-con looking for a handout. Except he wasn't looking for anything except to straighten things out.

He walked round the corner to a coffee shop, where he quickly downed two cups of strong black coffee. The waitress flirted with him. She had frizzy yellow hair and a faint shadow of a moustache. He ignored her, lit a cigarette and headed back to the house, where he waited across the street.

At two fifteen Tommaso emerged, setting off along the sidewalk with a purposeful stride.

Michael crossed the road, and fell into step beside the heavy-set man. 'Tommaso,' he said. 'Long time outta sight.'

'Jesus Christ!' Tommaso said, startled. 'I thought you got eight years.'

'Y'know how it is,' Michael said. 'Out in five for good behaviour.'

'So,' Tommaso said gruffly, 'you're back.'

'Looks like it.' A beat. 'I, uh, tried to see Mr G, got told he was busy.'

''S right,' Tommaso said, nodding his bullet head. 'Mr Giovanni is a *real* big shot now. You gotta plan a meet six or seven weeks ahead of time.'

'I do, huh?'

'That's the way it is,' Tommaso said, still walking.

Michael lit up another cigarette. 'I got a coupla questions for you.'

'Yeah?'

'I had a lot of time t'think bein' locked away for five years. Y'know what it's like – a man's got nothin' much else to do.'

'What questions?' Tommaso said abruptly.

'It's like this,' Michael said, expelling a stream of smoke. 'When I met with Mr G's lawyer, he informed me Mr G knew zilch about the truck thing. Now ain't that somethin'?'

'There was a truck thing?' Tommaso said, staring straight ahead as he continued to trudge down the street.

'The truck hijacking *you* sent me out on,' Michael said. 'Remember?'

'Dunno what you're talkin' about,' Tommaso replied, a totally blank expression on his beefy face.

'You don't, huh?'

'Got no clue.'

'You *prick*,' Michael said, in a low and steady voice as he grabbed the big man by the collar. 'You set me up to get me outta the way. Why? 'Cause I was gettin' too close to Mr G? Is that how it went down? Is that fuckin' *it*?'

Roaring with anger, Tommaso shoved him away. 'Mr Giovanni don't have time for punks who go off on their own an' pull shitass jobs,' he said, red in the face. 'He don't like it when you try draggin' *his* name into it. So don't come near him again. An' sure as shit don't bother me, 'cause if you do, you got my word you'll be *real* fuckin' sorry.'

'I will, huh?'

'Wanna try it?'

'Fuck you,' Michael said, and walked away, smart enough to know that at this particular moment it was a no win situation.

But revenge would be his. In jail he'd become a patient man. And a much smarter one. One day Tommaso and Roy would pay the price. Oh, yes, they certainly would.

Chapter Twenty

Dani: 1970

The teenage boy hovering outside the stage door was shaking with nerves. 'Excuse me, Miss, can I have your autograph?'

'Certainly,' Dani replied graciously. 'What's your name?'

'M-Mark,' the boy stuttered, hardly able to believe his luck.

'Nice name,' she said, accepting his rather battered autograph book. *To Mark, with love, Dani Castle*, she wrote, with a stylish flourish, using her professional name, because 'Dani Froog' had hardly seemed suitable, and Sam hadn't minded that she'd chosen not to use his surname. 'Castle' had a nice ring to it – she'd got it out of a travel magazine.

'Gee . . . thanks,' the boy stammered, blushing beet red.

'You're welcome,' she said, flashing him a warm smile.

Dani was now one of the lead showgirls in the Krystle Room at the Magiriano, an enormous luxury hotel where they treated their talent like human beings and paid them well too. Working at the Magiriano was a big step up from dancing in the chorus at the Estradido. The show was a lavish extravaganza, and the costumes amazing. Every day she realized how fortunate she was to have landed such a dream job.

After giving birth to her son, whom she'd named Vincent, she'd returned to work at the Estradido. Shortly after that, she'd been plucked from the chorus by a talent scout from the Magiriano, who'd immediately hired her. It had taken a lot of work and endless rehearsals, but gradually she'd risen to be one of the main showgirls – a coveted job.

Her life was her son and her work. And then there was Sam, her husband, who went on regular drinking binges.

Not only did Sam drink, he'd also taken up gambling, and with her money.

She kept him on a strict allowance, refusing to let him get his hands on her paycheck. After putting a down payment on a small house, she was saving her money to make sure that Vincent received the education she'd never had. And she was entitled to save, because now *she* was the family breadwinner since Sam had given up work altogether.

This suited her fine, because it meant he was there to look after Vincent, who was now almost five, and the most gorgeous child in the world. She couldn't take him out without people stopping her to admire his long silky eyelashes and deep-set dark eyes. 'He's going to be a lady-killer when he grows up,' was the general comment.

Not if she had anything to do with it.

He looked exactly like Michael, which in a way was good, because he was so handsome. In another way it was bad, because he was a constant reminder of her one-night stand.

As far as she was concerned, Michael was dead, and she hoped she'd never have to set eyes on him again.

She was twenty-two now, not so naïve, and quite well versed in the ways of men.

When she looked back, she saw herself as an innocent lamb being led to the slaughter. How Michael must have laughed at her naïveté. *Pretty virgin Dani. I'll take her by the hand and lead her up to my hotel room. She'll love every minute of it. Then I'll move on to the next innocent flower.*

Damn him!

But she'd had the last laugh – she'd got married, given birth to a healthy son and had a rewarding job. What more could she ask for?

A little love and romance. Because after their one jack-rabbit sexual encounter, Sam had never made love to her again. He'd tried a few times, but had been unable to maintain an erection.

It didn't bother her. In fact, she was relieved. Sex did not interest her. She was perfectly content with the way things were.

The good news was that Sam truly believed Vincent was his.

The bad news was that when he was drunk, he was unreliable, and she couldn't trust him with her boy.

The only person who knew that Vincent was not Sam's son was Angela, and since Angela had left the Estradido chorus line, they'd lost touch – although Dani had heard that her ex-roommate had given up dancing and taken to hooking full-time. Apparently she was doing very well at it.

Dani had acquired a new best friend; Gemini, a pretty French brunette who performed alongside her. Gemini was a divorced mother with a son, Nando, who was a few months older than Vincent. The two children often played together, and Dani and Gemini had plans for them to attend the same nursery school.

Sam didn't like Gemini – he wasn't fond of anyone he considered a threat. He wanted Dani and Vincent to himself and was fiercely jealous of outsiders. His jealousy manifested itself in an occasional petulant outburst, which Dani tried to ignore.

Basically, Sam was on a downward spiral. He'd never got over Emily's disappearance, and there was nothing she could do to help him forget. Emily was always there, hovering between them. Dani had learned to accept that this was the way it was.

Vincent was her saviour. To look into his handsome little face and see the love there was everything she'd ever needed. 'Love you, Mommy,' he said every night, when she tucked him into bed and read him a story before going off to do her show.

'Thank you, sweetheart,' she said, kissing him. 'Mommy loves you too. In fact, Mommy loves you the whole wide world!'

Sometimes, when Sam was on one of his drinking jags, she hired a babysitter to stay with her son.

Sam didn't approve. 'Are you saying I'm not capable of looking after the kid?' he yelled.

'If you want to go out, there *has* to be someone here,' she said. 'You *cannot* leave Vincent alone.'

He'd done it one night, and when she'd come home and found her child alone, she'd been hysterical. She was determined that it would never happen again. Sometimes she wondered how things might have turned out if Emily hadn't vanished. Would Emily and Sam have remained a happy couple? Would Sam have started drinking? And would *she* have got pregnant with Vincent? Because with Emily to advise her, she probably would've been wiser.

It wasn't worth thinking about, because it didn't matter. She had Vincent, and he was everything to her. One day, while walking home from the market with Vincent, she thought she saw Manny Spiven. It was a horrible moment. She clutched Vincent, tightening her grip on his small hand.

'Whassamatter, Mommy?' he asked, big eyes gazing up at her.

'Nothing,' she answered as Manny Spiven scurried past, barely noticing her. Of course he wouldn't recognize her. It was years later and she looked quite different. Onstage she was a gleaming goddess. Offstage she tied back her long blonde hair, put on no makeup, wore granny glasses and understated clothes.

Seeing Manny brought back all the memories. The night she'd spotted him in the audience with Michael, and then the next day Michael repeating the horrible lies Manny had made up about her. Then Michael returning a few weeks later, and their one night of unforgettable passion.

Damn! She had to stop thinking about him.

You think about him because he's Vincent's father, her inner voice informed her. *And you named him after Michael.*

I did not.

Yes, you did. Surely you remember that when you were sitting with Michael in the coffee shop at the Estradido, he told you that his given name was Vincenzio Michael Castellino?

Yes, she remembered, but it had nothing to do with her naming her son Vincent. It simply happened to be a nice name, a popular name.

When she got home, Sam greeted her full of enthusiasm. 'I've come up with a scheme,' he announced excitedly. 'We're gonna make millions.'

This was his new thing, coming to her with schemes that he tried to persuade her to invest in.

'What is it this time, Sam?' she asked, unloading the groceries in the kitchen as Vincent played on the floor with his train set.

'Windmills,' he said. 'Everybody wants windmills. It's a new tax dodge. And . . .' a triumphant pause '. . . guess what? *I'm* gonna build 'em.'

'You're going to build windmills?' she said patiently.

'Yeah,' Sam said, pacing up and down. 'I met this guy an' he's gonna show me how to do it.'

'You're going to build windmills with your own hands – is that what you're telling me?'

'No. I'll put together a team, an' I'll supervise.'

'It sounds like a good idea,' she said, thinking it was a stupid idea.

'Pleased you like it,' he said, beaming. ''Cause all you gotta do is hand over ten grand.'

Oh, yes, naturally it involves me and my money.

'I don't *have* that kind of money, Sam,' she said evenly. *And even if I did, I certainly wouldn't be giving it to you to put into windmills.*

'No, no, honey, you don't get it,' he said, waving his arms in the air. 'Windmills are gonna be big. Like I told you, we'll make millions.'

She didn't say a word. They were headed for another fight and she hated him for doing this in front of Vincent.

'So,' he said belligerently, 'you gonna come up with the money or not?'

'I told you,' she repeated, wishing he'd stop this nonsense, 'I don't *have* ten thousand dollars.'

'You must have,' he said, beads of sweat glistening on his upper lip. 'You sock it away every week, an' you're getting paid top dollar. You sure as hell don't spend it on me.'

'I told you what I do with my money,' she said quietly. 'I put it in the bank for Vincent's college education.'

'Why d'you wanna send him to college anyway?' he demanded. '*We* did okay without goin'.'

'Maybe *you* did, but I would've given anything to go to college.'

He threw a malevolent glare her way. 'So you're not gonna help me?'

'It's not a question of helping you.'

'I'm outta here,' he said, scowling. 'Get a babysitter for the night.' And he slammed his way out the door.

She couldn't win with Sam. It was quite obvious he didn't want them to be happy. The only time she saw a smile on his face was when he took Vincent to the park and played ball with him, and he didn't do that too often.

'Daddy's cross,' Vincent said, zooming his train round the wooden track.

'No, he's not,' she assured him, cheerful as always.

'Cross! Cross! Cross!' Vincent sing-songed.

She didn't know what their future held. She refused to allow her son to grow up in an atmosphere where there was no love or respect, and as each day passed, she and Sam seemed to argue more and more.

She had to make a decision. And the sooner she made that decision, the better it would be for all of them.

Chapter Twenty-one

'I can't breathe,' Natalie said, gasping for air. 'I think I'm about to faint.'

'Don't!' Madison said. She was equally scared, but desperately trying not to show it. Her face was splattered with blood and there was a tight knot of horror in her stomach from the senseless murder she'd just witnessed. She kept on thinking of Jake, and wishing he were there to protect them.

The gunman, in a fit of anger and frustration, suddenly ripped off his ski mask and threw it on to the ground. He was pale and thin-faced, with pointed features and a long nose. His hair was cut close to his head, Marine style, his skin was shiny with sweat, and he had wild, staring, stoned eyes.

He looks like one of those neo-Nazis, Madison thought. *Or one of those skinheads who hate everybody.*

'See what you made me do!' he screamed. 'See what you mothafuckers made me do! Get me a fuckin' van, or I'll shoot another of you.' He retreated to the other side of the room, where he and his two cohorts formed a tight group.

Cole removed the cloth from one of the tables and draped it over the girl who had been shot. She was obviously dead.

The women hostages were wailing and sobbing. The male ones were just plain scared.

'He's a kid,' Madison whispered to Cole. 'Did you see his face?'

'I saw it all right,' Cole said grimly. 'Wish I hadn't.'

'I know,' she agreed. 'He can't be more than seventeen or eighteen.'

'Listen,' he said, in a low voice, 'I'm gonna try an' talk to some of the guys, see if we can take 'em.'

'No, Cole. He's got an Uzi, he could kill every one of us.'

'I don't think so,' Cole said.

'Why not?' Madison said urgently. 'He's already killed twice, he's got nothing to lose.'

'We can take him, Maddy. Like you said, he's a kid.'

'Surely you *know* what kids are capable of?' she argued. 'Remember the Columbine School massacre?'

'Then what're we *supposed* to do?' Cole asked, completely frustrated. 'Sit here and take it? Give him a chance to pick us off one by one?'

Cole was right: they had to do something. But then, it was foolish to take risks.

'I need to talk to that hostage negotiator again,' she said, feeling strangely brave. 'It appears they have no intention of getting a van here. Maybe I can convince them.'

The main gunman swaggered into the centre of the room. Now that he'd removed his ski mask he seemed boastful and triumphant. He surveyed his captives.

Madison raised her hand. She noticed white powder on the tip of his nose and her stomach flip-flopped.

'What the fuck *d'you* want?' he yelled, eyes glittering dangerously.

'Let me speak to the negotiator again.'

'You did shit last time.'

'I know I can help,' she said, her words almost tripping over each other. 'Please, can I give it another try?'

'Yeah,' he sneered. 'Tell 'em what went down here. An' tell 'em that in fifteen fuckin' minutes I'm shootin' another one.'

'I don't want to be alone tonight,' Sofia said, as the Bentley pulled up in front of the boarding-house she was staying in.

'Excuse me?' Gianni said. He had never met anyone like Sofia before: she was a girl full of surprises.

'I don't want to be alone tonight,' she repeated, biting her lower lip. 'Have you got a floor or something I can camp out on?'

He raised an eyebrow, surprised. 'Are you asking to come home with me?'

'You're trustworthy, aren't you?' she said, deciding that he was. 'And anyway,' she added, 'you *know* what I can do if you're not. Scream bloody murder.'

'I'm staying in a hotel. If you like, I will book you into a room.'

'You don't understand,' she explained. 'It's not that I need a room, it's, like, I can't be alone right now.'

'You can't be alone,' he repeated.

'Sometimes I get totally freaked in the middle of the night and have bad dreams.'

'You wish to sleep with me?'

'Not *sleep* with you,' she corrected. 'Be in the same room.'

'You are making no sense, young lady,' he said sternly.

'Hey, c'mon, don't call me young lady like you're some old dude ready for the graveyard. How old are you anyway?'

'Forty-six. I'm sure, as far as you're concerned, forty-six *is* an old . . . dude.'

'Are you gay?' she asked, fixing him with a direct gaze.

'Do I *look* gay?' he replied, affronted.

'No,' she said, thinking that he looked like he'd stepped out of a magazine ad for expensive male fashions. 'Thing is, these days one never knows. Actually,' she added, with a sigh, 'I wish you *were*.'

'You do?'

'Jace, one of my best friends, was gay. The problem was there was no way I could keep tabs on him. We were travelling round Europe together, and he kept on, like, *totally* getting himself into weird situations.'

'What sort of situations?'

'Stuff you wouldn't approve of.'

'May I ask how old *you* are?'

'Um . . . uh . . . eighteen.'

'How long have you been travelling round Europe by yourself?'

'It's cool,' she said, not wishing to get into a discussion about her travels.

'If you were my daughter it wouldn't be . . . cool.'

'My dad doesn't give a shit,' she said, shrugging. 'He's probably glad to be rid of me.'

'Where is your father?'

'Who knows?' she said vaguely. 'Sometimes he's in New York, sometimes Vegas. That's where I'm from, y'know, Las Vegas.'

'People are actually born there?'

'What did you think? That everyone goes there *just* to lose their money?'

'Las Vegas is an odd place.'

'You ever visited?'

'Once, for a special charity event.'

'Of course,' she said sarcastically. 'Why else would a dignified man like you be caught dead in a hokey place like Vegas?'

'Excuse me?'

'You're, like, so up yourself,' she said, shivering.

'I *beg* your pardon?'

'Mr Uptight. It wouldn't kill you to chill out.'

'I am very relaxed. It's you who are nervous.'

'So,' she said, dreading the thought of being alone, 'can I sleep with you or not? I mean, y'know, just kinda, like, stay in the same bed or something, so long as you don't come anywhere near me.'

'Sofia, my dear, as tempting a proposition as it is, I do not imagine my girlfriend would approve.'

'You have a girlfriend?' she said, startled.

'Why do you sound so surprised?'

'I dunno, you seem like, uh . . . asexual.'

'That's an extremely insulting comment to make to an Italian man.'

'Sorry.'

'Why would you think that?'

'I dunno,' she said, fidgeting on the plush leather seat. 'You're, like, so all put together, with your expensive suit and your snooty attitude. I can't imagine you getting it on with anyone. Who *is* your girlfriend anyway?'

'A famous model.'

'Oh,' she said, giggling. 'So you fuck the help – is that it?'

'You're an extremely rude girl.'

'Some people get off on that.'

'Not me, Sofia.'

'Well, I guess I'll have to sit in my bed by myself and have freaking nightmares. Not that *you* care,' she said, reaching for the door handle.

He put his hand over hers. 'No,' he said. 'You can stay with me.'

'What about your girlfriend?'

'She's in Paris.'

'Then that was just a ploy to get rid of me?'

'*Am* I getting rid of you?'

'No.'

'Very well.' He tapped on the glass separating him from his driver. 'Mañuel, to the hotel, please.'

'And what hotel is that?' she asked.

'The Marbella Club,' he replied.

'Where else?' she murmured.

If Vincent had had a gun, he would have shot Andy Dale right in his movie star face. How dare the short, untalented actor think he could get away with this kind of repugnant behaviour?

And what was Jenna thinking? Naked in a Jacuzzi with another man, in *his* hotel? She was insane. She'd lost it totally, and he knew he would have to divorce her. She'd disrespected him, and that was the worst thing she could've done.

'Get out of there!' he said, barely able to say the words.

'Honey,' she said, putting on her little-girl voice, 'I'm *so* sorry. I know I was supposed to come back to the table, only I bumped into Andy and Anais and they invited me up here. I was about to call you, see if you cared to join us.'

'I repeat, get out!'

She stared back at him defiantly. 'And what if I don't?' she said, testing him.

'Surely you can't be *that* dumb?' he said. And then, turning his attention to Andy Dale, he continued, 'You get out, too. Take your girlfriend, your belongings, and leave my hotel.'

'Are you talking to *me*?' Andy said, eyebrows shooting up.

'Yes, I'm talking to you.'

'Do you know who I am?'

Christ! Hadn't they recently had this same conversation?

'Do you know who *I* am?' Vincent said.

'Yeah,' Andy sneered. 'Some schmuck whose wife doesn't give a shit.'

He'd taken enough for one night. Striding over to the Jacuzzi, he grabbed Jenna by the arm, and hauled her out. She was half naked, having kept on her thong underwear, which was now totally transparent.

'You hurt me!' she complained.

'Get dressed,' he hissed.

'You can't treat me like this,' she objected. 'I'm not a possession, I'm your *wife*.'

'Yes, my wife,' he said harshly. 'And *my wife* is sitting half naked in a Jacuzzi with this no-talent actor.'

'Hey,' Andy objected. 'Who're *you* calling names? I won a Golden Globe last year, and don't you forget it.'

'I'm not forgetting anything,' Vincent said. 'Now, get your skinny ass out of there.'

'I'll get out when I'm good and ready,' Andy said. 'In the meantime I'm calling my manager. This hotel's gonna get the worst publicity it ever had.'

'I don't give a shit what you do,' Vincent said. 'I'm sending somebody up here to throw you out. You are *not* staying on my premises.'

'You're being so *mean*,' Jenna wailed, her pretty face crumpling into tears of self-pity. 'It's all *my* fault. Andy didn't do anything!'

Vincent glared at her. 'Be quiet,' he said, 'and put your clothes on.'

Sulking, she reached for her dress.

'Are we going somewhere?' Anais inquired, stretching languidly, her large nipples startlingly erect.

'No,' Andy snapped.

'Yes,' Vincent said. And with that he physically dragged the actor out of the tub and threw him down on the floor, a sprawling wet mass.

'Shit!' Andy whined, trying to cover his privates. 'I'll have your ass for this. I'll sue you *and* the fucking hotel.'

By now Jenna had wriggled into her dress.

Vincent picked up her shoes, took her by the arm and led her from the room.

'I'm staying here,' Michael said, getting out of bed. 'Cancel your maid service or whoever you've got coming in.'

'That's what I like about you, Michael,' Dani said, sitting up in bed, 'the way you take my feelings into consideration.'

'I always do.'

'Did I *say* you could stay here?'

'You don't want me to, Dani?' he said, pulling on his pants.

'Does it matter?' She reached for her robe.

'C'mon, sweetheart, let's not fight. I need a place to think things out. *You're* that place.'

'I'm *always* that place,' she said, wondering why she continued to put up with him after all these years.

'This is what I want you to do,' he said, all business. 'Get me Vincent.'

'It's late.'

'He's in the casino, isn't he? Or his restaurant.'

'I don't keep tabs on him, Michael.'

'See if you can reach him. I need to see him.'

'Now?'

'No, in a week or two would be fine.'

'There's no need for sarcasm, I'll see what I can do.'

She picked up the phone and called the manager of the hotel. 'Is Vincent round, Mario?'

'I do believe he was in the casino earlier, Mrs Castle. He said something about visiting the penthouse. We have quite a few celebrity guests here. Maybe he was going to a party.'

'Vincent doesn't party,' Dani said. 'We all know that.'

'I . . . I actually think he was looking for the other *Mrs* Castle, his wife.'

'Ah . . .' Dani said. 'When you see him, please ask him to phone me. It's urgent.'

'Yes, Mrs Castle.'

She put down the phone. 'Satisfied?' she said to Michael.

'I'm always satisfied when I'm round you.'

'Oh, *please*,' she said. 'Don't start with me.'

'Come in the other room and I'll fix us a drink,' he said.

She followed him into the living room.

'What were you doing with that jerk tonight anyway?' he said, going behind the bar. 'You know I can't stand him.'

'I've told you many times, Dean is *not* a jerk. He's a very nice man who's always helped me.'

'When did *you* ever need help, Miss Independent?' Michael said, pouring her a shot of vodka and adding ice.

'Michael,' she said sternly, 'I'm not in the mood.'

'Okay. Calm down,' he said, grinning.

She hated that he didn't take anything seriously. And yet when he smiled she'd never been able to stay mad at him.

'Does Madison know you're on the run?' she said, reminding him of his situation.

'Is that what I am? On the run?' he said wryly. 'Has it come to this?'

'If there's a warrant out for your arrest and they can't find you, you're on the run.'

'Should I call her?' he asked, handing her the glass of vodka.

'She's *your* daughter.'

'I'll call her,' he decided. 'And while I'm doing that, you'd better try to reach Sofia. And when you do, tell her to get back here immediately. I'm having Vincent arrange protection for all of you.'

*

When Madison was eight, she made up an imaginary family. There was Daddy, who was always around when she needed him. There was Mommy, a warm and loving person. And there was a big, protective brother, whom she adored. She named him Cooper.

It was Cooper she spent most of her imaginary time with. She and Cooper had incredible adventures. They would laugh and play, and do things together. Most of all they always stood up for each other.

The truth was that, when she was eight, Madison was an extremely lonely child. Stella was a distant mother figure, blonde and beautiful with her Marilyn Monroe-esque stance, and her way of always having a headache when Madison needed anything.

And Michael, so handsome, was often away on some kind of business trip.

Whatever nanny her parents hired was the key person in Madison's life. And they came and went on a regular basis. So her imaginary brother became her very best friend, the only person she could *really* depend on.

When she'd met Vincent it had been a total surprise to discover that she actually had a real-life half-brother, one she'd never known about. A brother who strongly resembled her and looked exactly like Michael. It was quite a shock.

Now, as she sat in the middle of Mario's, in the intense heat with the killer gunman and a bunch of hysterical hostages, she wished that Cooper were there to save her. And if not Cooper, perhaps her real-life brother, Vincent. Or Jake – her wonderful Jake.

But none of them was round, so she had to try and make things work out herself. Screw it! She was going to get through this. She had to.

'You *must* let me talk to the negotiator again,' she repeated to the gunman, who was strutting up and down the room, Uzi swinging from one hand.

'You do that,' he said, eyes burning with hate, 'an' if you don't get action, you'll be the next fuckin' bitch t'get a bullet in your head.'

She shuddered. This was turning out to be the most frightening night of her life.

Chapter Twenty-two

Michael: 1970

After failing to get in to see Vito Giovanni, and then his tense exchange of words with Tommaso, Michael tried to decide on his next move. He needed to explain things to Mr G and get his job back. What else could he do where he made that kind of money? Besides, he kind of missed being around the Giovannis; the two of them had been like family to him. He'd certainly had more in common with Vito than he'd ever had with his real father. And Mamie wasn't so bad when she was in one of her good moods.

Unfortunately, getting back wasn't going to be easy, and when he *did* get in to see Vito, who would the big man believe? Him or Tommaso?

He finally reached the conclusion that Mamie was his only chance of getting through to Mr G, and *she'd* not given him the warmest of welcomes.

In the meantime, he was stuck on Max and Tina's couch, listening to them both get on his case.

Max had persuaded Tina's dad to offer him a job at the car dealership. 'He knows you've been in the joint,' Max explained, 'but he'll give you a chance anyway, so long as you give *him* your word you're goin' straight.'

'Hey,' Michael said, thinking there was no way he planned on selling cars for a living, 'you know me, I'm not cut out for a nine-to-five job.'

Max was immediately affronted. 'Are you sayin' no?'

'Hey, listen, I gotta figure things out for myself. Right?'

'You know what your problem is?'

'Spit it out.'

'You're an ungrateful prick.' But Max said it with love in his voice, because Michael was the brother he'd never had, and he did indeed love him.

A few days before his release from prison, Karl Edgington had made sure Michael still had the number he'd given him to call. 'Trust me,' Karl had said. 'You can make yourself a lot of money.'

Was he supposed to trust a man who'd embezzled two million dollars? It was a move he wasn't sure about, but he kept the number, just in case.

Tina had plans to introduce him to some of her girlfriends.

'Gimme a break, Tina,' he groaned. 'I *know* your friends. We were all in school together, right?'

'No, not right,' Tina said, determined to fix him up. 'I have other friends now. Girls you should meet, *decent* girls,' she added pointedly.

'I gotta get off your couch first,' he said. '*Then* I can start thinkin' about girls.'

'I like having you on our couch, Michael,' she replied, flirting mildly.

He'd noticed she'd been doing that a lot lately. He hoped it didn't piss Max off.

Every day when Max left for work, Tina and he were alone in the house with the kids. She usually sat the two children in front of the TV in the living room, where they nibbled cookies while watching an endless stream of cartoons.

'Is that okay for them to do?' he asked. 'Shouldn't they be goin' out to the park or somethin'?'

'If it keeps 'em quiet, it's okay,' she replied. 'Come in the kitchen, I'll make us coffee.'

He was sure that deep down Tina had never quite forgiven him for breaking up with her. Every now and then she made bitchy comments, alluding to the fact that they could have been together.

He decided he'd better address the subject before she said something she might regret. 'Y'know, it's a real kick seein' you and Max so happy,' he said, sitting down at the kitchen table. 'An' Jeez, Tina,' he added, tossing a compliment her way, 'even after two kids, you still got that babe thing goin' on.'

His words pleased her. 'You think so?' she asked, spooning instant coffee into two mugs, and adding hot water.

'I *always* thought so.'

'Hmm . . .' she said, handing him his coffee. 'If I'm such a babe, how come you broke up with me?'

'C'mon, Tina,' he said, reaching for the sugar. 'We were kids. Didn't know *what* we wanted.'

'*I* did,' she said, fixing him with a meaningful look.

'I know *you* did,' he said quickly. 'An' it was marriage an' all that goes with it. I wasn't into gettin' serious.'

'Why?'

''Cause I'm not Max,' he explained. 'Max is a stand-up guy. Look at the two of you, with the house an' the kids. It's great the way everythin' worked out.'

'Maybe,' she said noncommittally, sitting down at the table opposite him.

'Don't give me that "maybe" crap.'

'It's just that . . . well . . . you and I, Michael, we were something together, weren't we?' she said, suddenly going all dreamy-eyed.

This conversation was *definitely* heading in the wrong direction. 'I repeat,' he said firmly, 'we were kids. And thank God you were smart enough not to put out.'

'Even though you were begging!' she said with a knowing smile.

'Yeah, even though I was beggin',' he admitted, grinning at the memory. Talk about blue balls! Tina had been an expert at not giving it up.

She fingered the rim of her coffee mug in a suggestive way. 'Perhaps it's not too late . . .'

'Whoa!' he said, holding up his hand. 'Stop right there.'

'I'm teasing!' she said, laughing.

'Yeah – if I remember right, you were always good at that.'

That day, Max came home early from work, and the two of them went over to visit their old friend, Charlie, who was still living at home and looked like shit.

He wasn't the same Charlie that Michael remembered. The big, burly Charlie with the Elvis sideburns and happy-go-lucky attitude was long gone. In his place was a haunted twenty-five year old with horror in his eyes, a Marine crewcut, and liquor on his breath – even though it was only four in the afternoon. He'd lost a leg in Vietnam, along with his will to live. Michael recognized the look: growing up, he'd seen it every day in his father's eyes.

'How ya doin', man?' he asked, falsely jovial.

'How'd *you* be doin' with one freakin' leg?' Charlie replied.

'Sorry,' Michael said. 'It's a bum rap.'

'They gave me this piece a plastic shit t'wear,' Charlie complained. 'Hurts like hell.'

'Isn't there somethin' better than that?'

'Too expensive.'

The next day Michael found out the details, dug into his savings, and handed Max the money to arrange for Charlie to get a top-of-the-line prosthetic leg. 'Don't let him know it came from me,' he instructed.

'Where'd you get this kind of money?' Max wanted to know.

'I've been saving up for a rainy day.'

The following evening Tina had set him up with a date, refusing to take no for an answer. She and Max were making up the foursome.

Susie and Harry were settled in bed when the Delagado twins arrived to babysit: two young girls, both exotic beauties, petite and slender with burnished skin, wide-apart brown eyes, full lips and lustrous black hair. Catherine was the quiet and studious one, while Beth was somewhat wild.

'Where did you find *them?*' Michael asked, checking them out.

'They live next door with their Aunt Gloria,' Tina said, primping in the mirror. 'They came over from Cuba a few months ago. Their aunt gives Latin dance classes. I hear she's quite a mover; we should go some time.'

'Hot little babes, huh?' Max said, giving Michael a furtive nudge. 'Dunno why my old lady allows them around me – lucky me!'

'Listen to your wife,' Tina said, shooting Max a warning look. 'And remember these two words. Jail bait!'

'Yes, ma'am!' Max said, with a mock salute.

'How old *are* they?' Michael asked.

'Too young for you,' Max said, with a dirty laugh.

'Fifteen,' Tina announced triumphantly. 'Ten *years* too young for *either* of you.'

Beth didn't seem to think so. The moment she saw Michael she began coming on to him.

He pretended not to notice. She was a child in a woman's body, plus she had 'trouble' written all over her.

Michael's blind date was too tall, too serious, and

definitely not for him. Her name was April, and she worked in a bank.

The four of them went to a movie. As soon as they'd settled the girls in their seats, Max and Michael headed for the lobby to buy popcorn.

'Jeez!' Michael groaned, leaning against the concession stand. 'What've you *done* to me?'

'She's a nice girl,' Max said, grabbing a couple of candy bars and four cartons of popcorn. 'Very smart.'

'The last thing I need is nice,' Michael grumbled.

'Don't forget,' Max reminded him, 'the plain ones are always the most grateful.'

Did Max honestly think that because he'd been locked up for a few years he couldn't find his own date? This was crazy.

After the movie they went to the local diner. The girls sat there arguing about who was cuter – Paul Newman or Steve McQueen.

'I'll take McQueen any day,' Tina said, ordering a burger and french fries.

'No,' April said, shaking her head. 'Paul Newman looks like he has brains as well as brawn.'

So it's brains she's after, Michael thought. *Well, she certainly ain't getting them from me. I'm the jerk who allowed myself to get set up. The dumb fuck who sat in jail for five years.*

He was angry and frustrated, and as each day passed he was getting more so.

Had to come up with a plan. Had to do something soon. Couldn't sit around and do nothing.

A few nights later the Delagado twins came back. Max and Tina had already left for a wedding, and Michael was supposed to meet them later.

As soon as they arrived, Catherine went upstairs to check that both children were asleep, then she took out her schoolbooks and settled at the kitchen table.

Beth wandered into the living room.

'Hi, Michael,' she said, giving him a sexy smile as she perched on the edge of his chair.

'Hi, schoolgirl,' he answered.

He had to admit she was quite an exotic beauty, with her long black hair that hung below her waist, devilish brown eyes, and full pouty lips. She was wearing tight blue jeans and a checkered shirt tied at the waist, exposing a couple of inches of taut, tanned flesh.

'Missed me, did you?' she said, giving him a flirtatious look.

'Oh, sure,' he said, playing the game. 'Missed you desperately.'

'I'm not surprised,' she said, with a secret smile.

'How *was* school today?' he asked.

'Same as usual,' she replied, pulling a face. 'I have to sit in a class full of baby boys. Don't you *hate* baby boys?'

'What're baby boys?'

'Boys who don't know anything about girls,' she said vaguely. 'I like *men*. Real men.'

'You do, huh?' he said, wondering why there hadn't been any girls around like her when *he* was fifteen.

'Oh, yes,' she said, licking her full lips.

'And how many *real* men have you known?'

'You'd be surprised.'

'I bet I would.'

'Plenty,' she said confidently.

'Yeah?'

'Yeah,' she said, imitating his voice, her brown eyes throwing out a challenge.

He laughed. 'You're a nutcase.'

'Takes one to know one,' she retorted, playing with a delicate amethyst crucifix that hung round her neck on a thin gold chain.

'Fifteen, huh?' he said, yawning. 'You'll be somethin' when you grow up.'

'Believe me, Michael, I am *all* grown-up.'

'Says the schoolgirl,' he teased.

Her brown eyes flashed. 'In Cuba we grow up fast.'

'I can see that,' he said, getting up.

Her pouty lips got even more so. 'I break men's hearts.'

'Thanks for the warning.'

'I really do.'

'Don't doubt it.'

'My daddy told me I can get any man I want.'

'He did, did he?'

'Uh huh.'

'And where *is* your daddy?'

'He's a political prisoner in Cuba,' she said matter-of-factly. 'He arranged to get us out of the country. We've been here six months.'

'That was smart of him.'

'I think I like America – except for the baby boys. They're no fun. In Cuba the boys are more . . . adult.'

'You speak perfect English.'

'Our father taught us that education is important.'

'Another smart move.'

'Yes, we grew up learning several languages.'

'And your mom, where's she?'

'Ran off with another man when we were three. She was wild – exactly like me!'

'An' you're proud of that?'

'*You* can talk,' she said sharply. 'Weren't you recently released from prison?'

Jeez! Bad news travels fast.

'Gotta go,' he said, heading for the door.

'Too bad,' she said, following him.

He was half-way through the door when she called out, 'Had any pussy since you left prison?'

He stopped, quite shocked. '*What?*'

'Just asking,' she said innocently. 'No harm in that, is there?'

He shook his head in wonderment. This girl was something else. 'Ask me again in five years when you're all grown up,' he said.

'Ha!' she replied. 'You don't know what you're missing!'

Yeah, and he had no intention of finding out.

By the time he met up with Tina and Max, Tina had lined up two new prospects – a buck-toothed brunette and an anorexic redhead. They both leaped on him like ants on peanut butter, plying him with questions, and in between the questions telling him all about themselves. As if he cared.

'I'm gettin' an earache,' he complained to Max.

'I got a hunch you should bang the redhead,' Max said, with a ribald laugh. 'She needs it most.'

'*You* bang her.'

'*I'm* a married man.'

'You gotta tell Tina to stop fixing me up.'

'Why? You wanna get your rocks off, dontcha?'

'I can do it on my own time.'

'Then do it,' Max said. 'You've been out a week, or didya get a taste for somethin' different in jail?'

'Screw you, Max. That's not funny.'

'Then why aren't you horny?'

'You want the truth or a lie?'

'I'll take the truth.'

'I went to a hooker the day after I got out,' he lied. It was easier to tell a fib rather than start explaining why he wasn't in the mood for sex.

Max's eyes bulged. 'You did *what?*'

'Yeah. I paid for it. First time.'

'Why'd you do *that?*'

''Cause I don't need to take a girl out an' sweet-talk her into bed, make her think it means anything when it doesn't. Right now I gotta concentrate. So do me a big favour, no more of Tina's fix-ups.'

'Holy crap!' Max said. 'You *paid* for it. Jeez! What was it like?'

'Uncomplicated,' he said. 'And right now, that's the way it has to be.'

A few nights later, Tina announced that the Delagado twins' Aunt Gloria was having a party to celebrate the girls' sixteenth birthday.

'I promised her we'd drop by,' Tina said. 'She's quite a fabulous character. It'll be a blast.'

'We can't leave the kids alone,' Max pointed out.

'Yes, we can,' Tina replied, determined to go. 'What's the big deal? They're in bed asleep, and we'll be right next door.'

'I'll stay with the kids,' Michael volunteered. 'You two go enjoy yourselves.'

'That's not fair—' Tina began.

'You might as well make the most of me,' he said. 'Any day now I'll be outta here.'

'If you're sure . . .' she said, reluctant to leave him behind.

'I'm sure,' he said firmly. He had no desire to go to a sweet sixteen celebration – staying home was a far more tempting prospect.

Earlier in the day he'd met up with his old prison pal, Gus, who'd told him there was something coming up that he might be interested in.

'What?' he'd asked.

'I'll let you know,' Gus had said. 'It's a big-bucks job that'll pay good.'

'What'll I havta do t'make big bucks?'

'Drive. You can do that, huh?'

He was twenty-five with no job and a prison record. Did he have a choice?

Yes. He could call the number that Karl Edgington had given him. And maybe he would. Eventually.

Tonight, he decided, was going to be the last night he spent on Max and Tina's couch. He was getting lazy and too comfortable. Besides, leeching off his friends was not his style. If Gus came up with the job, he was definitely in. He needed to make some money, and fast.

The sound of Latin music began drifting over from next door. He put on the TV and tuned into Monday-night football.

After a while he must've fallen asleep, because the next thing he knew there were sirens and lights flashing outside the window.

Jumping up, he hurried to the front door and walked into the street. People were milling about on the sidewalk as two ambulance attendants carried a stretcher to the back of their vehicle.

He grabbed a fat woman in a floral dress. 'What's goin' on?' he asked.

'She's dead!' the woman wailed, clumps of thick black mascara dripping down her cheeks. 'The poor dear is gone!'

'Who?' he asked urgently. 'Who's dead?'

'Those little children will be all alone in the world,' the woman sobbed. 'It's a tragedy!'

Suddenly he spotted Max. His friend was sitting on the kerb with his head in his hands.

Jesus Christ! Something must have happened to Tina. Something bad.

Chapter Twenty-three

Dani: 1970

'There's someone I think you should meet,' Gemini said.

'What do you mean, meet?' Dani replied, quite flustered. 'Is it a man? Because I can't meet any men – I'm still married.'

They were sitting in the park watching Vincent and Nando playing in the sandbox. It was Dani's favourite thing to do, watching her son at play. He was so serious and intent, while Nando was all over the place.

'Oh, please,' Gemini said, in her lilting French accent, 'I know you do not love your husband, Dani. You are a woman, and you need to be fulfilled. It is time you left him.'

'I can't do that,' Dani said, feeling immediately guilty. 'Sam was there for me when I needed him.'

'I understand your guilt because he is the father of your child,' Gemini said quite seriously. 'However, if Sam does not give Vincent or you the love you deserve, then you must think of your future.'

'It's not that easy, Gem,' Dani said, frowning. 'It's complicated.'

'Everything is complicated. Look at me, I left Nando's

father, and he was from a very affluent family. However, I decided that happiness is more important than money.'

'Why *did* you leave him?'

'He abused me,' Gemini said simply. 'His father was a powerful man in Colombia, and Moralis was merely the son. Because of his circumstances he took his frustration out on me – mentally *and* physically. After I gave birth to Nando, I realized to survive I must get away from him, so I came here.'

'Why did you choose Vegas?' Dani asked. 'You could've gone anywhere.'

'I was a dancer in Paris when I met Moralis. I felt it unwise to return to France. Vegas seemed like a place where I could find a good job doing what I love to do.'

'Didn't he come after you?'

'I am sure he did. But I have learned that once a woman walks out on a man, it is never prudent to return.'

'I think about leaving Sam all the time,' Dani sighed, glancing over at her son, who was happily making mud pies with Nando. 'I can't stand his drinking, and he never works. We fight all the time. It's not the right atmosphere for Vincent to grow up in.'

'No, it's not.'

'And,' Dani continued, 'he's always asking me for money to invest in crazy schemes.'

'I hope you don't give it to him.'

'Of course not. I'm saving my money for Vincent's education.'

'You have quite a dilemma,' Gemini said. 'It is always better for a boy to have a man in his life.'

'I know,' Dani agreed. 'That's why it's taken me so long to make a move.' She hesitated a moment. 'You see, Sam rescued me and my sister from a terrible situation. I don't want to talk about it but, believe me, it was bad. Sam brought us to Vegas, and looked after us. Then later he married my sister. They were very happy, until one day she vanished, and we've never found her. After that, it was my turn to be there for Sam and get him through it.'

'And you did.'

'For a while. Then *he* took care of *me* when I was pregnant.'

'So he should,' Gemini said. 'It's his baby.'

'No,' Dani admitted. 'Sam is *not* Vincent's father.'

'Is this the truth?' Gemini asked, quite shocked.

'It's hardly something I'd make up.'

'Does Sam know?'

Dani shook her head. She wasn't sorry she'd revealed her secret. In a way it was a relief to share the knowledge with someone – especially since that someone was her closest friend.

'If he's not Vincent's father, then you have no responsibility towards him,' Gemini said. 'Why should you support this man for the rest of your life?'

Gemini was right: Dani had paid Sam back for everything he'd done for her. The tough part would be telling him that Vincent wasn't his son, because that was something she had to do. It was only fair.

'So,' Gemini said, 'after the show tonight I am having dinner with my business manager. I would love you to come and meet his friend from Houston. He's a very nice man.'

'If he's so nice, why aren't *you* dating him?'

'He's seen you in the show, Dani,' Gemini said with a slight smile. 'He is desperate to meet you.'

'I must be honest with you, Gem. I've had it with men, they fail to interest me. All I care about is my son – he's everything to me.'

'May I ask who his real father is?'

'A man I met when I was very young. I guess he wasn't that much older than me, although he had no idea I was only sixteen. I imagine he thought we were the same age.

211

He was probably nineteen or twenty. Unfortunately it turned out to be a one-night event.'

'And when you informed him you were pregnant, what did he do?' Gemini asked.

'I didn't tell him.'

'Why not?'

'Because after our one night together, I never heard from him again. So . . . I decided to marry Sam.'

'And pretend that Vincent is his?'

She nodded shamefacedly. 'Yes.'

'Perhaps something happened to your one-night lover. Life is like that.'

'Maybe.'

'At least if you'd told him you were pregnant, he could have helped support your son. Or do you not think he's entitled to know he has one?'

'No,' she said fiercely. 'He's not. Vincent is mine. *I'm* the one who's always been there for him, and I always will be.'

'If that's the way you feel . . .' Gemini said.

'Yes,' Dani said, nodding vigorously. 'That's exactly how I feel.'

'So . . . tonight, you will come?'

'I don't think so.'

'You're sure?'

'Very sure.'

A few weeks later she threw Sam out. He staggered home at four in the morning, completely drunk, falling over furniture and spewing obscenities. Wearily she got out of bed and hurried downstairs, hoping to shut him up before he woke Vincent.

He wasn't alone. There was a woman with him, a painted whore chugging from a half-full bottle of whiskey while draping herself all over him.

'Whassamatter?' Sam mumbled, giving Dani a bleary-eyed look. 'Dontcha wanna join the party?'

'Get out!' she screamed, suddenly losing it. 'Get out of my house and never come back!'

He left without a fight, the woman clinging on to him like a leech.

The next day Dani waited for him to come home, begging her forgiveness. Surprisingly, he didn't.

A few months later Gemini suggested dinner with her friend.

This time she agreed.

And so she met Dean King, and almost fell in love.

Chapter Twenty-four

Michael: 1971

'I'm getting an abortion and *you*'re paying for it,' Beth announced, tossing back her long black hair, a defiant expression on her young face.

'*What?*' Michael replied, in shock. She'd invited him over to the house, and *this* was what she'd had to lay on him.

'You heard,' she said, as if she'd casually mentioned she was about to have root-canal work.

'You *gotta* be kidding me,' he said, pacing round the room. 'I only slept with you once, and that was months ago.'

'We did it twice in one night,' she corrected. 'You knocked me up, and now *you're* paying to get rid of the kid.'

Christ! How had he ever got involved with this wild child? She was fucking insane! And so was he for going anywhere near her.

'What the hell makes you think it's mine?' he demanded.

She threw him a scornful look. 'Of course it's yours. If you don't believe me, we can take a blood test.'

He stared at this seductive child-woman, who was

accusing him of knocking her up, and attempted to get his thoughts straight. Everything seemed to have happened so fast. It wasn't Tina who'd been carried out to the ambulance that fateful night a year ago, it was the twins' Aunt Gloria. She'd suffered a fatal heart attack in the middle of a sexy tango with Max. Poor Max had been plagued with guilt ever since.

After Gloria's demise, the twins were on their own. The lawyer representing Gloria's estate had arranged for them to remain in the house next door, with Max and Tina as their legal guardians.

By this time Michael had found a small apartment, and moved out. He'd decided it wasn't worth trying to get back in with Vito Giovanni when he could be making good money elsewhere, so he'd taken the job Gus had offered him, and after a few successful runs, he'd become part of Gus's crew in the Lucchese family.

He'd also finally contacted the number Karl Edgington had given him. A woman had answered the phone.

'Michael Castellino,' he'd said. 'Karl told me to call.'

'About time,' she'd said. 'Discuss nothing on the phone. Meet me tomorrow, four o'clock, outside the Plaza.'

'How'll I know you?'

'*I'll* find *you*.'

And she had. Her name was Warner Carlysle and she was a definite uptown beauty, tall, with auburn hair and a confident attitude. It turned out, much to Michael's surprise, that she was Karl Edgington's mistress. She was also the keeper of his cash, a million dollars in unmarked bills that the detectives who'd arrested him had known nothing about.

'Karl wants to legitimize this money,' she'd said, 'and obviously *he* can't. So, for a return of ten per cent, he wants you to slowly invest it in the market over a period of time.'

'What if I blow it?'

'You won't. I'll give you Karl's instructions and a certain amount of cash at a time. This is a no-lose proposition.'

'How come he trusts *me*?'

'Karl is not as mild as you think. Screw him and you screw yourself. Follow instructions and everyone turns out a winner.'

Which is exactly what he'd done, and he was making plenty.

Christ! His one night with Beth had been a big mistake. However, it was *his* mistake, and now he had to pay the price.

She was seventeen and pregnant.

He was twenty-six and pissed.

'Take the goddamn test,' he said, reluctantly doing the right thing. 'If it's positive, I'll marry you.'

'Big deal,' she said, thrusting out her lower lip. 'I'm too young to sacrifice myself to marriage, and I'm *certainly* too young to have a baby. I'm getting rid of it, Michael, and *you're* paying.'

This girl had balls bigger than his. 'No,' he said sharply. 'I don't believe in abortion.'

'Who cares *what* you believe in?'

She was too much. 'Are you *listening* to me?' he said angrily. '*No* abortion.'

'My plans do not include getting stuck with a baby at my age,' she said, brown eyes flashing. 'If you really want to know, I'm going to be a dress designer. The biggest and the best.'

She'd already dropped out of school, and was attending a fashion institute. At least she had a mission, which was more than he could say about most of the women he dated. They *all* wanted to get married. They were *all* after the gold ring on the finger. So far, none of them had come close.

As far as *he* was concerned, marriage was a gold ring

through the nose, and not something he'd ever considered before. Now he was offering it to her, and she was turning him down. Unbelievable!

He confided in Max over a beer at their local bar.

'Jeez!' Max groaned. 'Why'd you havta screw her? She's *seventeen*, for crissakes. You didn't have enough pussy, you had to have her too? That's some dumb move!'

'Yeah, it was stupid,' he admitted. 'But she was always giving me the come-on.'

'An' you couldn't resist.'

'Guess not.'

'How was she in the sack?' Max asked, narrowing his eyes slyly.

'Get the fuck outta here,' Michael said, frowning. 'You *know* I never talk about the women I've been with.'

'Gee, thanks,' Max said indignantly. 'Here I am, married six years, an' *you* don't wanna tell me shit. Would it *kill* you to give a married guy a cheap thrill?'

'I'll tell you this,' Michael said, ignoring his comment. 'I'm sure as hell not allowing her to get rid of *my* baby.'

'What're you gonna do?' Max said sarcastically. 'Tie her to the bedpost?'

'You've got to get Tina to talk to her. Maybe after the baby's born she'll snap into some kind of maternal instinct thing. Isn't that what women do?'

'How would I know?' Max said, swigging his beer. 'If you were smart, you'd let her get rid of it.'

'That's not right, Max. How'd *you* feel if it was Susie or Harry?'

'Okay, okay – I get what you're sayin'.'

'Then you'll speak to Tina?'

'Sure. Only I'm warnin' you – my lovely wife'll have your balls for breakfast.'

'I hope she enjoys 'em.'

*

'You horny, disgusting *pig!*' Tina raged. 'Why couldn't you keep your slimy hands off her?'

He shrugged. 'You're right, I never should've gone near her. Believe me, it's my mistake.'

'And a big one,' Tina said, glaring at him. 'Don't you understand? Max and I are supposed to watch out for those girls. We're supposed to protect them from old leches like you.'

'I'm not exactly an old lech.'

'Well, *I* think you're *disgusting*. It's terrible what you've done to that poor little girl.'

'Oh, c'mon, Tina,' he said, defending himself. 'Beth is about the most street-smart kid I've ever come across.'

'You just said it, Mike – she's a *kid*, and you should have left her alone.'

'I didn't, an' now what happens?'

'You've got to marry her.'

'I've offered and she doesn't want that.'

'You offered to *marry* her?' Tina said, shocked.

'I certainly did.'

'And she said no?'

'You got it,' he answered wearily. 'Look, if she has the baby, I'll support them both. But I'm telling you straight – *no* abortion.'

'It's not your choice.'

'It's my baby.'

'How do you know?' Tina said, arching an eyebrow. 'Are you telling me she only slept with *you*?'

'She's willin' to do the blood-test thing, an' so am I. Besides, she swears it's mine.'

'And you believe her?'

'Yeah.'

'Okay,' Tina sighed. 'I'll talk to her. But not for you – for her. And, Michael—'

'Yeah?'

'In future keep your horny little dick to yourself.'

'*Little*, Tina?'

She couldn't help giggling. 'I never did find out, did I?'

Two days later Tina summoned him back to the house. 'How many times did you sleep with her?' she asked.

'Once.'

'Then you must be a one-shot wonder.'

'What d'you mean?'

'I took her to the gyno. She's five months' pregnant, so you must have slept with her right after you moved out of here.'

'Who remembers?' he said, remembering only too well.

It has been one of those hot summer nights and he'd been over at Tina and Max's for dinner. As he'd left their house, he'd spotted Beth sitting on the steps outside the house next door. She was wearing a skimpy red halter top and barely there shorts. 'Hi, Michael,' she said, waving at him.

He walked over. She was smoking a cigarette, drinking from a can of Coke and listening to Cuban music on her transistor radio.

'Miss me?' she said, flirting as usual.

He plucked the cigarette out of her hands. 'You're too young to smoke,' he said sternly.

She leaped to her feet. 'Give that back!' she yelled, hands on hips.

He took a drag, purposely teasing her. She sucker-punched him in the stomach and grabbed her cigarette from him.

'How are you?' he asked, grinning.

'Bored,' she answered restlessly, sitting down again and stretching out her long legs.

'Where's Catherine?'

'Away for the weekend.'

'Why didn't you come over to Max an' Tina's for dinner?'

'Then I'd be even *more* bored.'

'Why? I was there.'

'That's what I mean.'

'*You* are a piece of work.'

'Takes one to know one.'

'So,' he said, sitting down next to her, 'where are all your boyfriends tonight?'

'Ha!' she said disgustedly. 'I told you before – I don't like boys, I like *men*.'

'And *how* old are you now?'

'Old enough to do whatever I want,' she said, staring at him boldly.

'I don't think so. In my opinion you're gonna havta make do with boys for the next few years.'

'*Really*, Michael?' she said, giving him another provocative look.

'Yup.'

'Wow! It's hot,' she said, fanning herself with her hand.

He couldn't help noticing that her nipples were erect. The skimpy halter top did not hide much, and it was obvious she was not wearing a bra.

'The freezer thing at the top of our fridge broke and there's a big chunk of ice stuck there,' she said, aware that he was checking out her breasts. 'Can you please take a look for me?'

'Call the repairman,' he said briskly.

'Please, Michael, *please*,' she said, standing.

'Okay, okay,' he said, getting up and following her into the house, which had the same layout of rooms as Max and Tina's, although it was furnished differently, with colourful couches, bright abstract paintings, and ethnic rugs. Aunt Gloria had exhibited very flamboyant taste.

The kitchen was a mess. Dirty dishes and chaos everywhere.

'Catherine does the housekeeping,' Beth explained, bending down to pick up the cat's dish.

'Where's this ice problem?' he asked, trying to avoid staring at her butt, so snug and inviting in her short shorts.

She gestured towards the refrigerator. He walked over. She was right behind him, transistor radio blaring salsa.

He could smell her – a heady mixture of sweet vanilla perfume and fresh sweat.

'Michael,' she said.

'Yeah?' he answered, opening the fridge.

'I think you're *veree* sexy.'

'And *I* think you're *very* young,' he said, peering at a large chunk of ice jamming the door of the freezer section.

'I'm not a virgin,' she announced.

'Let's hang out the flags,' he said, attempting to dislodge the ice with his hand – a fruitless exercise. 'You got an ice-pick?'

'Will a hammer do?'

'Guess it'll have to.'

She fetched a hammer from the kitchen drawer and handed it to him.

As he turned to take it, she suddenly flung her arms round his neck and kissed him. A big, warm, wet one right on the lips with plenty of tongue involved.

'Beth—' he began. Too late. Like clockwork his dick sprang to attention.

She was no slouch. She felt his erection, and before he could even consider what was about to happen next, she unzipped his pants and inserted her hand.

Christ! What could he do? He was only human, after all.

Within seconds she was untying her halter top, revealing the most perfect small breasts with delectable erect nipples. 'I want you,' she murmured in a husky whisper. 'I want you, Michael. I want you now.'

He fingered her nipples. She moaned and began moving her hand on him.

The hell with how old she was! He was at the point of no return, and he wasn't going anywhere.

They sank down on to the cold linoleum-covered floor. He ripped off her shorts, only to discover she was wearing no underwear. Neither was he.

Her skin was hot, clammy, and inviting. After sucking on her nipples for a few moments, he thrust his hand between her legs, then mounted her.

She moaned with pleasure, moving under him, undulating her hips towards his, somehow writhing in time to the throbbing music.

It was a thrill ride for both of them. So good, that after a few minutes' respite he was ready to go once more. And he did.

Then, suffused with guilt, he never went near her again.

That had been five months ago. Now this.

'Anyway,' Tina said, in full take-charge mode, 'it's too late for an abortion.'

'That nails it,' he said decisively. 'She'll have the baby, an' I'll marry her.'

'Sorry to shatter your wonderful fantasy of every woman begging to be your wife,' Tina said, 'but, as you know, she doesn't want to do that.'

He wasn't in the mood for Tina's jibes. 'What, then?' he said shortly.

'She says she'll move in with you.'

'I don't get it,' he said, puzzled. 'One minute she won't marry me, an' now she wants to move in with me?'

'She thinks living with you is a good idea.'

'I don't want to live with anybody.'

'Why? You were willing to marry her.'

'That's different.'

'Well,' Tina continued. 'I imagine *this'll* teach you to

keep your pecker in your pants.'

Why did he have a feeling that Tina was enjoying every moment of his uncomfortable situation?

Businesswise, things were on the rise. Working with Gus and his crew suited him fine, and he was making plenty of money investing Karl Edgington's cash and skimming off ten per cent of the profits before transferring the balance to a numbered Swiss bank account. It was complicated, but Karl had the whole deal worked out. He never made a wrong call about what stocks to invest in. The man was a genius, and Michael was getting rich.

Meanwhile, Gus's crew was involved in everything from loan-sharking to the protection racket. Once in a while they pulled off a major hijacking. It kept Michael just busy enough.

'If anyone ever needs me to take anythin' to Vegas, it's what I used to do,' he said, passing the word along.

Gus laughed in his face. 'Mr Lucchese don't shift drugs that way,' he said. 'He's smarter than that.'

'Drugs? I thought I was carryin' cash.'

'Vito Giovanni had you runnin' narcotics,' Gus said. 'You're freakin' lucky you didn't get busted. You wouldn't be walkin' round today if the Feds had nailed your sorry ass.'

Shit! He'd been ferrying drugs back and forth across state lines without knowing it. What kind of an idiot was he? And why hadn't Mamie warned him? She was a bitch for not doing so.

He'd noticed that one of Dante Lucchese's men seemed to go out of his way to avoid him. The man's name was Bone, and that's exactly how he looked. Pale skin stretched over a skeletal face, with ice-pick eyes, droopy grey eyelids and a stooped frame. He had to be getting up there – almost fifty. Everyone knew he was Mr Lucchese's enforcer.

If someone needed to be terminated, Bone was the man who took care of it. Michael wasn't into that side of the business. Killing was not for him. The only killing he cared to make was in the stock market.

'Has Bone got a problem with me?' he asked Gus one day.

'What kinda problem?' Gus said, vigorously chewing gum.

'The asshole never says a word to me, never. I don't even get a nod.'

'Dunno,' Gus said, picking at a hangnail. 'You should try talkin' t'him. 'S matter of fact, he used to work for your old boss.'

'He did?'

'Yeah, he was with the Giovanni family. It must've bin before your time. I heard he was tight with the old lady's cousin.'

'Mamie Giovanni's cousin, Roy?'

'Yeah. Hey – ain't that the jerk you told me set you up?'

'Right.'

'Maybe Bone don't think you should be here.'

'How's that?'

'I dunno. Talk to him.'

But he didn't. There was something about Bone that did not invite conversation.

The Delagado twins had several relatives scattered across the country. This was useful, because while Beth was busy moving into the house Michael had found for them, Catherine elected to visit with a distant cousin. Catherine, the quiet twin, was most upset by Beth's pregnancy. She felt Michael had taken advantage of her sister.

'How come we're doin' this?' Michael asked Beth, as they unpacked boxes. 'It's crazy. We *should* be gettin' married.'

'Why?' she said simply. 'You don't love me, and I don't love you.'

''Cause we're havin' a *baby*,' he said, attempting to get through to her. 'An' we want this kid to grow up feelin' he's got parents, right?'

'What makes you think it's a boy?' she asked, busy removing T-shirts from a box and placing them in an untidy pile.

'It'll be a boy,' he said confidently.

'Don't be so sure,' she said, patting her stomach. '*I* think the sex is determined by the person who's the most dominating force.' A wicked grin. 'And that's *me*.'

'You would think that, wouldn't you?'

She smiled at him again, that tempting, tantalizing smile that had got him into trouble in the first place.

Recently he'd found himself visiting Max and Tina's more than usual. He enjoyed playing with the kids. Little Harry was a real toughie, and Susie was a cute tomboy. But girls weren't the same as boys, and he wanted a son, a boy he could teach things to, a mirror image of himself he could be proud of.

It wouldn't be like the relationship he'd had with his dad: Vinny had never given him any attention or love. *His* son would get the works.

'I'm getting so fat,' Beth wailed, catching a glimpse of herself in a mirror. 'I look like a big old hog.'

'No way,' he assured her, wondering what he was supposed to do about his other girlfriends now that they were moving in together. There were two or three he saw regularly. Was he supposed to give them up?

'Yes, I *do*,' Beth complained, turning sideways. 'Look at me, I'm a disgrace.'

'You're funny,' he said, amused at her dismay because there was hardly a sign of a baby growing inside her stomach – she still looked sensational.

Angrily she turned on him. 'Oh,' she said, narrowing her eyes, 'so *you* think being fat is funny?'

'You're somethin' else, Beth,' he said, laughing. 'When you grow up you'll make someone a very happy man.'

'And that someone is not you, is it, Michael?' she said, suddenly turning all serious.

'No, we both agreed this is a temporary arrangement until you have the baby. Then we'll figure out our next move. In the meantime, we're both free to do what we want.'

'*If* we want,' she corrected.

'Hey,' he said, 'I saw all the guys coming on to you when you lived next door to Tina and Max. You think I didn't notice? So go out, have fun. I'll do the same.'

'I never actually screwed any of them,' she said innocently. 'You were the only one I fucked. And someone in Cuba when I was fourteen.'

'Jeez – Beth!' he exclaimed. 'Anyone ever mention you got a mouth like a sailor?'

She tilted her head on one side. 'Something wrong with that?'

'You look so innocent sometimes, then whammo – you open that mouth of yours – an' watch out! Sailor alert!'

'Sorry, Michael,' she said sarcastically. 'Am I offending your tender ears?'

He wasn't in the mood for her smart-ass answers. 'Anyway,' he said, 'what's with the you-never-screwed any-of-them? When *we* got together, you were not a virgin.'

'That's right,' she said.

'So?'

'So I told you – there was a man in Cuba.'

'Who was he?'

'My secret lover.'

'Which I guess means you don't want to tell me.'

She grinned. 'Right.'

'I gotta go out,' he said. 'I've left money on the kitchen table. You'd better buy a crib and all that shit. We gotta get organized here.'

'You mean we're not doing it together like some newly married couple?'

'Beth, don't push me.'

'Hey,' she said vehemently, 'I'm having the baby for *you*, so don't *you* push *me*.'

'Let's remember that you're havin' the baby 'cause it's too late for you to get rid of it.'

'I hate you,' she said, suddenly acting her age. 'I really, really hate you.'

'Wow! Feelings. That makes a nice change.'

'I've *always* had feelings for you, Michael,' she said, switching moods. 'From the first time I saw you, I knew I'd get you. And now I've *really* got you.'

'I don't understand you,' he said, shaking his head. 'I would've married you, but no, you didn't want that.'

'It's better to see if we can get along without all that legal stuff, don't you think?'

And she looked at him with her big brown eyes, and it suddenly occurred to him that he might be falling in love with this sexy child-woman who was carrying his baby.

Sometimes he wondered what was really going on in her head. 'You're so casual about this,' he said.

'Why shouldn't I be?'

'By the way, for the record, you do *not* look disgusting. In fact, you look kinda beautiful. You got that glow thing happenin'.'

That smile again, lighting up her face. 'I do?'

'Yeah,' he said ruefully. 'Unfortunately for me, you are a very beautiful child.'

'You know I'm not a child,' she said, with a wicked grin.

'So you keep telling me.'

'Well,' she added seductively, 'since I'm pregnant

anyway, and it's quite obvious we've done the deed, shouldn't we maybe celebrate?' As she spoke, she put her arms round his neck, bringing her lips close to his ear.

'Beth,' he said, shaking his head, 'you are one big tease.'

'Michael,' she whispered, her tongue licking inside his ear, 'I am *not* teasing.'

Four months later, Beth awoke in the middle of the night and started screaming like a banshee. 'I'm having a baby!' she yelled hysterically. 'And it fucking *hurts*!'

Michael leaped up, dressed hurriedly, ran outside, hailed a cab and they got in and raced to the hospital. Beth continued to yell, scream and curse all the way.

The nurses were shocked. 'Kindly tell your wife to calm down, Mr Castellino. Her language is not acceptable.'

'She's not my wife.'

'Are you her uncle?'

'No.' He laughed. 'I'm the baby's dad.'

'Oh,' the nurse said, tight-lipped.

'Don't worry about it,' he said, as Beth's ear-splitting screams and curses filled the air. 'I offered to marry her. She told me no.'

'Silly girl,' the nurse said primly.

'I'd say so,' he agreed.

While the nurse wheeled Beth into the delivery room, he ran to a pay phone and called Max and Tina. 'You'd better get over here fast,' he announced. 'We're havin' a baby.'

'We're on our way,' Max assured him.

By the time they arrived, Beth had given birth to a healthy girl. The baby weighed eight pounds six ounces, and had a full mop of thick, black, curly hair.

'We're calling her Madison,' Beth announced, lying in the hospital bed holding her baby, her long, dark hair damp with sweat, a contented smile on her face.

'What kind of a name is that?' Michael asked.

'It's a special name,' she replied softly, 'for a special girl.'

'I don't got no say?'

'Get used to it.' Max laughed. 'That's the way it is. Married or not, the female always gets her own way.'

'Here,' Beth said, 'you take her.' And she handed Michael the newly named Madison.

Gingerly he took the baby and held her in his arms.

Madison.

She was a beauty, exactly like her mother.

Chapter Twenty-five

Dani: 1971

Recently Sam's lawyer had contacted Dani to inform her that Sam wished to arrange visitation rights with his son. When she confided in Gemini over lunch at the Desert Inn, her friend was adamant that she tell the lawyer the truth.

'I can't do that without telling Sam first,' Dani explained.

'I thought you *did* tell him.'

'No. After I threw him out I didn't see him again. It seemed pointless to contact him when he obviously had no plans to visit Vincent. I was under the impression he didn't care.'

'Apparently he does, so now you have to hire your own lawyer and only speak through him.'

'Surely that will cost a fortune?'

'Isn't protecting your son worth it?' Gemini asked.

'Of course it is.'

'Anyway, Dani, you should ask Dean's advice. He's a smart man, and rich. I'm sure he will help you.'

'You once told me that money isn't everything.'

'This is true,' Gemini said. 'However, Dean is not only rich, he also cares about you. The wise move would be to snap him up before someone else does. You're keeping him at a distance, and no man enjoys that. He's probably already beginning to feel rejected.'

'I'm not responsible for how he feels,' Dani said, wishing that Gemini would stop pushing Dean at her. If anything, it was making her back away even more.

Dean King lived in Houston, where he was president of a large oil company. He was thirty-three years old, unmarried, and extremely wealthy. He was also attractive, charming, kind, adored Dani, and was very fond of Vincent.

What more could she ask for? And yet there was something within her that prevented her allowing him to get too close.

'The man is crazy about you,' Gemini pointed out. 'Why are you holding back?'

'I'm scared,' Dani said, shivering at the thought of being intimate with another man.

'Of *what*?' Gemini asked, picking at her salad.

'Scared of him leaving me,' Dani admitted.

'Leaving you?' Gemini exclaimed. 'That's ridiculous.'

'I know I'm being foolish,' Dani said, speaking fast. 'I also know that I have to give it more time.'

'How much more time?' Gemini asked, as the waiter refilled her water glass. 'Dean won't stay around forever. I mean, how much longer do you think he'll wait before you sleep with him?'

'I can't do it,' Dani said, panicking.

'Why not?' Gemini demanded. 'It's a perfectly natural act. You're not a virgin. You've been married, you've had a child.'

'You don't understand,' Dani explained. 'Michael was the first man I slept with.'

'Who's Michael?'

'Vincent's real father, the man I told you about.

Anyway, Michael was my first, and after I married Sam, then he and I . . . well, we only did it once.'

'This cannot be true,' Gemini said, genuinely surprised.

'It is.'

'Are you telling me that you've only made love twice in your life?'

Dani nodded. 'I'm afraid sex is not for me.'

'Oh, my God.' Gemini sighed. 'You *poor* girl. You need professional help. And you also need a man who is gentle. A man like Dean. Now that I know this, I shall encourage it even more.'

'Please don't,' Dani said quickly.

Gemini had an endless supply of male admirers. Unlike Dani's former roommate Angela, Gemini was very picky. She would go out with a man once, and if he didn't measure up to her exacting standards, he was history. Dani admired the way she dealt with men. Personally she couldn't do it.

'I suggest you don't wait too long before asking Dean's advice,' Gemini said, signalling for the check. 'You're having dinner with him tonight, aren't you?'

'Yes, he's in town for the weekend.'

'Then do it.'

Gemini was right: if she didn't cement their relationship soon, it was quite possible she might lose him.

It didn't matter, because one of these days he'd leave anyway. Men always did.

They dined in Dean's penthouse suite atop the Stardust Hotel. Dean was extremely romantic, and tonight especially so. There were candles and a bowl of pink roses on the table set for two on the terrace, while a violinist played classical music quietly in the background.

'What's the occasion?' Dani asked.

'*You're* the occasion,' he replied, kissing her cheek. 'You're always the occasion.'

It was late, she'd performed two shows, and she would have preferred going straight home to Vincent, who was no doubt fast asleep. She'd hired a capable woman, who lived in, to take care of him. Although Vincent was fond of the woman, he'd told Dani that it wasn't the same as having his mommy round.

Vincent had never asked for Sam. Not once. Perhaps he sensed that Sam was not his real father.

'Make yourself comfortable,' Dean said, 'while I pour you a glass of champagne.'

'I don't drink,' she reminded him.

'Tonight is a special occasion,' he said, removing a bottle of Cristal from the ice bucket.

'Is it your birthday?' she asked, hoping she hadn't forgotten.

'No, it's not my birthday,' he said, filling her glass. 'You can have champagne once in a while, can't you?'

'I suppose so.'

He sat down opposite her and clinked glasses. 'Y'know, Dani, for someone so beautiful and, I thought, sophisticated, you're really just a homebody at heart, aren't you?'

'What made you think *I* was sophisticated?'

'You're one of the leads in a top Vegas show. Onstage you come across as so statuesque and glamorous.' He looked at her quizzically. 'That's not you at all, is it?'

'No, Dean, it's not,' she said, dazzling him with her smile. 'Gemini's the sophisticated one. I'm just a mommy.'

'Which makes you a very lucky woman indeed.'

'Why?'

'To have given birth to a child at such a young age. I've never found a woman I want to be with.' He gave her a meaningful look. 'Until now.'

She knew what was coming, hence the romantic setting. And, much as she liked him, she dreaded allowing him to get any closer.

'I've ordered all your favourite foods,' he said. 'Caviar to start, lobster, and then a chocolate soufflé – the chef's speciality.'

'Those are not my favourite foods,' she said, toying with her glass.

'They will be after tonight.'

'I've never tasted caviar.'

'Then this will be a first, won't it?'

Over dinner she brought up the subject of hiring a lawyer.

Dean listened to her carefully. 'Are you divorced yet?' he asked.

'No.'

He leaned forward, watching her carefully. 'Do you want to be?'

'Yes.'

'Unfortunately, your ex will have some visitation rights.'

'He will?'

'Of course. He's Vincent's father.'

She hesitated for a moment. 'What if he isn't?' she ventured.

'Excuse me?' Dean said, looking puzzled.

Should she tell him her whole sorry story?

Why not? She had nothing to lose.

'Dean,' she began. 'I've only ever told one other person this, and that was Gemini.'

'What is it?' he asked, anxious to hear what she had to say.

'Here goes,' she said, taking a long, deep breath. 'Sam is *not* Vincent's father.'

'He's not?'

'No.' And then she proceeded to tell him everything.

'So,' he said, when she'd finished, '*I* could be the father figure Vincent never had.'

'He *already* thinks you're the best.'

'Yes?'

'That's because you spoil him.'

'I know. He loves it, and so do I. He's a great little kid.'

'All those toys,' she scolded. 'What were you? A deprived child?'

'Not at all. I simply enjoy giving.'

'That's nice.'

'Now,' he said slowly, 'rather than waiting for the soufflé, I have something to ask you.'

'You do?'

'Dani,' he said, fumbling in his pocket and producing a Cartier ring box, 'will you do me the honour of marrying me?'

He popped the box open, and she found herself gazing at a magnificent emerald cut diamond solitaire ring.

She'd suspected it was coming, yet it was still a surprise. After all, she'd done no more than kiss this man good night, and now he was asking her to marry him.

'I can give you the life you've always dreamed of,' he continued, taking the ring out of its box and offering it to her. 'And not only you – Vincent too. He'll attend the best schools, the finest colleges. He can do whatever he wants. He can become a lawyer, a scientist, a football star, whatever.'

'I . . . I'll have to think about it,' she murmured, holding the ring.

Yes, I'll have to think about it, because my sex drive is in neutral – and I'm not sure I ever want to be with another man.

'What is there to think about?' he said, looking perplexed. 'Put the ring on, see if it fits. Let's get engaged, at least.'

'You have to give me time, Dean,' she said, handing him back the ring. 'I'm not even divorced yet.'

'I'll get you the best divorce lawyer in town.'

She lowered her eyes. 'Please know that I'm very flattered you've asked me.'

'Is that a no?'

'It's a maybe.'

He smiled. 'I can live with that.'

'I hope so,' she said softly. 'Because that's the way it has to be.'

'For now?' he said, taking her hand in his.

'Yes, Dean, for now.'

Chapter Twenty-six

Tuesday, 10 July 2001

'Get the damn van *here*!' Madison yelled into the phone. 'Stop screwing round. We're in a life-and-death situation. Two people are dead. Can you understand that? They've *killed* two people. Get it here *now*! Or, believe me, you'll be damn sorry. I'm a journalist, and I can promise you that I'll make sure your screw-ups appear on the front page of every newspaper in America. Now, do it!'

'Hey, baby,' one of the gunmen said, loping over and staring at her admiringly, 'you got stones.'

The ringleader shot him a warning look. But the gunman, who'd followed his leader and also removed his ski mask, was not to be stopped. 'Smokin' body, too,' he said, rubbing his crotch suggestively. 'This shit's makin' me horny.'

'You're not here t'get laid,' yelled the ringleader. 'You're here to get the fuckin' money. Now look in the sack, see what we scored.'

'We did good,' said the third bandit, the one who'd been collecting the loot in the black plastic garbage bag. 'There's a coupla Rolexes, eight cellphones, jewellery an' plenty of—'

'We gotta get the fuck outta here before they hang our asses,' the ringleader interrupted.

'They don't hang people any more,' Madison said, brushing a stray lock of hair out of her eyes. 'They fry them in the electric chair, and that's where you'll all end up if you shoot anyone else.'

'You think I give a shit?' he said. 'We could waste all you mothafuckers now, an' it wouldn't make no difference t'me.'

Madison realized they *didn't* care. This was just another day on the job to them, and if people got killed, too bad.

'Is this some kind of gang initiation?' she asked, noting that they were all young, white, and stoned. 'Because if it is, you'd be better off hitting a bank.'

'You dumb rich people make me laugh,' he sneered. 'Why bust a bank when you're all sittin' here with your rings an' your bracelets an' all your fuckin' shit?'

'Have you done this before?' she asked, ignoring Cole, who was over in the corner with the other hostages and silently signalling to her to shut up.

'It's so fuckin' easy,' the ringleader boasted. 'Walk in, zoom a few bullets in the ceilin', everybody on the floor, grab whatever they got, an' take off. If it wasn't for that mothafucker cocksucker pullin' a gun, we'd be gone.'

'Well, you're not,' she pointed out.

'So who'm I gonna take out next?' he said, his stoned eyes boring into hers. '*You?*'

She refused to allow him to intimidate her. 'The van's on its way,' she said, keeping her voice strong and steady.

'You'd better be right.'

'I am,' she answered confidently.

'What shit you write anyway?' he said, leaning across the bar and helping himself to a pack of Lucky Strikes.

'I write for a magazine,' she said.

'What kinda crap magazine?' he asked suspiciously,

rubbing his ear, which she noticed had three studs in it. Cancel out any kind of neo-Nazi group – these kids were operating on their own time, which made this situation all the more alarming.

'*Manhattan Style*,' she said, looking him right in the eye. 'Can I get a cigarette?'

'You got big balls, lady,' he said, but he handed her a cigarette.

She felt that was a step forward. 'You should tell me your story,' she said, appealing to his ego. 'If I were to write about you, people will be interested to hear why you do this.'

'It's pretty simple,' he said, tossing her a packet of book matches. 'I wanna get the shit I see on TV – the fuckin' car, the Rolex, the house, an' the fuckin' vacation in Hawaii.'

She studied his face, long, thin, and pale, with pointed features. 'Are you American?'

'What the fuck you askin'? 'Course I am.'

'Where are your parents from?'

'You a shrink too, like I seen on *The Sopranos*?'

Hmm . . . so he lived in a house or apartment that had cable. Probably with his parents, who had no clue what he did when they weren't watching.

'My guess is your parents are Russian or Polish,' she said, lighting her cigarette even though she'd given up smoking.

'Russian, *bitch*. That make you happy?'

'Why ya talkin' t'this ho?' the second gunman said, coming over again. 'This ho is tryin' t'suck you in so's you'll let 'em all go.'

'You think that's what she's doin'?'

'Yeah,' said gunman number two. He had mean eyes, and the tattoo of a black snake half-way up the side of his neck.

All the better to identify you, Madison thought. *That's if we ever escape from this nightmare.*

'Get over there with your old man,' the ringleader growled, snatching the cigarette from her hand. 'How come you married a black dude anyway?'

'This is America,' she said. 'In America there's a freedom you don't have in your mother country.'

'Don't gimme that mother-country *shit*,' he said, getting agitated. 'I'm an American, came here when I was five.'

'Which means you're Russian by birth.'

'I'm no fuckin' Russian,' he yelled, flushed with anger. 'I got nothin' t'do with that Bolshie shit my mom carries on about. I'm an American, and *this*, lady, is the American way. If you ain't got it – take it. Fuckin' works for me.'

Finally she was getting through.

Jenna did not know which would be the most effective ploy to soften Vincent up. Should she cry and sob? Beg forgiveness? Or should she be cold and nasty?

Since he wasn't talking to her anyway, it didn't matter.

They stood side by side in the elevator, travelling up to their penthouse apartment. They lived at the top of the hotel in an apartment she hated. When she'd married Vincent she'd imagined they would live in a magnificent house in a guarded and gated community like Jolie and Nando. But no, they had to live at the top of the hotel, where he could keep an eye on her at all times.

What had she done that was so terrible? She'd sat in a Jacuzzi with a movie star. Other people would think that was a sensational coup!

She wished she could've had her picture taken with Andy Dale. If Vincent wasn't such a pain in the neck, she could have got out her disposable camera and asked him to take few shots.

She couldn't wait to call her girlfriends and tell them

that she'd spent half the night in a Jacuzzi with Andy Dale – star of all their favourite movies. They'd be sick with jealousy.

Damn Vincent. He'd spoiled it. He always spoiled everything.

They entered their apartment in silence.

'Vincent . . .' she began, determined to have her say.

'I don't want to talk to you tonight,' he said, dismissing her coldly. 'Go to bed. We'll speak tomorrow.'

'You're not my daddy,' she said heatedly. 'Sometimes you talk to me as if you are.'

'Act like a child and get treated like one,' he said. 'How would *you* react if you found me in a Jacuzzi with Cameron Diaz or Catherine Zeta Jones?'

'You don't even know them,' she said scornfully.

'I could arrange to meet them tomorrow. *Then* how would *you* feel?'

'You're just jealous,' she said, pouting.

'It's not a question of my being jealous, Jenna. It's a question of respect. This is *my* hotel, and when people see *my* wife acting the way you did tonight, it's not proper behaviour.'

'You're so old-fashioned,' she said, continuing to pout. 'Anyone else would be thrilled to have a movie star in their hotel. And I'm sure they'd be even more thrilled if their wife entertained them.'

'And I suppose your idea of entertaining includes *screwing* the jerk?'

'Vincent! You are so crude! I was not screwing *anyone*.'

'You were sitting in a Jacuzzi with your tits out. That's *not* crude?'

'I'd look pretty foolish sitting in a Jacuzzi with my clothes *on*, wouldn't I?' she retaliated. 'And, anyway, in the South of France *everyone* goes topless. They're not ashamed of their bodies.'

'I hate to remind you, Jenna, but we are *not* in the South of France.'

'Well, when we were there on our honeymoon,' she said sulkily, '*all* the girls were topless. You didn't seem to have any objections then.'

This conversation was getting him nowhere. Right now he wanted her out of his sight, he couldn't stand to look at her. He should've listened to his mother and married a smart woman, not this dim-witted bimbo. 'I told you,' he said, 'I do not wish to talk about it tonight. Go to bed.'

She flounced into the bedroom.

He walked over to the window and gazed out at the sea of lights. Here he was, in a penthouse at the top of *his* hotel, and instead of enjoying everything he'd achieved, he was seething with anger.

It was Nando's fault. Nando encouraged movie people to hang out at their hotel, claiming it was good for business. What Nando failed to understand was that good business meant attracting big-time gamblers, high-rollers who were prepared to lose a fortune. Movie stars were nothing. You couldn't even give them markers without them not paying the debt.

He walked back into the living room, picked up the remote and clicked on the TV just in time for the news.

Another car chase. Another murder. Another hold-up in California – thirty people locked in a restaurant with armed gunmen in Beverly Hills.

The phone rang. He picked up.

'Mr Castle? Your mother would like you to contact her.'

'Thanks, Mario.'

It was unusual for Dani to call him so late. He punched out her number, wondering what she wanted.

Dani answered immediately. 'Vincent, I have a surprise for you.'

'What surprise?'

'I need you to come to my apartment right now.'

'Are you okay?'

'I'm fine.'

'Then *what?*' he said, irritated. 'Can't it wait until morning?'

'No, it can't.'

'You're sure?'

'Of course I'm sure.'

'I'll be there,' he said, not at all pleased.

'Good,' she said, and hung up.

Sofia followed Gianni into the Marbella Club where he was greeted on all sides with smiles and admiring salutes. Beautiful women waved and blew him kisses.

'Man, you're popular,' Sofia remarked, trailing behind him.

'Yes, and I'm sure they are all wondering who the drowned rat is dogging my footsteps.'

'Sorry,' she said rudely. 'Am I ruining your impeccable reputation?'

'Not at all.'

'I should've picked up some clothes from my place,' she ruminated. 'Do you have anything I can borrow?'

'I'm sure Anais has left something in the suite. She usually does.'

She followed him into his suite, which overlooked the ocean. There was a large blow-up poster of Anais propped against one wall. Her back was to the camera, and all she had on was a pair of low-rider, studded jeans. The heading across the poster read: *Black or white? Gianni or blue jeans?*

Sofia surveyed it, squinting her eyes. 'Gotta admit she's gorgeous,' she said at last.

'I know,' Gianni replied, putting on some classical music.

'Anais is your girlfriend, right?'

'Correct.'

'Isn't she kind of, like, *famous*?'

'She is a supermodel.'

'I've probably seen her in magazines.'

'So you read magazines?' he said, somewhat amused.

'And books. I *did* go to school, even though it was in Vegas.' She yawned: the events of the night were finally catching up. 'School sucked – I never learned anything. All I wanted to do was get out and discover the world for myself.'

'And have you?'

'Well, I gotta say, tonight was an education. Actually,' she added, grinning, 'I'm kinda psyched. I think I handled it very well.'

'Jumping out of a window is handling it very well?'

'I didn't jump out of a window,' she corrected. 'I jumped *into* a swimming pool.'

'Sofia, if you'd missed the swimming-pool and hit the concrete, you would be dead now, and we would not be standing here discussing this.'

'Hey,' she said cockily, 'I made the jump, hit the pool and now I'm totally psyched.'

'That's comforting to know.'

'So I suppose you're madly in love?' she said, flopping on to the couch.

'That's a very forward question.'

'Which means you're, like, *not?*'

'Anais is an extremely complex woman,' he said, lighting a long, thin Cuban cigar.

'How old is she?'

'Twenty-five,' he replied. 'In modelling years that's considered old. Sometimes it makes her insecure about her future. She wishes to try acting.'

'How long have you been together?'

'Why all the questions, Sofia?' he asked, expelling a thin stream of smoke.

'You were questioning *me* in the car. Now it's my turn.'

'You'll find a robe in the bathroom, go put it on before you catch cold. In the meantime, I'll order you something to eat. I'm sure you're hungry. What would you like?'

'A club sandwich. Unless they've got a burger and french fries,' she said, jumping up. 'I'd *kill* for an American-style burger.'

'Let us not get dramatic,' he said, half smiling. 'I'll see what I can do. When you've eaten, we should call your parents and perhaps you should think about going home for a while.'

She threw him a bold look. 'Is that *before* I come to see you in Rome, or after?'

'Then you *are* interested?'

'Depends what you have in mind,' she said, trying not to sound too intrigued – which she was, because the thought of flying to Rome and scoring a modelling job was quite exciting.

He indicated the poster of Anais. 'I need a new face alongside Anais for my next jeans campaign. Perhaps *you* could be that face. Of course, if you come to Rome, you'll have to test with my photographer. He'll know whether you possess the quality we need.'

'Oh, wow!' she said mockingly. 'Does this mean I'm being discovered?'

'Possibly,' he said, ignoring her attitude. 'If the camera loves you.'

'Cool,' she said. 'There's nothing keeping me here. So . . . will you take me to Rome?'

'You want *me* to take you?'

'Why not? It'll be an adventure.'

'Very well, Sofia. We leave in the morning.'

'What airline?'

'No airline, my dear. I have my own plane.'

'Of course. Why wouldn't you?'

*

Jolie was not into competition. She regarded Nando as a challenge – and the challenge was keeping him faithful. So far she was doing a pretty good job, but Jolie was a realist and Nando was a man, so the trick was keeping him as satisfied as she could at home. For his last birthday – his thirty-sixth – she'd had a stripper pole installed in their bedroom.

When Nando first saw it he'd yelled with laughter. But soon . . . when she'd begun showing him what she could do on it, the laughter ceased, and he was more turned on than she'd ever seen him. Now it was his private treat, something she reserved for special occasions.

Tonight Nando seemed like he could use a treat. He was so tightly wound up she could almost feel the tension.

'What's up, honey?' she asked, when they got home to their luxurious house in an exclusive, gated community.

'Vincent,' he said, going straight to the bar in their sunken living room with the over-size leopard-skin couches and huge marble coffee tables.

'Did he do something?'

'He did nothing. Vincent never does anything.'

'What do you mean?' she asked sympathetically.

'He's so freakin' rigid. Doesn't want movie stars in the goddamn hotel. Afraid to take risks. Doesn't think we should branch out. I got a deal that'll make us more money than even *you* can spend – an' he doesn't want to touch it.'

'Why?'

''Cause it involves drugs an' hookers. Big freakin' deal. This town wouldn't exist without drugs an' hookers.'

'Calm down,' Jolie said. 'You're all worked up.'

'Yeah. I'll never sleep tonight.'

'Yes, you will,' she murmured. 'Give me five minutes and meet me in the bedroom. By the time *I've* finished with you, you'll be so relaxed you won't know what hit you.'

*

Finally the van arrived. Madison experienced a brief moment of triumph. Had she persuaded the negotiator to get it there?

Whatever. It was there, that was the main thing.

'This is the way it's goin' down,' the ringleader announced. 'Pull the cloths off the tables, make holes for your eyes, an' put 'em over your heads. You,' he said, speaking directly to Madison, 'you're comin', an' your old man. An' you,' he added, pointing at Natalie.

'Leave her behind,' Madison said quickly. 'She's not feeling well.'

'Fuck that, she's comin',' he said, and singled out three more hostages – the young Italian waiter, the woman with the gash on her temple, and a middle-aged man. 'We go out with you surroundin' us. Anybody fucks with me, they get their shit-ass head blown off. Got it?'

Everyone nodded.

'The rest of you mothafuckers – over in the corner, an' stay quiet.'

Madison glanced at Cole. He gave an imperceptible nod – as if to say, *Do what he wants*. She pulled a cloth off one of the tables, and began making crude holes for her eyes with a table knife. Natalie started doing the same.

'This is a nightmare,' Natalie whispered. 'How'll we get through it?'

'We will,' Madison said reassuringly, sounding a lot braver than she felt.

'Where are they taking us?'

'Wherever this lunatic says.'

It was one thing telling Natalie not to worry, but Madison knew they were in great danger. One of the stoned gunmen could shoot them on a whim. Or maybe the police had sharp-shooters with itchy fingers dying to burst in.

Who knew what might happen?

All they could do was hope and pray.

Chapter Twenty-seven

Michael: 1972

Motherhood had mellowed Beth slightly, which did not stop her from complaining about being kept awake at night by the baby crying. She also flatly refused to breastfeed. 'Not my scene,' she said, wrinkling her nose. 'That's like – ugh!'

'Isn't it supposed to be better for the baby?' Catherine asked. She'd recently returned from her visit with relatives and was helping to look after Madison.

'That's crap,' Beth replied, shooting her sister a daggers look.

'Y'know, when Madison gets bigger, you gotta learn to control your language,' Michael commented.

'*Really?*' Beth answered coolly.

'It's a thought,' he said mildly.

He and Beth had settled into domestic life quite well. They lived together as man and wife, even though they weren't married. It suited both of them. Great sex and no wedding rings. He was a lucky man – or was he? Sometimes he thought marriage might work out. They had a baby together, so why not?

Since Madison's birth, he hadn't felt like seeing any of his old girlfriends. He was satisfied hanging out with Beth, the baby, and Catherine – who, once she'd got over her initial shock, had turned out to be a sweetheart. And Beth seemed to have curbed her wild ways, no longer running out to all-night parties and flirting outrageously with every man she saw. She loved Madison as much as he did, and although they fought a lot, they both agreed that Madison was the cutest baby in the world. She was a combination of the two of them, with her dark curly hair, sparkling green eyes and deep olive skin. She was truly beautiful.

Sometimes, late at night when Madison awoke for her bottle, Michael went into her room, scooped her out of her crib, and fed her himself. She was such a warm and trusting little bundle in his arms, her big eyes staring up at him so expectantly. When he looked at her, he felt a love he'd never experienced before. She was *his* baby. *His* future. She was the family he'd never had.

When Madison was six months old, Catherine moved in permanently. Although, like Beth, she was only eighteen, she seemed much older and more capable. Michael was pleased to have her around: she could keep an eye on Madison *and* Beth, so that when he was at work he could feel more secure. Especially since a lot of his work took place at night, and Beth claimed she felt nervous in the house by herself.

One morning Beth woke up, jumped out of bed, and decided she wanted to go back to the fashion institute to continue her studies. 'Will you pay for my tuition?' she asked. 'I promise you won't regret it.'

'If you're sure that's what you want to do,' Michael said, 'then I'll be happy to pay for it.'

'*Very* sure,' she answered. 'I'll be famous. You'll see.'

'You will, huh?' he said, amused by her enthusiasm.

'I'll make you proud, Michael.'

'You've already done that,' he said, indicating Madison, who was kicking and gurgling in her crib.

'I have?'

'You bet,' he said, hugging her.

And he truly meant it.

Word on the street was that Vito Giovanni and Mamie had split. Vito had caught Mamie with another woman in *their* bed, gone completely berserk and thrown her out. The rumour was that Vito now had a girlfriend – a twenty-two-year-old stripper who went by the name of Western Pussy.

One night, some of the guys were sitting round at the social club playing poker. Bone was there, so was Gus. When Michael walked in, they were sniggering about Mamie and her sexual predilections.

'She was always a tough-assed bitch,' Bone announced to the room. 'Her an' that douchebag cousin of hers, Roy.'

Michael figured this might be the right time to get Bone to acknowledge his existence. 'Oh, yeah, Mamie,' he said, pulling up a chair. 'She used to get it on with girls in Vegas. Everyone knew about it.'

Bone threw him a blank look. He was a tall, scary-looking man with yellowing, hang-dog teeth and a lethal scar running the length of his left cheek. 'You talkin' to me?' he said coldly.

'Some reason I shouldn't?'

'You're a fuckin' joke,' Bone sneered.

'Okay, okay, cut it out,' Gus interrupted. 'The war's outside this room, not in it.'

'Forget it,' Bone growled.

Michael was not prepared to forget it. 'You got some kinda beef with me?' he demanded later, blocking the older man on his way out.

Bone looked him over with his small, shifty eyes. 'You gonna stand there an' tell me you dunno what went down?' he asked. 'You really gonna do that?'

'Huh?'

'C'mon,' Bone taunted. 'You can't be *that* dumb.'

Michael stared at him blankly.

'Oh, *now* I get it,' Bone said, enjoying himself. 'Mamie never told you, did she?'

'Told me *what?*'

'About your mama,' Bone said. 'Y'know,' he added, fingering the scar on his cheek, 'I was there the night it happened.'

Michael felt a coldness in the pit of his stomach. 'What the fuck you sayin'?'

'*Mamie* set up the robbery that got your mom killed and your old man shot,' Bone announced triumphantly. 'Her and Roy was responsible. Roy fired the gun, while Mamie stood guard outside.' A long beat. '*Now* d'you get it?'

'That's impossible,' Michael said.

'Aren't you listenin'?' Bone said, with an evil leer. 'I told you, *I was there.*'

'You were there,' Michael repeated dully.

'I used t'fuck that cow, Mamie,' Bone continued. 'Turned out she's a bad one. Screwed me on a big deal.' He wiped his nose on the back of his hand. 'Oh yeah, I know plenty about Mamie an' her fuckin' scumbag cousin.'

'Roy killed my mother? Is that what you're tellin' me?'

'He sure did,' Bone said, picking his teeth. 'I was with 'em, only *I* wasn't carryin'. We scoped the place out in the afternoon, an' came back later. Shit – had no fuckin' clue Roy was gonna shoot anyone.'

'Christ!' Michael said, turning pale.

'Now you know – whatcha gonna do about it?' Bone challenged. ''Cause that bitch sure as shit made a monkey outta you all these years. You danced for her good.'

Michael didn't answer. He was trying desperately to remain calm and think rationally. *Never act on impulse*, that was one lesson he'd learned. Inside he was burning up with a barely controlled black rage. Could this be true? Had Roy shot his mom while Mamie waited outside?

In a horrible way it all made sense, and it certainly explained why Mamie had always been so interested in Vinny. It also explained why she'd befriended him. It must have amused her in a cruel and heartless way to know that *she* was responsible for his mother's death.

He turned and walked away from Bone without saying another word. If he stayed around, he'd probably kill the bastard.

When he got home that night, Beth was sitting on their bed painting her toenails silver while listening to the Rolling Stones on the new stereo he'd bought her. 'What's up?' she asked cheerfully, bouncing round to the raunchy sounds of Mick Jagger yelling 'Satisfaction'.

'Nothing you should worry about,' he said, going into the bathroom and staring at his reflection in the mirror.

'Never said I was worried,' she replied, shouting above the music. 'Isn't this track *amazing*? I *love* Mick. Don't you?'

He was desperate to talk to someone, and Beth was too young to burden with such grim information. He went downstairs to the kitchen, took a beer from the fridge, then sat at the table and considered telling Max.

Not a great idea, because Max was always on his case. 'You're working for another gangster,' Max had complained. 'Five years in the joint ain't enough? You want more, is that the deal?'

'Anybody with an Italian name and you automatically think they're connected,' he'd replied. 'How many times I gotta tell you? Dante Lucchese is a businessman.'

'An' what business would that be?'

'Waste disposal.'

Max had rolled his eyes.

So he couldn't confide in Max, and he certainly couldn't

confide in Charlie who, since getting his new leg was working in a bank and doing quite well. Besides, it was probably a good thing there was no one to try to talk him out of what he knew he had to do. Not only had the shooter, Roy, made Vinny into a cripple but, by killing Anna Maria, he'd robbed Michael of the childhood he might have had.

Pure fury was building inside him like a volcano. He realized he'd been waiting to get revenge for his mother's murder all these years. And now that he knew the truth, there was no more waiting. It was time to take action.

They would pay. All of them.

And they would pay soon.

Mamie had obviously got a good settlement out of Vito, because she'd relocated to a Park Avenue apartment and moved Roy in with her.

Mamie was a true survivor; she'd hired herself the best divorce lawyer in town, and was threatening to reveal certain aspects of Mr G's business interests if he didn't come up with the right amount of alimony. Meanwhile, she was spending her soon-to-be ex-husband's money at an alarming pace, and doing whatever and *whoever* took her fancy.

Michael began surveying her apartment building and checking out her movements, making sure she didn't spot him. He soon found out she had two dogs – a pair of spoiled white miniature poodles. They were walked three times a day by different people. The first walk, early in the morning, was taken care of by the front desk porter. Lunchtime, Mamie took them out herself. And late at night it was Roy's turn.

A couple of weeks after listening to Bone's revelations, Michael finally took action. It was time.

That night he waited in the park, stationing himself

behind a tree, half-way along the path where Roy usually walked the dogs. It was a cold, dark night, and the park was deserted, exactly the way he wanted it.

As he stood there, he was thinking about the Chronicle and everything Mr G's hit man had taught him. At last it was about to come in useful.

He stamped his feet as he waited, trying to stay warm. He thought about Beth, with her seductive smile. And his precious daughter, Madison. He loved them both. They were everything to him.

After about twenty minutes, he spotted Roy approaching. As soon as the man was close enough, Michael stepped out from behind the tree and stood in front of him, blocking his way. 'Hey, Roy,' he said, in a friendly tone. 'Remember me?'

Roy peered at him through the darkness. 'Who's that?' he asked, startled.

'Michael Castellino,' he said, moving closer. The dogs began to bark and pull on their leashes.

'What the hell *you* doin' here?' Roy mumbled bad-temperedly. 'It's the middle of the fuckin' night.'

'I was takin' a walk, saw you comin', an' thought it might be a good time to reminisce.'

'Reminisce?' Roy said, as the dogs continued to yap. 'What the fuck you carryin' on about?'

'Oh, y'know,' he said casually. 'Mamie an' my dad.'

'*What?*'

'Didn't Mamie used to go out with him? An' wasn't she kinda pissed when he dumped her an' married my mom?'

Roy made an attempt to kick one of the barking dogs with the tip of his shoe. 'Shut up, ya fuckin' rats,' he said sharply.

'I was wondering if you remembered my grandma's store,' Michael continued, feeling quite calm, although he knew what he had to do. 'Lani's convenience store. Bring back any memories, Roy?'

'What?' Roy repeated, distracted by the dogs which were now snarling at each other.

'There was a time my mom worked there, too,' Michael said, keeping his voice low and even. 'Yeah – she was pregnant with me.'

'You got a point?' Roy said, beyond irritated. ''Cause I'm standin' here freezin' my balls off.'

'Yes,' Michael said, 'as a matter of fact I do.' And very calmly, he took out his gun, aiming it directly at Roy. 'My *point* is that you're a piece of shit who doesn't deserve to live.'

Roy blanched. 'For crissakes!' he said, panicking. 'Put that away.'

'What's the matter?' Michael said mildly. 'You don't like guns? They scare you, do they?'

'Put the fuckin' thing away,' Roy repeated, his eyes bugging.

'I bet my mom was scared, exactly like you are now. And, as I said, she was pregnant with me, so she couldn't run, couldn't do anythin', could she? I guess she was a sittin' target. Do you agree?'

'Jesus *Christ*!' Roy said, spittle dribbling from the side of his mouth. 'I warned Mamie not to bother with you. Knew you'd be trouble one of these days. The dumb cunt wouldn't listen – she got off on havin' you round.'

'Until *you* got rid of me, right?' Michael said, his voice hardening. 'You set me up good, Roy. Eight years, an' I ended up servin' five. *That* must've been a disappointment.'

'It wasn't me,' Roy whined. '*She* wanted you outta the way – it wasn't *my* idea.'

'No?'

'I swear it wasn't, Mike,' he said, his hands beginning to shake. 'I like you – you've always bin civil t'me.'

'That's good to know.'

'So . . .' Roy whined '. . . whyn't you put the piece away before you hurt someone?'

'You think I should do that, Roy?'

'Yeah, yeah, I think ya should do that.'

'Just like you did for my mom, huh?'

'I never shot your mom.'

'You didn't, huh?'

'It was—'

'Remember the Chronicle?' Michael interrupted. 'An' Vito tellin' me I should learn to shoot? He was some guy that Chronicle – he taught me good.'

Raising the gun higher, he pointed it at Roy's face. 'Retribution is the name of the game. It's called paying the price. You killed my mother. Destroyed my dad. Now it's your turn.' A long silent beat. 'Remember my name, Roy. Michael Castellino. Remember it all the way to hell.'

And he shot him in the head.

Then, very calmly, he turned and walked away.

One down. Two to go.

Chapter Twenty-eight

Dani: 1972

'Y ou gave him back the ring?' Gemini exclaimed in amazement. 'Why?'

'Because I didn't say yes. Therefore there was no reason for me to accept it,' Dani explained.

They were standing in the wings getting ready to go on: two tall, spectacular young women, both blonde, wearing matching skimpy costumes of sequins, feathers, and lace, with plenty of flesh on show, and extravagant headdresses. The two of them together with their long legs and large bosoms were every man's fantasy.

'You're crazy,' Gemini said, licking her highly glossed lips. 'Surely you know that a girl *never* returns jewellery.'

'I couldn't lead him on.'

'You poor baby, you have *so* much to learn.'

'And I'm sure you're planning on teaching me.'

'I can see I'll have to.'

Several other girls jostled for position as the music started. Gemini and Dani hung back. They made their entrance a few minutes after the dancers. Statuesque, dazzling. Total glamour.

'How did you leave it?' Gemini asked.

'He had to fly to Houston,' Dani said. 'He'll be back in

257

a couple of weeks. I told him I'd try to give him an answer by then. In the meantime, he gave me the name of a lawyer to call.'

'Then what are you waiting for?' Gemini said, taking a quick peek in the backstage full-length mirror. 'Call the man.'

'I will,' Dani promised.

She'd been struggling with her feelings all day. How simple it would be to say yes to Dean, pack up everything, take Vincent and move to Houston.

Yet something held her back. She refused to get involved in another loveless marriage like the one to Sam. It wasn't fair to Vincent to bring someone else into his life who might not be permanent. She wasn't even sure she knew what love was. She'd murmured the words once in her life to Michael.

Ah . . . Michael. One magical night from her past, and she'd been no more than a child. Yet, hard as she tried, she couldn't forget him. How was it possible with Vincent there to remind her?

The next morning she and Gemini worked out in the gym, hardly the gorgeous, untouchable creatures of the previous evening: they now wore no makeup, hair in simple ponytails and had on work-out clothes. Staying in perfect shape was an essential part of their jobs, and they both toiled hard at it.

'Do you believe in love?' Dani asked, as she lifted light weights.

Gemini nodded, finishing a series of punishing sit-ups. 'Yes. Only you must never mistake passion for love,' she said, grabbing a towel. 'Unfortunately passion never lasts. When I married Nando's father, Moralis, he was *the* most passionate man I had ever met. I couldn't *breathe* when I was with him, I found myself thinking about him day and night.'

'That's how I felt with Michael.' Dani sighed, put down the weights and moved over to the treadmill.

'I hardly think it's the same,' Gemini replied. 'After all, you were only with Michael for what? One day, one night?'

'I know, but I've never had feelings like that before or since,' Dani said dreamily. 'And the way he made love . . .'

'It was your first time,' Gemini pointed out. 'You were hardly in a position to know whether he was a great lover or a bad one.'

'He was great,' Dani said, remembering every detail.

'Here's what you need to do,' Gemini said. 'Date a few different men, get some perspective.'

Dani shook her head. 'I'd feel I was being unfaithful to Dean.'

'Unfaithful!' Gemini exclaimed. 'You didn't even accept his ring.'

'That's true, but I can't see other men. It wouldn't seem right.'

'Then you'd better marry Dean,' Gemini said exasperated. 'That's my advice.'

A few days later Dani met with the lawyer Dean had recommended. Gemini accompanied her for moral support. The lawyer's name was Morgan Spelling Jones, and he was a flamboyant character. In his mid-fifties, he had a florid complexion, a hearty laugh, and big, smooth, well-manicured hands. A Texan with an extremely loud voice, he wore a ten-gallon cowboy hat with an off-white business suit and tooled leather boots. The look was eccentric to say the least.

'This must be my lucky day,' he said, beaming at the two women as they came into his office. 'The Lord surely smiled at me this morning to have two such beauties enter my domain.'

'Ms Castle is here about her divorce,' Gemini said,

settling into a chair opposite his desk and crossing her long legs.

'And Ms Castle will *get* her divorce,' Morgan said, his eyes lingering on Gemini's legs. 'That's if *I* have anything to do with it.'

'Dean King recommended that I see you,' Dani said, sitting down in the chair next to Gemini.

'He did indeed, and he spoke very highly of you, little lady. Now,' he said, picking up an expensive gold pen from his massive leather-topped desk and holding it over a yellow legal pad, 'I suggest you give me all the nasty details.'

'What did you think of him?' Gemini asked, the moment they left his office.

'He seems quite interesting,' Dani replied.

'Interesting or capable?'

'Both.'

'Hmm . . .' Gemini said. 'Don't you think that the combination of the cowboy hat and the boots lent him a certain . . . sensuality?'

Dani giggled. 'You're kidding?'

'No,' Gemini said, with a half smile. 'I like a man who has . . . quirks.'

Gemini liked him so much that they began dating, and within six weeks they were married. It was quite a rapid courtship – and one that Dani felt very much part of since she had been responsible for them meeting.

Dean flew in for the wedding, which took place at Morgan's large ranch a few miles outside town.

It turned out that Morgan Spelling Jones was rich, very rich indeed. A successful lawyer, he'd also inherited an old money fortune from his late parents. Gemini had not known this. She'd fallen in love with his style and couldn't care less that he was almost thirty years her senior. She *did* care about Nando, and fortunately he and Morgan hit it off, which was great for Dani because it meant that Vincent got to spend time at the ranch too – riding horses, swimming, and playing lots of outdoor games. He and Nando were inseparable.

The only downside was that being out of town at Morgan's ranch reminded Dani of her childhood and Dashell. How lucky she was to have escaped. What would her future have held if she hadn't?

Sometimes she wondered. There were many nights when she still experienced frighteningly vivid nightmares. And often she thought about going back and searching for her mother's grave.

She always decided that, no, it would not be a healthy thing to do. The past was just that. Letting go was the true freedom.

'It's your turn next,' Gemini whispered to Dani at the wedding. 'If I can take this step, so can you.'

Dean was pushing. She was still hesitant.

'Sleep with him at least,' Gemini urged. 'See if you are compatible in bed.'

Was *that* what she was supposed to do?

Yes. Because that's what everyone else did.

Sex was the big topic of conversation backstage – one girl had even slept with Frank Sinatra, making her the heroine of the week.

The truth was that sex didn't interest Dani; she'd shut off that part of her life. Sex only led to trouble – she knew that only too well.

Morgan had spoken to Sam's lawyer several times. 'The man's a shyster,' he informed Dani. 'Sam has made no requests to see the boy. All he wants is money, moola, big bucks.'

'How much?' she asked, disappointed that Sam had sunk so low.

'They're requesting alimony – and if not that, then a one-time payment of fifty thousand dollars.'

'Fifty thousand!' she said in amazement. 'Where am I supposed to get that kind of money?'

'It's not necessary to pay anything, Dani,' Morgan explained. 'However, my dear, it *is* the only guaranteed way of permanently removing him from our list of annoyances.' A beat. 'That, or we hire a hit man.'

'*What?*' she gasped, horrified.

'I jest, my dear, I jest.'

Dean came to the rescue. Without consulting her, he conferred with Morgan and paid the fifty thousand.

A week later she slept with him.

Sleeping with Dean wasn't the worst thing in the world. He was kind and attentive, and took things slowly. But Dani could not get over the feeling that she was only doing this because he'd paid the money to make Sam go away.

She felt like a whore. A very highly paid whore, but a whore all the same.

Dean was ecstatic. 'This definitely means we're getting married,' he crowed, producing the ring again.

'It means we're . . . we're engaged,' she said, as he slipped the magnificent diamond on her finger.

'You will never regret this, my darling, never,' he assured her, beaming. 'Whenever you can take a few days off, I'll fly you and Vincent to Houston to see my house. It'll be all yours to do with whatever you like.'

'That'll be great,' she said, already feeling pressured.

'Maybe you should quit your job,' he said. 'After all, there's no reason for you to work now that we're together.'

'Yes, there is,' she said quickly. 'I need my independence, Dean. One of these days I intend to pay back the money you gave Sam.'

'Think of it this way, Dani. When we're married, *my* money is *your* money. So what difference does it make?'

'It makes a difference to me,' she said quietly. 'This is a debt *I* should be responsible for.'

'We'll see,' he said, unconcerned about the money. 'I'm planning our engagement party. Start making a list.'

She nodded, and decided that since this was obviously her future, she'd better start being happy about it.

Chapter Twenty-nine

Michael: 1972

Scanning the newspapers, Michael had to work hard to find any mention of Roy's demise. Finally, twenty-four hours later, he discovered a small item tucked away at the bottom of page three.

Man Shot in Central Park
Assailant Unknown

Just as he was about to read on, Beth walked into the kitchen on her way to the fashion institute. He put down the newspaper quickly and picked up his coffee.

'What's our plan today?' she asked, dressed for action in tight black jeans, an off-the-shoulder peasant blouse, and backless high-heeled mules.

'I gotta meeting this afternoon, but after that I'm all yours.'

'Michael,' she said, tilting her head, a questioning look in her eyes, 'what is it you *do* exactly?'

'A little bit of this, a little bit of that,' he answered evasively, sipping his coffee.

It wasn't the first time she'd tried to find out what he did. When they'd first got together she'd questioned him non-stop until he'd warned her to drop it. Early on he'd decided that the less Beth knew about his business, the better. He especially didn't want her knowing about Warner Carlysle and the investments – which were going so well that he might retire soon from Gus's crew and concentrate on his own thing.

'That's what you always say.'

'Believe me, you don't wanna know – it's boring.'

'As long as you bring home the money, I suppose I shouldn't care,' she said, tossing back her long dark hair. 'Although I'd hate it if you ever got arrested again. That must've been horrible.'

She'd obviously been getting an earful from Tina and Max, which he didn't appreciate. 'Where's Madison?' he asked, changing the subject.

'Catherine took her to the park. We're going to the zoo later. Why don't you come?'

'I told you, I got a meeting,' he said, standing up and giving her a big hug, wrapping his arms round her slim body until she could barely breathe.

'What's that for?' she gasped.

'Something for you to remember me by today.'

'Oh,' she said, laughing softly. 'Mr Romantic.'

'I can be romantic when I want to,' he said, grinning.

'I know,' she said warmly. 'And I like it.'

'You do?'

'Yes, Michael. I do.'

She was smart, sassy, and sexy, and although she was still very young, she had an old soul. He was definitely falling for her big-time. A surprise. But one he was definitely into.

'I've been thinking, Beth,' he ventured.

'Yes?' she said, her brown eyes bright and alert.

'Remember before you had Madison, we were talkin' about gettin' married?'

'*We* weren't, *you* were,' she said pointedly.

'It's time.'

'For what?'

'Plannin' a wedding.'

'Oh, no, no, no,' she said. 'That's not for me.'

'C'mon, sweetheart,' he said persuasively. 'We got Madison to think about.'

'Madison is a very happy baby.'

'I know. But you gotta consider it.'

'Why?'

'Because.'

'Because *what?*'

Jesus! She could be stubborn. 'Hey,' he said, 'here's the good news. If you don't *like* bein' married, we can always get a divorce.'

She sighed and tilted her head on one side. 'You're funny, Michael.'

'*You're* even funnier,' he countered. 'You're the only woman I know who doesn't wanna get married.'

'In that case you should be jumping up and down with joy.'

'I'm not,' he said, exasperated. ''Cause I've decided you're gonna marry me whether you like it or not.'

'I am?'

'Yup.'

'Is that an order?'

'It sure is.'

'Okay,' she said meekly.

'Okay what? You'll do it?'

She grinned. 'I'll let you know.'

'You will, huh?'

'Maybe.'

'What a woman!'

'Oh, Michael,' she said with a great big smile, 'you *finally* called me a woman. I think I *will* marry you, after all.'

'That's my girl!'

'No,' she corrected him, still smiling. 'That's your *woman*.'

Most afternoons Michael hung out at the social club with some of the guys. They played poker or pool, sat around watching sport or the horse racing on TV, made a few bets and had a beer or two.

This particular day, Michael was feeling wary. He knew that Bone had to be suspicious that it was he who'd eliminated Roy. After all, Bone had revealed the details of the crime that had taken his mother's life, and two weeks later Michael had sprung into action. It didn't take a genius to work that one out.

But Bone wasn't there, and nobody else said a word about Roy's demise.

When he left, around five, he noticed two men standing by a black Cadillac parked across the street. Sensing they were watching him, he crossed the road casually and walked past them. He was not surprised when they stopped him.

'Michael Castellino?' one asked.

'Yeah?' he said, recognizing the man from the day he'd tried to get in to see Mr G.

'Mr Giovanni wants t'see you.'

'Now?'

'Yeah, now. Let's go.'

He got into the back seat of the Cadillac. He was apprehensive, but what could Mr G do to him? There was nothing tying him to Roy's murder. He'd got rid of the gun, weighted it down in a black plastic garbage bag with some bricks, and thrown it into the East River. 'Never off anyone and keep the piece,' the Chronicle had drummed into him. 'It's cheaper to buy a new one than to hang on to somethin' could incriminate you.'

Good advice. He'd taken it.

Neither of the men in the car said anything as they drove to Vito Giovanni's house.

As soon as they arrived, he got out of the car and walked up the steps by himself. Another man opened the door and ushered him inside.

Michael had not seen Vito Giovanni in six years. The man had aged. Once so dapper in his fine cashmere coats and flowing silk scarves, he was now older and greyer, with heavy glasses and a bad set of extra white false teeth.

'Mike,' Vito said, clapping him on the back. 'Look at you, all grown-up.'

'Yeah,' he said warily. 'All grown-up.'

'It's nice t'see ya ugly face. Wanna drink?'

'I'll have a Jack.'

'I'll have a Jack,' Vito repeated. 'You got the lingo down. Mr Cool. Mr Good-lookin'. You didn't lose the looks, you got better.'

'Thanks,' he said awkwardly, wondering what the hell he was doing there.

'Hey, Luigi,' Vito called out. 'Fix Mike a Jack Daniel's on the rocks, an' one for me, too.' He turned back to Michael. 'It's Sinatra's favourite drink. Had the pleasure of meetin' the man a few months ago. What a swinger! My kinda guy.'

Michael was not into Sinatra, he preferred Elvis or Beth's wild salsa sounds.

'You're probably wonderin' why I asked ya here,' Vito said, lighting a big fat cigar with a solid gold lighter.

'Yeah.'

'I got someone wants to talk t'you.'

'Who would that be?'

'Another old friend of yours,' Vito said, snapping his fingers for Luigi to open the door.

Luigi did so – and enter Mamie. What a sight!

Yellow teased hair with inch-long, jet-black roots,

swollen red eyes, slightly heavier, and she still dressed like a teenager with her short leather skirt, tight orange sweater, and hooker heels.

Michael stared at her with contempt. Now that he knew the truth, he hated her.

'Ya probably heard that Mamie an' me, we're no longer together,' Vito explained, puffing on his cigar. 'However, since Mamie was my wife for many years, I keep the respect, an' if *she* comes t'me with a problem, that means *I* got a problem. *Capisce?*'

Michael nodded, wondering where this conversation was leading.

'So, ya see,' Vito continued, sitting down in his favourite armchair, 'Mamie's got a *big* problem.'

'She has?'

'You *know*,' she said furiously, glaring at Michael. 'My Cousin Roy. My best friend. Him an' me was like brother an' sister.'

'Somebody offed Roy,' Vito said, as casually as if he was talking about a lost wallet. 'An' word on the street is that that somebody might have been you.'

'Why'd *I* do somethin' like that?' Michael said, making sure his expression stayed blank.

Luigi walked over and handed him his drink. He took a swig. He needed it.

Vito let out a weary sigh. 'Lemme tell you the story that's goin' round,' he said. 'It seems many years ago your mama got herself shot in a robbery, an' people are sayin' you might've thought Roy had somethin' t'do with it, so you offed the little prick.'

Keeping his face blank, Michael said nothing.

'This is the first I'm hearin' of it,' Vito continued, slurping his drink. 'My wife,' he added, indicating Mamie, who was now slumped on the couch, still glaring at Michael, 'she comes to me hysterical. Take a look at her.'

Michael stared straight at Mamie, his eyes sending her a message. *Yes, I shot Roy. And I'd shoot him again if I had the chance.*

'Roy was everythin' to me,' she snivelled. 'I *want* the person who shot him. I want revenge.'

'I know how you feel,' Michael said, repressing the urge to spit in her over-made-up face. 'I'd like revenge for my mom's murder.' He took a long beat, his mind racing. How had the story got out so fast after all these years of silence? Was Bone responsible? And, if so, why? 'An' while we're talkin' about word on the street,' he continued, deciding to go for it, 'I heard a mention that *you* might've had something to do with that robbery. Bullshit, Mamie? Or the truth?'

She glanced quickly at her husband. 'Where'd you hear that?' she asked, narrowing her red-rimmed eyes.

Now it was Vito's turn to stare at her. '*Didya* have anything to do with it, Mamie?' he demanded. ''Cause if you did, you'd better fuckin' 'fess up.'

'No,' she said guiltily.

'Doesn't it seem to fit?' Michael said, pressing ahead. 'You were datin' my dad. Then he met my mom, knocked her up, married her, an' the next thing, somebody's robbing the store. The newspapers said the cops were lookin' for a blonde woman an' two men.'

'Mamie,' Vito said, his voice hardening, 'you'd better tell me the fuckin' truth here.'

'I came to you for help, not to get the third degree from this punk kid,' she spat, full of venom.

Vito laughed suddenly. 'You did it, didn't you?' he said incredulously. 'You fuckin' did it.'

'No, I didn't,' she said through clenched teeth.

'Oh, yeah, you *did*,' he said, putting down his cigar and getting up. 'You never was good at lyin'. What happened – Roy pull the trigger?'

'It wasn't Roy,' she said spitefully, letting out her venom. 'Roy couldn't handle a piece. It was Bone killed the tramp, an' only 'cause she was tryin' to attack him. He *had* t'do it. It was self-defence. There!' She glared at Michael. 'Satisfied?'

He stifled a desire to smash her fucking face in. 'You sick *bitch*!' he said. 'How can you live with yourself?'

'So that's the thanks I get for takin' care of you all these years,' she said, her face contorted with fury.

'You didn't take care of me. You *used* me t'try an' get rid of your guilt.'

'Ungrateful loser!' she shouted. 'You're exactly like your no-account daddy. You're *both* losers!'

'Jesus Christ, Mamie!' Vito exclaimed in disgust. 'Get the fuck outta here.' He clicked his fingers. 'Luigi, drive her home.'

'An' what'll you do to *him?*' she asked, pointing at Michael, her voice rising. 'He *murdered* my Roy. My own cousin. You're not lettin' him get away with it, are you?'

'Retribution is a strange an' wonderful thing,' Vito said. 'It always has a way of comin' back an' bitin' you on the ass.'

'You'll pay for this,' Mamie screamed at Michael, as Luigi took her arm and began leading her from the room. 'You'll pay good.'

'Women – you can never trust 'em,' Vito said, as soon as she was gone.

'I'm sorry—' Michael began.

Vito held up his hand. 'No apologies. You did what ya thought was right. Only now you'd better take care of Bone.' He laughed drily. 'You might've got yourself a new job.'

'What job would that be?'

'You wanna be a hitter? You'll get paid plenty.'

'It's not what I do,' Michael said slowly.

'You're happy to be nothin' but part of a crew in the Lucchese family, huh?' Vito said, cradling his drink.

'I got no complaints,' he said, not about to reveal his other lucrative business.

'I was thinkin' you might wanna work for me again,' Vito said. 'There was a time I had big plans for you.'

'That's what I thought,' Michael said, 'so as soon as I got outta the joint, I came t'see you. Problem. I was told I had to make an appointment six weeks in advance.'

'Didn't know nothin' about that.'

'I would've come back to work for you, even though it was Tommaso an' Roy set me up.'

'They did?'

'You must've known about it.'

'Shit, no.'

Michael wasn't sure whether he believed him or not. 'Where is Tommaso anyway?' he asked.

'In the hospital,' Vito said. 'Poor bastard got caught in the crossfire.'

Michael nodded. A couple of weeks ago he'd read in the newspaper about a shooting outside a gambling parlour. Apparently the shooter had missed Vito, and the bullet had caught Tommaso in the shoulder. Too bad it wasn't a direct hit.

'How about it?' Vito said. 'You comin' back?'

'I'm makin' good money where I am.'

'You'll make better money with me.'

'I always liked being close to you, Mr G. I felt a loyalty. Thing is, when I couldn't get near you, it kinda soured me.'

'Loyalty,' Vito said, rubbing his hands together, 'that's what's important. When you got power, you gotta have people watchin' your back. People who care.'

Michael nodded his agreement.

'You wanna think about it?' Vito said.

'I'll do that.'

'Good, good. Only don't make me wait. I'm not a patient man.'

There was something Michael had to do, and much as he dreaded it, he got on a plane and flew to Miami, where his father had taken up residence in an oceanside apartment. He knew exactly where Vinny was living, he'd kept tabs on him over the years, even though they'd not spoken since Vinny had packed up and left him with three hundred dollars and nothing else.

When he told Beth he was planning on visiting his father, she'd pleaded to go with him.

'No,' he'd said. 'It's not necessary.'

'Oh, yes, Michael, please!' she'd said, throwing her arms round his neck. 'It *is* necessary. Miami. The sun. The music. The food.' A long, meaningful pause, and then that seductive smile of hers. 'The sex.'

'No, Beth,' he'd said firmly. 'You're stayin' here.'

'Does he know about Madison?' she'd asked, playing the family card. 'Surely he'd like to see her? After all, he's her grandfather.'

'Vinny's not the grandfather type. He's . . . y' know, got a bad attitude. Besides, I don't want him knowin' anythin' about Madison.'

'That's not fair,' she'd said, sulking. 'I *want* to come to Miami. It's a cool place, it'll give me inspiration for my designs.'

'Sorry, honey. Fair or not, you'll just have to live with it.'

'Fuck you, Michael,' she'd said, brown eyes flashing major danger signals.

One thing about Beth, she certainly had spirit. And a mouth. She was completely different from any woman he'd ever known, and he loved her for it. 'I'll be home tonight,' he'd said. 'Don't wait up.'

'Like I'll be waiting up,' she'd said scornfully. '*I'm* going out. Catherine will babysit.'

'Why can't you stay in?'

'Why should I? You'll be in Miami without me.'

'What's that got to do with anything? I'm seein' my dad.'

'I know, Michael, so while *you*'re there, *I'll* hit the town with friends. After all, as *you* pointed out, we're not married.'

Why had he suddenly felt jealous?

There was something about Beth that made him want to keep her all to himself.

Miami was hot and humid. Michael took a cab from the airport straight to Vinny's apartment. It pulled up outside a sturdy old building painted a lurid pink. He paid the driver and walked into a musty lobby. Then he got into the elevator, which smelt of overcooked cabbage and stale cat piss. It slowly creaked its way to the third floor, where he got out and knocked on the door of Vinny's apartment. He was startled when a woman opened it.

'Yes?' the woman said, in a none too friendly tone. She was in her mid-forties, thin, with lank brown hair and a long nose. She wore an old flowered housecoat and once pink fuzzy slippers on her feet.

'I'm lookin' for Vinny Castellino,' he said, wondering if he had the right address.

'You're not the only one,' she said sharply.

'Excuse me?'

'If you're lookin' to collect on a debt, you're outta luck. He went bankrupt last week, so screw off!'

This was not exactly the greeting he'd had in mind. 'I'm Michael,' he said quickly, blocking the door with his foot before she slammed it in his face. 'Vinny's son.'

'Oh,' she said. 'In that case . . . you got any money?

'Cause your daddy's stone broke.'

'How can he be broke? He sold the house an' the shop. He must have plenty of money.'

'Medical bills,' she said vaguely. 'Crap like that.' A weary sigh. 'An' then there's the gambling.'

'Gambling?'

'A man's gotta have *some* pleasure in life, don't he?'

'Is he around?'

'You'd better come in,' she said, throwing open the door.

The apartment was bright enough. So bright that he immediately noticed thick layers of dust on all the surfaces, and a kaleidoscope of stains decorating the worn carpet. A large balcony overlooked the ocean.

Vinny sat out on the balcony in his wheelchair, a portable TV perched on his lap, a mangy orange cat curled up by his feet.

Michael approached him warily. 'Dad,' he said, the word almost sticking in his throat.

Vinny turned his head. Not a flicker of surprise crossed his once-handsome face. 'I heard you was in jail,' he said brusquely.

Nice greeting. Michael hadn't expected anything else.

'Wasn't surprised,' Vinny continued. 'Your grandma always said you was gonna turn out no good. I tried to keep you on the straight and narrow. Trouble is, you wouldn't listen to nobody.'

'I came here to talk to you.'

'About what?'

Michael glanced at the woman who was hovering by the balcony door, eager to hear every word. 'It's personal,' he said. 'Do you mind?'

'Get lost,' Vinny said, waving her away.

She marched inside.

'Your, uh, ladyfriend said you recently went bankrupt.'

'Don't tell me y'came here expectin' money?'

'*You*'re the one took all the money and left me with three hundred lousy bucks, an' you're *surprised* I got into trouble,' he said heatedly. Then he realized he was getting off track, and that was not his intention. 'No,' he said, determined to forget old grudges. 'That's not why I'm here.'

'Spit it out, son.'

He groped in his pocket for a cigarette and lit up. 'You never really told me exactly what happened that night.'

'What night would that be?' Vinny asked, squinting at him.

'The night Mom was shot.'

Vinny fiddled with the TV aerial. 'What's left to tell?' he said at last.

'Plenty,' Michael said. 'I need to know the details.'

'Told you everything.'

'No, you didn't. I asked, an' you never wanted to talk about it. Neither did Grandma.'

'What's so important that you wanna know now?'

'I have my reasons.'

'Dunno why I havta go through it all again,' Vinny grumbled. 'Don't want to. Don't have to.'

Michael placed his cigarette in an old tin ashtray on a rickety table, slid his hand into his pocket and produced a wad of money. He counted out ten crisp hundred dollar bills. 'Here,' he said, offering Vinny the money. 'Maybe this'll help you remember.'

'Where'd *you* get this kinda money?' Vinny asked suspiciously.

'I robbed a bank,' Michael deadpanned. A beat. 'Seriously, Dad, it's legit. I got lucky in the stock market.'

'Whadda *you* know about stuff like that?'

'Plenty,' Michael said, getting impatient. 'You want the money or not?'

Vinny couldn't resist. After a moment's hesitation he grabbed it, shoved it in his pants pocket, and started talking.

'I was in the shop by myself when two punks busted in an' started shovin' me round. One of 'em puts a gun to my head while the other one's robbin' the cash register.'

'Go on,' Michael said, encouraging him.

'Then Anna Maria comes walkin' in,' Vinny continued. 'She was supposed to be home. It was snowing, she had flakes of snow in her hair an' on her coat. Anyway, when she saw what was happenin', she threw herself at the one with the gun.' A long pause while he recalled memories of that fateful day. 'I yelled at her not to, but she did it anyway.' Another long pause. 'Then the bastard shot her.' His voice began to quaver. 'I tried to save her, it was too damn late. They shot me, too, snatched the money, an' ran.'

'Tell me about the guys.'

'What about 'em?'

'Were they tall? Short? Fat? Thin?'

'One was shortish, the other one was a tall bastard. I saw them well enough. Described 'em to the cops. They never caught 'em.'

'Which one had the gun?'

'The tall, skinny one with the crazy eyes an' the long thin scar down his cheek.'

Damn! Vinny had just described Bone.

'You're *sure?*'

''Course I'm sure. I'll never forget that night.'

So Mamie had been telling the truth for once. Bone was the shooter. Bone was responsible for his mother's death and Vinny being in a wheelchair. Christ! He'd shot the wrong man.

'What's all this about?' Vinny asked. 'Why're you dredging up somethin' I'm tryin' t'forget?'

'Remember your old girlfriend Mamie?'

'Who?'

'Mamie. She married Vito Giovanni. Turned up at Grandma's funeral an' pissed you off.'

'Oh, yeah,' Vinny said, scowling. '*That* cow.'

'She was with them that night. One of the two men was her cousin Roy.'

'You're makin' this up,' Vinny said, turning pale.

'No, I'm not. It's somethin' I found out recently. Mamie was waitin' outside the store. It was her set the whole thing up.'

'That lousy no-good *cunt*!' Vinny screamed.

'Don't worry, I'm takin' care of it.'

'How'll you do that?'

'Better you don't ever know.'

Chapter Thirty

Dani: 1972

Vincent was a serious child, and gorgeous, with his long, silky black eyelashes and deep green eyes. He was smart too – by the time he was two he could recite his ABCs and count to one hundred in English and Spanish. Nando was also smart. Quick-witted and very bright, he refused to take anything seriously. He was into exploring, experimenting, and getting into trouble. The two of them balanced each other out. They were as close as brothers, and even though they were only seven, they exhibited a fierce loyalty towards each other.

At school, Vincent excelled, while Nando lagged behind. Sometimes it worried Dani that Nando might be a bad influence on her son. She didn't act on it: the boys were so close it would be unfair to try to separate them.

Shortly after marrying Morgan, Gemini gave up her job at the Magiriano Hotel. Dani was upset; she knew she would miss the companionship of seeing her friend every night. 'We'll still get together during the day,' Gemini promised. 'Except when we're travelling. Morgan loves to travel, and I have to be available to go with him.'

They'd made a deal that whenever Gemini was away, Dani would take care of Nando.

Friday morning, Gemini and Morgan left for a long weekend in Chicago, dropping Nando off on their way to the airport.

Later that day, Dani took the two boys to the children's area in the park. She sat on the bench watching Nando show off as he attempted to stand on his head on the roundabout; some of the smaller kids who were playing in the sandbox screamed with delight.

The boys were getting too big for park activities: they preferred hanging out at the ranch where they could ride horses and run wild.

Dani didn't notice the man approaching her until he was standing right next to her.

'Excuse me,' he said, startling her.

She glanced up. He was a slim man, quite attractive, dressed in jeans, a blue sports jacket, and a white shirt open at the neck. He had dark blond hair that curled round his collar, a stubbled chin, and unfocused, faintly bloodshot eyes. He did not look American.

'Can I help you?' she asked.

'You're Dani Castle, is that right?' he said, in a hardly detectable foreign accent.

'That's right,' she said, thinking that he must recognize her from the show and was about to ask for her autograph.

'You have something that belongs to me,' he said, cracking his knuckles.

'I do?' she said, glancing round to see if there was anyone who might come to her assistance if he got crazy on her. Sometimes fans did – although this man did not seem to be a fan. 'And what would that be?'

'My son,' he said.

'Your son?' she repeated.

'I'm Moralis,' he said, his eyes darting round the playground. 'Gemini's ex-husband. I'm sure she has informed you what a bastard I am.'

Actually, Gemini had said very little about Moralis, except that he was the son of an extremely rich man, that he'd abused her both mentally and physically, and that after their divorce was final they'd both agreed never to see each other again. Now here he was.

Uninvited, he sat down beside her and proceeded to tell her how he'd been searching for his son for the last four years, and had only recently, with the help of a private detective, discovered that Nando was in Vegas.

'I – I thought you and Gemini worked everything out,' Dani said, not wanting to get into the middle of this.

'After I paid her a fortune, she disappeared with my son,' he said bitterly. 'Left my country without informing me where she was going. It has taken me all this time to find her.' He stood up. 'Where is Nando? I must see him.'

'You'll have to wait until Gemini gets home in a couple of days.'

'I don't think so,' he said forcefully. 'I came here to take my son, and that's what I'm doing.'

'You can't,' she said quickly.

'Who'll stop me?'

'*I* will.'

'Oh, *you* will,' he said, almost laughing in her face.

'Gemini has custody of Nando,' she explained, hoping he'd listen to reason. 'If you want to share that custody you'll have to go through the courts.'

'Do I look as if I'm prepared to do that?' he said edgily.

'Let me see if I can contact Gemini and ask *her* what to do.'

'Don't you understand what I'm telling you?' he said, getting angry. 'She took my *son* away from me! In my country that is not legal. In my country a man has rights.'

There was something unsettling about this man, and until she had Gemini's permission, there was no way she was allowing him to take Nando.

'Perhaps you can tell me where you're staying, and I'll be in touch,' she said.

'I want my son,' he answered, an angry gleam in his eyes. 'And I want him now.'

'That's not possible. Nando is in my charge, and I can't release him.'

'*Bitch!*' he said, suddenly snapping. 'You fucking American women are all bitches. You're as bad as the French ones.'

Dani stood up. She was as tall as him and unafraid. 'You'll need a court order to take Nando, so go away,' she said firmly.

'No, I will not go away,' he said, staring her down.

Out of the corner of her eye she observed a police car cruising by. 'If you cause any more problems, I'm flagging down that police car and you'll be arrested.'

'Are you *threatening* me?' he said, the anger in his eyes turning dangerous.

'I'm merely trying to make this a pleasant experience for everyone concerned. I'm sure you want to see your son. However, you must understand my position.'

'I understand shit,' he said abruptly. 'I'm takin' my kid.' And he marched towards the boys on the swings. 'Nando!' he called out. 'Nando, it's your papa. I've come to get you.'

Nando stopped what he was doing and turned to see who was calling him.

Quickly Dani ran over and waved down the police car. She leaned into the window, and was happy to recognize one of the cops. His name was Burt, and he attended her show regularly.

'Hey, Dani – how's it going?' Burt asked.

'Not good,' she answered. 'That man over there is Gemini's ex-husband. He's trying to take her son. Can you do something?'

'Sure,' Burt said. 'We'll go have a word with him.'

Burt and his female partner got out of their patrol car and approached Moralis, who by this time had picked Nando up and was swinging him round in the air. The little boy didn't seem at all perturbed. On the other hand, he didn't recognize Moralis – but, hey, an adventure was always fun, and Nando lived for fun.

'I'm your papa,' Moralis kept on repeating. 'Remember me? Your papa.'

'Can I talk to you, sir?' Burt said.

Moralis was not in a good mood. 'I'm busy,' he said.

'Put the boy down, come over here, and we'll talk,' interjected the female cop, a tough-looking redhead.

'Screw you,' Moralis snapped.

Vincent, who'd been watching all this, ran over to Dani. 'Who's that man, Mommy?' he asked. 'Why's he got Nando?'

'It's nothing, baby,' she said, quickly taking his hand.

'Why's Nando *with* him?' Vincent persisted.

'He's a . . . relative. We have to wait until Auntie Gem comes back, then we'll sort everything out.'

'Wanna get down,' Nando yelled suddenly at Moralis. 'Lemme *go*.' And he kneed him in the stomach.

'You little shit!' Moralis shouted, and went to slap the boy.

Before he was able to, Burt grabbed his arm, Moralis lost his balance, and a scuffle ensued.

Dani didn't wait round. She rushed over, grabbed Nando, and hurried the boys to her car. 'Get in quickly,' she commanded. And without looking back, she drove them home, where her housekeeper informed her that a Mr Sanchez had been asking for his son, and she'd directed him to the park.

'*Never* do that again,' Dani said. 'Do not tell *anyone* where I am unless you know who they are.'

She instructed the boys to go upstairs, ran to the phone,

and called Gemini and Morgan in Chicago. They were not in the hotel. Next she phoned Dean in Houston. He was there. She relayed the story.

'Don't panic,' he said. 'Drive the boys out to the ranch and warn your housekeeper not to tell anyone where you are. In the meantime, I'll contact Morgan. He'll know how to handle this.'

'Thank you, Dean,' she said gratefully.

'The guy didn't threaten *you*, did he?'

'No, but there was definitely something weird about him.'

'Don't worry, I'll take care of it.'

That's what she loved about Dean: he was always ready to take care of anything she asked, even though she was still reticent about getting married.

'We're engaged,' she'd said to him the last time he'd asked. 'Let's enjoy that for a while.'

'What kind of an engagement is it when you're in Vegas and I'm in Houston?' he'd said.

He was right, but she couldn't bring herself to take the final step.

'I'm not going to wait forever,' he'd told her.

'I know, Dean. I promise – soon.'

And that's how they'd left it.

When Gemini returned from Chicago, she cautioned Dani not to tell Morgan anything that Moralis had said, other than his request to take Nando.

'I thought you'd worked everything out with him,' Dani said, over lunch at the ranch.

'Not exactly,' Gemini replied.

'According to Moralis, you took off with Nando four years ago, and he's been looking for you ever since.'

'It's a long story,' Gemini said, and sipped some iced tea. 'I left a trail that ended in Paris. I thought he'd search

Europe for a couple of months, then forget about us.'

'Apparently he hasn't.'

'Moralis is full of demons,' Gemini said earnestly. 'Look what *you* went through with Sam.'

'That's different,' Dani said. 'Sam isn't Vincent's real father. Plus Sam turned out to be a drunk – that's hardly comparable to being filled with demons.'

'I had to get away,' Gemini explained, her face clouding over. 'Nobody has any idea how violent Moralis can be. When he loses his temper, he doesn't care what he does. You're lucky he didn't attack *you*.'

'I have a feeling he was about to. Fortunately, I saw the police car and waved it down.'

'Do you think Nando remembered him?' Gemini asked.

'He didn't seem to.'

'Thank God!'

'Is he likely to come back?'

Gemini shook her head. 'With the police involved, I'm sure he won't dare.'

'Do you honestly think one little incident with the police will make him go away?'

'When he finds out he can't treat me the way he used to, he'll leave. I have Morgan to protect me now.'

It crossed Dani's mind that maybe Gemini had married Morgan for exactly that reason. An older, powerful, rich man who could protect her. Close as she was to Gemini, there were obviously things she didn't know.

'If you ever want to talk about it, I'm here,' she offered.

'Thanks, Dani, you're a good friend.'

'I try to be.'

Several weeks passed and there were no more Moralis sightings.

Gemini was relieved. 'Morgan says if he comes back again, he'll have him arrested.'

'Is that possible?'

'Anything's possible,' Gemini replied, secure in her marriage to a powerful man.

Dani wasn't sure that Moralis would give up so easily. She'd seen the look in his eyes: he was a determined man and an angry one.

Dean flew back into town and began pressuring her again. Since she'd slept with him once, he expected she would do it again. She demurred, coming up with many different excuses.

'Dani,' he said to her one day, 'are we doing this, or not?'

'Doing what, Dean?' she asked, although she knew exactly what he meant.

'Getting married,' he said flatly. 'Because if we're not . . .'

'Yes?'

'If we're not, I have to move on.'

Move on? What was he talking about? 'Excuse me?' she said.

'I have needs, Dani, and you're not meeting them.'

'Are you asking me to give you back your ring?'

'No.'

'Then – what?'

'Love *me* like I love you. Is that too much to ask?'

'I . . . I'm not sure I can,' she said hesitantly.

'Why not?' he demanded.

'I need time.'

'You've *had* time.'

She knew she had to make a decision. If she didn't marry Dean soon, he *would* move on.

She consulted with Gemini, who told her that Morgan had mentioned Dean was seeing someone in Houston. The news came as a blow.

Dean was hers. Always there. Always faithful.

Or was he?

She waited until his next trip and, over a quiet dinner after her show, agreed that they should set a date. Then she stayed the night at his hotel, cementing the deal.

In the morning he was ecstatic. 'You'll never regret it,' he said.

'Let's do it next week,' she said, afraid that she might change her mind.

He was surprised. 'Don't you want to plan a big wedding with all the trimmings?'

'No,' she said. 'If Morgan and Gemini agree, we'll do it at the ranch.'

'Whatever you say, my darling. I'm all yours.'

The day before the wedding, Dani moved out to the ranch with Vincent to spend the night. She couldn't believe it had all happened so fast. One day she'd said yes, and now, six days later, it was the eve of her wedding. She'd purchased a dress, given in her notice at the Magiriano, sold her car, and leased her house to a nice young couple from New Orleans.

Soon she and Vincent would move to Houston to live in a house she hadn't even seen. It was crazy. Or was it? Dean was kind and caring, he genuinely loved her *and* Vincent, and if all went well, they would be extremely happy.

Vincent was *not* happy about leaving Nando, the ranch, his school, and all his other friends to go live in Houston. Dani assured him they would visit often.

Morgan decided to spend the night in town with Dean. 'I'll leave you girls alone to plot and plan devious women things,' he boomed. 'Weddings are the damnedest events. A person has to prepare – especially the ladies.'

'You just want a night of freedom,' Gemini teased, smiling affectionately. 'Remember, you can look, not touch.'

Morgan adjusted his stetson and beamed. 'I married a

smart woman who understands men. That makes *me* a very smart man.'

An hour after he left, Moralis phoned. Gemini took the call, although Dani advised her not to.

'He doesn't frighten me any more,' Gemini said, a determined thrust to her chin. 'There is *nothing* he can do to me.'

'You should find out where he is and have Morgan call him back,' Dani suggested.

'No,' Gemini said firmly. 'He has to hear it from me. He cannot take Nando, and that is final.'

Dani shrugged, she had problems of her own. Vincent was refusing to try on the suit she'd bought him to wear at the wedding. He was behaving like a brat, and Nando was encouraging him. Maybe a break from each other would be good for both of them.

Gemini stayed on the phone for some time. When she emerged from the bedroom, her face was streaked with tears.

'What's the matter?' Dani asked sympathetically.

'Nothing,' Gemini said, close to tears again. 'It's so damn difficult.'

'What did he say?'

'Everything's fine,' Gemini said. 'He's agreed to go away.'

'Then why are you so upset?'

'Well, you know, the past and everything. We did experience a passion that is very difficult to forget.'

'Mommy!' Vincent yelled. 'Come see Nando's dog. It's got *huge* fleas. Can we get a dog, Mommy? Nando says *his* dog *eats* fleas. *I* wanna dog that eats fleas.'

She hurried outside to inspect the flea-ridden mutt Nando had rescued from the pound.

The dog was enormous, with a big shaggy coat. Vincent had draped himself all over the panting animal.

'Get *off*,' Dani ordered. 'The poor dog is not a horse.'

'*You* can ride him, Mommy,' Vincent said encouragingly. '*I* do.'

'Off,' Dani repeated.

'Piss.' Vincent giggled.

'What did you say?' Dani asked, quite shocked.

'Piss off,' Nando said, screaming with laughter.

'Get it, Mommy?' Vincent said, giggling uncontrollably.

'No, I do not get it,' she said sternly. 'That is not nice language, and I do not expect to hear it again.'

'Piss off,' both boys shrieked in unison. 'Piss off! Piss off! *Piss off*!'

'Inside! Now!'

They followed her into the house.

Mrs Braxton, Morgan's long-time cook, was busy in the kitchen preparing hamburgers and french fries for the boys.

The manicurist Gemini had arranged for was in the dining room setting up her equipment. Gemini had also booked a masseuse, a facialist, and a hairdresser. They would all be arriving any minute.

'It's the night before your wedding,' Gemini had said. 'I am making sure you are thoroughly pampered.'

'Where's Gemini?' Dani asked Mrs Braxton.

'She asked me to tell you that she had to pop out.'

'Did she say where she was going?'

'She mentioned she'd be back soon.'

Dani didn't start to worry until an hour had passed. Then two, then three. By that time she was seriously worried. All the beauticians had come and gone and it was almost eleven.

Had Gemini 'popped out' to meet Moralis? Where else would she have gone?

Dani picked up the phone and called Dean. Neither he nor Morgan were at the hotel, so she left a message for them to call her immediately they returned.

This was supposed to be a happy time for her, and yet she felt exactly the same as she had the night Emily disappeared. Sick and apprehensive.

She sat in the front room, her eyes shifting from the clock to the front door. Midnight came and went. She tried to reach Dean and Morgan at the hotel again. Still no answer from either of their rooms. They were out celebrating, while Gemini was . . .

She didn't know.

She only knew that the sick feeling in the pit of her stomach told her that once again something bad had happened.

Something really bad.

Chapter Thirty-one

Michael: 1972

The news that he'd probably shot the wrong man did not sit well with Michael. Although, when he thought it through, he was able to accept it, because all three of them eventually had to pay the price.

He'd killed a man in cold blood. It didn't seem real to him, and yet he'd done it. And he would do it again if he had to.

For his mother.

For the woman he'd never met.

For her honour.

Bone must've figured that by getting him to eliminate Roy, the truth would never come out. The scumbag hadn't reckoned on Mamie and her big mouth.

Another thought. How *had* Mamie heard it was him who'd shot Roy? Bone was a dangerous bastard, and he probably had something else in mind. The problem was, who knew what that something was?

What should he do now? Switch sides and move over to the Giovanni family?

Maybe. Vito Giovanni understood what revenge was all about.

It was almost midnight when he arrived back at the

house. Catherine was sitting in the front room knitting a sweater. Like her sister, Catherine was quite beautiful and very young, only she had none of Beth's fire. 'Hi, Michael,' she said, holding a finger to her lips. 'Ssh . . . Madison's asleep.'

'Where's Beth?' he asked, looking round.

'She went out with friends.'

'What time's she comin' home?'

'*You* know Beth,' Catherine said, putting down her knitting. 'I can't control her, and neither can you. Neither of us should try.'

'*I* don't want to,' he said pointedly.

'Yes, you do.'

Sometimes Catherine got on his nerves. 'Did she happen t'tell you we were talkin' about gettin' married?' he said, thinking that would shut her up.

'No, she didn't mention it.'

'Didn't mention it, huh?' he said, aggravated. 'Gee, she must've been really excited.'

'Michael,' Catherine said, in a sanctimonious annoying tone, 'Beth adores you in her own way. But you have to understand that when our father was arrested and taken off to a political prison, it kind of put her out of control.'

'How's that?'

'She's always been a little wild, but after that . . . Well, you *do* know you're not her first man?'

'You're lucky she already told me,' he said sharply, ''cause if she hadn't, you'd be *way* outta line.'

'Sorry,' Catherine said, getting up quickly. 'Shall I give Madison her bottle when she wakes, or do you want to?'

'What I want t'know is where my fuckin' girlfriend's gone. The mother of my child,' he said, full of frustration. 'Who are these friends she's out with?'

'People from the fashion institute.'

'Girls? Boys? What?'

'A mixture.'

'If I ever catch her with another man,' he said ominously, 'I'll kill her.'

'Don't *say* things like that, Michael.'

'I mean it.'

'Anyway,' Catherine said crisply, 'she's not with another man, she's merely having fun.'

'Fun, huh?'

'It's not easy for her, Michael. She has a baby to care for, a house to run, and—'

'C'mon, Catherine,' he interrupted. 'Cut the bull. *You* do everything round here. Beth gets dressed up and goes off to some fancy school with her fancy fuckin' friends, an' now she's out all night with them.'

'I'm sorry I told you.'

'Yeah, well, I needed to know the truth.'

'How was your father?'

'The same old loser,' he said. 'Look, I'm not sittin' round here waitin' – I'm goin' out.'

'I'm sure Beth will be home soon.'

'Hey, she wants to do her thing, that's okay – I'll do mine.'

He left the house filled with anger, drove round for a while, and eventually went to a neighbourhood bar, where an attractive girl with huge breasts sat down next to him. 'I'm a lingerie model,' she informed him with an inviting smile. She had pearly white teeth, curly auburn hair, and a snub nose. 'How about coming back to my place for a nightcap?' she suggested. 'I promise I won't bite. Not unless you ask me to!'

The invitation was there, staring him in the face.

He simply wasn't interested. Beth was the only woman he wanted.

After throwing down another couple of Jack Daniel's, he went home alone.

Beth was still out.

He lay down on the bed, switched on the TV, lit a cigarette and fumed. Eventually he fell into a restless sleep.

In the morning Beth was asleep beside him, her dark hair spread out across the white sheets, one long leg stretched out and exposed.

He was angry and turned on all at the same time. Without saying a word, he got on top of her.

'Michael,' she murmured, half opening her eyes, 'what're you doing?'

'Fucking you,' he said forcefully. 'Is that okay?'

'No, it's *not* okay,' she said, beginning to struggle. 'Get . . . off . . . me.'

He was having none of it. Pinning her arms back, he pounded into her until he came.

Afterward, he was regretful. He'd just committed a purely selfish act. It wasn't *her* fault he was jealous.

Jesus Christ! She had him out of control.

He glanced over at her. She'd moved away and was lying with her back towards him.

'We're announcing our marriage this week,' he said gruffly. 'That's the way it's gonna be.'

'I hate you,' she said, rolling over to face him, big brown eyes flashing undisguised anger.

'No, you don't.'

'Yes, I do. You – you *rapist*!'

'Sorry, baby,' he muttered. 'Dunno what came over me.'

'Ha!'

'Miami stank, an' when I got back you weren't home,' he said, making excuses.

'I *told* you I'd be out.'

'I know that.'

She moved a little closer to him. 'I suppose seeing your father upset you?'

'No,' he lied.

'Yes, it did.'

'Okay,' he admitted. 'It made me crazy.'

'I knew it! Told you I should've gone with you.'

'You were right. You're always right,' he said, nuzzling close to her. 'How come for someone so young you're pretty damn smart?'

'Just lucky, I guess.'

'Sorry if I was rough with you. I didn't mean it. It's . . . I dunno . . . Guess I missed you.'

'Did you now?'

'Ain't *that* something?'

She sighed and cuddled closer. 'I like it when you miss me, Michael. It means you care.'

He sat up and reached for a cigarette. 'I never felt this way about anybody before, Beth. Never. You're it.'

She flashed him her seductive smile. 'Good.'

'You'd better believe it,' he said. And to make up for before, he began caressing her breasts the way he knew she liked.

'That's nice.' She sighed. 'Umm . . . *veree* nice.'

He slid down the bed, spread her legs, and began tonguing her the way she'd often asked him to, though he'd declined, because going down on a woman didn't seem a very manly act. And yet . . . if you loved that woman, and she did the same for you, why not give her pleasure?

Her excitement and her smooth firm thighs turned him on again. He resolved to stop the jealous crap and start treating her better.

A few nights later he drove down to the fashion institute to pick her up. He planned to surprise her, take her to dinner at their favourite restaurant and present her with the ring he'd got her – a five-carat diamond direct from Tiffany's via a friend of Warner's in the jewellery business.

Beth emerged shortly after five. His beautiful, soon-to-be child bride.

She was arm-in-arm with a young guy, not much older than her. They were so busy talking and giggling that she didn't even see him waiting patiently in his car like Dumb Schmuck of the Year.

Beth. His Beth with another man.

A black fury overtook him. He could barely see straight. He wanted to smash the asshole's brains in.

Instead he did nothing. He watched them walk out of sight, and then he went home.

Catherine had gone to stay with a girlfriend for the weekend, leaving a babysitter in charge of Madison. As soon as Michael arrived home, he paid the girl and told her she could leave.

'Where's the babysitter?' Beth asked when she got home, two hours later, and found Michael sitting in the kitchen bouncing a gurgling Madison on his knee.

'Sent her away,' he replied. 'Figured we didn't need her.'

'You *know* I need help when Catherine's away,' Beth complained, shrugging off her short, embroidered jacket.

'Got a hunch you'll manage for one night.'

'Damn, Michael.' She opened the fridge. 'I wish you wouldn't do things like that without checking with me.'

'Like what?'

'Sending the babysitter home when I need her.'

'Why'd you need her, Beth?' he asked, barely able to contain his anger.

''Cause I'm tired,' she said, pouring herself a glass of milk.

'Tough day at school?' he said, scrutinizing her face.

'As a matter of fact, yes.'

'How come you got home so late tonight?'

'We have finals coming up. I've got to present my first collection on paper.' Her brown eyes sparkled. 'It's so exciting. Next year I'll be designing actual clothes.' She took Madison from him and began showering her with kisses. 'What a *cute* baby!' she said, grinning. 'Who's the *most* gorgeous little girl in the *world?*' Madison rewarded her with a gummy smile. 'Guess what?' Beth continued, hugging her baby. '*Daddy*'s going to bathe you tonight. Won't *that* be fun?'

'Can't,' he said abruptly. 'Gotta go out.'

'You're kidding?'

'No. Gotta take care of business,' he said evasively.

'You *know* I hate being here alone when Catherine's away.'

'I forgot.'

'That's not fair.'

'That's the way it goes, babe.' A beat. 'By the way, how *was* school today?'

'You've asked me that already. And, besides, it's not *school*, Michael,' she replied, placing Madison in her bouncy chair, 'it's a fashion institute.'

'Anything interesting happen?'

'Yeah,' she teased. 'I gave a blow job to three of my teachers. Is that interesting enough for you?'

'Beth!' he said sharply. 'Watch what you say.'

She giggled. 'You're such a prude!'

Nobody had ever called him *that* before.

'Well,' she said, 'I suppose that since you're deserting me, I'd better get this little angel to bed.'

'You do that,' he said, simmering about her blow-job comment. Maybe that's exactly what she'd done with the jerk he'd seen her leaving the institute with. His Beth with another man. He couldn't take it.

She looked at him curiously. 'Is something the matter, Michael?'

'Why'd you think that?' he snapped.

'You seem kind of . . . pissed off.'

'I was thinking,' he said, regaining his composure, 'I should meet some of your friends. We could all go out for dinner one night.'

'You wouldn't like them,' she said, dismissing the idea. 'They're not your kind of people.'

'They're not my kind of people, but they're yours, huh? Is that what you're tellin' me?'

'No, it's simply that *I* have something in common with them.'

'And *I* don't.'

'Michael,' she said mockingly, 'I didn't know *you* wanted to start designing clothes, too.'

He hated it when she came at him with attitude. 'Hey, Beth,' he said coldly, 'have a good evening. I'll see you.'

'*Please* don't be late,' she said, picking up Madison again. 'If you're very lucky, I'll wait up.'

'Don't bother,' he said, and left the house with no idea where he was going: he only knew he had to get out before he exploded.

Tomorrow he'd confront her.

Tonight she could suffer – let her wonder what was wrong.

He ended up at the social club, hanging out with Gus.

Bone was still on the missing list. According to Gus, he hadn't been round for several days. 'He's probably trackin' a job for Lucchese,' Gus said, when he asked. 'Why you interested?'

'Who's interested?' Michael replied. 'It's a pleasure not to look at his ugly face.'

'Yeah,' Gus said, laughing. 'He's a plain motherfucker.'

'Where'd he get the scar on his cheek?'

'Told me his dad cut him when he was a kid.'

'Then he's had it a long time?'

'Yup,' Gus said, getting impatient. 'Are we playin' poker or what?'

'Count me in.'

Too many shots of Jack Daniel's, he'd lost his ass at poker, and on top of everything else he felt like crap.

When he got home he'd ask Beth what the fuck kind of game she was playing. He'd had enough. If she was screwing around on him she'd better confess.

Then what?

Shit! Falling in love was not for weaklings.

All he really wanted to do was hold her in his arms and stay close. She was part of his life now, with her seductive smile and sassy comebacks.

So was little Madison. His own daughter. His own flesh and blood.

God! How he loved having her. It didn't even bother him that Beth hadn't given birth to a boy. They had plenty of time.

Jeez! What was wrong with him? If he really thought about it, he knew that Beth wouldn't screw around on him. She loved him and they were planning on getting married.

He drove home slowly, wary of getting stopped by the cops. It was two a.m. and the street was deserted. He wished he'd spent the evening at home, instead of losing money and getting tanked.

Fortunately there was a parking spot directly outside his house. As he walked up the front steps, he thought he heard a noise. A cat raced past, startling him.

Tomorrow he'd have a monster hangover.

The porch light was out. Had to get that fixed.

Unsteadily, he put his key in the lock, deciding that he'd wake Beth and tell her how much he loved her.

As he walked inside, something or someone fell on top of him, taking him completely by surprise.

He was on the ground, his mind fuddled, reaction slow.
Then he heard it. One single gunshot.
And everything turned to black.

Chapter Thirty-two

Tuesday, 10 July 2001

'Stick together. Don't panic,' Cole said, grim-faced. 'Everyone, remember to keep your head down.'

The hostages making the break with the robbers were gathered by the back exit of the restaurant, cloths over their heads and down past their waists. The gunman had made the men remove their ties in the restaurant, then he'd tied the hostages together, making it impossible for any of them to break loose. They were sweating and nervous as he began herding them into place round him and his two cohorts, making sure they'd be surrounded and couldn't be picked off by sharp-shooters.

'You're drivin',' he instructed Cole. 'Everyone else in the back.'

'Where we heading?' Cole asked.

'You'll find out.'

Madison wished that Natalie didn't have to go with them. She'd feel much more secure if they could've left Natalie at the restaurant with the others.

'When I say move – do it!' the ringleader said. 'Any of you mothafuckers get outta line, I got a bullet waitin'.'

Madison prayed that the police would not attempt to do anything foolish. She also hoped they'd sent a big enough van. What kind of a joke would it be if they couldn't all fit inside?

As they reached the back door of the restaurant, the leader spotted bright lights shining outside.

'Tell 'em to turn those fuckin' lights off,' he yelled angrily at Cole, 'or we ain't comin' out.'

'Turn the lights off!' Cole shouted, knowing that his voice would make them think he was one of the bandits.

Nothing happened.

'Turn the lights off or we aren't coming out,' Cole shouted a second time.

A beat of three and the lights were switched off. Madison's stomach turned over. This was such a perilous situation. What if the keys weren't in the van? What if it didn't have a full tank of gas? What if the police marksmen began shooting?

Anything was possible. She remembered a robbery that had taken place in Beverly Hills a few years ago at a jewellery store on Rodeo Drive. As soon as the hostages left the store and were in the parking lot, gunfire had started. At least one of the hostages had been killed.

The unruly procession, looking like a giant moving tent, began heading down the alleyway towards the van.

In the middle of the night, Sofia awoke from a violent nightmare. She sat up, shivering and scared.

Gianni had tried to insist that she sleep in the bed and he would take the couch. She'd uttered a firm no. 'If I'm in your bed, you'll get another room as soon as I'm asleep,' she'd said accusingly, 'and that's not cool, 'cause I can't be alone tonight.'

'Very well,' Gianni had answered patiently. 'I'll take the bed and *you* will sleep on the couch.'

Now here it was, pitch black, and she was frightened. Ever since she was a little girl she'd experienced nightmares.

It probably had something to do with the fact that her mom was always out working and Vincent was never around because he was so much older than she and was busy doing his own thing – which meant that most of the time she was left alone with different babysitters. She'd never liked any of them: they were always mean and nasty. There was one who had been particularly nasty, but she didn't care to go there.

She got off the couch, clad in a big white T-shirt Gianni had loaned her. Then, tripping over a foot stool, she made her way into the bedroom.

Gianni was asleep in bed, a book propped in front of him, his reading glasses half-way down his nose.

She removed the book and glasses. He didn't stir. Next she turned off the bedside light and crawled into bed beside him.

Sometimes she was overcome with loneliness. It was as if there were nobody in the world who cared about her. And yet, in spite of their differences, she knew her mom cared, and Michael – in his own way. And big brother Vincent, who'd always been very protective of her. When she'd started dating as a teenager, he'd practically killed one of the boys she was seeing.

'You're thirteen, too young to date,' he'd warned her.

'I'm not too young to do anything,' she'd answered back, realizing it was impossible to lead a normal life with an overbearing brother like Vincent watching her every move.

Actually, she'd always fancied Vincent's best friend, Nando. Sad to say, Nando had never so much as glanced in her direction: she was far too young for him to bother with.

She edged closer to Gianni. He wouldn't notice if she cuddled up to him, would he?

And that's exactly what she did. She cuddled up to a man she'd known only a couple of hours, spooned into his back, and fell into a deep sleep.

*

Jolie had a special song that always put Nando in the right mood, a combination of soul with just a touch of rap: it was Usher's 'Good Ol' Ghetto'. The beat was perfect – slow and funky. And Usher's raspy sexy voice put *her* in the right mood for fun.

She went to her closet and took out the appropriate items of clothing – a skimpy pink bandeau top and short black rubber skirt. Under the clothes she wore a crotchless thong, a front-fastening nippleless bra, and thigh-high lace stockings. Shiny leather boots and a gold coin on a chain round her neck completed the look.

Living in a city jammed with strip clubs, lapdancers, naked women, and lavish nude shows, Jolie had come up with the perfect answer to keep her man happy at home, or at least try to – because Nando was hardly the faithful type.

She shook out her long raven hair, spritzed Angel from head to toe, switched on the Bose CD player, and entered the bedroom.

Nando was lying on the bed, hands behind his head, an anticipatory grin on his face.

Attitude. She had it down as she swayed towards him, undulating her hips to the throbbing beat, running her hands up and down her thighs, thrusting her pelvis at him.

'Oh, *babee*!' he crooned. 'Take . . . it . . . *off*.'

Slowly, in time to the music, she began peeling down her top. Then, leaning over him, she encouraged him to unfasten her bra. Her breasts tumbled out.

'Nice titties,' he said, leering, as if it was the first time he'd seen them.

They'd been married three years. The sex still sizzled.

She grazed his mouth with her nipples, then pulled up her rubber skirt and straddled him.

He was still fully dressed, so she dry-humped him in true lap-dancer style.

He enjoyed every minute, especially when she unzipped his fly and gave him a memorable hand-job. What a wife! She understood everything. She especially understood that sometimes a man liked to feel as if he were fourteen again.

When they were finished, he reached into his bedside drawer and handed her a thousand bucks.

She took it.

'Cheap at the price,' he said, still grinning.

'I know,' she said, with a secret smile. 'I'm thinking of raising my rates.'

'Get dressed, we're goin' out,' he said.

'Where?'

'I'm takin' you to meet my future partners.'

'What about Vincent?'

'Fuck him.'

'Surprise,' Michael said, greeting his son at the door.

'Jesus Christ!' Vincent exclaimed. 'Where did *you* come from?'

'Nice greeting.'

'Why didn't you tell me you were coming?'

'Complicated story.'

'Where's Mom?'

Dani emerged from the bedroom. She'd put on a pale blue shirt, sleek black pants, and secured her long blonde hair on top of her head.

Vincent was always struck by his mother's incandescent beauty. Time had not dimmed her glow.

He often thought what a fool Michael was not to have married her. Whenever he asked *why* they hadn't got married, they both came up with the same evasive answers.

It was stupid, because it was so blatantly obvious they belonged together. Dani, who was usually so on top of everything, turned to mush round Michael. And *he* treated *her* as if they'd been married for years.

'Something not so good has happened,' Michael said, clearing his throat.

'What?' Vincent asked, immediately thinking it must be something to do with Sofia.

'It's a tough one.'

'So tell me what it is.'

'Your father is being accused of killing Stella and her boyfriend,' Dani blurted out.

'Come *on*,' Vincent said disbelievingly.

'There's a warrant out for my arrest,' Michael said. 'It probably won't be long before they come sniffing round here.'

'Jesus Christ!' Vincent repeated. As if this evening hadn't been bad enough, he now had to hear that his father was on the run from a murder charge.

'I didn't do it, in case you're wondering,' Michael said. 'It's a set-up.'

'Who set you up?'

'I have enemies – long-time enemies. Grudges that go way back.'

'This is insane.'

'I know.'

'So what am *I* supposed to do?'

'Look after your mother. Contact Madison and Sofia. I think they should both come here for a while.'

'To do what?'

'Be protected,' Michael said. 'You can arrange that, can't you?'

'Yes. Only I should point out that I have no idea where either of them is.'

'Madison's in New York,' Michael said, reaching for the phone. 'I'll call her now.'

'You think she'll fly out here?'

'If I tell her it's important, she'll come.'

'How about Sofia?'

'Find her. If *you* don't, somebody else might. And, Vincent, believe me, that could be deadly.'

When Jenna heard the front door slam and realized that Vincent had gone out, she couldn't believe it. How dare he nag and scream at her, then leave her alone in the apartment? She was livid.

She came out of the bedroom and took a good look round. He was definitely gone.

Quick as a flash, she ran to the phone. 'Andy Dale's suite,' she said to the operator.

'One moment, please,' the operator replied.

Anais answered the phone – or, at least, it sounded like her.

'Is Andy still round? This is Jenna Castle.'

'Hey, baby,' Anais said, sounding real friendly, 'we're packin' up an' blowin' this dump. You wanna talk to the man?'

'Yes, please.'

'Sure, babe. You gonna party with us later?'

'Maybe,' Jenna said, hopefully.

Andy got on the phone. He did not sound happy. 'I'm sick of your freakin' husband chasin' me everywhere I go,' he complained.

'I called to apologize,' Jenna said. 'Vincent gets into silly moods sometimes. It's not as if anything was going on between you and me.'

'It's not like I don't *want* something to go on between us,' Andy said, warming up.

'Really?'

'Didn't you feel the vibe?'

'Yes . . . I did,' she said excitedly. 'Where are you going now?'

'I got a suite at the Bellagio. Wanna join us? We're ready to party, only *don't* bring your old man. An' *don't* tell the asshole where you're going, okay? 'Cause I'm not into another confrontation.'

She took a long, deep breath. Andy Dale was a huge movie star, and this was her big opportunity. Was she supposed to pass it up simply because Vincent was jealous?

No way.

'I'll be right there,' she said.

'You got it, foxy.'

The procession made its way down the darkened alleyway towards the big black van parked there. Madison realized that this was probably the most dangerous time of all.

Once they reached it, she was relieved to see that it was probably large enough. Hopefully it had a tracking device in it.

A voice boomed out of a nearby loudspeaker. 'Whyn't you give it up now? Let the hostages go, drop your weapons and surrender.'

The ringleader nudged Madison in the ribs with his gun. She could smell his sweat and fear. He might act tough, but she knew he was nervous. 'Keep moving,' he muttered.

She did as she was told, along with everybody else, wondering if they'd encounter a roadblock when they drove out of the alley.

Roughly he shoved her into the van. The rest of them squeezed in too.

Cole got behind the wheel, the main gunman crowded up next to him, while Madison sat on his other side. Everyone else was crammed into the back.

It occurred to her that if the cops started shooting, she and Cole were prime targets. Cole especially, because he was in the driver's seat.

Cole started the engine. The gunman leaned forward, checking to make sure the gas tank was full. 'Let's fuckin' go,' he yelled. 'Move it!'

'Where?' Cole asked.

'Turn on to Beverly an' floor this mothafucker.'

'Yes,' Cole said, doing as he was told. And they roared off.

Silently Madison began reciting a prayer, knowing that within minutes there was a strong possibility that they could all be dead.

Chapter Thirty-three

Michael: 1974

It was Madison's third birthday. She sat with a dozen other toddlers in the garden of Tina and Max's new house, which was now her home, and watched in fascination as a funny man, dressed like a clown, blew up different coloured balloons and twisted them into animal shapes. Susie, Tina and Max's daughter, sprawled on the grass next to her. At seven, Susie was a cute little girl, with two missing front teeth and a sweet smile. Harry, her eight-year-old brother, was not so nice. His favourite occupation was pulling Susie's hair, destroying her dolls, and teasing her until she screamed.

Tina was constantly nagging at him to behave himself.

Max was constantly telling Tina to shut up. 'He's a boy,' he said. 'That's what boys do.'

'Not this boy,' Tina retorted.

Michael arrived late and stood at the kitchen door, watching his daughter. She was such a little beauty. So full of life, so like Beth. Thank God for Max and Tina. They'd been there when he'd needed them – they were true friends, always behind him. Unlike Catherine, who'd accused him of murdering her sister.

The last two years had been a living nightmare. Coming

home that night drunk, getting hit on the head, and then, when he regained consciousness, he'd been holding a gun – *his* gun. And the police were standing over him.

Beth was dead, shot in the back of her head. Madison was asleep in her crib, the press were outside the house, and he was read his rights and arrested for Beth's murder.

It wasn't true. He hadn't done it. Once more, he'd been set up, and once more he'd had to struggle to prove his innocence.

This time Vito Giovanni supported him, hiring the best criminal defence attorney and paying for everything.

Vito was a wise man. He knew Mamie was in some way responsible, and because he was genuinely fond of Michael, he'd felt a sense of guilt.

Mamie denied she'd had anything to do with it. Not that Michael had had a confrontation with her, but Vito had, and she'd sworn she was not involved.

They both knew she was lying.

'My lawyers will get you off,' Vito had promised. And they did.

He'd still had to go through the media blitz. The press anointed him Vito Giovanni's blue-eyed boy. Except that he didn't have blue eyes, and he wasn't anybody's boy. So, not only did he have to bear the grief of Beth's death, he'd also had to endure the constant exposure that the press decided to bestow upon him.

The day he was arrested was a slow news day, and his extreme good looks put him right on the front pages.

The headlines were lurid and without merit.

PRETTY BOY KILLER
THE MAN WITH THE GOLDEN SMILE

Fame, even if it was only transient, was horrifying. Women began to write him – thousands of letters, sending pictures of themselves in scanty outfits – claiming they wanted to marry him, have his children, save him. There were a lot of nuts out there.

He endured it – what else could he do? He had no choice.

After spending several months in jail there was a trial, and eventually he was acquitted.

He'd never forget Catherine's face the day she stood in the witness box claiming he'd told her that if Beth so much as looked at another man he'd kill her.

Sure he'd said it, he'd been angry that day. But he hadn't meant it. And Catherine knew that.

Other witnesses came forward. People he didn't know, people who'd attended the fashion institute with Beth. Many claimed she'd often said that the man she lived with was insanely jealous. He could just imagine Beth saying that – it was her way of getting attention. She'd always got off on creating havoc.

His lawyer destroyed the witnesses one by one.

Tina and Max took Madison in, treating her as if she were one of their own children. He'd never forget their kindness.

After Beth's death, Catherine had attempted to gain custody of Madison. She had not succeeded.

He had no idea where Catherine was now. He hated her. She actually believed he'd killed Beth – the love of his life. It was unthinkable she could believe such a thing.

Sometimes, when he relived that night, the horror was too much to bear. And the sadness . . .

Now time had passed since he was acquitted, and he wanted his daughter back.

'She's better off staying with us,' Tina informed him.

'No, she's not,' he argued. 'She should be with me.'

'You live in some crummy hotel,' Tina pointed out. 'Who'll look after her?'

'I'll get an apartment, hire a nanny.'

'Is that how you want your daughter raised, by a nanny? That's not fair to Madison. She's happy round Susie and Harry.'

'I know, Tina, and I appreciate it, only I gotta claim my life back – and Madison *is* my life.'

After his acquittal he'd legally changed his name from Castellino to Castelli. He'd torn up all the letters and photos he'd received, and tried to stay out of the limelight. People had short memories: it was only a matter of time before they'd forget the notorious headlines and he could slide back into obscurity.

Bone had left town. According to Gus, he'd moved out to the west coast. He knew beyond a doubt that Bone and Mamie were responsible for Beth's murder. The two of them together had hatched some kind of diabolical plot. But why? That was the question. What had Beth done to them? Did they hate him so much that they had to murder the one woman he loved?

Vito Giovanni had counselled him. 'Look at it this way,' Vito had said. '*You* whacked Roy. Then someone did this unfortunate thing to you. Now ya gotta leave it alone – you're even.'

Even! Was Vito fucking crazy? They'd *never* be even.

'Michael,' Tina said, interrupting his thoughts, 'can you help me bring out the cake?'

'Sure,' he said.

'Can't wait for Vegas this weekend,' she said excitedly, as he followed her into the kitchen. 'It'll be so much *fun*!'

What was fun any more? He didn't know. He didn't care. He'd promised Tina and Max a weekend in Las Vegas to celebrate their wedding anniversary, and he would try to make it fun for them.

Everyone sang 'Happy Birthday' while Madison jumped up and down squealing with excitement. Harry made a futile attempt to shove her face in the cake. Susie slapped him away. Tina began yelling at them both. There were kids and toys and balloons everywhere.

'Love you, Daddy,' Madison lisped, bestowing a big, sticky kiss on his mouth. 'Love you *sooo* much!'

He picked her up and hugged her to him. 'You're my world, baby,' he said. 'You know that? You're my whole wide world.'

'I'm my daddy's whole wide world,' she repeated proudly. 'Love you, Daddy.'

'Yes, kitten,' he said, putting her down. 'Ain't *that* the truth.'

He'd never get over Beth, but at least he had his precious daughter. That was something.

Returning to Vegas with Max and Tina brought back a rush of memories. Fortunately, none was of Beth. He'd managed to compartmentalize his life, and Beth was not part of his memories of Vegas.

They'd left the children with Tina's parents, so he felt secure that Madison was in good hands.

The moment they landed, Tina was in heaven. 'Oh, my God! Oh my God!' she said, hyperventilating. 'Can we go see Elvis?'

'We'll never get tickets,' Max said, always the pessimist.

'I can arrange it,' Michael said. 'I got connections here.' He was boasting, but why the hell not? If Tina was hot to see Elvis, that's exactly what she would do.

He wondered if Manny Spiven was still round. Then, for some unknown reason, he began thinking about the blonde. What was her name? Dani. Yeah. Dani.

That was a long time ago. A one-night stand. Why was he thinking about *her*? He wondered if she was still in the chorus line at the Estradido.

No, she was probably long gone, married and living in Omaha with three kids and a fat husband.

'I want to see *everything*,' Tina enthused, as the airport cab drove them into town. 'I want to go to every hotel, every casino. I want to drive up and down the Strip. This is so exciting! You have no idea.'

Vito Giovanni had arranged for them to have their rooms comped at the Estradido Hotel. He'd got them the best, for which Michael was grateful. It helped that he'd recommended a market buy to Vito – a stock that had doubled over a three-week period.

'Where'd you learn about this shit?' Vito had asked.

He'd shrugged. 'Just lucky, I guess.'

'I want you t'do more for me.'

'Fine with me.'

Karl Edgington's picks were always right on the money, and over the last few years he'd been making himself a small fortune. He didn't have to work for anyone any more, he was his own boss – with the help of Karl who, according to Warner Carlysle, was due to be released any day now.

'There's a Jacuzzi in the living room,' Tina giggled to Michael, when they all met downstairs for a drink after checking into the hotel. 'Can you *believe* it?' she said, wide-eyed. 'In the *living* room. Max is the happiest man around!'

'I am?' Max said, sounding surprised.

'Yes,' Tina said, ''cause you can take a bath *and* watch TV at the same time.'

'Maybe I'll take a bath with you,' Max said slyly.

'Don't be disgusting,' she snapped.

'Did you notice the mirrors on the ceiling above the bed?' Max asked, giving Michael a quick nudge.

'Guess I missed that.'

'Take a look. Sexy, if you ask me.'

It seemed that lately Max found everything sexy. He was definitely experiencing the married-man itch.

'Tomorrow I'll score tickets for Elvis,' Michael said.

'If you take me to see Elvis, I'll love you forever!' Tina swooned.

'How about *me*?' Max asked.

'Oh, *you*. You're my husband, I'll always love *you*.'

'Tonight I thought we'd have dinner at the hotel,' Michael decided. 'We can see the show, then take a look around.'

'I don't want to have dinner *here*,' Tina said petulantly. 'Can't we go to the Sands, or the Desert Inn, or the Magiriano? My girlfriend stayed at the Magiriano, and *she* says it's the best. Apparently there's an amazing show.'

'Whatever you want. I'll arrange it.'

Tina nodded enthusiastically.

'Two nights in Vegas an' you'll be screamin' to go home,' Michael said, laughing at Tina's genuine excitement.

'As long as I get to hit the tables,' Max said.

'You'd better remember what happened last time,' Michael reminded him.

'That was a long time ago,' Max said cockily. 'I know what I'm doin' now.'

'He's got a hundred dollars to play with, and that's *it*,' Tina said, in true wifely fashion.

'Yes, honey,' Max said, the five hundred dollars he'd managed to smuggle from home itching to leave his pocket.

Before they went upstairs, Tina decided she should play the slots. She hit a lucky streak, and after forty-five minutes and two jackpots, she came away with fifteen hundred dollars.

'Oh . . . my . . . *God*!' she exclaimed. 'This is the most fabulous place on earth! I wish we could come here every weekend.'

'Well, we can't,' Max said, surly because he'd already blown a hundred. 'Lend me some of your money – *I* wanna play.'

'No, it's mine. You go play with your hundred dollars.'

'Selfish,' he muttered.

'I'm *not*,' she countered. 'I won it, and I'm spending it on the kids.'

'Yeah, that's right – spoil 'em.'

'You two gonna fight?' Michael said. 'I thought we came here to relax.'

'We *did*,' Tina said, shooting Max a baleful look.

'Okay,' Michael said. 'So I'll make reservations for dinner and the show at the Magiriano. We should leave here in an hour. Maybe you wanna go upstairs an' shower.'

'Why?' Max joked. 'Do I smell?'

'Get *outta* here,' Michael responded.

Tina and Max took the elevator to their room, still arguing, while Michael made his way to the main show room. There was nobody round, so he went backstage. A stage manager informed him the girls hadn't checked in yet.

'I was, uh . . . looking for Dani. Is she still working here?'

'We don't have a Dani,' the stage manager said.

'How about Angela?'

'We got two Angelas.'

'What time do they usually come in?'

'You a relative?'

'Yes.'

'The girls are here by five.'

'Thanks,' he said, hoping that one of the Angelas could fill him in on Dani.

Why was he looking for her anyway?

No reason. Anything to pass the time.

Angela was not the Angela he'd had in mind. Nor was the second Angela – a faded brunette who tried to persuade him to come back after the show, promising she'd show him the sights.

'Sorry,' he said.

'So am I!' she said, with a jaunty wink.

Is that all women saw, his good looks? When he was younger and hoping to get laid every five minutes it had worked for him. Now, at almost thirty, with everything he'd experienced, one-night stands were a thing of the past. He craved love and companionship, a woman who excited him and kept him alert. A woman like Beth.

Only problem, women like Beth did not exist.

When Tina arrived downstairs she was all dressed up for her big night out in Vegas. Short black cocktail dress, three-inch heels, rhinestone jewellery and teased hair.

'How about my wife?' Max boasted. 'Ain't she somethin'?'

'She sure is,' Michael agreed.

'And *I* am escorted by the two handsomest men in Vegas,' Tina said, preening as they made their way through the casino to the front of the hotel where they took a cab to the Magiriano.

Tina loved the Magiriano. She stopped to admire the dancing fountains and the caged cockatoos, while Max tried to sit down at one of the blackjack tables on their way through the casino to the Krystle Room.

'No!' said Tina, dragging him off his seat. '*After* the show, not before.'

Michael palmed a twenty to the *maître d'* so they would be assured a front table.

'I'm so happy!' Tina squealed. 'This is my dream!'

Michael nodded. It was nice that someone still had dreams.

Chapter Thirty-four

Dani: 1974

'Goddamn it!' the young girl screamed. 'Some moron stepped on my fuckin' train!'

The girl was nineteen years old, six feet tall and spectacular. Her name was Penelope and she had a mouth on her. She was Gemini's replacement and worked next to Dani. The only problem was, nobody could replace Gemini.

Dani had been back at work for a year. She needed to keep herself occupied, and nothing did that better than two shows a night at the Magiriano, where she was considered a veteran.

Twenty-six and a veteran. That was Vegas for you. No history.

'Calm down, dear,' said Eric, the assistant stage manager. He was a sweet gay guy, who always looked out for Dani. 'You're upsetting everyone with your uncouth language.'

'Uncouth?' exclaimed Penelope. 'Listen to you, faggo, you must've heard four-letter words before.'

Penelope was a total pain. Engaged to a young Mafioso type, she thought everyone should kiss her fine nineteen-year-old ass.

Dani had tried to keep the feelings between them neutral. It simply wasn't possible. She missed Gemini. She thought about her every day. The night before her wedding, Gemini had indeed gone to see Moralis. Why she'd done so in view of their history together, nobody could quite figure out. She'd gone to his hotel room, where he'd been his usual violent self, locking her in the room, attacking her, raping her and, finally, in a fit of fury, throwing acid in her face. After that terrible act, he'd kept her a prisoner in the room for three days in excruciating pain, until eventually a maid became suspicious and called the police.

By the time the police got there, it was too late. Gemini died on her way to the hospital.

Morgan was a broken man. He blamed Dani for allowing Gemini to leave the ranch that night, even though it was clearly not her fault.

Moralis was arrested and locked in a cell overnight. Somehow or other he managed to hang himself.

Over the following months Dean attempted to comfort Dani. It was no good, she was inconsolable. 'I can't marry you, Dean,' she'd finally told him. 'I bring people bad luck. First Emily. Now Gemini. I cannot do it to you.'

He stayed by her side for a long time, trying desperately to persuade her to change her mind. It was no good, she was adamant. Eventually she told him she couldn't see him any more, and he returned to Houston. Three months later she heard he'd married someone else.

She didn't care. Relationships were not for her. Not even friendships. So Penelope behaving like a complete diva did not bother her.

Occasionally Dean phoned, even though he was now a married man. 'How are you doing?' he would ask.

'Fine,' she would answer.

'We'll always be friends, won't we, Dani?'

'As long as your wife doesn't mind.'

She was glad Dean had found somebody who seemed to be good for him – a nice Southern girl with money of her own.

A few days after Moralis killed himself, his millionaire father, Esai, had flown in from Colombia to collect his grandson and take him home. Dani tried to persuade him to allow Nando to stay in Vegas. 'Mr Sanchez,' she'd pleaded, 'Nando is better off staying with us. He doesn't *know* you. My son loves him like a brother – he'll be very happy living here.'

'I think not,' Esai had said, cold as ice. And that was his final answer.

Nando leaving town upset Vincent deeply. He missed his best friend, and although he was only nine years old, he chose to be a loner, refusing to make any more close friends. He excelled at school, getting As in most of his classes. He also shone at sports. Dani and he were as close as a mother and son could be. The two of them went to movies, rode bikes, and sometimes they took a boat out on Lake Mead, while other times they drove into the desert and spent the day exploring.

'Will ya look at my fuckin' train,' Penelope screamed again. 'It's ruined!'

'It's not ruined, dear,' Eric said, fussing with her elaborate train. 'It's perfectly fine. You'll go onstage and do a *fantastic* show.'

'Screw off, you little faggot,' she said rudely.

'Don't talk to Eric like that,' Dani intervened.

'Are *you* telling *me* how to behave?' Penelope demanded, giving her an imperious look.

Dani shrugged. 'Somebody should.'

'Who the *hell* do you think you are?' Penelope ranted. 'My boyfriend could *buy* this hotel if he wanted to. Then I'd have *your* ass fired.'

'Go ahead,' Dani said. 'I don't care.'

'Stuck-up *bitch*!' Penelope spat.

'*She*'s the bitch,' Eric whispered in Dani's ear.

Sometimes on stage Penelope attempted to sabotage her. It was all very subtle, but Dani knew exactly what Penelope was doing. After getting tripped up several times, she decided to play Penelope at her own game. One night she flung out her arm and knocked Penelope's headdress flying. The following night she did the same thing. The sabotage soon stopped.

Penelope received plenty of attention. Men loved her, but not as much as they loved Dani. She had a very loyal fan following, especially when the conventions came to town – the same groups of men returning twice or three times a year, and always coming to see her in the show.

Shortly after she had returned to work, the company director had called her into his office and said, 'Dani, the time has come for you to go topless.'

'You know I won't do that,' she'd answered.

'It'll be very tasteful,' he'd assured her. 'You'll wear the same lavish costumes, make the same extravagant entrances, except you'll show your breasts. Is that such a terrible way to make twice your salary?'

'I– I don't know,' she'd said hesitantly.

'What've you got to lose, my dear? You're famous as it is in Vegas. You're one of the most beautiful showgirls in town. So cash in and make the big bucks while you can.'

'Isn't it kind of sleazy?'

'Not any more. All the big hotels are taking their best girls topless. We're an expensive, classy show. We have to keep up with the competition.'

'I'll think about it,' she'd sighed.

She'd thought about it for a couple of weeks, and then decided she had nothing to lose. The costumes were expensive and gorgeous, and she knew they'd present her in a stylish way. Plus, there was no man around to get upset and jealous and, as the company manager assured her, the nudity would be brief and tasteful.

The lure of making twice her salary finally convinced her. She was putting away everything she earned for Vincent's education, and the extra money would be an enormous help. Being a single mother was not easy, so . . . if showing her breasts would double her savings, why not?

When she informed the company manager her answer was yes, he was delighted. 'You're gonna kill 'em, Dani,' he'd said. 'They'll be flocking to see you.'

And that was the truth.

Her loyal fans were also delighted, they even started an official fan club.

She enjoyed her two separate lives. Life one: mother of Vincent, going to PTA meetings, swim meets, and little-league baseball, no makeup, no fancy clothes, just another mom who baked cookies on open school day. Life two: Dani Castle, famous showgirl, glamorous, gorgeous, a lurer of men, all of whom she rejected.

Which life did she prefer? There was no choice, she'd choose being Vincent's mom any day. If it wasn't for the money, she'd give up all the glamour in a second.

Earlier that night, between shows, a man had appeared in the dressing room she shared with Penelope, and handed her his card. He was a representative of *Playpen* – a glossy magazine for men. 'I've heard plenty about you,' he'd said, 'and we'd love to photograph you for the magazine.'

'I'm not interested.'

'You should be. We pay a lot of money, and only deal with the top photographers. You show it on stage, why not show it in our magazine?'

She'd taken his card and said she'd think about it. Her standard answer.

Perhaps that was why Penelope was in such a bad mood, because he had not approached *her*.

Eric was fussing around, trying to fix Penelope's train. 'For God's *sake*!' Penelope kept on complaining. 'You're as clumsy as a hog!'

Their intro music started, and Eric backed away thankfully. 'Heads up, tits out, have a good show,' he said.

'Not if *you* have anything to do with it,' Penelope sniped, grabbing a handful of ice to liven up her nipples.

And so they made their entrance to the strains of 'The Most Beautiful Girl in the World'.

Chapter Thirty-five

Michael and Dani: 1974

Michael ordered a bottle of champagne. He had every intention of making this trip special for Tina and Max since they'd done so much for him. Earlier he'd slipped the bell captain at the Estradido a hundred bucks to get them tickets for Elvis the following night. 'Do it, an' there's more where that came from,' he'd promised.

A female photographer stopped by their table.

'Yes, please!' Tina exclaimed, posing between her two men, big smile firmly in place.

After an excellent dinner of steak, lobster and chocolate soufflé, the show started. First a line of gorgeous dancing girls. Then an extremely clever magic act, followed by a group of astounding Chinese acrobats, who made the audience gasp in amazement.

Michael's eyes scanned the chorus line – just in case. Max was practically frothing at the mouth, while Tina was guzzling champagne like it was going out of style.

And then came the showgirls, parading to the strains of 'The Most Beautiful Girl in the World'. Six tall, statuesque, topless beauties, clad in satin and lace, with flowing marabou-trimmed chiffon trains and *faux*-diamond tiaras.

In high heels they were all six feet tall, moving with stately grace as they glided down the magnificent double staircase and struck a pose.

Max let out a low, appreciative whistle. Tina elbowed him in the ribs.

Michael was transfixed. The girl on the left was Dani. The girl from his past. The one-night stand he'd never forgotten. She was a little older, probably a whole lot wiser, and breathtakingly radiant.

For the first time since Beth's murder he felt something – an attraction that was undeniable. It must be almost ten years since they were together – she'd probably forgotten all about him, or wouldn't speak to him. Maybe she was engaged. Or married.

He had to find out.

As soon as the show was over, he was on his feet.

'What's your rush?' Tina asked. 'Let's finish the champagne. We can't waste it.'

'Gotta go see an old friend,' he said. 'I'll meet you in the casino.'

'What old friend?' Max wanted to know.

'Where in the casino?' Tina asked.

'Don't worry about it, I'll find you.'

'Michael—'

He didn't hear her. He was already on his way backstage.

A strange thing had happened to Dani while she was onstage. She thought she saw Michael Castellino.

Standing in position, attempting to stay as still as possible, she checked out the audience, and tonight there was a man at one of the front tables who looked remarkably like him. She couldn't see that well, what with the stage lights and all, but still . . .

No. It couldn't be. Too much time had passed, and she

didn't want him coming back into her life, finding out about Vincent and trying to stake a claim.

She looked away, hoping that would make him vanish. But when she glanced back a few minutes later, he was still there.

Only it wasn't him. The bright lights were playing tricks with her vision. She paraded round the stage, head held high, moving like a queen.

When she got off the stage and returned to the dressing room, she was furious to find Joey, Penelope's boyfriend, lounging on the couch. She'd informed Penelope on countless occasions that she didn't want him in there. Being topless on stage was one thing, but returning to her dressing room and having Joey ogling her at close quarters was unacceptable.

'Like he'd want to look at *you* when he's got *me*,' Penelope had argued. 'Get a fuckin' *life*!'

Dani realized she would have to take it up with the company manager. Enough was enough.

'How ya doin', doll?' Joey said, jumping up and leering at her. He was all greasy black hair and pointed white teeth.

'Not so good,' she answered crisply. 'Do you mind waiting outside while I change?'

'You don't got nothin' I ain't seen a thousand times,' Joey said, eyes fixed on her nipples.

'I'd appreciate some privacy.'

'Don't be like that, doll,' he said, edging closer. 'Where's my Penny?'

'On her way, so take your dirty little eyes off me,' she said, grabbing a towel to cover herself.

'Jeez! It wasn't like I was gonna *touch* 'em,' he said indignantly.

'Out!' she yelled, suddenly losing it.

He slouched to the door and stepped into the hall. She quickly slammed and locked the door behind him.

Soon Penelope was hammering and shouting outside.

Dani took her time removing her heavy stage makeup and changing into her street clothes. When she was finally ready, she unlocked the door and a furious Penelope burst in.

'What the fuck—' Penelope began, quivering with fury.

Ignoring her, Dani headed for the stage door.

'*Bitch!*' Penelope yelled after her.

On her way out Dani grabbed Eric. 'Either she goes into another dressing room or *I* do,' she said. 'Call me when it's done or I'm not coming back.'

It felt good to assert herself, and why not? She had a fan club and magazines chasing her to take her photo. It was about time she started enjoying her success.

She walked outside.

Standing there, smoking a cigarette, was Michael Castellino.

'Where did Michael go?' Tina asked, as they trooped out of the Krystle Room along with the rest of the audience.

'Dunno,' Max replied, more interested in hitting the blackjack tables than anything else.

'Should we wait here?'

'No, Tina. He said *he*'ll find *us*.'

'So what shall we do?'

'Dunno what *you're* doin', but I'm hittin' the tables.'

'Then I'll play the slots.'

'Have fun.'

'Don't lose your money.'

'I *never* lose.'

And happily they went their separate ways.

She didn't back away. She didn't run, although she wanted to.

Michael Castellino was standing there as casual as if

328

they'd seen each other the day before.

'Hey,' he said, flicking his cigarette to the ground. 'Remember me?'

Remember him. She'd never got him out of her mind. And now, almost ten years later, he was back.

'I'm sorry . . .' she said, faking it.

'Michael,' he said, stepping closer. 'Michael Castelli.'

'Castellino,' she corrected. And she could have kicked herself for coming out with his name.

'So you *do* remember,' he said. 'That's nice. Oh, and by the way, I changed my name to Castelli.'

'What are you doing here?' she asked, keeping her tone cool and impersonal.

'Right now I'm wondering if I can buy you a drink.'

'I don't think so.'

'You don't think so,' he said, giving her a quizzical look. 'Hey, that's better than a flat no. At least I got a fifty–fifty chance.'

They stood there. Two strangers who'd conceived a child together. And yet *he* didn't know. He had no idea he was the father of an amazing nine-year-old boy.

Don't just stand here, get moving, her inner voice urged.

She couldn't move. Her legs wouldn't allow her to.

'I guess this is kinda awkward,' he said. 'We spent one great night together, then you never heard from me.'

'That about sums it up,' she said coolly.

'Believe me,' he continued. 'there were circumstances, things that prevented me coming back.'

She was silent, refusing to help him out.

'Uh . . . are you married or something?' he asked, feeling awkward – a new sensation for him.

'Divorced,' she answered quietly. 'And you?'

'No. Never did get married.'

'I see.'

'You look great.'

So do you, she wanted to say, but she didn't. He was *so* damned handsome.

'One drink, Dani. How about it?'

'I don't drink.'

'I'll buy you a milkshake.'

Damn! He was attractive. What harm was there in having a drink with him? He was just another man, and she knew exactly how to deal with men.

'Fine,' she murmured, giving in. 'One milkshake. Chocolate. And then I have to get home.'

An hour later they were on the bed in his hotel room at the Estradido, making wild passionate love.

She had *never* felt this way before. *Never*. Sex was something other people did. Not her. She wasn't interested.

Yet here she was – with Michael. And it was as if the world had stopped and he was the only person who mattered.

His touch made her moan and shiver with pleasure. The way his body felt up against hers. His lips, so insistent, covering every inch of her flesh.

She was transported to another time, another place. She was truly happy.

For the first time since Beth's tragic murder, Michael could feel the pain lifting away. There was something about Dani, something warm and nurturing. Suddenly he felt at peace. It seemed that being in her arms was the right place to be.

The sex was incredible, too. It wasn't as if he was scoring, more like connecting. He knew she felt the same way. She had to.

Afterwards they lay on the bed, side by side, silent, peaceful and content.

'Wow!' he said at last. 'That was something.'

'Yes, it was,' she agreed.

'You were . . . *are* . . . sensational.'

'Isn't it about time you got dressed and left?' she said, deciding she couldn't allow this to go any further.

'Huh?'

'Y'know, repeat performance. See you again in ten years.'

'Ouch!' he said, sitting up. 'I explained to you where I was. Didn't think you'd appreciate the "Dear Dani, I'm in jail" letter.'

'I might've appreciated *something*.'

'Yeah,' he said, reaching for a cigarette. 'I know.' A long beat. 'Hey – it wasn't as if I didn't *think* about you.'

'That's comforting.'

'Dani,' he said seriously, 'we were both kids then.'

'Yes,' she said. 'I was only sixteen.'

'*What?*'

A slight smile. 'Didn't want to scare you.'

'Jeez!' he said, shaking his head. 'I coulda bin *arrested*.'

'You were,' she said drily.

'Yeah, but not for sleepin' with a juvenile.'

She reached over and touched his face. The same nose, eyes, lips as her little Vincent. My God, if he ever saw him he'd know at once. She had to make sure that never happened.

'You were pretty spectacular onstage tonight,' he said admiringly. 'I got such a kick when you walked out.'

'You did?'

'Yeah. I'd been over at the Estradido lookin' for you. Then I figured you'd got married an' were long gone. You can imagine my surprise when you appeared on stage.' He stared at her intently. 'It's like fate, huh?'

'Kind of,' she said hesitantly.

'Yeah,' he said, nodding to himself. 'It was meant to be.' He smiled at her. 'Dani Castle. That's quite a name. I was reading about you in the programme.'

'You got a programme?'

'I picked one up on the way out. Where did you come up with Castle?'

'Saw it in a magazine and it seemed like a good name.'

'Dani Castle,' he repeated.

'Michael,' she said, throwing all inhibitions aside. 'I do believe you're talking too much.'

He grinned. 'I am, huh?'

'Yes – you am,' she said softly, running her fingers lightly across his stomach.

'Well . . .' he said, touching her breasts. 'In that case . . .'

The second time was even better. Dani tried to figure out what it was. With Sam the sex had been a disaster. And with Dean, even though he'd tried to be a caring lover, she'd lain there like a log, completely unaffected by his ministrations.

How come Michael was the only man capable of lighting her fire?

She didn't know, she didn't care. She simply surrendered to the moment.

Tina successfully managed to lose all her earlier winnings in the space of two hours. When she looked at her watch she was shocked to discover how much time had passed. Where the hell was her husband? She'd been so caught up playing the slots that she hadn't noticed he was missing. And why hadn't Michael come looking for them?

She got up and began searching the casino for Max, finally tracking him down at one of the blackjack tables, where he was winning. This was a reversal of fortunes – one moment she'd been up, and he was down. Now it was his turn.

'Honey,' she said, coming up behind him. 'You're winning!'

'Sure am,' he said excitedly. 'Don't stand too close – you might change my luck.'

'Thanks a *lot*,' she said indignantly, taking a step back.

'Ssh . . . I gotta concentrate.'

'Can I have some money to play with?'

'No,' he said, protecting his stack of chips with both hands.

'What do you mean, *no*?'

'You said no to me, so why should I give *you* money?'

'You're so selfish,' she argued. 'I was planning on spending *my* money on the children.'

'Then go do it.'

'I can't.'

'Why?'

'I lost it all.'

'Jeez!' Max said. 'Here's a hundred. Go lose that.'

'Oh, Mr *Generous*,' she said sarcastically. 'How much are you up anyway?'

'I dunno. Go away.'

'Where's Michael?'

'Around somewhere.'

'Okay, I'll take this hundred and win all my money back.'

'Sure, baby, that's the spirit.'

Hmm, she thought. *Max at the tables is a different man. Assertive, sexy, in charge. I like it!* She'd win her money back, then drag him upstairs. They'd been married a few years now, and he wasn't as enthusiastic in the bedroom as he used to be. Maybe tonight she'd light a few sparks.

'Do *not* order Room Service,' Dani said, smiling.

Michael stretched and gave a lazy grin. 'I thought, y'know, maybe champagne, caviar.'

'*That's* a change.'

'From what?'

'Surely you remember? Last time it was ice cream and strawberries.'

He laughed. 'You can order whatever you want.'

'I can?'

'Certainly.'

'Shrimp and french fries. Ice cream and strawberries.'

'Nice,' he said, grinning.

'Tonight was nice,' she murmured. 'One nice night with you, and I'll see you again in ten years.'

'Come on, Dani.' He groaned. 'Don't keep on rubbing it in. I told you, I was locked up for five an' when I came out it seemed like too much time had passed.' He took a long beat, choosing his next words carefully. 'Then I had, uh . . . more trouble.'

'What kind of trouble?'

'You didn't happen to read about me a while ago, did you?'

'Read about *you?*'

'I was all over the papers in New York. Guess it wasn't a national story, thank God!'

'What was it about?'

'Something I was accused of that I didn't do.'

'Is that why you changed your name?' she asked curiously.

'I needed a fresh start. People knew who I was. Hey, do you mind if we don't get into it now?'

'No, I don't mind.'

'Thanks.'

'When are you going back to New York?'

'I'm supposed to leave the day after tomorrow, but I was thinking I might stay a few extra days. Would you like that?'

'I don't know, Michael,' she said unsurely. 'This is not something we should take any further because—'

'I know, I know,' he interrupted. ''Cause I'm not reliable. Right?'

'You don't have to stay over for me,' she said quietly. 'I came up here tonight by choice.'

'Are you sayin' that last time I forced you?'

'I was a virgin. I had no idea what to expect.'

'Oh, great,' he said, half joking. 'That's right, make me feel guilty.'

'That wasn't my intention.'

'Hey – remember what you told me?'

'No,' she said, remembering only too well.

'You told me you loved me. I never forgot that.'

'You see what a foolish little girl I was?' she said lightly.

'You weren't foolish, you were wonderful. You still are.'

'I'd better call home.'

'Who's waitin' up?'

'Didn't I tell you? I have a child.'

'You do?' he said, surprised. 'Boy or girl?'

'A little boy.'

'No kiddin'? I've got a daughter – she just turned three. Maybe we should get 'em together.'

'I thought you told me you never married.'

'I was living with someone. She was very young. When we've got more time I'll tell you all about it.'

'Where is she now?'

'She . . . uh . . . died.'

'I'm sorry.'

'Hey, life goes on,' he said, determined not to burden her with his pain. Besides, the love story between him and Beth was private.

'Where is your daughter?'

'She's been living with my friends Max and Tina. Now I'm planning on taking her back to live with me.'

'So you should, she's your child.'

'Madison's a great kid.'

'Madison. That's an unusual name. Does she look like you?'

'Yeah,' he said, laughing. 'Poor kid.'

'Do you have a photo?' she asked, wondering if his daughter looked anything like Vincent.

'Would I sound like a proud dad if I said yes?'

'There's nothing wrong with that.'

He got out of bed, padded across the room and picked up his wallet from the table.

She admired his body as he walked back towards her. He was lean and muscular, with broad shoulders and hard abs. He was certainly one great-looking man.

She sighed and wished this night would last for ever.

Only she knew it wouldn't. He'd leave. And that would be that.

Unless she told him.

Max was trying desperately to stay cool as he won hand after hand at the blackjack table. But staying cool was tough when all he really wanted to do was stand up and yell!

He kept on hitting twenty-one. It was unbelievable.

'Card?' the dealer asked.

He nodded.

Shit! Twenty-one again.

He could do no wrong!

'Gotta go find my friends before they blow their bankroll,' Michael said, jumping out of bed. 'Come with me, I'd like you to meet them.'

'Are you sure?'

'Wouldn't ask if I wasn't.'

They got dressed and took a cab to the Magiriano, holding hands all the way. When they got there, he was just in time to haul Max away from the blackjack table before he blew his winnings.

'Be smart,' Michael said, getting a firm grip on Max's arm. 'You gotta learn when to walk away.'

For once, Max listened.

'Say hello to Dani,' Michael said, as soon as they were a safe distance away from the blackjack table.

Max stared at the beautiful blonde holding Michael's hand. He recognized her immediately. She was the gorgeous topless babe in the show they'd just seen, the second girl from the left. How did Michael do it? Lucky bastard.

'Hi, Dani,' he said.

'Hi, Max,' she said, remembering him from his one night of lust with Angela.

'How do you two know each other?'

'Guess you've forgotten about your bachelor night,' Michael said, grinning.

Max looked blank. 'Huh?'

'Wasn't her name Angela?'

'Jeez!' Max said, eyes nervously darting round the casino. 'For God's sake, don't let Tina hear you.'

'If you hadn't been so bombed, you would've remembered that Dani was Angela's roommate. *Now* do you get it?'

'Oh, yeah, *Dani*. She's the girl you used to talk about.'

'You see?' Michael said, smiling at her. 'I used to talk about you all the time. Max thought I was nuts.'

'Why did you think that, Max?' she asked.

''Cause, uh, well, he'd talk about you, an' you weren't there. An' I kinda figured he'd get on a plane and come back to see you. Then he, uh, had other things goin' on.'

'It's all right,' Michael said. 'She knows what happened to me.'

'She does?'

'Yes, I do,' Dani said.

'She also knows I'm out of that line of business now,' Michael said. 'An', by the way, with that investment thing I got going, you should give me your four thousand bucks, I can double it for you.'

'I'd better ask Tina.'

'D'you havta get her permission to take a piss too?'

'Screw *you*.'

'Where is Tina anyway?'

'Losing *my* money on the slots.'

'We should go find her.'

The three of them went searching for Tina, and discovered her playing her last ten dollars.

'Lose it an' quit,' Michael ordered. 'Oh, an' Tina, meet Dani. We're all going for a drink.'

'Who *is* she?' Tina hissed at Max, not thrilled that their cosy threesome was now a foursome.

'She was in the show,' Max whispered back. 'Mike knows her from years ago.'

They were sitting in one of the lounges drinking champagne to celebrate Max's four-thousand-dollar win. He was flushed with success, but Tina was livid: not only had she lost all *her* money, she'd also lost the hundred dollars Max had given her to play with.

Besides, she was feeling disconcerted. *She* was usually the prettiest girl in any group. Now this tall, beautiful blonde had joined them, and everyone was looking *her* way. This did not thrill Tina.

'I don't like her,' she whispered to Max.

'I don't think Michael cares,' Max retaliated.

'What do you mean by *that*?'

'He's fucking *her*, not *you*.'

'God! You are *so* vulgar. What makes you think he's sleeping with her?'

'Take a look at the two of 'em.'

'I should think he'd have more respect for Beth's memory.'

'Beth's been gone for almost two years. A man has to get it on.'

'Sometimes you are *so* disgusting.'

Meanwhile Dani decided she should try to get to know Michael's friends. 'What do you do?' she asked Tina.

'Me . . . I, uh . . . look after my kids,' Tina said. 'And *he*'s a lot of work,' she added, jerking her thumb at Max. 'Dumps his clothes on the floor, never does anything around the house, leaves his empty beer cans on the table . . .'

'Hold on a minute,' Max objected. 'It's *me* you're talking about. I get up every morning at dawn and go to work sellin' cars for a living.'

'Perhaps you can advise me, Max,' Dani said. 'I'm thinking of buying a new car.'

'You are? What do you drive now?'

'A Cadillac. I was considering something more sporty. My son keeps on trying to persuade me to get a Corvette.'

'Oh, you have a son?' Tina said, making an attempt to warm up.

'Yes.'

'How old is he?'

'Nine. What about your kids?'

'Susie's seven, Harry's eight – the little monster. What am I telling you for? I guess you know all about boys.'

'Actually, mine's quite studious.'

'Lucky you!'

To Michael and Max's relief the women were suddenly on mutual ground.

'I thought they weren't gonna get along,' Michael said to Max, in a low voice. 'Only now Tina's started complainin' about you, we're on Easy Street.'

'Max mentioned that you knew Michael a long time ago,' Tina said, dying to find out more. 'Where did you meet?'

'Where *did* we meet, Michael?' Dani questioned, throwing the ball to him.

'Uh . . . a mutual friend introduced us.'

'You can tell Tina the truth,' Dani said, laughing. 'I was sixteen and a virgin. Then along came your friend Michael and took advantage of me.'

Tina shot him a spiteful look. 'Oh, yes, our Michael's very fond of sixteen-year-old virgins.'

Michael returned her look with one of his own that said, 'Shut the fuck up!'

Tina got the message.

Later, at Michael's urging, Dani called her housekeeper and informed her she would not be home that night.

While Dani was on the phone, Michael warned Tina not to mention Beth or what had happened. 'I'll tell Dani in my own time,' he said. 'I can't risk frightening her off.'

'Whatever,' Tina said. 'Only I think you're making a mistake.'

'It's *my* mistake, so *I'll* make it. Okay?'

When Dani returned from making her phone call, they took off on a tour of all the big hotels, finally arriving back at the Estradido at three a.m.

'This was *so* much fun!' Tina exclaimed, as they rode up in the elevator. 'Can we do it again tomorrow?'

'Sleep – I need sleep!' Max groaned. 'Gimme a bed!'

'They're such a nice couple,' Dani said, as soon as they reached Michael's room.

'Yeah,' he agreed. 'Max is a real stand-up guy, we've been through a lot together. And Tina's a character. She nags the crap outta him, an' he gets off on it.'

Dani walked over to the window and gazed out at the spectacular view. 'Listen, Michael,' she said quietly, 'I've been thinking that you *should* go back to New York with them. If you really want anything to happen between us, then come back by yourself. That way I'll know I'm not a one-night stand.'

'You really think you're that?' he said, quite hurt.

'It's just—'

'I don't *have* to go,' he interrupted.

'*I* want you to.'

'What is this?' he said quizzically. 'A test?'

'I suppose it is.'

'Jesus, don't you trust—'

Now it was her turn to interrupt him. 'Do it my way, Michael,' she said softly. 'Please.'

'Whatever you say,' he said, putting his arms around her.

This is insane, she thought. *I'm spending the night with a man I barely know. And I'm happier than I've ever been.*

The day they left, Dani hired a limo as her treat, and rode with them to the airport. By this time she and Tina were fast friends. They'd spent the last twenty-four hours together having a fantastic time, the highlight being Elvis Presley's amazing performance at the Hilton where they'd had stage-side seats, and Tina had almost fainted with excitement.

'You gotta come visit us in New York,' Tina said. 'I can't believe you've never been there.'

'Maybe I will,' Dani said, glancing shyly at Michael.

'Yeah, she will,' Michael said. 'That's if *I* have anythin' to do with it.'

'Good,' Tina said. 'Can't wait to show you *our* town.'

At the airport, Tina and Max got out of the limousine and went on ahead into the terminal. Dani and Michael also got out and stood beside the limo. He leaned her against it, pressing his body up against hers.

'I don't know about you, but I've had the best time,' he said, stroking her hair.

'Twenty-four hours longer than last time,' she murmured.

'I'll be back in two weeks.'

'Try not to get arrested.'

'I told you,' he said, 'I'm not into that business any more.'

'Glad to hear it.'

'I was thinkin', maybe I could stay with you next time. What d'you say?'

'No, Michael, that's not possible. I told you, I have a son.'

'Yeah,' he said. 'A son you wouldn't let me meet.'

'Perhaps when you come back.'

'So what you're tellin' me is that you don't have men stay over?' he said, raising an eyebrow in disbelief.

'I don't have men, period.'

'Really?'

'I'm not that kind of a girl.'

'Star of a Vegas show with every guy in town after her, and she's not that kind of a girl,' he said, shaking his head. 'Should I believe that?'

'Believe what you want.'

'What I *want* is to kiss you.'

'Go ahead,' she said breathlessly.

He did so until she felt his erection pressing against her leg.

Gently she pushed him away. 'You're insatiable,' she murmured.

'You make me that way.'

'I'm glad,' she said, smiling.

'Uh, Dani,' he said, suddenly turning serious. 'There's things I gotta tell you. Stuff I don't want to get into now.'

'I'm not going anywhere.'

'I'll call you,' he said, kissing her again, knowing that he'd finally found some kind of peace, and that meant everything.

Chapter Thirty-six

The van ricocheted down the back alley. Madison stared straight ahead through the front window, eyes alert, ready to duck if she spotted anything blocking their way. A helicopter hovered above. It was probably from a TV station. There was no way the cops could control the media, they ran their own game.

'Make a left at the end of the alley on to Beverly,' the gunman said. 'Anybody gets in your way, hit the mothafuckers.'

Madison turned her head to see if Natalie was okay. The woman with the gash on her temple was sobbing quietly.

This is crazy, she thought. *Where the hell does he think we're going? What's his plan? He'd have been better off staying in the restaurant and giving himself up.*

Cole swerved on to Beverly, side-swiping a Jaguar.

'You see any red lights ahead,' the ringleader shouted, 'jump 'em. Don't even think about it.'

'We could all be killed,' the woman in the back wailed.

'If he don't do what I'm tellin' him, you'll all be dead anyway.'

*

343

'You're actually taking me to a business meeting?' Jolie said, pleased. This was a first and she liked it.

'Hey, babe, thought you should see how the professionals do it,' said Nando.

'How the professionals do what?'

'I'm taking you to a strip club I might buy into.'

'You're taking *me* to a strip club?' Jolie said, raising an eyebrow eloquently.

'Got a feelin' you'll find it very educational,' Nando said, grinning.

'Are you intimating that I need lessons?'

'That's the last thing *you* need. I want you to meet these guys I might partner with, see what you think.'

'And how is Vincent involved?'

'He's not.'

'Why?'

''Cause Vincent is livin' in the past. He doesn't get that Vegas is changin'.'

'Do you honestly think it is?'

'Sure it is. We're goin' back to the basics – girls an' sex, that's the coming wave.'

'Whatever happened to family?'

'That side of the business is over.'

'Tell *that* to the mom-and-pop brigade.'

'Now, honey,' Nando said, in his most persuasive voice, 'this place I'm takin' you to is kind of sleazy, but knowing you, you'll see the potential. With your eye for style – you'll imagine how it can look when you redecorate, or do whatever it takes to make the place hot. If this works out, I might even give you a piece of the action.'

'You will?'

'Yeah,' he said magnanimously. 'Why not?'

'I've never heard you speak like this before, Nando.'

'It's amazing what a workout on the pole will do, huh, babe?' He laughed. 'When you meet these two guys you'll

344

hate 'em on sight. Bear in mind they are sittin' on a moneymakin' *machine*.'

'Am I correct in assuming that if Vincent went in with you, you wouldn't need partners? You'd buy them out, right?'

'And she's smart, too.'

'Maybe *I* should talk to Vincent,' she mused.

'You got influence with my best friend I don't?'

'I'm a woman, Nando. Sometimes it makes a difference.'

'Yeah, babe, you're a woman all right.'

'Tell me about these guys we're meeting?'

'They're a couple of black dudes who've been around a while. You'll charm the pants off both of 'em.'

'I do hope you don't mean that literally.'

'Baby, you ever *look* at another man, an' he'll be wearing his balls in the back of his throat.'

'It's nice to know you care, Nando.'

'Yeah, isn't it?'

'You've never done coke?' Andy Dale said, sounding as surprised as if she'd told him she'd never drunk a glass of milk.

Jenna shook her head, blonde hair swirling round her shoulders. 'No, my husband doesn't approve of drugs.'

'Drugs, my ass,' Andy said. 'Coke is not a drug – it's recreational, like smoking and booze. If doctors could, they'd give out prescriptions for it. It's that simple.'

'I thought it turned people into *drug* addicts.'

'Who told you that? Your old man?'

'Vincent says that drugs destroy anyone who takes them.'

'That's *hard* drugs, cookie. Heroin and all that shit. I'll tell you what happens when you take coke. You relax, lie back, have a good time. *And* you also have wild sex. Look at Anais.'

She glanced across the luxurious room at Anais, who'd decided to remove all her clothes, except for a minute thong and many gold crosses hanging on chains round her neck.

'Does she look like she's an addict?'

'No, Andy, she doesn't.'

'Then take a snort. You're too uptight. C'mon, I'll show you how.'

'I only came here to apologize for Vincent's behaviour. Sometimes he doesn't understand that people in the movie business are different.'

'*You* understand, don't you?' Andy said, grabbing her hand.

'Of course, I do. I mean, you're artistic, you're an actor, an *artiste*.'

'Yeah, that's what I am,' Andy said, pleased with her description. 'An *artiste*. Now,' he added, leading her over to the bar, where he'd set out several lines of coke, 'I'm gonna roll this bill, and you'll hold it to your cute little nose and, like, breathe in. Y'know, snort it. Can you do that?'

'Are you *sure* it won't have a bad effect on me?' she asked, feeling the tiniest bit insecure.

'Positive.'

She took the bill from him, gingerly snorted the cocaine, and sneezed immediately, scattering some of the white powder on to the floor.

'Jesus Christ!' Andy shouted. 'What the fuck are you *doing?*'

'Sorry,' she said, humiliated that she could have done such a thing.

'It's good I got plenty,' he grumbled.

Anais wandered over. 'Put some on my tits,' she commanded, thrusting her bare bosom at him.

'Later,' he said, waving her away.

'Now,' she said imperiously, a woman used to getting

her own way. 'And some on my pussy, too.'

'I'll be with you in a minute,' Andy said, frowning. 'I'm trying to teach Jenna how to snort without blowing everything all over the floor.'

'Order more champagne,' Anais said, not giving up with her demands. 'I want to wash my hair.'

'You're washing your hair *now?*' he said, finally paying attention.

'Yes.'

'Okay.'

Anais smiled dreamily. 'If my boyfriend knew I was here, he wouldn't be happy.'

'Who *is* your boyfriend?' Andy asked; he had been unaware that she had one.

'He's mega rich,' she said. 'Mega, mega, mega rich.'

'So am I,' Andy said, which wasn't strictly true, because by the time he'd paid his agent, publicist, stylist, manager, driver, and business manager, there was not that much left.

'Order *ten* bottles of champagne,' Anais said, distractedly touching her nipples, 'and I'll bathe in it.'

'Maybe you should just go wash your hair,' he said, turning back to Jenna, who by this time was feeling light-headed and adventurous. 'You ready to try again?' he asked.

'Yes,' she said eagerly. 'I'm ready.'

Michael tried calling Madison twice. He didn't leave a message on her answering machine because he did not consider it safe to alert anyone to where he was.

'At least you *know* where Madison is,' Dani said. 'How do we go about finding Sofia?'

'Good question,' Michael replied. 'When did you last hear from her?'

'A couple of weeks ago. She was in Marbella, in Spain.'

'I don't know why you allow her to travel around the

world by herself,' Vincent grumbled. 'You should *insist* that she comes home.'

'Have *you* ever tried telling Sofia anything?' Dani replied. 'Even when she was very young she wouldn't listen to reason.'

'The kid probably takes after me,' Michael said. 'Does things her way.'

'And look where it's got *you*,' Dani said.

'Did she give you an address or phone number in Marbella?' Michael asked, ignoring her remark. 'Somewhere we can reach her?'

'She said she was working as a photographer at a nightclub.'

'A photographer!' Vincent exclaimed. 'What kind of job is that?'

'Did she mention what club?' Michael said.

'She didn't say,' Dani replied. 'You know Sofia – every time she calls, she refuses to leave a number.'

'I'll get someone on to it,' Vincent said. 'We'll find her.'

'Hey,' Michael said. 'The good thing is, if *we* don't find her nobody else can.'

'You think it's that serious?' Vincent said.

'Yeah, it's serious.'

'What's *your* next move?'

'I'm flying to L.A. in the morning. There's someone I have to see.'

'Who?'

'Nobody you know,' Michael said abruptly. 'Take care of the things I asked you to – I'll be in touch. Anybody comes asking questions, I wasn't here, an' that includes your wife.'

'I know *that*,' Vincent said.

'Good.'

'How *is* Jenna?' Dani asked.

'She's fine, Mom,' Vincent said quickly. He knew how

his mother felt about his wife, and he refused to give her the satisfaction of telling her she was right. He'd work it out with Jenna in his own way. And if that meant a divorce, so be it.

In the middle of the night, Sofia awoke again. She was close to a man, a stranger, and he felt so good in his silk pyjamas. She snuggled closer, rubbing her hands over the smooth material, loving the feel of it.

Nobody wore pyjamas any more. Why wasn't he naked? She spooned even closer. He stirred in his sleep.

She moved her hands downward and felt that he was pleased to see her. By the time he awoke fully, she was making love to him, riding him in a wild fashion.

'My God!' Gianni gasped. 'What are you doing?'

'I'm not playing tennis.' She giggled. 'Shut up and enjoy it.'

He put his hands on her shoulders, vigorously pushing her off.

'Are you nuts?' she said. 'I'm making *love* to you. Isn't that what you want?'

'No, Sofia, it's *not*,' he said angrily, sitting up in bed.

'Of course it is,' she said accusingly. 'You were hard, you were ready.'

'I was *asleep*,' he said, reaching for the light switch.

'Oh, my God, you *are* gay, aren't you?' she gasped.

'No, Sofia,' he said. 'I am *not* gay.'

He got out of bed, marched into the bathroom, and slammed the door.

This was a first. A man who didn't want to get laid.

When he emerged from the bathroom a few minutes later, he had put on a bathrobe over his silk pyjamas and was still angry.

'Do you always make love with complete strangers?' he asked.

'You weren't exactly reluctant.'

'I told you before, Sofia, I was asleep. I thought I was dreaming.'

'Some cool dream, huh?' she said, beginning to feel a bit foolish.

'I do not indulge in casual sex. Especially with a girl I'm supposed to be in charge of.'

'In charge of?' she exclaimed. 'You've *got* to be kidding me.'

'If I was going to have sex with a woman, I would certainly want to know a lot more about her than I do about you.'

'Oh,' she said, insulted. 'You're perfectly safe. I don't have any sexual diseases or anything.'

'Is this the way you always behave with people you don't know?'

'Not always,' she said, deciding that she hated him and was glad they hadn't made love.

'You're lucky I didn't take advantage of you.'

'Are you saying I'm lucky you didn't *come* inside me?'

'You have an extremely vulgar way of putting things.'

'And I suppose your girlfriend, Anais, is the perfect lady.'

'Anais has nothing to do with you.'

'Look, I'm sorry,' she said, suddenly contrite. 'I thought it would be a nice kind of payment for you letting me stay here.'

'So now you're a whore?'

'Fuck *you*!' she yelled, leaping off the bed. How dare he say such a thing to her? Who the hell did he think he was?

He was silent.

'Look,' she said at last, 'I like you. I like being here. I was *happy* to get into bed with you. Why're you so uptight?'

'You need to realize that things are not always as easy as

you think. A thank-you is *not* sleeping with someone. I do not require sexual favours.'

'What are you?' she said rudely. 'Faithful to your girlfriend?'

He sighed. 'You don't understand, do you?'

'Most men would be very happy to sleep with me.'

'I'm sure they would.'

'Don't you find me sexy?'

'You're very sexy.'

'Well, then, *what*?'

'I'm too tired to argue, Sofia,' he said, yawning. 'You take the bed, I'll take the couch. We'll talk about this in the morning.'

'Whatever,' she said, glaring at him. 'We'll play it your way. I suppose everyone always does.'

'Call those mothafuckers an' tell 'em to get that helicopter outta here, or I'm throwin' one of you from the car.'

'I don't have a phone,' Madison said. 'You took it – remember?'

'Fuck! Ace,' he said, turning round, 'get me a fuckin' phone.'

At last a name. Ace. Probably a nickname.

Was Ace the one with the snake tattoo on his neck? No, Ace was the third – the shorter guy with the sack full of loot and a pierced nose.

Ace fished in the black plastic garbage bag jammed on his knee. He soon located a cellphone, which he handed to the front.

The gunman took it and thrust it at Madison. 'Call 'em. Do it now!'

'Please don't hurt us,' the girl in the back of the van moaned. 'Please, *please*, why can't you let us go?'

'Shut the fuck up!' he said, turning back to Madison. 'Come on, *bitch*! Make the call.'

'Who am I supposed to call?' she asked. 'Did they leave you a number?'

'Don't diss me, lady. Call nine-one-one. Tell 'em if the 'copter's not outta here in two minutes, one of you is gettin' thrown out.'

She took the cellphone and dialled 911. A dispatcher answered.

'This is Madison Castelli,' she said, as calmly as she could manage. 'I'm one of the hostages from the restaurant on Beverly Boulevard. We're in the van. Please listen carefully. You have to tell the cops that they've got to get the helicopter above us away. If they don't, they're throwing a hostage from the van.'

The gunman grabbed the phone from her and hurled it into the back. 'You'd better hope they do what you told 'em,' he said. ''Cause if they don't, one a you mothafuckers is gonna hit the sidewalk.'

Chapter Thirty-seven

Michael: 1975

B y the time Karl Edgington was released from jail,
Michael had accumulated a great deal of money of
his own. And since he was paying taxes on most of it,
it was perfectly legitimate. He'd followed instructions for
the last four years, and every time he made an investment
with Karl's money, he'd made one of his own. Now that
Karl was out, he wondered what would happen next.

Warner called and suggested they meet for dinner at 21.

'I thought Karl would prefer me to come see him,' he
said.

'No,' Warner replied. 'Karl feels a social occasion is a
better venue. So dinner it is.'

'If that's what he wants.'

'It's the safest way,' Warner assured him.

Michael had never been to 21, although he was well
aware that it was a very famous restaurant. He took a trip to
Saks and bought himself a new suit, shirt, tie, and shoes for
the occasion. He wanted to look his best. He also wanted
to continue working with Karl.

Over the last few months many things had happened.
He'd rented a decent three-bedroom apartment, hired a
nanny, and moved Madison in with him. She spent most

weekends over at Tina and Max's, but then so did he when he wasn't flying back and forth to Vegas.

His affair with Dani was going well. Every few weeks he got on a plane and visited her. She was always happy to see him, and they had a great time just hanging out. They always stayed at his hotel, even though Dani had a house. She never mentioned going there, and when he said he'd like to, she explained it was too soon for him to meet her son.

'Too soon for what?' he'd asked, last time he was there. 'We've been seeing each other for three months. Don't you think it's time I met him?'

'Maybe on your next trip,' she'd said. 'Only you still can't stay at my house.'

'How come?' he'd asked, perplexed.

'Vincent's too young. It wouldn't look right.'

'You really are an old-fashioned girl, aren't you?'

'Something wrong with that?'

He didn't mind. He liked that about Dani. She wasn't a tramp who'd been round the block a hundred times.

She wasn't Beth either, but then Beth had been unique. He'd been thinking very seriously about taking things further. Before he did that, he had to meet her son and get to know him. If things worked out, he expected Dani to give up her job and move to New York, which was for the best, because he wasn't crazy about her parading round the stage with her boobs on display.

Recently he'd persuaded her to request a week off so that she could come and visit him in New York. He liked the idea of being in a different environment where they could discuss their future together without the distraction of her appearing in her show every night.

She'd finally agreed. He was looking forward to her visit. She'd never met Madison, and he was hoping she'd fall in love with his adorable and smart little girl. If she did, and Madison liked *her*, then marriage was *definitely* an option.

'You're acting like the Queen is coming to town,' Tina complained, as they ran around purchasing new sheets and towels and dishes, preparing for Dani's arrival.

'Just making things nice.'

'This *really* must be love, huh?' Tina said, as they wandered round the bedding department in Bloomingdale's.

'You could say it's serious.'

'I'm glad for you,' Tina said, inspecting sheets. 'Uh, Michael,' she said hesitantly.

'Yeah?'

'Have you told her about Beth yet?'

'What about Beth?'

'You know,' Tina said awkwardly. 'The thing that happened, the, uh . . . murder.'

It was a subject he never cared to address. And yet he knew Tina was right: he had to reveal everything to Dani.

'I'm tellin' her this weekend,' he said abruptly. 'It's something I couldn't get into before.'

'You *have* to tell her, Michael,' Tina said, her pretty face grave. 'You were accused of *killing* Beth. I mean, you were all over the papers here. You're lucky nobody's mentioned it.'

'You're right,' he said. He knew what he had to do, he didn't need a goddamn lecture.

'We all know you didn't do it,' Tina continued.

'Thanks,' he said drily.

Later in the week he had dinner with Karl and Warner. Warner brought along her friend Stella, a beautiful young woman who could have doubled for Marilyn Monroe with her shoulder-length platinum hair, creamy skin, pouty lips, and voluptuous figure.

'What do *you* do?' he asked, making polite conversation.

'I'm a showroom model,' she said, sipping a martini, her

hazel eyes checking out the room. 'I model clothes for the out-of-town buyers when they come into the city. Warner used to model with me. Now she's getting her own costume-jewellery business together. Karl's helping her.'

'Sounds like a good idea.'

'It is. Warner's an excellent businesswoman. She's always been interested in designing.'

Designing. The very word reminded him of Beth. 'I'm going to be the biggest dress designer in the world,' Beth had boasted. If she'd lived, she probably would have made it. Beth could have accomplished anything she set her mind to.

'Are you and Karl old friends?' Stella asked, toying with the stem of her martini glass.

'Kind of,' he said, returning to the present. 'You're lovely, Stella, only I hope you realize this evening is *purely* business.'

'I didn't imagine it was a blind date,' she said caustically. '*I'm* here as a favour to Warner.' She sipped her martini. 'I wouldn't go on a blind date. Never have, and never will.'

'I can see that you wouldn't need to.'

She smiled, a dreamy Marilyn Monroe-like smile. 'You've got that right.'

When the girls went off to the powder room, Karl started talking. 'I'm pleased with the way you've handled yourself, Michael,' he said. 'You've done everything I've asked of you, and more besides. I hope you've made yourself a lot of money along the way.'

'I've done okay.'

'Then there is no reason why we shouldn't continue with this arrangement.'

'Why would you need me, now that you're out?'

'It's always good to spread one's assets around. Take my advice and do the same thing. Employ your friends, and give them ten per cent. You'd be surprised how well this works.'

Interesting man, Karl Edgington.

Getting on with his life and being a responsible father to Madison meant putting his past behind him, and that's exactly what he'd tried to do. Much as he wanted vengeance for his mother's death, and he certainly craved revenge for Beth's murder, he'd decided that the most prudent thing to do was nothing. He could not risk getting sent back to jail. Madison was his priority now: he had to be there for her.

That didn't mean that Mamie and Bone were forgotten. Eventually an opportunity would present itself, and if that opportunity was completely foolproof, he'd do something about it.

Once in a while he got together with Vito Giovanni, who was now living with his favourite stripper, Western Pussy.

'This girlie is the greatest,' Vito crowed. 'Come see her one night. I'm gonna make her a star.'

'A star of what?' Michael asked.

'Porno. It's all the rage. This kid can do anything.'

'You want your girlfriend to be a porno star?'

'Why not? She gets off on it. To tell you the truth,' Vito said, with a lewd wink, 'so do I.'

No accounting for taste.

The following night, Vito took him to the Gentlemen's Club, where Western Pussy was performing. Michael had no desire to go, but since he now handled all of Vito's investments, it seemed prudent to keep him happy.

When Western Pussy hit the stage, the male audience began whooping and hollering with enthusiastic delight. She was one of those in-your-face strippers with attitude, her most noticeable asset being her boobs, a fully enhanced 46D. Something Vito had forgotten to mention.

As she whirled round the stage, doing things that only a contortionist could usually manage, Vito chortled with laughter. 'Ain't she something?' he said, slapping Michael on the back. 'Greatest little girl in the world.'

'Little' was hardly the word to describe Western Pussy. Michael was transfixed. He'd never seen anyone quite like her. It had always amazed him that men were turned on by strippers. If you couldn't touch, what was the point of looking?

Later that night, Vito invited him to join Western and himself for dinner at his favourite steak house. Although Western was all over Vito, she couldn't resist nudging her leg up against Michael's thigh under the table.

Jesus! From Mamie to this. What next?

The moment he got home, he phoned Dani. Her kid answered the phone.

'Hi,' he said. 'Is your mommy around?'

'She's not back yet,' the boy said.

'This is Michael.'

He waited for the boy to say something like, 'Oh yeah, I know who you are, Mommy's told me all about you.'

Nothing.

'Michael, your mommy's friend,' he said. 'Has she mentioned me?'

'Nope.'

'She hasn't? Okay, well, you and I are gonna meet. What are you into? Baseball, football or basketball? What's your game?'

'I like 'em all.'

'Next time I come out there, we'll get together.'

''Bye.'

Michael replaced the receiver. Why hadn't she mentioned him to her son? They were going together, for God's sake. Okay, so he didn't live in the same city, but they *were* going together.

He got into bed, put on the TV, and fell asleep watching Johnny Carson on *The Tonight Show*. He dreamed about

Beth. Or, at least, he thought it was Beth, it might have been Dani. He couldn't remember which one it was when he woke up. Was that a good sign?

He didn't know.

Soon Dani would be here, and he could start figuring out their future. He couldn't wait.

Chapter Thirty-eight

Dani: 1975

Whenever Dean came into town, he took Dani to dinner.

'What does your wife think of all these trips?' she asked. As far as she was concerned they had settled into the perfect platonic relationship, which suited her fine. Only she wasn't sure how his wife back in Houston felt about him still seeing her.

'I have business here, Dani,' he explained. 'Morgan and I run a company together.'

'I wasn't aware of that.'

'I told you,' he said. 'Obviously you weren't listening.'

'Sorry,' she murmured.

'It's a business we started a year ago. Something to do with cattle.'

'That's interesting.'

'So interesting that you don't remember.'

'I *said* I'm sorry.'

'More important,' he said, leaning towards her, 'how are *you* doing?'

'Really good,' she said, sipping her wine.

'You look great. In fact, you look glowing.' He hesitated a moment, almost afraid to ask. 'Don't crush my heart and tell me you've met someone?'

'As a matter of fact,' she said, breaking into a helpless smile, 'I have.'

Dean felt a stab of jealousy. Even though he was married to someone else, he still had feelings for Dani. She was the one who'd got away and he'd always love her.

'Who is this mystery man?' he asked, trying to keep it light.

'He's not such a mystery.'

'No? Then how come you've never mentioned him?'

'I don't know,' she said vaguely. 'I think I wanted to make sure it was going somewhere.'

'And is it?'

She smiled. 'Be happy for me, Dean. I'm happy for *you*.'

'Sure, Dani. If you've found the right guy, that's wonderful. But I *would* like to know more about him.'

'What are you – my father?' she said, laughing.

'I watch out for you, Dani. This is a tough town.'

'You're telling *me*?' she said, putting down her wine glass. 'I've been meaning to ask you, Dean. How come you never bring your wife with you? I'm sure I'd enjoy meeting her.'

'You'll meet her.'

'When?'

'Soon,' he said impatiently, anxious to resume talking about Dani's boyfriend.

'We can all go out to dinner.'

'I saw the show last night,' he said, rapidly getting off the subject of his wife. 'You looked spectacular.'

'Really? Y'know, lately I've been thinking of giving it up.'

'What does *that* mean?'

'It means that the man I'm seeing wants me to spend time in New York.'

'Is he asking you to marry him?'

'Not yet, but he probably will.'

'Dani,' Dean said sternly, 'take my advice – do *not* give up *anything* until he puts a ring on your finger. You have a son, responsibilities.'

'I know,' she said, nodding. 'I'm flying to New York next weekend. I have a feeling we'll be discussing our future.'

'Well,' Dean said, 'in that case I wish you the best of luck.'

'I know you do, Dean,' she said warmly. 'You and I – we'll always be friends, won't we?'

'Yes, Dani, we always will,' he said, trying to hide his dismay that Dani – *his* Dani – was involved with another man. 'So . . . uh . . . what's this mystery guy's name?'

'Michael.'

'Michael who?'

'Why are you so full of questions?'

'I didn't know it was a secret.'

'It's not. His name is Michael Castelli.'

'Nice Italian name.'

'He's a nice Italian boy,' she said, smiling softly.

'Boy? How old is he?'

'Thirty.'

'Uh-huh. What business is he in?'

'Investments. Dean, I know you're trying to be helpful, but I do not appreciate this third degree.'

'Then I'll drop it.'

'Good.'

The moment he got back to his hotel room, Dean called his office in Houston.

'Put a search out on this name,' he said. 'Michael Castelli. Find out everything you can. It's a priority.'

If Dani was thinking of marrying someone, he needed to know everything about him.

*

Vincent was upset that his mother was going away without him, even though he was very fond of Reggie, their house-keeper, a cheerful Jamaican woman with children of her own.

'It's only for a week,' Dani assured him. 'You can manage without me for a week.'

'Can't,' Vincent said stubbornly.

'Yes, you can.'

'Can't!'

'Can!'

'Can't!'

'You impossible little monkey,' she said, wrestling him to the ground.

He giggled and fought back.

She'd made up her mind that it wasn't fair keeping Vincent from his true, biological father. When she got to New York, she'd decided to tell Michael the truth.

'Can I come with you, Mommy?' Vincent pleaded.

'No, darling, I'm sorry you can't.'

'Why not?'

'Because it's not a trip for little boys.'

'I'm not a *little* boy, I'm a *big* boy,' he said indignantly.

'You're almost ten, that's not big enough.'

'I wish Nando was here,' he said mournfully.

'I know, sweetheart. As soon as I get back I'll call his grandfather in Colombia, see if we can arrange for him to come visit.'

'Nando's my friend. The other boys at school are stupid.'

'Why are they stupid?' she asked patiently.

''Cause they call me names.'

'Why would they call you names?'

''Cause of you.'

'Me?'

'Mark Timson says you show your boobies on the stage.'

Oh, God, this was exactly what she hadn't wanted to hear.

'What did he say?' she asked.

'He told everyone his parents went to your show, an' they all saw your boobies. *Do* you show them, Mommy?'

'It's not like that, darling. I wear a beautiful costume. It's very glamorous and . . . let me put it this way, what I do is work. It's how I make money so that we can live in this nice comfortable house and have Reggie to look after you.'

'Can *I* come see your show, Mommy?'

'When you're older, of course.'

'When?'

'I just told you, when you're older.'

'Okey dokey,' he said, getting bored. 'Can I go watch TV now?'

'No more than half an hour. Then it's homework time.'

'Done it, Mommy.'

Of course he had. Vincent was always ahead of everyone.

Now she had the new worry of him knowing that she appeared on stage topless. She'd realized that she'd have to face up to it eventually, she simply hadn't expected it to be so soon.

She decided to discuss it with Michael, see how he suggested she handle it. Lately she'd been talking to him about everything. She'd mentioned the magazine that had asked her to pose. He'd warned her against doing it. 'They'll use the photos out of context,' he'd said. 'Don't start appearing in those kind of magazines, 'cause one of these days you'll regret it.'

She'd taken his advice and turned the magazine down. They'd retaliated by asking Penelope to pose.

'Guess *you* couldn't cut it,' Penelope had jeered.

She'd ignored her.

She had no idea what to pack. Michael had told her

it was raining in New York, and the last thing she possessed was rainy-weather clothes. She didn't even own a raincoat.

This was the first time she'd be getting on a plane, and she was excited. Michael had offered to fly out and fetch her. 'I'm a big girl, I can do it all by myself,' she'd assured him.

'Then I'll meet you at the airport,' he'd said.

She was leaving the next morning. The company director had generously allowed her a week off. Tonight she had one more show to do before she left. Vegas was experiencing a boom, and lately she'd been getting offers from other hotels. Even though she was being tempted with more money, she was happy at the Magiriano. Who knew what her future held, anyway? She suspected that Michael might possibly be planning on asking her to marry him. And if he did? Well, she was prepared to say yes.

Dean had called earlier to ask if he could take her to dinner again after the show. 'I have to pack,' she'd told him. 'Anyway, we had dinner two nights ago.'

'I know,' he'd said. 'However, I have something important to tell you.'

She'd finally agreed, meeting him in the cosy, all red bar-room restaurant at the hotel. It was one of her favourite places, where she and Michael had enjoyed several meals together.

Dean seemed agitated. She wondered if something was going on in his marriage. She hoped not, because she wasn't in the mood to start handing out advice.

'I can't make this a late night, Dean,' she warned him, as soon as she sat down. 'I'm leaving early tomorrow.'

'That's why I had to talk to you tonight,' he said, and ordered a bottle of wine.

'Concerning what?' she asked.

'Concerning your new friend.'

'Do you mean Michael?'

'Yes.'

She tapped her fingers on the table. 'You don't *know* Michael.'

'I know plenty about him.'

'What's on your mind, Dean?' she asked, sighing.

'Dani,' he said, trying to keep his voice in neutral, 'how much do you know about his past?'

'I don't think that's any of your business,' she said, beginning to get angry.

'*You're* my business, Dani,' he said earnestly. 'We're best friends, remember?'

She sighed again and attempted to remain calm. Dean was only trying to do what he thought was best for her, which wasn't such a bad thing, because at least he genuinely cared.

'If you're talking about the time he was in jail for hijacking a truck, I know all about it,' she said. 'Michael told me everything.'

'I wasn't talking about that.'

'Then what *are* you talking about?'

'He has a daughter, right?'

'Yes.'

Dean cleared his throat. 'Do you know what happened to the child's mother?'

'She died.'

'Are you aware of *how* she died?'

'No, actually I don't know, because Michael doesn't like to talk about it. I assumed it was an illness.'

'You *assumed*?'

Now she was getting really impatient. 'What exactly are you trying to tell me, Dean?'

'You're a smart woman, Dani,' he said quickly. 'However, as I've told you many times before, you have to think about your son as well as yourself. You cannot allow yourself to get caught in a situation that puts you and Vincent in danger.'

'Danger! Why would you say such a thing?'

'Don't hate me for telling you this, Dani, but there is a strong possibility that Michael Castelli, or Castellino, as he was formerly known, murdered his girlfriend.'

'*What?*'

'Shot her in the back of the head.'

The colour drained from Dani's face. 'Are you crazy?'

Dean picked up a large manilla envelope. 'It's all here in black and white. Read it for yourself.'

'I – I don't understand what you're talking about.'

'You'll know when you read the newspaper clippings. Yes, he was acquitted, but that was only because he had high-powered lawyers – paid for by his powerful Mob boss in New York.' A beat. 'I'm sorry to say this, Dani, but there's a chance that he may be guilty.'

'Oh . . . my . . . God,' she said, feeling faint.

'If this man has genuine feelings for you, he would have told you everything when you first got together.'

'I . . . I thought he did.'

'How long have you been seeing him?'

'Three months.'

'Three months, and he hasn't found a moment to mention this? I think that seems highly suspect, don't you?'

'You – you don't know him. He's—'

'He's *what*, Dani? According to the newspapers, he's a hit man for the Mob, who shot his girlfriend in the back of the head because he thought she was seeing someone else. This woman was the *mother of his child*. Is that the kind of man you're going to throw your life away for?'

'Give me the clippings and let me out of here,' she said, hardly able to breathe.

'I'll drive you home.'

'Don't bother,' she said, getting up. 'I'll take a cab.'

'Dani, I only found this out for your own good.'

'You think this is for my own good?' she said, tears filling her eyes. 'Can't you understand? I *love* him.'

'You must do what you see fit,' he said, following her from the restaurant. 'Only, I beg you, think of your son. He should come before anyone. Vincent is your priority, Dani. Do not put him or yourself in peril.'

Chapter Thirty-nine

Michael: 1982

'Where's your mom?' Jamie asked. She was a cute, flaxen-haired eleven-year-old girl with a pronounced overbite.

'Asleep,' Madison replied. She was also eleven, tall and gangly, with long dark hair and an inquisitive face. 'She sleeps a lot.'

'Why?'

'Dunno,' Madison replied vaguely, not that interested.

'I'm starving!' Jamie announced.

'C'mon,' Madison said. 'Let's go in the kitchen. I think the cook's made brownies.'

'Yum,' Jamie said. 'If I stay over, are we allowed to watch *Remington Steel*?'

'We can do whatever we want,' Madison replied airily. 'Dad's away, and Mom doesn't care what I do.'

'Lucky *you*,' Jamie said enviously.

'Yes, lucky me,' Madison agreed, although she often wished for a mother who paid her more attention.

'*My* mom's all over me,' Jamie said, following Madison into the kitchen. 'She hardly *ever* lets me watch TV.'

'That sucks,' Madison said.

'You bet,' Jamie said. 'My mom thinks I should still be

playing with Barbies. She doesn't understand that *boys* are *much* cooler.'

''Cept the boys in our school,' Madison remarked, pulling a face. 'They suck.'

'When does your dad get home?' Jamie asked, helping herself to a warm brownie.

'Soon, I hope,' Madison said. 'He always brings me a ton of presents.'

'I told you,' Jamie said enviously. 'You're the luckiest girl I know.'

'You think?' Madison said, munching a brownie.

'Oh, yes,' Jamie said.

Later that afternoon, Michael surprised his daughter and arrived home early. Just as she'd boasted to Jamie, he was loaded down with presents.

'Hey, girls,' he said, greeting Jamie too. 'What are you up to?'

'Waiting for you, Daddy,' Madison said, her big green eyes staring up at him, filled with love.

'Good. 'Cause I've bought you plenty of *stuff*.'

'What have you got me this time, Daddy?'

'Well . . .' he said, teasing her '. . . I was gonna get you a lynx coat or a Cadillac. Then I thought you might prefer this Sony video recorder, and a Radio Shack colour computer.'

'Daddy! That's *so* cool! You are the best!' she said, throwing her arms round him.

'There's a bunch of other things in my bag,' he said. 'Records an' books. Take your pick.'

'Oh, Daddy, you always spoil me so much.' She sighed, shooting a glance at Stella, who had just emerged from her bedroom.

Stella stood in the doorway, surveyed the two girls, gave them a weak smile, waved at Michael, and retreated back to the bedroom, murmuring that she had a headache.

'Mommy's got another headache,' Madison announced, in case he hadn't heard.

'Yeah?' Michael said. 'What else is new?'

Madison giggled. Michael grinned at his precious daughter. She was smart. As smart as any boy. He loved everything about her.

'You girls had dinner?' he asked. 'If you haven't, I'll take you out to 21.'

'I *don't* think!' Madison said, still giggling.

'Hey, one of these days I will. When you're old enough.'

'I *wanna* go to 21, Daddy,' Madison pleaded. 'I hear it's the finest restaurant in town.'

'Listen to you, madam,' he said, laughing at her way of putting things. How many other eleven year olds would come out with a sentence like that?

'Do you get the best table, Daddy? Do they treat you like a king?'

'Of course they do, sugar.'

'Your dad is *sooo* good-looking,' Jamie said admiringly, when they reached the privacy of Madison's bedroom, dragging all the loot behind them.

'Looks like a movie star, doesn't he?' Madison said proudly.

Jamie nodded. She so envied her best friend, who got to do everything she didn't and had such a great-looking dad.

'He's cool, too,' Madison added.

'The coolest,' Jamie agreed.

Madison went over to her record collection and started riffling through it. 'Cyndi Lauper or the Go-Go's?' she asked.

'The Go-Go's!' they both yelled in unison, and collapsed giggling on the floor.

Michael walked into the bedroom. Stella was lying on the bed leafing through *Harper's Bazaar*.

'*Another* headache?' he said.

'A migraine,' she replied, putting down the magazine.

'You should see a doctor about your headaches.'

'I will,' she murmured.

'So,' he said, sitting on the edge of their king-size bed, 'did you get to spend a lot of time with Madison while I was away?'

'Of course,' she lied.

Actually, she'd spent no time with Madison at all. That's why she always made sure there was a capable housekeeper in the apartment and an excellent cook. Child-friendly staff were absolutely essential.

Stella was *not* child-friendly. And pretending to be Madison's mother for all these years was getting her down. Materially she had everything she desired, but she knew that Michael put Madison first, and that drove her a little bit crazy.

'You know, darling,' she said, 'Madison is growing up very fast.'

'I realize that,' he said, loosening his tie.

'She's so smart,' Stella continued. 'And, quite frankly, *I* don't think the school she's attending is good enough for her, so I've been investigating other possibilities.'

'You have?'

'Yes, and I've found a top-rate boarding-school I think we should send her to. A talented child like Madison needs academic excellence.'

'A boarding-school?' he said unsurely. 'Have you spoken to her about this?'

'She's too young to know what's good for her. However, I *have* discussed it with some of my friends, and they all agree that she should be getting the best education possible. The boarding-school I'm suggesting *is* the best.'

'Where is it?' he asked, not sure if it was such a great idea.

'Connecticut.'

'So she could come home every weekend?'

'If she wants to.'

'I don't know . . . she won't like being away from Jamie.'

'Jamie's a little giddy, don't you think?' Stella said. 'Madison's much more mature for her years.'

Michael nodded. He trusted Stella's judgement. After all, he'd married her, hadn't he?

He walked into his wood-panelled dressing room and removed his jacket. Michael Castelli, businessman, investments, real-estate mogul. Boy, had he moved up in the world.

After Dani had dumped him in such a heartless way, he'd turned to the nearest woman, who happened to be Stella, Warner's good friend.

Stella was there for him. She'd given him all her attention, comfort, and plenty of sex. None of it meant that much, but he'd begun to see her as the woman who might make a great mother for his child. He *refused* to allow Madison to grow up without a mother the way he had. His child was going to have it all – and that included responsible parents.

After a couple of months of seeing each other, he'd broached the subject to Stella. She'd been quite amenable when he'd told her what he had in mind. 'Here's the deal,' he'd said. 'If I marry you, then Madison has to grow up believing that you are her natural mother.'

'What about her real mother?'

'Beth's gone. And I don't want Madison ever finding out what happened. As far as she's concerned, *you* are her mother.' In his mind he'd decided that Madison would always come first. He'd allow no half-brothers or -sisters to compete with her. 'And, Stella, one more thing,' he'd added.

'Yes?'

'You have to promise me that you'll never have children.'

She'd agreed, and they'd got married on a spring afternoon in New York with Karl and Warner as witnesses.

He didn't love her. He was not prepared to love again.

Stella had neither Beth's fire nor Dani's sweetness. What she did have was great beauty. In a physical way she sometimes reminded him of Dani.

Talk about being left at the altar. Dani hadn't exactly left him at the altar, but he *was* left at the airport, waiting for her to fly in.

She'd never arrived, and when he'd called Vegas to find out where she was, her housekeeper had informed him that Dani and her son had gone away for a while and would not be back anytime soon.

The next day he'd received a letter via FedEx.

Dear Michael:
Circumstances have changed. I cannot see you any more.
Please do not try to contact me.
Dani

He had no idea what had happened to make her feel that way, but he had his pride, and even though he'd considered getting on a plane and confronting her, he had not done so.

Four months later, he had married Stella.

The last seven years had been good to him. His fortune had grown, and financially he was able to do more or less anything he wanted.

Stella was addicted to their lifestyle: a luxurious Park Avenue apartment; vacations in the Bahamas; shopping trips to Paris and London. The only thing she did not love was having a daughter. Especially an extremely smart eleven year old whom her husband adored more than he did her.

It was infuriating. However, she never let on to Michael how she felt, and whenever he was round, she acted out the perfect-mother role.

After a while, Tina and Max had refused to visit. 'You want me to be frank with you, Michael?' Tina had said. 'Stella's a cold bitch. She doesn't like *me*, and *I* don't like her. So we're not hanging out any more. You want to see us, come over and bring Madison.'

So that's what he did. Every other weekend he drove over to their house with Madison, and they spent the day together.

Soon Stella put the pressure on, and his visits to Tina and Max became less frequent. He felt guilty about not seeing as much of them as he would've liked. After all, Max was his best friend and they shared a long history together. However, Stella was his wife, and more than anything he wanted a happy marriage for Madison's sake.

Gradually Stella began drawing him into a whole new social circle. She had many friends in the arts, and soon he'd found himself attending the opera, theatre, and ballet. They went to gallery openings, parties and all the hot new restaurants. At first he kind of enjoyed it, although he did not enjoy the ballet and the opera – he considered them one big yawn. However, since Stella loved doing it so much, he went along for the ride. And she always looked like a million bucks hanging on to his arm wearing the designer clothes he paid for, the fur coats and the expensive jewellery. Diamonds were definitely Stella's best friend.

Sometimes he imagined what things might have been like if Beth had lived. Far different from his current lifestyle.

And what would have happened if he'd married Dani? He could picture them lying in bed, munching on hamburgers, watching TV, just hanging out and having fun. In spite of her Vegas fame and glamour, Dani was a simple girl. Stella wasn't. The only time Stella lay round was when she had a headache or wanted to study her magazines, finding out what was new and exciting in the beauty world. She was very into the latest beauty treatments and heavy maintenance. Manicurists, facialists, and masseuses were always in and out of the apartment, ministering to her every need. She had tried to get him into it. One pedicure and he'd run out screaming.

Business became his focus, building a financial empire. And he was good at it, he'd learned well. First, in a small way, from Grandma Lani. And then the real deal from Karl Edgington. Money was his passion: he had a genius way with numbers.

Over the years, he and Karl had partnered in many ventures. They owned buildings, shopping centres and real estate. He'd also kept up his association with Vito Giovanni. He took care of Vito's investments. Vito trusted him and sent plenty of money his way. He'd heard that Mamie had given up her New York apartment and moved to the West Coast. Vito was still living with Western Pussy – a woman almost forty years his junior.

Financially, Michael could do just about anything he wished. He had an office on Wall Street and employed a small staff of competent people, including his old friend Charlie, who was now working for him as his accountant. Several years ago he'd paid for him to take a business course, and Charlie had come up trumps. Now Charlie was making plenty of money, had a secure job, and he'd even got married to a pretty girl who worked in the office.

Michael was very fond of Charlie, although they didn't socialize. Stella did not consider it prudent to mix business with pleasure.

Basically he had it all: a beautiful wife, a smart daughter, and enough money to do whatever he wanted. So why wasn't he happy?

He didn't know.

Max, who now owned several car dealerships, had informed him one day while they were having lunch that it was because he was living a lie.

'What kinda shit remark is that?' Michael asked.

'Stella's a big snob,' Max had said. 'An uptown bitch with attitude.'

Michael was so offended by Max's criticism that he'd stopped seeing him. Which was a shame because, apart from Charlie, Max was Michael's only true friend from the old days.

He missed the old days. He missed hanging out with Tina and Max, goofing off.

Work compensated. He was obsessed.

Stella decided that he should be the one to inform Madison that they were sending her away to boarding-school. When he told his daughter she burst into tears. 'I don't *want* to go, Daddy,' she sobbed.

'It's for the best, princess.'

'No!'

'You'll soon get used to it.'

'I won't!' she said adamantly.

'I promise that you will.'

She stared at him with her big green eyes – *his* eyes. They looked alike, although her deep olive skin and lustrous dark hair always reminded him of Beth.

'I'll go, Daddy,' she said at last. 'But I promise you this, you'll *really* miss me.'

And he did, in spite of Stella's social efforts, which seemed to escalate with Madison's absence.

He began making more and more business trips – inspecting a shopping mall here, a piece of property there. And so his empire grew.

Michael Castelli was a very successful man.

Michael Castellino was just a distant memory.

Chapter Forty

Dani: 1982

'If *you* don't marry me, there's somebody else who will,' Dean threatened.

'I wish her luck,' Dani said, smiling.

'You know it'll happen one day. Why do you insist on waiting until we're old and grey?'

'Because.'

'Because what?'

'Because,' she said patiently, 'I have to pay you back the money I owe you first.'

'At the rate *you're* going, we'll both be dead!'

'Are you two fighting again?' Vincent asked, entering the brightly lit kitchen. 'The way you go at it, you might as well be married.'

At seventeen, Vincent was undeniably handsome. He was also a dead ringer for Michael. Black hair, worn long. Perfect features. Six feet tall and a great body. The girls were crazy for him, which didn't do them much good since he was more interested in studying and sports.

Dani, who was in her early-thirties and still a knock-out, could not believe she had a grown son. The boy needed a father, so thank God for Dean, who – although he and Dani were no longer romantically involved – had stepped into the breach and spent as much time with Vincent as he could. Which wasn't easy, considering he still lived in Houston.

His divorce had helped. Dani had never asked him why his marriage hadn't worked out, because she knew why. Dean had never got over her. His crush was a lifelong thing. But, although she loved him in her own way, he was more like a big brother to her.

Over the last seven years she had not exactly been celibate. Although she had not resumed her affair with Dean, there *had* been other men. None of them had measured up in any way whatsoever, and currently she was not seeing anyone. Somehow she was so much happier by herself.

Recently Vincent had received news that Nando's grandfather had died, and that Nando was planning to visit. Vincent was totally psyched. 'This is gonna be so cool, Mom,' he enthused. 'I can't wait!'

'You haven't seen Nando in a long while,' Dani warned. 'Don't expect too much – he's probably changed.'

'No way,' Vincent scoffed. 'Nando and me are like brothers. He'll be exactly the same.'

Dani was still appearing in the show at the Magiriano, only now she was a featured player. She made two grand entrances during the course of the show, and her fan base kept expanding. Dani Castle, the staggeringly beautiful showgirl, had become quite a legend in Vegas.

The fact that she walked around topless on stage embarrassed the hell out of Vincent. '*When* are you going to quit, Mom?' he kept on nagging. 'You're too old to be taking your clothes off.'

'Don't tell me what to do,' she said. 'My job has put bread on the table and *you* into the best school. The day you graduate college is the day I'll quit.'

'So you'll still be doing it when you're forty?' he complained. 'That's *gross*.'

'Thank you, Vincent dear. I love it when you pay me compliments.'

'C'mon, Mom, it's just not cool. And I sure don't want Nando finding out.'

'Then don't bring him to the show.'

'Believe me – I won't. But there's photographs of you all over the hotel.'

'Then don't go to that hotel.'

Dean was on Vincent's side. 'Maybe you *should* give some thought to retiring,' he said.

'Why? Don't you think I look good any more?'

'You *always* look beautiful,' Dean assured her.

'Then why should I give it up? I have no other skills.'

'Marry me,' he said, always hopeful, 'and you won't need any.'

There he goes again, she thought. And yet she couldn't help feeling flattered.

Vincent went to the airport to meet Nando. He was excited. He couldn't wait to see his childhood best friend. Then he began wondering if Nando *had* changed.

When Nando strode off the plane carrying a tote bag and a stack of magazines, there was *no* mistaking him. He had that I-am-trouble glint in his eyes. His hair was even longer than Vincent's, and he was wearing the tightest of ragged jeans and a black shirt. Only Nando could get away with wearing a black shirt in the middle of summer. Not conventionally handsome, he was attractive in a quirky, offbeat way, and very skinny.

Vincent took a deep breath. How did men greet each other? He didn't know, he'd never had a father to teach him.

Nando waved, dropped half his magazines, picked them up, and raced over. 'Son-of-a-*bitch*!' he exclaimed. 'You've gotten more handsome. Screw you, asshole!'

'Screw you, too,' Vincent retorted.

Then they hugged.

'Sorry to hear about your grandfather,' Vincent said as they walked from the airport.

'Forget it,' Nando said. 'Esai was a miserable old bastard.'

'He was?'

A pretty girl walked by and Nando made appreciative sucking noises. The girl ignored him.

'The good news is that when I'm twenty-one I inherit everything. I'm a rich kid now.'

'You?'

'Yeah, me,' Nando boasted. 'The money's in trust, so I can't get my hands on it yet, but when I do – watch out!'

'Wow!' Vincent said. 'Cool.'

'Yeah,' Nando said, winking at another girl. 'I'm buyin' me a *Ferrari*!'

'Red?'

'Naw. Black. An' you and me are gonna take a trip around the world.'

'We are?'

'Betcha ass.'

'What about college?'

'Who wants to waste time in college?'

'My mom's planning a trip back East to take a look at colleges there.'

'Your mom still a babe?'

'She's, uh, looking good.'

'Hot lady,' Nando said.

'Don't talk about my mom like that,' Vincent said, frowning.

'Sorry,' Nando said, whistling at a passing brunette in a short red dress.

Vincent hoped fervently that Nando would not find out about Dani's topless appearances at the Magiriano. It was bad enough that he'd had to take so much ribbing at school. Nando seeing her like that would be too humiliating.

Back at the house, Dani greeted the two of them warmly. '*You* sure grew into a big boy,' she said, giving Nando a hug.

'Yes, Mrs Robinson,' he answered, with a cheeky grin, holding the hug for a few seconds too long.

'Excuse me?'

'Joking!' Nando said, still grinning.

Vincent took him upstairs to his room.

'Got a cigarette?' Nando asked, prowling round.

'Don't smoke.'

'Any grass?'

'Don't do drugs.'

'Jesus!' Nando exclaimed. 'Thank your lucky balls *I'm* back to give you a freakin' *life*.'

'Not in *this* house,' Vincent said quickly. 'My mom would have a fit.'

'Don't tell me she's made you into a mommy's boy?'

'Mom works very hard, so I try not to give her a hard time.'

'You got laid yet?' Nando asked, throwing himself down on the bed. 'Had any prime pussy come your way?'

'I do okay,' Vincent said evasively, although the truth was he had *not* got laid.

'Okay doesn't cut it,' Nando said, yawning. 'I can see I gotta give you an education. An' one that *doesn't* take place in school.'

Dani wasn't sure that the return of Nando was a good thing. She could tell that he was still a wild one, only now he was no longer a child. Even though he was only seventeen, he looked older. He was staying with them for a month, which meant that she'd have to watch both of them. She hoped he wasn't going to be a bad influence on Vincent.

Dean was flying back to Houston the next day, so that night they had their usual dinner together after the show. Over dessert she confided her fears.

'Vincent won't get into trouble,' Dean assured her. 'He's a decent kid.'

'Do you think so?' she asked anxiously.

'Yes, Dani, and *you*'re quite a woman.'

'I don't know, Dean,' she worried. 'I feel I've done the best I can, raising him by myself. Then sometimes I look back on mistakes I might have made.'

'What mistakes?'

She picked up her wine glass and took a sip. 'The thing with Michael.'

'You're dragging up Michael again?' he said, always reluctant to address the subject of the man he considered his chief rival. 'I showed you the clippings and you made your own decision. You put your son first, which was the right thing for you to do.'

'Sometimes I'm not so sure . . .'

'Did he ever come back and try to change your mind?' Dean asked forcefully.

'No,' she murmured.

'Then what are you worrying about? Doesn't it prove to you that you didn't mean anything to him?'

'Thanks, Dean,' she said sarcastically. 'You make me feel like a million bucks.'

'I'll make you feel even better if you'll marry me and stop this nonsense.'

'What *nonsense*?'

'Independent woman, still insisting on paying me back, have to keep on stripping in a show—'

'I do *not* strip,' she said frostily. 'I am a showgirl. I glide round the stage in gorgeous outfits. Something wrong with that?'

'Vincent isn't happy about it.'

'Vincent should realize that what I do keeps us in the style to which *he* has become accustomed,' she snapped, fed up with criticism.

'Yes, *ma'am.*'

'When will you be back?'

'I'm not sure,' he said, hesitating for a moment. 'There's a woman I've been seeing.'

'Are you getting married again?' she asked lightly.

'If *you* won't have me, probably.'

'Hmm . . . then perhaps this time you should try and remember to get a pre-nuptial,' she teased.

'Yes, dear.'

They smiled at each other. They had an intimate friendship. And over time it seemed to strengthen and get better.

Nando's visit turned into Dani's nightmare. Just as she'd thought, he was wilder than ever, and an extremely bad influence on Vincent. Running round town was his activity of choice.

'You're too young to play in the casinos,' she warned him.

'Wouldn't do that, Mrs Castle,' Nando replied, pseudo innocent to the hilt, fake ID stashed firmly in his pants pocket.

She didn't believe him. And she knew he was smoking pot: the smell permeated the house.

'Vincent,' she asked her son, 'does Nando do drugs?'

'No, Mom.'

'I can smell grass.'

'Oh, yeah,' Vincent answered vaguely. 'That's Nando's special cigarettes. He has to smoke them for his, uh . . . throat.'

'What *are* you *talking* about?' she said, frowning. 'Do you think I'm a complete idiot?'

'No, Mom, honestly – they're medicinal.'

'Not in *this* house. Tell Nando he cannot smoke here, medicinal or otherwise.'

'C'*mon*, Mom. I'll look like a real jerk if I tell him that.'

'Should *I* tell him, then?'

'No way,' Vincent said sulkily. 'I'll do it.'

Nando was into the Rolling Stones. He played their music day and night at full volume. The raunchy rock-and-roll sounds reverberated throughout the house, giving Dani a permanent headache.

God knows what they got up to while she was at work. Unfortunately she was unable to watch them twenty-four hours a day.

One night she came home and there were girls in the house. Not one, not two, but five, all sitting round in her kitchen, smoking, drinking wine, and generally enjoying themselves. They were in their twenties and looked suspiciously like hookers in barely there outfits.

'Vincent,' she said, standing at the kitchen door, feeling like a prison guard, 'can I see you for a moment?'

He emerged, unsteady on his feet. 'Yeah, Mom?'

'Have you been drinking?'

'No.'

'What *is* going on?'

'Huh?' he mumbled, obviously drunk.

She was furious. 'Who are these girls?' she asked.

'Friends of Nando's,' he explained, a stupid grin on his handsome face. 'I said it was okay for them to hang out.'

'Well, it's not.'

'You mean I can't have friends over to the house?' he said, spoiling for a fight.

'I'm not saying that.'

'Then what *are* you saying?'

She didn't want to create a scene in front of people – it certainly wouldn't help matters to humiliate him. 'Make sure they stay in the kitchen,' she said firmly. 'Do *not* take them upstairs to your room.'

'Sure, Mom,' he mumbled sarcastically. 'Wouldn't wanna do anything to upset you.'

It was at that precise moment it occurred to her that Vincent definitely needed a strong man to control him. He needed a father.

The truth was he *had* a father. Michael Castelli. A man she'd sent away. Only now was she beginning to regret it. Oh, yes, he'd been accused of a murder, and Dean seemed to think that he'd done it. But according to the newspapers he had been acquitted, and she hadn't even given him a chance to explain *why* he hadn't told her.

She was beginning to realize that it wasn't fair to deprive Vincent of his real father.

Sometimes, when she thought about Michael, she was overcome with deep feelings of regret. She'd never fallen out of love with him, and that was something she had to face up to.

As soon as Nando left, she was taking Vincent to New York, where they were going to check out some college campuses. In her mind she made a major decision. When she got to New York, she would contact Michael and tell him the truth.

Vincent deserved to know who his real father was. It was time.

Chapter Forty-one

Tuesday, 10 July 2001

The van hurtled down Beverly Boulevard at full speed. Madison was scared that if they crashed she'd be thrown through the windshield. She wished she could reach for a seatbelt. Kind of a stupid thought in view of the circumstances.

Cole wasn't saying a word: he was concentrating on his driving, which was good. Unfortunately the helicopter still hovered above them, shining lights in the black sky.

'Get that fuckin' 'copter outta here!' the gunman yelled.

'It's not in my control,' Madison responded.

'Fuckin' *bitch*!' he muttered. 'Think you're so fuckin' smart.'

'There's nothing I can do,' she said, through clenched teeth. 'It's the media – they play by their own rules.'

'They better get the fuck outta here. 'Cause two more minutes, an' one of you mothafuckers leaves this van.'

The young woman in the back began to moan.

'Don't you have any conscience?' Madison asked, staring at him angrily. 'You've already *shot* two people. What kind of an animal are you?'

'*I* got nothin' to lose,' he jeered, small, pig eyes full of

387

hate. '*You*'re the fuckin' losers. It ain't *my* fault if you can't control shit.'

The Manray was an extremely spacious and noisy establishment, with blow-up photographs of naked girls displayed outside and a man on the street doing his best to lure customers inside.

Nando pulled up his Ferrari at the door and handed the parking valet twenty bucks. 'Keep a watch on this car, and there's another twenty for you when I come out.'

'Yes, *sir*.'

'Well,' Jolie drawled, surveying the scene, 'this looks like a pleasant little place.'

'Remember what I told you,' Nando said, taking her arm as they walked inside. 'Sure, it's sleazy now, but here's *my* thinking. We can make it into the hottest strip club in town. A place where guys can spend their money and not feel as if they're gettin' ripped off.'

Jolie was hardly prepared for the amount of nudity that assailed her. Naked girls were everywhere. The waitresses had no clothes on as they went about their business, lap dances were taking place all along the side of the stage, and on the stage ten females were doing their thing, totally nude and uninhibited.

'This is a cesspit,' Jolie said, wrinkling her nose. 'The girls aren't even attractive.'

'What did you expect? The Folies in Paris?'

'Why do you think the owners will consider partnering with you?'

''Cause everybody gets off on makin' a buck. And I can guarantee this place three times the amount of revenue it's taking now.'

'I still think you should bring Vincent in on it.'

'Oh, yeah, Vincent. Mr Pure.'

'What's he done to upset you?'

'Look,' Nando explained, 'I grew up with Vin. I know him better than anybody. He was repressed by that mother of his.'

'Don't you like Dani?'

'She's okay. Problem was she stifled the shit outta him.'

'Is that why you think he's uptight?'

'*Now* you're getting it. He *is* uptight,' Nando said, leading her through the vast room. 'He probably fucks with the lights off.'

'They must be making a fortune,' Jolie remarked. 'The place is packed.'

'Yeah, with a bad crowd who don't have two bucks to rub together. We can make it into the classiest strip club in town. We'll put in private rooms, a VIP area, hire gorgeous girls. I'm tellin' you, babe, this is a major moneymaker.'

'I don't feel comfortable here, Nando,' Jolie said as a skinny black waitress with enormous boobs swayed past them, balancing a tray of drinks.

'We're not sittin' around socializing,' Nando pointed out. 'You gotta agree, the space is unbelievable. Remember what I've always told you—'

'I know.' Jolie sighed. 'Location, location, location.'

'Here come the guys, Leroy and Darren. Now be nice.'

'Aren't I always?'

'Am I *stoned*?' Jenna giggled, totally stoned.

'You're just in a good mood,' Andy said, stroking her arm.

'No, I think I'm stoned,' she said, starting to giggle again. 'I feel all kind of tickly and tingly.'

'That's 'cause you got too many clothes on,' Andy said, tugging at her dress. 'Here, let me help you.'

'That's all right,' she said, backing away.

'C'mon, cookie, don't be shy.'

'I'm *not*.'

'Then let me see those beautiful little titties you've been thrusting at me all night.'

'I haven't been thrusting anything at you.'

'C'mon,' he coaxed again. 'Look at Anais – *she*'s not shy.'

Jenna glanced over at the beautiful black girl, who was once again lounging on the couch, legs spread, ebony skin glistening.

'Did you know that Anais likes girls?' Andy said, moving close and nibbling on her ear.

'I like girls, too,' Jenna said. 'I've got lots of girlfriends.'

'I didn't mean in *that* way,' he said, pushing back a lock of his trademark dirty blond hair. 'Have you ever made out with a girl?'

'What do you mean?' she asked, widening her eyes.

'God!' Andy said. 'You are young, aren't you?'

'I'm twenty-two,' she said matter-of-factly. 'How old are *you*?'

'Same,' he mumbled.

'What's your star sign?'

'It doesn't matter.'

'Yes, it does,' Jenna said earnestly. 'A person's star sign is the key to their personality.'

'Take off your dress. I wanna look at your boobs.'

'I don't think—'

'I've seen 'em once tonight in the Jacuzzi, remember? So what's the harm in showing me again?'

'Okay,' she said agreeably, beginning to disrobe.

'*That's* more like it,' Andy said, rubbing his hands together in anticipation.

Dani walked into the bedroom and lay down on the bed. She needed to rest, her mind was buzzing. There was so much going on, what with Michael turning up unexpectedly and the new accusation against him – which couldn't help reminding her of the last time he'd been accused.

First Beth.

Now Stella.

She was sure he was innocent, but how strange for it to happen twice.

She could hear the murmur of conversation as he talked to Vincent in the other room. Father and son bonding. She loved it when they were together.

Reaching for the TV remote, she clicked on the news. Almost immediately she heard Madison's name mentioned, and her photograph was flashed on the screen.

'Michael!' she called out, abruptly sitting up. 'Michael, Vincent – quickly, get in here!'

'What?' Michael said, entering the bedroom, Vincent right behind him.

The newscaster – a prettier-than-a-movie-star blonde – relayed the latest. 'A high-speed chase is currently taking place in Hollywood. Journalist Madison Castelli is one of the captives in the van with four other hostages. There are three gunmen involved, and apparently two hostages have already been shot.'

Michael stared at the screen and paled. 'Jesus!' he said. 'They must've got to her before we did. Those *bastards*!'

Sofia couldn't sleep. She felt embarrassed about what had happened, and she also didn't care to face Gianni in the morning. This was the first time a man had rejected her, and she couldn't believe it.

Stealthily, she got out of bed, found her clothes and dressed. Then she left his suite.

At the front desk she asked the concierge to call her a cab.

'May I ask where you will be going?' the concierge inquired, a snooty man with attitude.

'Ask away,' she said, 'because it's really none of your business.'

The concierge gave her a superior look and informed her that the cab would arrive in fifteen minutes.

'I'll wait outside,' she said.

She walked from the entrance of the luxurious hotel and sat down on the kerbside.

Goodbye, Gianni. Sorry it didn't work out.

'Fuck!' the gunman said, as the helicopter continued to track them, spotlights shining down from the dark sky. 'Slide open the side door.'

'Huh?' Ace said, from the back seat.

'Slide open the fuckin' door, an' shove that whinin' bitch out.'

'I'll pull over,' Cole said, swerving the van.

'Yeah, if you want a bullet in your head.'

'No!' The girl in the back started to scream, as the two gunmen began manhandling her. 'No, no, *no!*'

It was too late.

Ace and the other guy slid open the side door and tossed her from the moving van like a sack of garbage.

Her frantic screams hung in the air.

Chapter Forty-two

Michael and Dani: 1982

Michael was in his office when his assistant, Marcie, informed him there was someone called Tina on the phone. He could tell that Marcie – who was very protective, did not want to put her through. 'She *says* it's personal,' Marcie said, with a disbelieving curl of her lip.

'I'll take it,' he said, picking up the receiver.

'Michael?' a female voice said.

'Tina?' he responded, genuinely pleased to hear from his old friend. 'How you doing?'

'Fine, thank you very much,' Tina replied crisply, adding a succinct 'Not that *you* care, since we never see you any more.'

'That's not true.'

'Yes, it is, and Max is fine, too, in case you're interested.'

Good old Tina, snippy as ever. 'It's great to hear your voice,' he said.

'I'm surprised you would say that.'

'C'mon, Tina,' he groaned. 'It's not *my* fault you don't get along with Stella.'

'And whose fault is it that you never see your best friend Max any more? Do you understand how hurt he is?'

Here it came, the lecture. Tina was a master at breaking

a man's balls. 'You didn't hear what he said about Stella,' Michael said.

'Whatever it was,' she argued, 'I'm sure it wasn't bad enough to end a friendship.'

'Stella's my *wife*, Tina. I have to show her respect.' God! Shades of Vito Giovanni. Had the man really had that much influence over him?

Yes.

And sometimes he still did.

'Anyway,' Tina continued, 'that's not the reason I'm calling.'

'What is?'

'Somebody's looking for you.'

'And who would that be?'

'Remember Dani?'

Did he remember Dani? Yes, he certainly remembered Dani.

'What about her?' he asked, trying to sound disinterested.

'She's here in New York, and she called me.'

'She did, huh?'

'Yes. She wants to see you.'

He took a deep breath, reached for a cigarette, and lit up. 'Dani wants to see *me*?'

'Yep. I promised I'd pass the message on. In case you're interested, she's staying at the Plaza.'

'Nice of you to tell me, Tina. Only aren't you forgetting that I'm married now? So I don't think I'll be calling her.'

'She said there's something she has to talk to you about.'

He inhaled deeply. 'Did she say what?'

'No, but she asked me to tell you it's important.'

'Will *you* be seeing her?'

'She might come over to the house with her son.'

'At least *you* get to meet him.'

'You mean *you* didn't?'

'No. That was one of the bones of contention between us. She didn't want me meeting him,' he said, placing his cigarette in a marble ashtray. 'I guess it's one of the reasons she took off. Who knows? She's my past, and I'm not planning on revisiting.'

'Are *we* part of your past, Michael?' Tina asked, suddenly sounding needy.

'No,' he said warmly. 'You, Max and the kids are always in my heart.'

'That's so sweet.'

'I can be a nice guy when I want to,' he joked.

'We hear about you from Charlie. You're Mr Big Shot now.'

'C'*mon*, Tina,' he said, embarrassed.

'How's Madison doing?'

'She's unbelievable,' he said, picking up his cigarette and taking another deep drag. 'Eleven years old and the smartest kid you've ever come across.'

'Is Stella a good mother to her?'

'Stella's a wonderful woman,' he said, exhaling smoke.

'I'm sure,' Tina said sarcastically. 'When she finds the time.'

'What does *that* mean?'

'I read the society columns, Michael. Your wife is never home; she's always out and about at some big opening or charity event.'

'Stella gets off on doing good deeds.'

'Sure.'

'Anyway, Tina, we'll get together soon. That's a promise.'

'Max would love to see you. Only don't tell him I told you 'cause he's bound to give you a hard time.'

'I can take it.'

'I know.'

Thoughtfully he put down the phone. Dani Castle. Seven years of silence, and now she wanted to speak to him. What could she possibly want?

In a way he was intrigued, on the other hand he knew he shouldn't go anywhere near her, because what would happen if he did? All they had to do was look into each other's eyes and that was it. Chemistry. They had it in spades.

Not any more. He was married, it was a whole different ballgame. Stella was Madison's mother, and he wouldn't mess with that.

A beat of two, and he picked up the phone. 'Get me the number of the Plaza,' he said to Marcie.

Jesus Christ! Aren't you even going to think about it?

Apparently not.

Marcie gave him the number. He wrote it on a pad on his desk and stared at it for a few minutes before picking up his private line.

When the hotel operator answered, he requested Dani Castle. Even saying her name brought back a flood of memories, most of them good.

'There's nobody in the room at the present time,' the operator said. 'Would you care to leave a message?'

'I'll try again later,' he said, and replaced the receiver.

Plain fact of life. He wanted to see her. He had to know why she'd dumped him.

Not that he cared.

Or did he?

That night he and Stella were due to attend another boring opera. He simply wasn't into her social scene any more. At first it had been a kick, now it was plain work – and not the kind he enjoyed either. He wasn't into her friends. The women were so thin they could slide through a crack in a wall. They were mean-spirited too – all they did was gossip about one another and try to outdo their best friend's jewellery. He was well aware that the men looked down on him in spite of his success. He simply did not come from the right background.

He called Stella at home, and informed her that he wouldn't be able to make the opera.

'You have to,' she said, her voice frosty.

'No, I don't,' he answered evenly. 'What I have to do is attend an urgent meeting.'

'Oh, God, Michael, this is *so* aggravating,' she said, sounding upset. 'You know how I hate going to these things alone.'

'Take your walker,' he said, mentioning a gay art dealer who sometimes stood in for him when he was unable to accompany her to functions.

'Very well,' Stella said, in an uptight voice. 'I'll do that.'

He waited an hour before trying the Plaza again. Still no answer in the room.

He had no intention of leaving his office until he reached her.

Dani Castle. He'd never expected to hear from her again.

'Well,' Tina said, throwing open the door of her house, 'it's only taken you seven years to get here.'

Dani stood there smiling. 'I encountered a few problems along the way,' she said, observing that Tina had put on about fifty pounds although she was as pretty as ever. 'This is my son, Vincent,' she added, giving Vincent a little shove.

He stepped forward, reluctantly shaking Tina's hand. Lately he had not been getting along with his mother, finding her far too controlling. It had taken Nando's visit to open his eyes.

As soon as Tina got a look at him she did an immediate

double-take. 'Oh . . . my . . . God!' she gasped, shooting a quick glance at Dani. '*Now* I know what you want to see Michael about.'

Dani frowned, to shut her up. Tina got it.

'What a lovely house,' Dani said, walking inside.

'Yeah,' Tina said proudly. 'Max did okay for us. He recently bought me a new Corvette. I figure the kids are so old that if I don't get a Corvette now I swear I'll *never* get one.' She took another long look at Vincent. 'How old are you, dear?'

'Seventeen,' he answered, wondering who the hell this woman was and why they had had to go see her.

'You must meet my son, Harry, he's sixteen,' Tina said. 'Can't believe I'm the mother of a teenager!'

They all trooped into the large, comfortable living room. There were dogs, cats, oversize couches, books and magazines everywhere. It was a real home.

'I made that call,' Tina said quietly. 'The one you asked me to.'

'Thanks,' Dani said, glancing at Vincent, who was prowling restlessly round the room.

'So, uh, Vincent, is this your first trip to New York?' Tina asked.

'Yeah,' he said. 'First time out of Vegas.'

'Las Vegas is *spectacular*,' Tina raved. 'Did your mom ever tell you about the time we went to see Elvis? I *still* remember it as the most exciting night of my life. And that *includes* my wedding night!'

They all laughed.

Harry slouched into the room. Overweight with an abundance of freckles, he had a permanent sneer and a fiendish sense of humour.

'Say hello to Vincent,' Tina said cheerfully. 'He's from Las Vegas. And this is his mom, Dani.'

'Hi,' Harry mumbled.

'Maybe you can take Vincent upstairs and show him your room.'

'My room,' Harry said, making a face. 'Dontcha mean my pigpen? That's what you usually call it.'

'Harry!' Tina said warningly. 'We have company.'

'All right, Mom,' Harry said. 'C'mon,' he added, beckoning to Vincent.

A reluctant Vincent followed him upstairs.

'Oh my Lord!' Tina said, turning to Dani. 'He's Michael's son, isn't he?'

'Is it so obvious?'

'Obvious!' Tina said, her face all flushed. 'For God's sake! He's the spitting image!'

'I suppose he is.'

'How come you never told Michael?' Tina asked excitedly. 'He doesn't know, does he?'

'No, he doesn't,' Dani said, shaking her head.

'And now you're going to *tell* him?'

'I finally decided it's only fair.'

'You *do* know Michael is married?'

'No, I didn't know that,' she said, experiencing a sharp stab of regret. 'It doesn't matter, though. This is strictly about him and Vincent.'

'You broke Michael's heart when you left him waiting at the airport,' Tina confided. 'Can I ask what happened?'

'I found out about Beth.'

'Oh, God!' Tina exclaimed. 'I warned him that he should tell you.'

'Unfortunately he didn't,' Dani sighed, 'and when I found out, it was quite a shock.'

'He didn't do it, you know,' Tina said quickly. 'He was set up by certain lowlife people he was involved with. Y'see, Michael's mom was shot in a robbery before he was born, and Beth's murder was some kind of complicated revenge thing.'

'I knew about his mother. I didn't know about Beth.'

'You should've called me. I would've explained every-thing.'

'I didn't think about doing that.'

'Y'know, Michael's a great guy,' Tina said earnestly. 'He'd never hurt anyone. Ask Max, he'll vouch for him.'

'Too late now,' Dani said wryly.

'Anyway,' Tina continued, 'the problem is, *how* will you tell him? You can't walk in with Vincent like you did here, he'll know immediately. And I wouldn't think his wife will take it too well.'

'What's his wife like?' Dani couldn't help asking.

'A major cold bitch!'

'She is?'

'Oh yeah. Nobody can figure out why he married her, except I suppose she *is* beautiful. The deal is he wanted a mom for Madison, and Stella's it. Michael adores his little girl. He used to bring her over all the time, but now we never see them.'

'How do *you* think I should handle this?'

'Tell him straight. Say, "Listen, Michael, you've got a seventeen-year-old son". No point in dragging it out.'

'You're right.'

'Does Vincent know?'

'I haven't got round to telling him yet.'

'Wow, Dani. You've sure got a whole lot of explaining to do.'

'I know,' she said, realizing how right Tina was.

'Wish I could help.'

'You can't, although I appreciate the offer.'

Later, back at the hotel, the phone rang. Dani quickly picked up.

'This is Michael. Tina said you wanted to speak to me.'

'Uh, yes, I do,' she said, glancing over at Vincent, who

was busy flicking through TV channels with the remote.

'So, I'm calling you. What is it?'

He sounded cold and distant and angry. She didn't blame him.

'Can we meet?' she asked in a low voice.

'Is that necessary?'

'Actually, it is. I have something important to tell you.'

'And you can't tell me on the phone?' he said, not making it easy.

'No.'

'It's ten of nine,' he said abruptly. 'I can meet you in the bar of your hotel in fifteen minutes.'

'I was thinking maybe dinner tomorrow night.'

'At the bar in fifteen minutes, or forget it,' he said brusquely.

'I'll be there,' she said, understanding his anger, but saddened by it all the same.

'Where're you going, Mom?' Vincent asked.

'I have to meet an old friend downstairs in the bar,' she said, pulling out her favourite blue dress from the closet. It matched her eyes.

'Then why're you getting all dressed up?'

'I wish you wouldn't ask so many questions,' she said, choosing a pair of small gold earrings and clipping them to her earlobes. 'Can't I look nice to see an old friend?'

'Yeah, but you're, like, all nervous, spraying on perfume and shit.'

'Don't use language like that, Vincent,' she said sternly.

'Mom,' he said, throwing her a disgusted look, 'I'm seventeen. If I can't use it at home, where can I use it – school?'

'It's not proper,' she said, fussing with her hair.

'Nando says you keep too sharp a watch on me.'

'Nando says that, does he?' she said, irritated.

'Yeah.'

'Maybe it's because Nando doesn't have a mother to watch *him*. Could be he's jealous, don't you think?'

'Nando? Jealous of me?' Vincent said, hooting with laughter. 'No way.'

'Anyway, why don't you watch TV? I won't be long.'

'Great! We fly to New York, and *I* gotta sit in a hotel room watching TV while *you* go out.'

'I'll be back soon.'

'Nando's offered me a trip to Colombia,' he said, knowing it would piss her off.

'*What?*'

'He's sending me a ticket.'

'If you think I'm letting you go to Colombia by yourself, you can think again.'

'I'm going, Mom,' he said, challenging her. 'You can't stop me.'

This was not the time to get into a fight. 'Watch TV,' she said, grabbing her purse. 'Don't drive me crazy.'

Vincent was right. Why was she getting all dressed up to see an old friend? Except Michael was more than an old friend – he was the love of her life, and he always would be.

Still, she had to remember he was married, and she would respect that, even though Tina had called his wife a cold bitch.

She checked her appearance in the mirror one last time. Had she changed that much?

No, she still looked the same.

'Order whatever you want from Room Service,' she said, heading for the door.

'Gee thanks, Mom,' he answered sarcastically.

Michael took a cab from his office. He'd sent his car and driver home so that the man could drive Stella and her escort tonight. He didn't mind taking cabs – in fact, he

quite enjoyed it. Having a car and driver was not *his* idea –
it was Stella's. 'This is New York,' she'd pointed out. 'It's
impossible to park, therefore we should have a driver.'

Why not? All her friends did.

He wondered what Dani wanted after all this time. In
a way he was excited to see her, and in another way he
would have been quite happy never to have heard from
her again.

Dani Castle. A vision from his past.

When Dani entered the bar, men turned to stare. It was not
unusual: she always had that effect on the male sex. She
spotted a table in the corner, went over and sat down. After
a few minutes the waiter came to take her order.

'A glass of white wine,' she said, realizing that her hands
were shaking.

Michael was late. Was he going to turn up? She
wouldn't be surprised if he didn't.

A beat of ten and a tall man with a beard hovered by her
table. 'May I buy the beautiful lady a drink?' he asked, the
smell of his aftershave overpowering.

'That's very generous of you,' she said coolly. 'However,
I don't think my husband would appreciate it.'

'Whoa – sorry,' the man said, rapidly backing away.

She tapped her fingers on the glass-top table, grabbed a
handful of nuts, and began stuffing them nervously into her
mouth.

The waiter brought her wine. She took several gulps for
courage. This was an impossible situation to be in. It was
one thing telling Michael he had a son, but how was she
going to tell Vincent? He was under the impression that
Sam Froog was his father, a father he'd never seen much of:
once Sam had got the settlement money he'd vanished out
of their lives.

She glanced up, and there he was. Michael Castelli.

Striding into the bar, looking more handsome than ever in a dark suit, white shirt, and pearl grey tie.

God, he always had such an incredible effect on her. The very sight of him made her feel warm all over.

His dark eyes surveyed the room until he spotted her. Then he walked towards her, threading his way purposefully through the tables until he reached her. 'Dani,' he said, standing by her table.

'Hi, Michael,' she answered.

No physical contact, not even a handshake.

He pulled up a chair and sat down. 'What're you drinking?'

'White wine.'

He clicked his fingers for the waiter, who hurried over. 'Jack Daniel's on the rocks,' he said. 'And another glass of wine for the lady.'

'Yes, sir,' the waiter answered, responding to his authoritative manner.

'So, Dani,' Michael said, slightly warmer than he had been on the phone, but still cool all the same, 'what brings you to New York?'

'I'm here with my son,' she said. 'We're checking out college campuses.'

'How *is* your son?' he asked politely.

'Very well, thank you. And Madison?'

'Great.'

'She must be big.'

'She's eleven,' he said, taking a very obvious look at his watch – which she noticed was an expensive gold Rolex. 'I've got fifteen minutes,' he said briskly. 'Then I have to be somewhere.'

'I thought that maybe we could spend the evening together,' she said tentatively. 'Although I quite understand if you don't want to.'

'You understand, huh?' he said, his voice edgy.

'Listen, Michael,' she said, speaking fast, 'I know what I did was unforgivable, but you should have been honest with me.'

'About what?'

'Beth.'

'Oh,' he said, suddenly deflated. 'How did you find out about that?'

'A friend of mine showed me the newspaper clippings.'

'Some friend,' he muttered.

'It was very upsetting to find out that way. I thought we were close, and I . . . I couldn't risk flying to New York to be with a man I obviously didn't know.'

'And of course you couldn't discuss it with me, call me up and say, "Hey, Michael, why the fuck didn't you tell me?"'

'It wasn't right, Michael. You were keeping secrets.'

'I guess you didn't give a shit that I was acquitted?' he said, stony-faced.

She sighed. Obviously this was going to be short and not so sweet. 'I can see that you're not interested in spending time with me,' she said. 'I don't blame you. So I'll come right out with what I have to tell you.'

'Good.'

'Prepare yourself,' she said quietly. 'It'll be a shock.'

'Nothing you do or say can shock me, Dani. You dumped me – remember? I must admit *that* kinda shocked me at the time, so now, whatever you do – fuck it, I don't care.'

She hated his cold indifference. This was difficult enough without having to deal with his negative vibes.

'You probably wondered why I never introduced you to my son.'

'What's that got to do with anything?'

'There *is* a reason.'

'And that would be . . .?'

She took a long slow beat, and then came out with it, just as Tina had advised. 'Vincent is *our* son.'

'*Excuse* me?' he said, looking at her as if she were crazy.

'The first time we slept together I got pregnant,' she said, her words tumbling over one another.

'Jesus *Christ*!'

'I had a baby, Vincent – he's your son as well as mine. I never told you because you obviously didn't care about me. Then when you *did* come back several years later, and we got together, I thought I'd tell you then. I was going to do it when I came to New York.' She took a deep breath. 'Oh, God, Michael, I *know* I should've told you. I feel so guilty now because Vincent really needs his father. I'm so sorry.'

'I don't fucking believe this,' he said, shaking his head.

'It's true,' she said, close to tears. 'I never slept with anyone else – you were the only one.'

'You got married, didn't you?' he said harshly.

'I married Sam because I was pregnant,' she explained. 'I made him believe the baby was his.'

'Talk about *me* keeping secrets,' Michael said, giving her a long, hard stare. 'How devious can you get?'

'You mustn't punish Vincent because of my mistakes.'

'I don't even *know* Vincent.'

'I kept the two of you apart because he looks so much like you. When I took him to Tina's today, she was amazed.'

'*Tina* knows, and you're only *just* telling me? This is fucking unreal.'

'I have to tell Vincent. Then I thought that maybe tomorrow the two of you can finally meet.'

'Are you out of your freaking *mind*?' he said angrily. 'I'm married, Dani. *Married*. As far as Madison is concerned, Stella is her *mother*. And believe me, anyone who tells her otherwise will be very sorry indeed.'

'I understand,' she said meekly.

'Good. 'Cause I think it's great that you're coming to

me seventeen years later and telling me I've got a son. Only you know what? It's too goddamn late. I don't *want* to meet him. I don't *want* to have anything to do with you. And right now I'm getting up and walking out of here. So . . . do us both a big favour, and *never* contact me again.'

Chapter Forty-three

Michael and Dani: 1982

'I said come visit, only I didn't reckon it was going to be this soon,' Tina said, standing at the door of her house.

'I need to talk,' Michael said, shoving past her.

'I wonder why,' Tina said, following him. 'We're eating late tonight and are in the middle of dinner.'

'I don't want dinner.'

'I didn't offer.'

'Thanks!'

'You'd better say hello to Max, otherwise he'll think something strange is going on.'

'Something strange *is* going on, Tina,' he said, turning on her. 'Why the hell didn't you warn me?'

'I guess this means Dani told you?'

'Damn right.'

'What are you going to do?'

'Why should I do *anything*?' Michael responded, his handsome face grim. 'She raised a son I knew nothing about. Now I'm supposed to believe he's mine. Fuck that shit.'

'Hey,' Max said, emerging from the dining room, 'what's going on? Jeez!' he said, spotting Michael. 'A ghost from the past.'

'Nice greeting,' Michael said.

'What do you want – a hug and a kiss? Look at you, all dressed up, Mr City Freakin' Big Shot.'

'Cut the crap,' Michael said. 'I know we haven't seen each other in a while, but I'm here because you're my friends. And I don't need to hear shit.'

'Oh,' Max said. '*Finally* he discovers he has friends.'

Tina, who had not filled her husband in, quickly shushed him. 'Let's go into the living room,' she said, taking Michael's arm.

'I need a drink,' Michael said.

'So fix yourself one,' Max said, adding a sarcastic, 'Sorry, the staff are all on vacation.'

'Where do you keep the booze?' Michael asked, ignoring Max's crack.

'In that cupboard over there,' Max said. 'You want ice, get it from the kitchen.'

'Max,' Tina scolded, 'stop behaving like a jerk. Michael had a big shock tonight.'

'What kind of shock?'

'The kind of shock where a woman comes back seventeen years later and tells you you've got a son,' Tina said.

'*What?*' Max said, sitting down.

'I was going to tell you later,' Tina said. 'Here's the fast version. Dani's son, Vincent, is Michael's.'

'How come she didn't tell me when we started seeing each other again?' Michael said tersely.

'She must've had her reasons,' Tina said, shrugging.

'What're you gonna do?' Max asked.

'It's not *my* problem,' Michael said, pouring himself a hefty drink. 'It's *her* fucking problem.'

'She said the boy needs a father,' Tina interjected.

'She should've thought of that before.'

'Does that mean you won't see him?'

'Why would I?'

'I think you should,' Tina ventured. 'After all, it's not *his* fault.'

'I gotta figure this one out on my own,' Michael said.

'That's true,' Max agreed.

'Hey, listen, sorry I barged in on you tonight – didn't know where else to go.'

'How about home to your *wife*?' Tina suggested.

'Jesus!' Michael said. 'If Stella finds out, she'll go nuts.'

'Oh, yes, I imagine she would,' Tina said, quite enjoying the thought of an out-of-control Stella.

'Let's not discuss my wife,' Michael said shortly. 'We'll get together when she's not around, okay?'

'Yes, Michael,' Tina said. 'And if you want my advice – which you probably don't – you *should* see your son. It's the right thing to do.'

Dani felt like a total failure. Not only had she failed to connect with Michael, but when she'd told Vincent the truth, he'd yelled at her and run out of the hotel. She had no idea where he'd gone.

She didn't know whether or not to call the police. Instead she called Tina.

'Don't worry,' Tina reassured her. 'He'll come back.'

'How do you know?'

'He can look after himself,' Tina said. 'Don't believe everything you read about New York. If he's not back in the morning, *then* start worrying.'

'I'm sorry to bother you in the middle of the night.'

'That's okay,' Tina said, adding a casual, 'By the way, Michael dropped by.'

'How was he?'

'Angry and frustrated.'

'I know,' Dani said sadly. 'He didn't take it well.'

'Give him time,' Tina said. 'I know Michael, he'll come round.'

'I don't have that kind of time,' Dani said. 'We're only here for five days.'

'Michael's tough on the outside, soft on the inside. He won't turn his back on his own son.'

'I hope not,' Dani whispered.

Eventually, at three a.m., Vincent returned to the hotel. Dani was awake. 'Where have you been?' she asked.

'Why do *you* care?' he said.

'Look, I know you're upset, but you've got to realize that everything I did I thought was for the best.'

'Jesus, Mom,' he said, throwing her a look, 'you must've been a real tramp. A one-night stand and you got yourself knocked up. How come you didn't get an abortion?'

She tried to remain calm. 'We wouldn't be having this conversation if I'd done that, would we?'

'You should've,' he muttered.

'I didn't abort you because I wanted you. Is that good enough?'

'How come you didn't tell him?'

'I didn't know how to reach Michael. I was very young and scared, so I married Sam. How did I know he was going to turn out to be a drunk?'

'You certainly made bad choices,' Vincent said, and marched off into the other bedroom.

In the morning, when she awoke, he was gone again. Fury overcame her. How was she supposed to deal with him? The situation was becoming impossible.

Michael was drinking coffee and staring out of the window when Marcie knocked on the door and entered his office. 'There's a young man here to see you,' she announced.

'Who?'

'He said his name is Vincent. Wouldn't say what he wants.' She looked at him curiously. 'Do you have a relative by that name?'

He sighed. 'Why are you asking, Marcie?'

'There's quite a strong resemblance.'

'Send him in,' Michael said.

Now his mind was really racing. The kid had actually come to see him. Had Dani sent him? What did they want from him? Money? Okay, so he'd give the boy a cheque. Big fucking deal.

When Vincent walked into his office, Michael could hardly believe it. Everyone was right: it was almost like looking into a mirror twenty years ago.

They stared at each other. Vincent was obviously equally startled.

'Shut the door, Marcie,' Michael said gruffly. 'And hold my calls.'

'Yes, Mr Castelli,' Marcie said, intrigued by this new development in her normally routine life. She left the office, shutting the door behind her.

Michael indicated a seat. 'Take the weight off,' he said.

Vincent sat down. They regarded each other warily for a moment.

'So . . . what can I do for you?' Michael said at last.

'Is that all you've got to say to me?' Vincent said, biting his lower lip.

'Look, I saw your mother last night for the first time since she dumped me seven years ago,' Michael explained. 'And you know what she says to me? "Seventeen years ago when you and I had a one-night stand, we made a kid."' He took a beat. 'Only problem, she forgot to tell me about this until last night. And *you*'re that kid, right?'

'She never told me anything until last night either,' Vincent said, his eyes darting round the well-appointed office. 'I thought my father was some drunk who'd run off with a shitload of money. Now I'm told it's you. I don't know who you are, which means I don't know who I am, do I?'

'What is it that you want from me?' Michael asked, deciding to end this fast. 'Money?'

'Is that what you think I came here for – money?' Vincent said, giving him a cold look. 'My mom's worked hard all these years to make sure I had everything I needed. I guess she never got a dollar from you.'

'Weren't you *listening*?' Michael said, exasperated. 'I *didn't know* I had a kid until last night.'

'Like that's my fault,' Vincent muttered.

'So what I'll do is write you a cheque, and you can take it home to your mom and tell her this is the money I owe her for raising you. Now, since I don't know who the hell you are, or anything about you, that'll be the end of our commitment to each other.'

'You *bastard*,' Vincent said, jumping up.

'How come *I'm* the bastard?'

''Cause *I'm your son*,' Vincent said. 'How do you think *I* feel? I came here hoping to find a dad, someone I can look up to and respect. And it sure as hell isn't you.'

An image of Vinny sitting in his wheelchair glued to the TV swam before Michael's eyes. He remembered his father never giving him a moment's attention, because as far as Vinny was concerned his life had ended when his wife was shot and he'd lost the use of his legs. Was he going to do the same to *his* kid? Ignore him. Send him away. Give him nothing except money.

'Listen—' he began.

'No,' Vincent interrupted angrily. 'I don't have to listen. You're not interested in *me*. You don't want to take any kind of responsibility. So screw you.'

'That's not—'

'We don't want your lousy money,' Vincent shouted. 'I'm going back to my mom – at least *she* cares.'

'How many times I gotta tell you?' Michael said, exasperated. 'I didn't *know* you were my son.'

413

'Sorry I've bothered you,' Vincent said, heading for the door. 'I hoped we might've had some connection. Now I realize coming here was a bad idea.'

'Hey, wait a minute,' Michael said, standing up and moving out from behind his desk. 'You're right. We're kind of like innocent parties in this. Dani should've told us both, but she didn't. So now I'm blaming you, and *you're* blaming me. And the truth is, we're both wrong.' He paused. 'Does Dani know you're here?'

'She'd be pissed if she thought I'd come to see you.'

'Tell you what, kid, I'm gonna take you out to lunch, and we'll get to know each other. How's that?'

Vincent hesitated for a moment. 'I'd like to know you,' he said tentatively.

'Then we'll do it, huh?'

'As long as you stop calling me kid.'

'That's a deal.'

'Should we call Mom? She's probably going crazy wondering where I am.'

'Why not?' Michael said, picking up the phone.

Dani answered immediately. 'Vincent, is that you?'

'No, it's me, Michael.'

'Oh.'

'Vincent's here with me. We're doing some family bonding.'

'I thought you—'

'Don't worry about it, Dani. He's spending the day with me. I'll drop him back at the hotel round six.'

'But, Michael—'

'I *said* don't worry about it.'

'Fine,' she said, and put down the phone.

Things were looking up.

Chapter Forty-four

Michael and Dani: 1982

After her evening at the opera, Stella decided that the time had come for her to spend a few days at a health farm. She did this on a regular basis, placing her beauty treatments above all else.

Michael was relieved. Now that he'd got used to the idea of having Vincent around, it helped that Stella was absent, and since Madison was away at school, he had no commitments.

He'd spent the last three days with Vincent, and discovered that the son he never knew he had was a smart kid, able to converse on any subject, and interesting to be with.

Vincent spoke a lot about his friend Nando, in Colombia, and how they were planning to do stuff together.

'Isn't Dani expecting you to go to college?' Michael asked, as they stood in a men's store, trying on jackets.

'Did *you* go to college?' Vincent retaliated.

'Naw,' Michael said, grinning. 'I dropped outta school at fifteen to run the family convenience store. I should tell you about your great-grandma Lani – what a character!'

'How about *your* dad?' Vincent asked, picking out a

black leather motorcycle jacket with silver studs. 'What was *he* like?'

'That's another story. We'll get into it one of these days.'

'So what's the deal?' Vincent said, reminding Michael of himself at the same age. 'Why do I have to go to college?'

''Cause it's what your mom wants,' Michael replied, trying on a dark blue Armani sports jacket that suited him admirably.

'You said it,' Vincent said heatedly. 'It's what *she* wants, not what *I* want. Nando and me, we're gonna travel around the world.'

'You are?'

'Hey, if I don't do it now, when'll I *ever* get the chance?'

'And how can you afford to do that?'

'Nando inherits a shitload of money when he's twenty-one,' Vincent said enthusiastically. 'He figures he can score an advance from the bank.'

'I see,' Michael said. 'So you're gonna travel around the world on somebody else's money – is that it?'

'Nando and me are like brothers.'

'Word of advice: never take advantage of a friend's dime.'

'College is not for me,' Vincent said, shrugging off the leather jacket. 'I know what I want to do.'

'Yeah, what's that?'

'Something in Vegas with Nando. We've been talking about it. We want to open our own place.'

'What kind of place?'

'A bar or a restaurant. Maybe even a hotel.'

'I like it,' Michael joked. 'He thinks small.'

'We can make it work if I don't have to waste my time in college. Will you talk to Mom for me?'

'Okay, okay.'

'You'll do it?'

Michael nodded thoughtfully. 'Maybe the three of us

should have dinner tonight,' he said, thinking it wouldn't be such a bad thing to see Dani again.

'That'd be great,' Vincent said.

'I'll call her later,' Michael said, wondering if he was making a wise move inviting Dani to dinner. She'd looked so beautiful the other night. He'd tried not to be influenced by that – an impossible task. But now, having spent time with Vincent, he'd kind of got used to the situation, and he had to admit that Dani had done an excellent job in raising the boy, and she'd done it all by herself. They could be friends, couldn't they?

He decided he should give her money – money he would have been sending her over the years if he'd known she'd had his child.

The sales assistant came over, a gay man thrilled to be dealing with two such handsome customers. 'Well?' the young man questioned. 'Have we decided?'

'Whatever my son wants,' Michael said. 'And I'll take the Armani.'

'Of course you will,' the sales assistant murmured admiringly. 'It looks *so* good on you.'

Later that day Michael sat at his desk considering how much he should give Dani. He finally made her out a cheque for two hundred and fifty thousand dollars. Whether she'd accept it or not was another matter. He'd insist. She couldn't say no.

His next problem was where to go for dinner. It would not be wise to take them anywhere Stella's friends might see them, so he called Tina and requested suggestions.

'Come over here,' she said. 'Max is barbecuing. It'll be all family and fun – or chaos, depending.'

'You sure?'

'Why not?'

'We'll be there.'

'Is everything going okay?'

'It's an odd situation, but you're right, I *should* get to know Vincent, so that's what I've been doing.'

When he finally called Dani, she was initially reluctant. But after Vincent got on her case, she called Michael back and agreed to come for dinner.

That night he picked them up in a cab at their hotel. As usual, Dani looked breathtakingly gorgeous in a white silk pantsuit, her long blonde hair piled on top of her head, gold hoop earrings hanging from her ears.

'Hey—' he said, thinking about the good memories they'd shared.

'Hi, Michael,' she murmured, wondering why she'd agreed to do this, although relieved to see that he was obviously in a much better mood than the other night.

Deep down Michael knew that Dani would have been a more caring mother to Madison. Only he couldn't allow those thoughts to live in his mind. *Stella* was Madison's mother, and that's the way it had to stay.

At Tina and Max's house, everyone was gathered in the backyard. Harry had a bunch of his friends over shooting hoops, while Susie was sitting round with a couple of her teenage girlfriends, who took one look at Vincent and immediately began to nudge one another and giggle self-consciously.

'I can see it's family night,' Michael said, wishing Madison were there with him, so that she could enjoy it too.

'Hey, Vinny,' Harry yelled, 'get over here an' play ball.'

'I've never heard him called Vinny before,' Dani remarked, watching her son as he joined Harry and his friends.

'You *did* know it was my father's name?' Michael said, wondering if it was his imagination or were her eyes even more startlingly blue than he remembered?

'No.'

'My name too,' he said, pursuing the subject.

'Your name's Michael,' she stated.

'Vincenzio Michael Castellino,' he announced. 'That's what's on my birth certificate.'

'Really?'

'You named him Vincent and you didn't know that?' he said quizzically, not believing her for a second.

'Maybe I did,' she said offhandedly. 'I think you might've told me once.'

'Yeah, but isn't Vincent kinda formal?'

'He doesn't like it when people shorten it.'

'Well, well, well, this is just like old times,' Max said, strolling over. 'Anyone want a beer?'

'Sounds good,' Michael said, as Tina joined them.

'Why don't you two go sit over there?' Tina said, pointing to a large picnic table set up next to her three prized rosebushes and a large patch of grass.

Michael took Dani's arm and steered her to the table. It felt so good being with him, she thought, and yet she knew this could lead nowhere.

'He's a great kid, Dani,' Michael said, sitting down. 'You've done quite a job.'

'Thanks,' she answered coolly, adding quickly, 'Have you told your wife yet?'

'*Not* a good idea,' he said. 'It's better she doesn't find out about Vincent.'

'Why?'

'Y'see, Dani, I really want him in my life, only I gotta keep him separate from what I got going on here. Can you understand that?'

'If Vincent understands, then I suppose I can.'

'I'll be there for him. That's a promise.'

'It's definitely what he needs,' she said, relieved that things seemed to be working out.

'No,' Michael said firmly. 'What he needs is some freedom.'

'Excuse me?'

'He tells me you're always on his case – making him study and work hard.'

'That's what he's supposed to do, Michael.'

'He was telling me about his friend Nando – the one he wants to visit in Colombia. Says you're against it.'

'I am,' she said, not liking the direction this conversation was heading.

'Why?'

'Nando's a bad influence.'

'What's a bad influence?' he said restlessly. 'The kid hasn't even got laid yet.'

'Michael!'

'He's seventeen. You and me got together when you were *sixteen*. Don't make him into a mommy's boy.'

'I'm not,' she said stubbornly.

'You are.'

'I have to protect him.'

'From *what*?'

'Life.'

'Dani, you can't protect anyone from living. I'd think you'd understand that better than anyone.'

She looked away, thinking about everything she'd gone through. She realized he was right, of course, but could she let Vincent go so easily?

'Anyway,' he added, leaning towards her, 'I'm sorry about giving you a hard time the other night. It can't have been easy for you.'

'It wasn't.'

'So,' he said, grinning suddenly, 'here we are, sitting around like an old married couple arguing about our son. That's something, huh?'

'*You're* the old married one,' she pointed out. '*I'm* still single.'

'You are, huh?'

'Yes,' she said casually, and threw in provocatively, 'even though Dean is always begging me to marry him.'

'Who's Dean?' he asked, frowning slightly.

'Oh, didn't I tell you about him? Dean is a very special friend.'

'How special?'

'We've known each other a long time.'

'You sleeping with him?'

'I really don't think that's any of your business.'

'Is he the one who told you about Beth?'

'As a matter of fact, yes. How did you know that?'

'Just a hunch,' Michael said, deciding that whoever Dean was, he was a prick.

Max ambled over with several bottles of beer and dumped them on the table. 'Who's gonna help me with the barbecue?' he asked.

Michael stood up. 'I will.'

'You'd better be good at it, 'cause I make the best damn barbecue sauce known to man. So if you screw up the steaks, you're in *big* trouble.'

After the barbecue, Harry asked if he could take Vincent off to a party.

'I don't think so,' Dani said.

'I think so,' Michael said, taking Dani's arm and walking over to the side. They looked at each other and Michael burst out laughing. 'You *told* me you wanted him to have a father in his life. Well, here I am.'

'Yes, but—'

'Let the kid go to a party,' he interrupted. 'How many times is he gonna be in New York?'

'And exactly how will he get back to the hotel?' she asked, knowing she sounded like an uptight, overly protective mother, but she couldn't help herself.

'He's seventeen, for crissakes. He'll find his own way.'

'Only if he's back by midnight,' she said, compromising. 'We do agree he should have a curfew, right?'

'Midnight, one in the morning, what difference does it make?'

'It makes a difference to me.'

'Hey,' Michael said, 'you know what I was doing when I was seventeen?'

'I'm sure you were a wild one.'

'*You* weren't exactly Miss Prim and Proper, if I remember correctly.'

'You took advantage of me, Michael,' she said, flushed.

'Yeah?' he said, his eyes meeting hers.

She couldn't help smiling. 'Well . . . maybe I encouraged you.'

'*You* were a naughty little girl,' he said, grinning again.

'And you *did* encourage me,' she countered.

'C'mon,' he said, standing up. 'I'm taking you to your hotel while *our* son goes out and has himself a great time.'

They said goodbye to Tina and Max, and while Dani was thanking Tina, Michael slipped Vincent a hundred bucks and told him to enjoy himself.

They took a cab to the Plaza, and when it pulled up outside the hotel, Dani said, 'You don't have to get out.'

'Yes, I do,' Michael replied, paying the driver, and escorting her into the lobby.

'Well . . . Michael,' she said, 'this was nice.'

'Let's go to the bar and have a drink,' he suggested, once more taking her arm.

She found herself nodding, even though she really knew she should say no. Having a drink with Michael always seemed to lead to other things.

'Vincent really likes you,' she said, as they settled at a table.

'I really like him, too,' he said, and ordered a bottle of champagne.

'So I did the right thing?'

'Looks like it.'

'I'm glad.'

He reached in his pocket, took out a pack of Lucky Strikes and offered her one. She shook her head.

'Here's the deal,' he said, lighting up. 'You gotta give the kid a chance to see the world before he goes to college. I'll finance his trip, he shouldn't have to depend on Nando. He's gotta get out and experience things for himself. You can't hold him back, Dani.'

'Sending him to college is holding him back?' she said stiffly.

'He doesn't want to go.'

'How do you know?'

'He told me.'

'He's too young to make that kind of decision.'

'No, he's not. And now that I'm in Vincent's life, you *do* know that I have a say legally.'

'*What?*'

'You wouldn't want me getting my lawyer involved, would you?'

She looked at him incredulously. 'I don't believe you said that.'

'Then let's not talk about it any more. We should just sit here reliving old times, 'cause seeing you is *very* special.'

'Don't change the subject.'

'I want you to think about it. The kid has my genes, he wants to find things out for himself. All I'm askin' is for you to give it some thought.'

'Okay,' she said reluctantly.

The waiter brought the bottle of champagne, and opened it with a flourish. After he'd filled both their glasses, Michael toasted her. 'To old times and new ones,' he said.

'How's married life?' she blurted, bringing him back to reality.

'It's, uh . . . interesting,' he said guardedly.

'I'm sure you're very happy.'

'No,' he said, gazing into her eyes. 'It should've been you and me – we both know it.'

'Maybe . . .' she murmured. Oh, God! She was falling under his spell again, and she couldn't let it happen.

'So, here we are,' he said, reaching over and taking her hand.

'Yes,' she answered softly. 'Here we are.'

'By the way, this is for you,' he said, reaching into his pocket and handing her an envelope.

'What is it?'

'Don't open it now. Wait until you get back to Vegas.'

'Okay,' she said, figuring he'd written her a letter of apology, because his attitude was so different from the other night.

Two glasses of champagne later, and Dani was feeling quite lightheaded. Michael still exerted the same old irresistible charm, a charm she couldn't seem to escape. Then she thought, *Why should I? I'm a grown woman. I can do anything I want.*

So when he suggested they go upstairs, she didn't argue. Why fight a losing battle?

'You wait here. I'll go book us a suite,' he said. 'That way we can relax, and you won't be worried about Vincent walking in on us.'

'I don't know, Michael,' she said, suddenly overcome with doubts. 'You're married. It's not right.'

'Dani,' he said, fixing her with his incredible green eyes, 'you were in my life long before Stella. I want to be with you, and not just for one night.'

She nodded quietly, aware that saying no to Michael was an impossibility.

Chapter Forty-five

Tuesday, 10 July 2001

The van raced along the freeway, narrowly missing other vehicles as it wove in and out of the lanes. The gunman kept on leaning out of the window to see if he could spot the helicopter. When he finally realized it had gone, he chortled with laughter. 'Mothafuckers,' he sneered. 'All it takes is action.'

'You *threw* a girl out of the van,' Madison said, staring at him with loathing. 'Don't you have any mercy?'

'Shut the fuck up,' he snarled. 'You talk too much. How d'you put up with her?' he asked Cole, whose eyes stayed fixed on the road ahead.

'That poor girl,' Madison continued, her voice filled with disbelief. 'You tossed her out of the van like a dead animal.'

'Yeah,' the gunman said, chuckling as if it was a big joke. 'You got that right. Roadkill! Some fuckin' trip!'

'Your mother must be very proud of you.'

'You leave my fuckin' mother outta this,' he growled.

'I hope I get to meet her one day, so I can tell her what a fine son she raised.'

'Keep talkin' an' you're next, *bitch*!' he threatened.

His words were ominous. She took a quick look at Cole, who was still concentrating on his driving.

She remembered watching a movie involving a hostage situation. *Never get into a vehicle with a gunman, because chances are you'll end up dead.*

One piece of advice had been to crash the car if you found yourself in such an unfortunate position. That's what Cole should do – smash the van into the centre divider.

Of course, being on a freeway, an accident like that could kill all of them.

Still, anything was better than this journey of certain doom.

Leroy Fortuno was an extremely large black man in his thirties, dressed rapper-style, while Darren Simmons bore a strong resemblance to Snoop Doggy Dogg – tall, thin, and emaciated-looking with gnarly dreadlocks and darkly hooded eyes. They both wore Sean John sweats, Nike running shoes, and big diamond crosses hanging round their necks.

'My God,' Jolie gasped, as they approached, 'they look like a couple of major drug dealers.'

'They're in the record business,' Nando explained. 'Everyone looks like that.'

'Are you *certain* you want to be partners with these people?' Jolie asked.

'I got no choice. If Vin refuses to come in with me, there's no way I can swing it on my own.'

'You could be making a big mistake.'

'It pisses me off when you're negative,' he said, shooting her a look. 'I'm offering you a piece of the action here, so be quiet, and be nice.'

'Hey, bro,' said Leroy, high-fiving Nando, who came up with the appropriate response. 'Let's go park it in the crib.'

'This is my wife, Jolie,' Nando said.

'Hey, baby,' Darren said, giving her a perfunctory check from head to toe. 'Lookin' hot.'

Jolie felt a shiver of annoyance run up and down her spine. She was not a snob, but these two were the lowest of the low, and it didn't take a detective to figure *that* out.

Naked, uninhibited, and wallowing in a coke-induced haze, with Andy Dale pounding into her, and Anais sucking on her nipples, Jenna lay spreadeagled, imagining herself in a huge house in Bel Air, with many servants to do her bidding and several luxury cars parked in the garage. Of course, there would be an entourage of famous people, all of whom would want to be her best friend, because she was Andy Dale's wife.

These fantasies flitted through her head as she murmured an automatic, 'Oooh, Andy, you are *such* a sensational lover.'

Even as she said it, she realized that he wasn't. Andy Dale was not particularly well endowed, whereas Vincent Castle *was*.

However, Andy Dale was a movie star, and that compensated for a few missing inches.

'You're not so bad yourself, cookie,' he said, pounding into her with as much finesse as a pile-driver.

'I'd really love . . .' Jenna gasped '. . . to have my photo taken with you.'

'Yeah. Why not?' A long drawn-out groan. 'Spread 'em, baby. I'm coming!'

Vincent arranged for a private plane to get Michael to L.A. as fast as possible. Dani suggested that she go with him, but he told her, under no circumstances.

'Where can I reach you?' she wanted to know.

He gave her the number of his cellphone.

'Vincent,' he said, 'you're responsible for keeping your mom safe, finding Sofia and getting her back here.'

'I've already got people on it,' Vincent said. 'Are you *sure* I shouldn't come with you?'

'If I need you, that's when you'll hear from me.'

Dani put her arms round Michael's neck and kissed him on the lips. 'Be careful,' she murmured.

'You know I will,' he said. 'Because when I get back, there's things we should discuss.'

'What things?'

He gave her his magical grin – the one that made him look thirty again. 'Good things,' he said.

And she loved him more than she ever had.

It was eight a.m. Wednesday morning by the time Sofia arrived back at her beach-front lodging house in Marbella. Her landlady Mrs Flynn, a flamboyant English woman who drank too much, greeted her in the kitchen clad in a bright orange floor-length caftan.

'Out all night, dear?' Mrs Flynn said with a saucy wink. 'Have a good time, did you?'

'I had a lousy time.'

'Was he cute?'

'No,' Sofia said.

'You *do* know you're a week late on your rent,' Mrs Flynn reminded her. 'I'll need something today.'

'Do you mind if I use your phone?' Sofia asked. She was suddenly experiencing a strong desire to speak to her mother. Maybe Gianni was right. Maybe it *was* time she went home.

'Go ahead, I'll add the charge to your rent,' Mrs Flynn said obligingly.

I bet you will, Sofia thought. *You're a mean old cow.*

She picked up the phone and called Vegas, even though it was probably midnight there. Dani answered immediately.

'Hi, Mom,' Sofia said, as if they'd spoken yesterday. 'Hope I didn't wake you.'

'Thank God!' Dani exclaimed. 'We've been trying to track you down.'

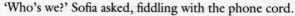

'Who's we?' Sofia asked, fiddling with the phone cord.

'Your father and Vincent.'

'Why?'

'There's an ongoing emergency concerning your father. You must come home immediately.'

'Can't do that, I'm broke.'

'You have no money at all?'

'Nada.'

'Go to the local American Express office. I'll arrange for a plane ticket to be waiting for you.'

'You can do that?'

'Of course I can.'

'Is Daddy okay?'

'It's not something I can discuss on the phone.'

'Sounds ominous,' Sofia said, adding vaguely, 'actually, I was thinking I might fly to Rome.'

'Listen to me,' Dani said sternly. 'I know you don't like being told what to do, but this is important. Come home immediately. You could be in danger.'

'Wow!' Sofia said, intrigued. 'You're making this sound like a James Bond movie.'

'Pick up the ticket, Sofia, I'll arrange it now.'

'Okay, Mom, I'm on my way.'

'Hit the next exit,' the gunman instructed.

Madison had no idea where they were. She knew that they'd been driving for almost half an hour, and the helicopter had not been in evidence for a good twenty minutes. That didn't mean it wasn't out there somewhere, trailing them without lights.

'Where are we heading when we get off the freeway?' Cole asked.

'Keep drivin'.'

'You okay, Nat?' Madison said, stretching her head to see in the back.

'I'm doing fine,' Natalie replied. 'You?'

'Oh, we're having a wonderful time,' Madison said.

'Did I *say* you could have a fuckin' conversation?' the gunman said, switching on the radio and pressing the buttons until he tuned into a rap station. He turned the volume up high and began drumming his fingers on the dashboard. 'Move this mothafucker!' he yelled, as Cole began to slow down. 'Gettin' off the freeway don't mean you gotta drive like an old lady. Fuck it!' he crowed. 'I'm the king – the fuckin' king!'

And he laughed. A crazy, stoned laugh.

Chapter Forty-six

Michael and Madison: 1987

'Get packed, we're going to Miami for the weekend.'

'Are you *serious?*' Madison said, her emerald green eyes sparkling with excitement at the thought.

'Yup,' Michael responded, grinning at his long-legged sixteen-year-old daughter, whom he rarely saw any more. 'We're doin' it.'

'Wow! Is Stella coming?'

'Stella's not feeling great,' Michael explained. 'She'll stay in New York.'

'Wow!' Madison repeated. 'You mean it's just you and me?'

'You got any objections?'

'No *way!*'

Madison was especially excited because she was away at boarding-school for most of the year, and long vacations were usually spent at summer camp. Michael was always travelling so much and Stella's health was somewhat delicate; she suffered from bad migraines, especially when her husband was out of town.

Madison had learned to survive on her own. Early on she'd figured out that that was the way it was. Stella had

Michael. Michael had Stella. She was just round occasionally. The kid. The daughter.

Not that they didn't love her, she was sure that they did, especially Michael, who was the best father a girl could have. She adored him, so the thought of spending the weekend in Miami with him was thrilling.

Last week she'd celebrated her sixteenth birthday. No big deal. Stella had booked a table at Tavern on the Green and sent her there with a few of her girlfriends. After an early dinner they'd gone to the theatre and seen *Starlight Express*. It was all very uneventful. Michael had been away on a business trip, which was disappointing because she would've loved to have spent such a special day with him. He'd sent her a gold watch from Tiffany's engraved with a meaningful message.

Now this surprise – a weekend in Miami with her father. How radical was *that*!

Michael was pleased to see his daughter so cheerful. Although Stella assured him Madison was doing well in school, he'd noticed there were times she seemed quite melancholy, and although her grades were always high, he wondered if she was really happy being away from home.

'Don't be silly,' Stella had told him, when he'd questioned her. 'Madison loves school. She's an extremely well-adjusted young lady.'

Michael travelled a lot. He didn't have to, but spending time away from home had become a habit.

And then there was his other habit – Dani and his second family. Meeting up with Dani again in 1982 and discovering that he had a son had turned out to be one of the high points of his life. He loved Vincent – he saw much of himself in the boy. Although Vincent was no longer a boy: he was a handsome, clever twenty-two-year-old man who knew exactly what he wanted.

Michael's opinion had prevailed with Dani, so instead of

going to college, Vincent had taken a trip round the world with Nando. When the two of them got back to America, they'd immediately set to work trying to put something together. Nando had his inheritance, and Vincent was catching up fast. Unbeknown to Michael, his son was a world-class gambler, the kind casinos eventually ban from playing in their establishments. Before that had happened, Vincent had made a killing. Like Michael, he was a genius with numbers. And, smartly, he'd invested his winnings.

With a little financial help from his father, Vincent had formed a partnership with Nando, who'd moved permanently back to Vegas, and they'd opened a restaurant and bar on the Strip called *The Place*. It was a big success with the young hip crowd.

Michael saw plenty of Dani. Every few weeks he flew to Vegas to be with her. He loved her, and she loved him. He also had another reason for spending so much time with her. Six weeks after they'd got together in New York, Dani had informed him that *they* were pregnant. 'You and your magic bullet,' she'd said, laughing. 'What is it with you and me?'

'Huh?' he'd said, not quite sure what she was getting at.

'We're *pregnant*, Michael,' she'd said, beaming. 'And this time we're doing it together.'

Rather than responding with shock and horror, he'd been delighted, because not only did he want to spend time with Dani and Vincent, he *definitely* planned on being a big presence in his new child's life too.

Dani gave birth to a daughter in 1983. They named her Sofia.

Dani understood that Michael couldn't marry her. He'd explained at great length that there was no way he would ever disrupt Madison's life. 'When she's grown, I'll leave Stella. *Then* you and I can be together,' he'd promised.

'I'm not sure it's what I want,' Dani had said with a lazy smile. 'I kind of like being the mistress.'

'You do, huh?'

'Yes, I get treated better that way.'

She'd given up work and Michael paid for everything, including a luxurious new house in a gated community and a gleaming silver Mercedes.

Recently he'd arranged for her and Sofia, who was now four, to take a week's vacation in Miami. Then he'd thought about flying down there with Madison.

Not that he planned on introductions, but at least he'd be near them.

Madison couldn't have been happier. She was a great kid, with a high IQ and a passion for writing. When Michael thought about his own humble beginnings, he was filled with pride to see how his offspring were turning out. Vincent with his successful restaurant, and Madison brimming with so much ambition. It gave him a very satisfying sense of having done *something* right.

Jamie came over to the apartment with the sole purpose of helping Madison pack. She was a natural blonde, tall and willowy. 'Wish I was coming with you.' She sighed enviously, sorting through a pile of skirts, jeans, and T-shirts.

'So do I,' Madison said, more exotic-looking with her smooth olive skin, green eyes, and long, dark hair. 'What's going on at school?'

'The same old crap,' Jamie said. 'Boys, boys, and more boys.'

'That can't be all bad.'

'It *is*! They're *so* gross,' Jamie said, making a face. 'And stupid. I dig older men, not dumb-ass adolescents.'

'I know,' Madison agreed. 'So do I.'

'You'll have a great time with Michael,' Jamie said wistfully. 'I wish I could call *my* dad by his first name.'

'You're lucky, you've got terrific parents,' Madison said. 'They never sent *you* off to boarding-school.'

'Agreed. But look at all the freedom you get. I don't get *any*. *You* can do whatever you want.'

'I think my dad was kind of a wild kid himself,' Madison said thoughtfully, 'so he doesn't believe in discipline.'

'What about your mom?'

'Stella doesn't care, as long as I stay out of her way. She's much too busy getting her legs or pubes waxed. That's if she's not having silicone pumped into her face.'

'Sounds painful!'

'Our apartment is more like a beauty salon than a home. I'm kind of *glad* I'm never there.'

'It's so cool the way you get to call them Michael and Stella.'

'That was *her* idea,' Madison said. 'She thinks being called Mom makes her sound old.'

'Ego alert!' Jamie giggled. 'She *is* old.'

Madison nodded. 'In her thirties.'

'How old's your dad?'

'Forty-something.'

'Ancient!'

'Ha!' Madison said. 'Bet *you* wouldn't turn him down.'

'That's so *rude*!' Jamie giggled, blushing.

'You've always had a crush on him. 'Fess up.'

'He's your *father*, Maddy.'

'I could definitely go for an older man.'

'Like who?'

'Michael Douglas. Kevin Costner.'

'Wow! Cool! They're both *sooo* sexy.'

'Even Clint Eastwood.'

'*Too* old,' Jamie said, wrinkling her nose.

'Not for me,' Madison said.

'I was so jealous of you when we were little,' Jamie sighed.

'You still are,' Madison teased.

'I suppose I am,' Jamie admitted. 'You've got to tell me all about Miami. Maybe you'll get laid.'

'Oooh, exciting!' Madison said. 'I *don't* think!'

Madison talked nonstop on the flight to Miami. She told Michael about her teachers, the thesis she was working on, a journalism course she was planning to take, and how much she was looking forward to college.

'I *really* want to be a writer, Michael,' she said earnestly. 'What do *you* think?'

'I think I'd be the proudest dad in the world,' he said. 'You have no idea where I come from, sweetheart. To have a writer in the family – well, that'd *really* be something.'

'Yes?'

'Oh, yeah.'

'You'll see, I *will* make you proud. That's a promise.'

'It is, huh?'

'Yes, Michael,' she said determinedly. 'It is.'

He picked up a copy of *Time* magazine and began reading. Madison gazed out of the window, imagining herself as a published author along the lines of Tom Wolfe or Mario Puzo. She loved their books. *The Godfather* was her all-time favourite, and she'd just finished reading *Bonfire of the Vanities*, which she'd devoured over two nights. Then again, she wouldn't mind being a journalist, covering wars and world events.

I can do anything, she told herself. *Anything I set my mind to.*

Michael had taught her that. Michael had instilled in her a confidence that achievement started in the mind.

She adored her father. He was the best.

Chapter Forty-seven

Dani and Vincent: 1987

Shortly before Dani left for Miami, Dean dropped by her house. 'You're insane, you know that?' he said, trailing her into the kitchen.

'*I'm* insane?' she replied. '*You're* the one who's been married twice, and I understand you're about to embark on your second divorce.'

'Where did you hear that?'

'Word gets around, Dean,' she said, pouring him a cup of coffee.

'Why you ever got back together with Michael Castelli is a mystery to me,' he grumbled, reaching for the cream and sugar. 'And then to have another baby. Wasn't one enough?'

'I don't need a lecture,' she said, walking into the living room. 'I'm extremely happy.'

'Happy because he won't marry you?' Dean said, following her.

'Don't go there, Dean,' she warned. 'I've told you many times, it's none of your business.'

'You *are* my business, Dani. And as much as you fight it, you always will be.'

'Why?'

'Because I love you,' he said simply. 'And nothing you do or say can ever change that.'

He didn't have to tell her, she was well aware of how much he loved her. And over the years she had to admit that it was quite comforting to know he was always there, ready to catch her if she fell. Dean was her safety net, and they both knew it. So did Michael who, although the two men had never met, hated Dean. 'That loser just wants to get into your pants,' Michael often informed her. 'Why do you still see him?'

'He's not a loser. He's my friend.'

'Some friend,' Michael usually muttered. He had never forgiven Dean for showing her the press clippings regarding his arrest for Beth's murder, thereby separating them for seven long years.

Dean put down his coffee and began pacing around the living room. 'You're throwing your life away, Dani,' he said.

'Why?' she responded crisply. 'I'm with a wonderful man who loves me. I have two great children. I live in a beautiful house. So tell me, exactly *how* am I throwing my life away?'

'You're with a married man who only sees you when it suits him. He has a *wife* and, whatever you think, he'll always put her first.'

'Not necessarily,' she said, a defensive thrust to her chin.

'He uses you. Surely you know it?'

'Our relationship isn't like that.'

'I think it is.'

'Quite frankly, Dean, I couldn't care less *what* you think. I'm happy, and that's it. So, if you'll excuse me, I have to get ready for my trip.'

Sofia toddled into the room, all curly hair, dimpled cheeks, and enormous eyes. 'Hi, Uncle Dean,' the little girl said, flirting outrageously.

'Hi, Crunchie,' he said – his nickname for her.

'Wanna play dolls?'

'Not right now.'

'Blow bubbles?'

'Next week.'

Sofia wandered off.

'Things weren't meant to turn out this way,' Dean said. 'It should've been you and me.'

Where had she heard *that* before? From Michael. Only Dean was always proposing marriage, and Michael wasn't.

She understood. Michael had explained it to her enough times. He'd made an irrevocable pact with himself to stay with Stella for Madison's sake, and there was nothing she could do about it.

She pretended not to care. Only sometimes, late at night, when she hadn't seen him in a while, she cried herself to sleep, because maybe Dean was right – perhaps he *was* using her.

Anyway, he certainly kept them in great style, never denying her anything she wanted.

She couldn't help it, she loved him with every fibre of her being. What was so bad about that?

Later, Vincent came by to wish them a safe trip to Miami. Vincent. So tall, dark, and handsome, exactly like Michael.

He picked up his baby sister and began tossing her in the air. Sofia squealed with delight.

'Careful, you'll drop her,' Dani warned.

'Yeah, yeah, like *I'm* gonna drop her!' Vincent said, throwing Sofia even higher.

'Enough!' Dani said.

'More!' Sofia begged.

'Are you staying for dinner?' Dani asked, hoping his answer would be yes, because she did not get to spend enough time with her handsome son.

'Can't,' he said apologetically. 'Got a date.'

'Who is she this time?'

Vincent grinned – he had Michael's grin along with everything else. 'You know you don't want to know.'

'That's true.' She sighed. 'I wish you could meet a nice girl.'

'They're nice enough for me.'

'That's the problem.'

'You're beginning to sound like a mother.'

'I *am* a mother.'

'Gotta go,' he said, tickling Sofia until she screamed for mercy. 'Have a great trip.'

'I wish you were coming with us,' Dani said wistfully.

'Too busy.'

'I know.'

She watched from the window as Vincent jumped into his black Corvette – a twenty-first birthday present from his father – and roared off.

He drove too fast. He'd inherited *that* particular skill from Nando, who was into race cars, and often encouraged Vincent to join him on the practice track.

She'd given up worrying about Vincent. Michael had taught her that worrying did absolutely no good at all.

Vincent was leading a bachelor's dream life and he knew it. Girls, girls, girls. Blondes, brunettes, redheads. He had his pick.

Unlike Nando, he did not care to indulge in sex with a different girl every night. He tried to be more discerning than that. Only it wasn't easy: the girls who came into their restaurant bar were begging for it. He and Nando were prizes: score with one of them and it meant you were *really* a hot chick.

Vincent liked girls. In fact, he loved them. But sometimes he yearned for a girl who wasn't so damn available.

Nando laughed at him when he tried to discuss it. 'Take

it when you can get it,' was Nando's philosophy.

So he did, but not as much as Nando, who seemed to possess an alarmingly active libido. Two or three girls a night was not unusual.

Vincent enjoyed the restaurant business: he ran a tight operation while Nando was Mr Personality, luring the prettiest girls and the guys with money to hang out at their place. Vincent preferred to take a back seat, although somehow he got to do all the work. Nando was into the music and the look and the minor details, while Vincent made sure the chef ordered wisely, the bartenders didn't steal too much, the waiters kept a high standard, and the bills were paid on time.

They both wanted more. Their dream was to build their own hotel and casino. And one of these days Vincent was convinced they would achieve their dream.

Chapter Forty-eight

Michael and Madison: 1987

The hotel in Miami was big and luxurious. Michael had booked them into a suite. Naturally. He always did things in style.

As soon as they arrived, Madison ran round inspecting everything, from the two huge marble bathrooms to the spacious, palm-decked terraces overlooking the ocean.

'This is *so* wild!' she exclaimed. 'Can we go down to the beach and take a walk along the shore?'

'What's so interesting about the beach?' Michael asked, enjoying her excitement.

'I've never been to the ocean before.'

'First time?'

'You *know* it is, Michael.'

This was his second trip to Miami. The first time had been when he'd visited Vinny. He hadn't seen his father since, although he knew that Vinny was still living in the same place. He sent him a cheque every month, a cheque that was always cashed.

'*You* go take a walk along the beach,' he said. 'I've got a couple of calls to make.'

'Oh, no! Business!' Madison said, making a face. 'You *promised* no work.'

'Only two calls, sweetheart, then we'll have a wonderful dinner together. Just the two of us. You like lobster?'

'Who doesn't?' she said, already hungry.

'So . . . will you be my date?'

'You bet!'

As soon as Madison left the suite, he called Dani. 'How was the flight?' he asked.

'Uneventful,' she replied, always delighted to hear his voice.

'That's my girl.'

'Who? Me or Sofia?'

He laughed. 'Hey, look, after you've put Sofia down tonight, leave her with a babysitter and drop by the restaurant in my hotel. I'm having dinner with Madison. I'll see you walk past, pretend you're an old friend, and ask you to join us. How does that sound?'

'You don't think Madison will suspect anything?'

'What's she gonna suspect?'

'How would I know? She's *your* daughter.'

'Do it,' he ordered. 'I'm not staying here without seeing you.'

'And how will you cope if Sofia spots you on the beach tomorrow and runs over yelling, "Daddy, Daddy"?'

He laughed. 'That's the reason I booked us into different hotels.'

'Clever.'

'So . . . later?'

'Whatever you say.'

'Michael? Michael Castelli?'

Beautifully executed. He couldn't have done it better himself.

He stood up from the table. 'Dani Castle, what a pleasure to see you again.'

Madison glanced up, green eyes on alert. Who was this

beautiful blonde woman talking to her father, interrupting them while they were trying to enjoy a quiet dinner for two?

'Are you by yourself?'

Shut up, Daddy, we do not need company.

'As a matter of fact I am,' Dani replied. 'Business trip, you know.'

'Then why don't you sit down and join us?' Michael said, making it sound as if it had only just occurred to him. 'This is my daughter, Madison. Say hi to Mrs Castle, dear.'

Dear? When had he ever called her dear? Damn! This woman appearing out of nowhere was a big pain in the butt.

'Well . . . if you're sure I'm not disturbing you,' Dani said, and sat down at the table.

Shit! Madison thought. *I cannot believe this woman has the temerity to sit down at our table, when I am having a private dinner with my father.*

Michael didn't seem at all put out. Madison threw him a narrow-eyed glare – just to let him know that *she* was.

'Dani's a friend of mine from Las Vegas,' Michael explained. 'We've known each other for years.'

'Oh,' Madison said, totally uninterested.

'I'm in Miami for the jewellery show,' Dani offered.

'Where's your husband?' Madison asked bluntly. *And why the hell isn't he with you?*

'He, uh, doesn't like to fly.'

'I see,' Madison said. Although she didn't see at all. What was this rather glamorous woman doing travelling by herself when she should be at home with her husband? This was a big fat *drag*.

'We've ordered lobster,' Michael said. 'Would you like some?'

'Actually, I haven't eaten,' Dani said, 'so that would be very nice. Lobster is my favourite.'

Oh, crap! She's staying for dinner.

'Are you a friend of my mom's?' Madison asked rudely, suddenly feeling a little protective of Stella.

'No, actually we've never met.'

'Dani's husband is a business associate of mine in Vegas,' Michael explained.

'Have you ever been to Vegas?' Dani asked, all sweetness and big blue eyes.

'Nope,' Madison said, shaking her head. 'I never go anywhere except school, and summer camp, and home. Daddy and I came here for a weekend together, just the two of us. Didn't we, Daddy?'

Michael raised an eyebrow. Madison never called him Daddy, it was always Michael. Suddenly he was Daddy. He had a feeling she was marking her territory. 'That's right, sweetheart,' he said. 'I'll take you to Vegas one of these days. It's quite a place.'

'I gotta go to the john,' Madison announced, abruptly standing up. 'See ya.'

As soon as she was out of earshot, Dani said, 'I don't think she likes me.'

'What do you mean?' Michael replied. 'She doesn't *know* you. If she knew the real you, she'd love you.'

'No, I mean I don't think she likes me being here,' Dani said, sipping her wine. 'Wasn't this weekend supposed to be just you and her?'

'It *is* me and her. I'm spending the whole weekend with her. I can see you once, can't I?'

'Is this the only time I get to see you?' she asked, leaning forward.

'God! I love being with you,' he said, studying her face. 'Right now I wish we were lying in bed, eating hamburgers, making love.'

'In that order?' she asked, smiling.

'No.' He grinned. 'We'd make love first, *then* we'd order hamburgers.'

'You're funny, Michael,' she said warmly. 'I love you so much.'

'It's the greatest when we're together,' he said contentedly. 'I feel no pressure. When I'm round Stella there's always pressure. She's got so much going on, what with her social events and all that shit. She's working on a hundred different agendas.'

'You don't *have* to stay with her, Michael,' Dani reminded him gently. 'Madison *is* sixteen.'

'I can't tell Madison the truth,' he said, his tone hardening. 'It's not going to happen, Dani.'

'That's fine,' she said, instantly backing off. 'No pressure from *me*.'

'How's Vincent doing?'

'Surrounded by girls – as usual. They won't leave him alone.'

'That's good.'

'No, it's not. I don't want him knocking up some little bimbo.'

'I knocked *you* up, didn't I?'

'That was different.'

'Yeah, when it's you and me it's always different. Right?'

She smiled. 'Can I hold your hand under the table, Michael? Is that allowed?'

'As long as it's only my hand.'

'Oooh – naughty, naughty.'

'Hey, maybe when Madison's asleep, I'll slip out and come by your hotel.'

'You think so?'

'Yeah. I *definitely* think so.'

Madison made her way to the ladies' room, where she studied her reflection in the mirror. Tall, blonde women always made her feel inadequate. Her mother was tall and blonde. In fact, there was a slight resemblance between this

Dani woman and her mom. Except Stella was more refined-looking, not as glamorous as Dani Castle.

Madison knew she looked like her father, with her dark skin, green eyes and black hair. It didn't thrill her. Why couldn't she be more like Jamie? Jamie was gorgeous: boys *always* took notice of her.

Madison had not experienced much success with boys. She was too smart. Besides, the boarding-school she attended was girls only. So were the summer camps she went to. Therefore, she didn't know much about boys – unlike Jamie who, according to her, was constantly fighting them off.

I'm sixteen, she thought. *It's about time I did something wild and exciting. I'm a woman, I should be fighting off gorgeous guys. Or not fighting them off – depending how I feel. I'm a writer, I need the experience.*

She splashed cold water on her face and applied a dab of lip gloss.

I still look gawky and awkward, she thought. *I look about fourteen. Fourteen and an inexperienced jerk.*

Maybe I should dye my hair blonde, that would make boys notice me.

She walked out of the ladies' room and bumped straight into a man in a white suit, a man who closely resembled Michael Douglas. Unfortunately it wasn't Michael Douglas, whom she'd just seen in *Fatal Attraction* and with whom she had fallen madly in love.

'Sorry,' she mumbled.

'Not looking where you're going, young lady?' the man said. He had sandy-coloured hair and a deep suntan. Maybe there was a bit of Robert Redford mixed in with Michael Douglas.

'I was thinking.'

'And what would a beautiful young lady like you be thinking about that made you appear so earnest?'

Wow! Is this older man actually coming on to me? This man, who is probably the same age as my dad. Wow!

'Uh . . . I was thinking how nice it is here, and how I'm going to write about it.'

'Are you a writer?'

'Yes,' she lied. 'I sometimes write for *Rolling Stone*. Bits and pieces, you know.'

'I'm very impressed.'

They stared at each other. This older man and this young, exotic-looking girl.

'Is this your first trip to Miami?'

'It certainly is, and I love it – well, what I've seen so far.'

'I live in the penthouse,' he said. 'It's my permanent home.'

'Cool.'

'If I can show you around at all, just let me know. My name's Frankie.'

'Frankie,' she repeated.

'Frankie Medina. And you are?'

'Madison Castelli.'

'Pretty name. Pretty girl.'

'Has anyone ever told you that you look like Michael Douglas?' she blurted.

'Only better-looking, I hope,' he said, smiling.

He had nice teeth, capped probably, but nice all the same.

'Of course,' she said quickly.

'Yeah, I've been told that,' he said with a lazy grin. 'Only I'm not looking for a fatal attraction.'

She laughed. Glenn Close was a blonde in the movie. She definitely had to change her hair colour.

'If you get lonely later,' Frankie Medina said, 'give me a call.' And he handed her a little gold card with his name embossed in black and a phone number.

'I might do that,' she said boldly.

'You *are* very pretty,' he said.

Oh, my God! He is coming on to me. 'I just washed my hair,' she said. *Like, what a stupid thing to say.*

'What did you use? A magic shampoo that makes you even prettier?' She giggled. 'Call me,' he said. 'I'll give you a ride in my Porsche.'

Hmmm. A penthouse and a Porsche. How very sexy.

'What do you do?' she asked.

'What do I do?' he repeated, with a big smile. 'I'm a playboy – what else?'

At which point a gorgeous blonde emerged from the ladies' room – yes, another blonde – and immediately clung possessively to his arm.

'See ya,' Madison said, and quickly took off.

Back at the table, Michael and Dani Castle seemed to be getting more than friendly. Madison could almost feel them move apart as she approached.

'Where were you?' Michael asked. 'I was gonna send out a hunting party.'

'Guess what?' she said. 'I bumped into an old friend, too.'

'You did?' Michael said.

'Yes,' she said, surreptitiously sliding Frankie Medina's card into her purse.

To Madison's annoyance, Dani Castle hung round all through dinner. She ate lobster, she drank wine, she talked to Michael. Too bad! What could have been a wonderful dinner was ruined.

As soon as they were finished, Madison excused herself. 'I'm kind of tired,' she said. 'Do you mind if I go upstairs?'

'You sure, sweetheart?' Michael said.

'I really am. I want to wake up early and hit the beach,' she said, getting up from the table. 'Night, Mrs Castle.'

'Good night, Madison,' Dani said warmly. 'It was a pleasure meeting you.'

Yeah, well, Madison thought, *the pleasure is all yours.*

She walked away from the table and wandered outside. She was not tired at all – she was just tired of watching her father cosy up to the tall blonde.

The beach beckoned, so she decided to take a long walk, which she did, enjoying every second of the roaring ocean and the feel of the sand on her bare feet.

When she arrived back at the hotel, it was quite late. Frankie Medina was standing in the lobby, resplendent in his white suit and deep suntan.

'Hey, here comes that beautiful girl again,' he said. 'The one with the lonely eyes.'

'Do you think I have lonely eyes?'

'Yes.'

Hmm . . . Poetic too. A poetic playboy. Just what I feel like.

'What're you doing?' he asked.

'I took a walk along the beach. It was great.'

'I used to do that when I first moved here.'

'Where did you move here from?'

'You don't wanna know.'

'About that Porsche you were telling me about . . .'

'Would you care to take a ride?'

'Why not?'

Now, *this* was an adventure.

His Porsche was low-slung, black, and very sexy. It also featured a great sound system. He put on Frank Sinatra's *In the Wee Small Hours.*

'Don't you have any Bon Jovi or Janet Jackson?' she asked, disappointed by his choice of music.

'Listen and learn. Sinatra is the greatest.'

He was rather sweet. Old, but sweet.

He zipped her around town in his Porsche, pointing out the sights, Sinatra crooning away.

'You're a regular tour guide,' she said, enjoying every moment.

'How old are you, Madison?'

'Eighteen,' she lied, like her father before her.

'You're a baby.'

'No, I'm not,' she said indignantly. 'Eighteen is hardly a baby. How old are *you*?'

'Forty,' he lied, shaving off five years. 'You want to come up and see my penthouse?'

'Do I need my passport to get up there?'

'Just bring your luscious self.'

Luscious self. Wow!

'What happened to that blonde you were with earlier?' she asked.

'They come and they go,' he said vaguely. 'Interchangeable blonde babes – I got a dozen of 'em.'

'Oh, that's *right*, you're a *playboy*.'

He laughed. 'Yeah, that's exactly what I am.'

'Then maybe I should write about you,' she said archly. 'Profile of a playboy. What do you think?'

'I think you're cute.'

'Thanks!'

His penthouse was the most beautiful apartment she'd ever been in, far nicer than their place in New York, which she considered over-decorated and too antiquey – Stella's taste. The penthouse featured an enormous living room furnished in white modern minimalist style, vast walls of windows overlooking the ocean, and a fantasy bedroom with an oversized waterbed covered in rose petals. It was the most glamorous place she'd ever seen.

'What's with the rose petals?' she asked as he gave her the tour.

'They're an aphrodisiac.'

'Right,' she said, reminding herself to look up

'aphrodisiac' in the dictionary, although she had a vague idea that it had *something* to do with sex.

After sipping a glass of cold champagne with peaches floating in it, she turned to him and said, 'When are you going to make a move on me?'

'Eighteen's a little young for me,' he answered. adjusting the sound on his stereo by remote.

'Oh, c'mon,' she challenged. 'You're a playboy with a Porsche and a penthouse. You can make a move on me.'

'I'd feel like a dirty old man.'

'You *are* a dirty old man,' she said. And she threw her arms round his neck and started to kiss him.

'Madison,' he said, trying to extract himself from her, 'even *I've* got *some* principles.'

'Well, drop 'em,' she said. ''Cause I'm in Miami to have fun.'

'Then the first thing you'd better do is learn how to kiss.'

'*Excuse* me?'

'Kiss, baby. Pucker up. I'm about to give you a lesson you will *never* forget.'

The weekend went by only too quickly. Michael noticed that Madison seemed to be in an extremely good mood and, even better, she gave him plenty of time to himself.

'I thought we were spending this weekend together?' he asked quizzically, after she'd been missing from yet another lunch.

'We are,' she said. 'Only I met this friend from school, and we're having such a great time exploring. You don't mind, do you?' she added innocently. 'That's what us writers like to do.'

He didn't mind at all. Madison's absence allowed him to spend plenty of time with Dani and the adorable Sofia, who looked like Madison had at the same age. There was something in his genes that produced matching kids.

Meanwhile Madison was experiencing an adventure she could only have imagined in her wildest dreams. Frankie Medina was teaching her everything an aspiring writer needed to know. And her education was *not* taking place between the pages. Far more exciting – it was taking place between the sheets.

Madison was a very willing pupil indeed.

Back in New York, Marcie informed Michael that Vito Giovanni needed to see him urgently.

Vito never changed. When Vito wanted something, he wanted it immediately. He was not a patient man.

Michael gave him a call. 'What's up, Vito?'

'Gotta see you, Michael,' Vito replied in his familiar gravelly voice. 'Come by the house.'

'How's six o'clock tonight?'

'That'll suit me.'

Michael skipped going home and had his driver take him straight from the office to Vito's brownstone. He hadn't seen Vito in several months – it wasn't necessary since they conducted most of their business by phone.

Vito was sitting in his favourite chair in his living room. He looked like he'd shrunk, or that his chair had grown larger.

'Mike, come in,' Vito said, waving him into the room. 'You want a drink? Jack Daniel's. I never forget a man's drink.'

'Yeah,' Michael said, feeling right at home. 'I'll have a Jack.'

'I'd have one with you, only my doctors say I shouldn't drink. Fuckers!' Vito said morosely. 'Always tellin' me shit about what I can't do.'

A henchman fixed Michael a drink, while Vito indulged in a short coughing fit.

'You okay, Vito?' Michael asked.

'I got a few health problems. Nothin' major. Had oral surgery the other day – that's what they call it now when they yank your fuckin' teeth out – oral surgery.'

Michael was well aware that over the years, Vito Giovanni had risen to become very high up in the hierarchy of mobsters. Michael was glad that he'd made it on his own, and had never had to ask Vito for any favours – although Vito had always played fair with him, and in return he'd made the old man a lot of money in investments and the stock market. Legitimate money.

'How's everythin' goin', Mike?' Vito asked. 'A kid like you from the streets, you did well for yourself.'

'Took a lot of hard work.'

'Yeah, an' you had your setbacks along the way. But I'm glad you took my advice.'

'About what?'

'About that girl of yours who got shot,' Vito said, adjusting his oversize reading glasses. 'You could've gone chasing after whoever you thought was responsible. You didn't, an' that was smart. Like I told you at the time, you was even.'

Vito *still* didn't get it. He was not even. He would *never* be even. Sometimes he awoke in the middle of the night and there was Beth, sitting at the end of the bed staring at him. *What are you doing about getting revenge for my murder?* she always asked, her dark eyes vengeful. *You need to do something, Michael. One of these days you need to do something.*

And one of these days he would. He didn't know where or when, he only knew that the opportunity would present itself.

Mamie had moved to Los Angeles, so had Bone. Every time Michael flew to Vegas, he thought about making a side trip to L.A. and blowing their fucking brains out.

He didn't, because he had responsibilities. Madison, Vincent and Sofia. His three wonderful children. And Dani, of course. He could never risk letting any of them down.

He'd amassed dossiers on both Mamie and Bone. He knew exactly where they were and what they were doing. Seven years ago they'd got married – his two arch enemies. It made him sick to imagine them together. Not only had they got married, but they'd entered the business of moviemaking, partnering with a porno king who made explicit sex videos for Japan and Europe. Apparently, it was a business that suited Mamie just fine. Bone took care of the finances and Mamie was involved with the creative side. Yeah, he could just imagine it.

As if that wasn't enough, they'd also opened a series of sex shops across the country.

Vito never mentioned Mamie any more, so Michael didn't either. As far as he knew, Vito considered her history.

'You gotta do somethin' for me next week,' Vito said.

'What's that?' Michael asked.

'Be best man at my wedding.'

'Your *wedding*?' Michael said, somewhat surprised. Vito was over seventy years old and looked it. 'Who are you marrying?'

'Western, of course,' Vito said, chuckling happily. 'The old broad is finally makin' an honest man of me.'

'Congratulations.'

'You'll be my best man,' Vito repeated.

Michael understood that it wasn't so much a request, more like an order. He didn't mind, he was used to Vito's ways.

'You planning a big wedding?' he asked.

'Nah, we'll do it privately. Just a few friends. No fuss.'

'I'll be honoured to be your best man,' Michael said, wondering if that was the only reason Vito had requested his presence.

'There's somethin' else you gotta do for me,' Vito said.

'If I can.'

'I'm gonna have the guys put a coupla locked suitcases in your car. I'll give you the combination.'

'What's in them, Vito?' Michael asked, not embracing the thought of lugging around a couple of Vito's suitcases filled with God knows what.

'Money,' Vito said. 'Two million bucks in cash. You'll make it legitimate for me.'

'Wait a minute,' Michael said. 'Two million in cash, I mean—'

'You'll keep it until I give you instructions,' Vito interrupted. 'I trust you, Mike – I trust you as if you was my own son.'

'Jeez, Vito, I don't know—'

'You'll do it. *Capisce?*'

Michael nodded. He felt seventeen again. Besides, why argue? He always ended up doing whatever Vito wanted.

It was their dance. And it never changed.

Chapter Forty-nine

Tuesday, 10 July 2001

Wedged in the front seat of the van, her hands braced on the dashboard ready for impact should they crash, Madison began reviewing her life. This was all so surreal. How had she ended up in this position?

Just luck, I guess, she thought wryly.

She closed her eyes for a moment, trying desperately to take herself to another place, just like she used to do when she was a child visiting the dentist. *Close your eyes and it will all go away. Michael used to tell me that.*

This last year had been such a mess. Finding out that Stella wasn't really her mother, and shortly after that Stella's murder. And then her tortured relationship with Michael. One moment she loved and trusted him, the next she didn't know what to think because he'd made up such stories about her past. It wasn't fair of him to do that: he had no right to play God with a person's life. She might be his daughter, but she deserved to know the truth.

Then there was her relationship with Jake. A rollercoaster love affair with an extraordinarily sexy and interesting man. Now, for all she knew, he could be lying dead, or kidnapped by Colombian drug-dealers. She missed her apartment in New York. She missed her dog, Slammer. She missed her friends, her work. She missed everything.

The van was racing down dark side streets. She had no idea where they were, although the gunman seemed to be aware of their destination.

Fifteen minutes after getting off the freeway, he instructed Cole to pull over. They were in an industrial area, a dimly lit back-street filled with tall, deserted warehouses, somewhere downtown.

'You mean stop the van?' Cole asked.

'What the fuck do you think I mean?' the gunman snapped. Everyone's patience was wearing thin.

Madison felt dread in the pit of her stomach. Was he going to kill them? Was that his plan?

Where are the police? Where's the fucking helicopter? Where are the hostage negotiators?

This was a bad joke.

They were totally on their own, and there was nobody to help them.

They were sitting in what Leroy and Darren referred to as their office, although Jolie considered that it looked more like a flophouse for drug addicts. She was trying hard not to breathe, realizing that if she took one more breath she'd be as stoned as the rest of them. The scent of marijuana hung heavily in the air. And Nando, being Nando, had immediately accepted a joint.

That's not the way to do business, she wanted to warn him. *If Vincent was here, you wouldn't have dared.*

The reason Vincent and Nando were such excellent partners was that Vincent knew how to keep control of a situation. Nando didn't. Her husband was one of life's great adventurers. He saw something he wanted and he grabbed it. Unfortunately, he'd never learned the word 'no'.

Now he wanted to make this dump into the hottest strip club in Vegas. Why? They had the hotel and gambling casino. Vincent and he were doing great. Personally she agreed with Vincent: why move into the sleazy side of the business when they didn't have to?

She also knew that however involved she was, it would not sit well with her if Nando was dropping by a strip club every night, even if that club belonged to them. She'd installed a stripper pole in their bedroom. What more did she have to do to keep him at home?

Darren kept on shooting her sneaky sideways looks, as if he were summing up her potential as one of his girls. He looked like a pimp. He acted like a pimp. He probably *was* a pimp.

What the hell were they doing here?

And why had Nando brought *her* along for the ride?

The phone was ringing when Vincent walked into his apartment. He grabbed it quickly before it woke Jenna.

'Good news,' Dani said.

'What happened?'

'Sofia called. I told her to get the next plane home.'

'That *is* good news,' Vincent said. 'By the way, I've sent someone over to stay outside your apartment. Don't get alarmed if you see him.'

'Do you think that's necessary?'

'If Michael says it is, then it is. We can't take risks.'

'I find this excessive,' she complained.

'Hey, you know him better than anyone.'

'That's true,' she said ruefully.

'Then don't argue. Michael gets what he wants, he always has.'

'Oh, yes,' she agreed. '*That*'s certainly true.'

'I'm home now if you need to reach me. I'll stay here until I hear from Michael.'

He put down the phone, went to the bar and fixed himself a drink.

Maybe he'd been too hard on Jenna earlier. She was only a kid, after all. The truth was that she didn't know any better. Christ! He had so much to teach her. That was the problem with marrying an innocent girl who didn't understand the rules.

He walked into the bedroom ready to forgive her.

Their large double bed was empty.

He opened the door to her bathroom. She was not there.

For a moment he thought about raging out of the hotel, tracking down Andy Dale, and beating the crap out of the dumb little movie star.

Then he thought better of it. Jenna had a lesson to learn. And that lesson was, do not screw round with Vincent Castle.

Sofia had decided that the only sane thing she could do was skip out on Mrs Flynn and her demand for the late rent. She simply didn't have any money. The deal was to walk out casually as if she were going to work, then not come back.

She collected a few precious things that meant something to her, stuffed them into her oversize shoulder-bag, then yelled casually at Mrs Flynn, 'I'm going out. I'll be back later with your money.'

'Good on you, dearie,' shouted Mrs Flynn, the trusting old dear, already on her second glass of wine.

As soon as she got outside, Sofia realized she had no idea where the American Express office was. Damn! She should have made a call.

Then, to her surprise, up rolled Gianni in his gleaming chauffeur-driven Bentley.

The car pulled to a stop beside her. Gianni lowered the back window. 'Jump in,' he ordered.

'Excuse me,' she said.

'Jump in. We're on our way to Rome.'

And it seemed silly to argue because with Gianni by her side it would be so much easier to get back to America.

What did she have to lose?

Absolutely nothing.

'I think I'm going to throw up,' Jenna wailed.

'No, you're not,' Andy Dale said, pumping away on top of her.

'Yes . . . I think I am.'

'Then don't do it all over me.'

She managed to shove him off and run to the bathroom, whereupon she threw up in the basin. She retched for several minutes, feeling as though she'd been punched in the stomach by a mule.

When she was finished she lay down on the cold marble floor, rolling herself into a tight, naked ball. Nobody came in to see if she was all right. Not Andy, not Anais.

From the other room she heard the sounds of music, laughter and tinkling ice.

She had never felt this bad. 'I want to die,' she groaned.

Where was Vincent? Where was her husband when she needed him?

Oh, God, she couldn't let him see her like this – sick and having just made love to Andy Dale, if love was a word she could use in connection with the way Andy Dale had treated her.

He wasn't very nice. In fact, he was a big bully. While they were making out he'd slapped her hard on the bottom several times with the palm of his hand. It had hurt.

'I don't like that,' she'd cried, his slaps stinging.

'*I* do,' he'd said, sniggering.

She wondered how she could collect her clothes from the other room and escape. Spying a white terry-cloth

461

bathrobe behind the door, she got up gingerly and slipped it on.

Now what? She couldn't go back inside, it was too humiliating.

Of course, she could always tell Vincent that Andy Dale had raped her. Knowing Vincent, he'd probably beat Andy to a pulp, and she didn't want it to go that far.

Still . . . she refused to go back into the other room, which meant there was no way she could get out of the suite unless Vincent came to rescue her.

There was a phone next to the basin. She picked up the receiver.

When Vincent answered, she began to cry. 'Help me,' she sobbed. 'Please come and get me. I need help.'

Sitting on the plane Vincent had chartered to fly him to L.A., Michael was totally calm on the outside and churning up on the inside.

Mamie and Bone.

He should've finished them off years ago, exactly like they deserved.

They were scum. Two old pieces of shit who needed eliminating.

And he would do it. There was nobody to stop him.

Before this night was over, Mamie and Bone would be history.

'Everybody get the fuck out,' the gunman said. 'An' no smart moves.'

Hurriedly everyone got out of the van. Madison put her arms round Natalie and hugged her. 'We'll be all right,' she whispered. 'I promise you, we'll be all right.'

Natalie nodded. She was shivering and shaking. Cole came over and embraced the two of them, giving them a solid hug.

Madison looked round: there were two other hostages, five altogether, including them.

Just as they were all wondering what was about to happen next, an old black Cadillac came cruising down the street, loud rap music blasting from the windows.

'You,' the gunman snarled at Madison, 'in the back.'

'What are you talking about?' she said, her heart pounding.

'Do it, *bitch*. Get in the fuckin' car.'

And he grabbed her arm, twisted it behind her back, and shoved her into the back seat of the Cadillac. Then he jumped in after her.

There was nothing she could do. As soon as she was in, the car took off, racing away into the night.

Chapter Fifty

Michael and Madison: 1995

'I want you to look at this,' Madison said, racing into Michael's office, waving a magazine in front of his face.

'What?' he said, always delighted to see his daughter.

'Remember years ago when we were in Miami, and I told you I'd make you proud?' she said, perching on the edge of his desk.

'Yeah?'

'Well, take a look at this,' she said, triumphantly thrusting a magazine called *Manhattan Style* at him. On the front cover was her byline, *Profiles in Power by Madison Castelli*.

'Jesus, kid,' Michael said, staring at the magazine. 'All those years in college finally paid off.'

'They certainly did,' she said excitedly. 'Guess who my first subject is?'

'Who?'

'Would you believe Henry Kissinger?'

'Holy shit!' Michael said. 'This I gotta read!'

'And,' she said, 'I'd like you to note that my picture is included at the beginning of the magazine.'

Two years ago, fresh out of college, she'd been

discovered by Victor Simons, the editor of *Manhattan Style*. He'd seen a small piece she'd had published in *Esquire* about the still rampant double standard between men and women. Victor had read it, liked it, and taken her out to lunch. He'd encouraged her to get more experience then come back to see him.

'Why don't you hire me now?' she'd asked boldly. 'Grab me while you can.'

'No, but one of these days I will,' he'd said.

And, true to his word, he had. She'd been working at *Manhattan Style* for several months, and this was her first big assignment with her own byline.

'Sweetheart, this is great,' Michael said, studying the piece, a big smile spreading across his face. 'Has Stella seen it?'

'I haven't shown her yet.'

'Call and tell her. She'll be excited.'

'Oh, c'mon, Michael – when have you ever seen Stella excited?'

Stella and Madison did not enjoy the warm and wonderful mother/daughter relationship Michael had hoped for. Instead, things were somewhat strained between them.

'You're her daughter, Madison,' he said. 'I'm telling you, she'll be very happy for you.'

'*You* show her. Take this copy home.'

'How about we go out to dinner tonight and celebrate?' he suggested.

'Can't. I've got plans with the girls.'

'What girls?'

'Natalie's in town from L.A. and Jamie's set something up. I can't let them down.'

'Where are you going?'

'One of the clubs. Why? You want to join us?'

'I've had my club days,' he said ruefully.

'Really? Well, *I* still think you're the most handsome man around.'

'And out of the mouths of daughters . . .'

'Anyway,' she said happily, 'I couldn't wait to show you.'

'Thanks, sweetheart. I'm glad you dropped by. I'm *very* proud.'

As soon as Madison left his office, he instructed Marcie to call Vito Giovanni.

'I've left messages for Mr Giovanni three days in a row,' Marcie stated.

'I know that, Marcie,' he said patiently. 'That's why we've got to keep trying.'

'Perhaps he's out of town.'

'Who answers anyway?'

'An answering-machine,' Marcie said.

'Okay, give it another shot.'

He needed to talk to Vito about the two million dollars he'd invested for the old man. Over the years the money had almost doubled, and Vito had expressed no interest in how he was supposed to get it back.

Michael didn't feel comfortable holding the investments in his name. Even though he'd buried it and nobody could ever trace it to Vito, the fact remained that it was Vito's money.

Marcie tried again, once more getting the answering machine.

'I'm going over there,' Michael decided, grabbing *Manhattan Style* and heading out of the door. 'Call my driver. Have him meet me outside.'

Travelling down in the elevator, he began reading Madison's profile on Henry Kissinger. Unfucking believable! His daughter, a published writer – a journalist interviewing an important politician in a big-shot magazine. Jesus! What a thrill.

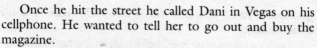

Once he hit the street he called Dani in Vegas on his cellphone. He wanted to tell her to go out and buy the magazine.

Sofia answered. 'Hi, Daddy.'

'Hi, chicken. Is your mom round?'

'She's out. When are you coming home, Daddy?'

'Soon.'

His other family. His secret family. Stella and Madison knew nothing about his second life in Las Vegas. And, for now, that was the way it had to be.

Sometimes, even though he was married to Stella, he never really felt he knew her. Half the time she was suffering from migraine headaches, the other half she was out socializing, buying clothes and jewellery at an alarming rate. They rarely had any interaction together. In fact, they didn't even make love any more. He'd sold their New York apartment and bought a house in Connecticut to please her and maybe bring them closer together. It hadn't worked.

Every month he managed to spend a week in Vegas. Things were different with Dani. He *always* wanted to make love to Dani. If it hadn't been for Madison he would have moved to Vegas a long time ago. However, Madison truly believed Stella was her mother, and even though he'd promised Dani that when the time came he'd leave Stella, he found it impossible to do so.

He often imagined what Madison's reaction would be if she ever discovered that she had a half-brother and -sister. She'd either be furious or delighted. There was no in-between with his feisty daughter.

Lately he'd realized that Dani was becoming disillusioned with their arrangement. 'You told me that when Madison went to college, you'd leave Stella,' she'd said, the last time he'd seen her. 'Then you told me that as soon as she got *out* of college, you'd leave. And now Madison's graduated, has a job, and *still* you're with Stella. I don't understand it.'

'I can't explain it to you,' he'd said, trying his best to say the right thing. 'It's . . . difficult.'

'*What's* so difficult, Michael?' she'd answered heatedly. 'I've been waiting for you all these years. I raised your family. We *should* be together.'

'Why ruin something so good, sweetheart?'

She'd glared at him. Wrong use of words.

A housekeeper at the Giovanni house informed him that Mr and Mrs Giovanni were away on vacation in the Bahamas. He had to admire the old guy – nothing slowed Vito down, he was always up to something.

It was becoming increasingly obvious that Vito didn't care about his money. He must be so rich that it didn't matter to him.

'Tell Mr G I'll be in contact when he returns.'

Madison met Jamie and her other best girlfriend from college, Natalie, at a downtown club. Jamie was even more wistfully beautiful than ever in a white linen suit and Manolo heels. Natalie, short, curvaceous and glowingly pretty, was in a sexy red dress, while Madison wore a slinky, pale beige Ralph Lauren suit, clouds of dark hair framing her oval face.

'Hey, look at you,' Natalie said, as Madison walked in. 'Dressed for success.'

'Is this my celebration dinner?' Madison asked, sitting down and grinning. ''Cause I am now officially a great big deal.'

'Yeah, yeah,' Jamie said dismissively. 'You're a star.'

'I flew in for tonight,' Natalie interjected, 'so it *better* be a celebration!'

Jamie had organized everything with her usual style. She

was studying interior design, and with her father to finance her she was hoping to eventually open her own place. She'd recently got engaged to Peter, a handsome blond man. Everyone referred to them as the golden couple.

Natalie was living in L.A. with her brother, Cole, trying to get a TV celebrity journalist career off the ground.

Madison was the first one to achieve her dream. She was a published writer at a very prestigious magazine – a magazine that consistently outsold *Esquire* and *Vanity Fair*.

'So,' Natalie asked, grabbing a handful of potato chips, 'did you tell Michael?'

'I showed him the article.'

'And?' they both asked.

'He was kind of psyched.'

'I *bet* he was,' Jamie said, laughing. 'Is he still as handsome as ever?'

'Hmm . . .' Madison said with a knowing smile. 'You always had a crush on him, didn't you?'

'Yes,' Jamie admitted. 'However, now that I'm getting married, my crush will have to be a thing of the past.'

'Are you inviting him to your wedding?' Madison inquired. 'So he can admire the bride?'

'Of course,' Jamie said, refusing to be teased. 'I've known both your parents forever.'

'How *is* the lovely Stella?' Natalie asked.

'She spends most of her time in Connecticut,' Madison said, 'and when she comes into the city, she's either shopping or sick. I hardly ever see her.'

'Then I guess things are the same as ever,' Jamie said.

'I get off listening to you privileged kids discuss family shit,' Natalie said. 'Me, I'm the one who had to struggle through college, working as a waitress and all that crap.'

'You *never* worked as a waitress,' Jamie said jokingly. 'You did one week in a hamburger joint and ran screaming to the hills when you broke a nail. You had so many boyfriends there wasn't *time* for work.'

'Now you're making me sound like a hooker,' Natalie objected.

'They were lining up outside the dorm,' Jamie giggled. 'Seven little hard-ons all in a row!'

'Yeah – and that was for *you*,' Natalie said succinctly.

In college the three of them had been nicknamed the Beauty (Jamie), the Brain (Madison), and the Sexpot (Natalie). They'd been inseparable.

Jamie ordered a bottle of Cristal. As soon as their glasses were filled, she lifted hers and toasted Madison. 'How does it feel to be famous and successful?' she asked, tucking a strand of wheat-blonde hair behind her ears.

'Unfuckingbelievable,' Madison said, using one of her father's favourite words.

'Unfuckingbelievable,' Natalie repeated. 'Girl! I like it!'

'So how *was* Dr Henry Kissinger?' Jamie asked.

'Very charming. And extremely clever.'

'Can you please interview Denzel Washington next?' Natalie pleaded. 'Or Sidney Poitier, my hero?'

'Too old,' Jamie said.

'Don't you mean too *hot?*' Natalie contradicted. 'That man has got it goin' on!'

'I'll try,' Madison said, sipping her champagne. 'Apparently he's a hard get, doesn't like doing interviews.'

'So I'll settle for Denzel.' Natalie sighed. 'That man is sweet as molasses.'

Later, at home in the small apartment Michael had bought her the day she graduated from college, Madison propped the magazine up against the mirror in her bathroom.

Profiles in Power by Madison Castelli.

Life couldn't get any better.

Chapter Fifty-one

Dani and Vincent: 1995

'You look great in a hard hat, Mom,' Vincent said, mildly teasing her.

'Excuse me?' Dani replied.

'No, really,' he said, taking her arm and steering her round a fenced-off area. 'It suits you.'

'I can assure you that it's not going to be my mode of dress every day. Only when I visit my son's construction site.'

'Can you believe it?' Vincent said, shaking his head as if he couldn't quite believe it himself. 'Our own hotel.'

'I must say, much as I disapprove of Nando, the two of you deserve it. You've both worked hard to achieve this.'

'You're telling me,' Vincent agreed. 'It's taken two years to build, and when it's finished – man, it'll be worth all the stress and hard work.'

'How much longer?' Dani asked.

'I reckon another six months.'

'Incredible,' she said. 'And you do know I'm ready to help you in any way I can.'

'Good, Mom. 'Cause I'm depending on you to sit down with the interior designer, see he doesn't get carried away. You have great taste.'

'It's all in the finishing touches,' she said modestly. 'I can help choose the paint colours and the fabrics. I want the rooms to be stylish and comfortable.'

Vincent nodded. He wasn't really concentrating. He had too much on his mind – so many details and everything had to be perfect: there could be no mistakes. Nando and he were risking everything on the success of their hotel, which Nando had generously suggested should be called The Castle Hotel and Casino. 'That name's got a lucky feel to it,' Nando had said, displaying a refreshing lack of ego. Vincent felt the same way.

A group of investors had put up the money to build the hotel, including Michael, who'd insisted on being involved. Reluctantly Vincent had agreed to his father's participation. If the hotel was a flop he would simply kill himself. There was no way he could let Michael down.

'It's exciting, huh?' he said, as he walked Dani back to his car.

'It would be even *more* exciting if you found yourself a nice girl and settled down,' she remarked.

'What's with the settling down?' he said, knowing that that was the one thing he had no intention of doing. 'I'm perfectly happy the way I am.'

'I know you are, Vincent,' she said, wishing he'd listen to her. 'But wouldn't it be nice if you had a baby?'

'Oh, c'mon, Mom,' he said, laughing, 'you're not the grandma type.'

'I'd be a sensational babysitter.'

He grinned at his beautiful mother and wondered how she'd managed all these years by herself.

Michael's visits were becoming less frequent, and he knew it upset her. He felt like *he* was the man of the family now, because Michael had this whole other life in New York.

It was weird knowing that he had a half-sister out there

somewhere, a sister who, if Michael had his way, he'd never get to meet.

His other sister, Sofia, was twelve. She was into Madonna, makeup and lots of girly clothes. She already looked like a teenager, so Vincent was aware that he had to keep a strong watch over her, especially since Michael wasn't round to do so.

'Inspection over,' Dani said, removing her hard hat and getting into his car. 'Can we go to lunch now?'

'I always like buying my mom lunch,' Vincent said, settling behind the wheel. 'She's the hottest date in town.'

'I wish,' Dani said wryly.

'I remember when I was growing up. God! Every boy in school had the hots for you.'

'Vincent!'

'They did. And then one night someone's parents spotted you in the show. The next day I was *so* embarrassed. It was all over school that my Mom took her clothes off.'

'Sorry if I embarrassed you,' she said drily. 'Don't forget that taking off my clothes paid all our bills.'

'Listen, Mom,' he said sincerely, 'I *know*, better than anyone, how hard you worked *and* the sacrifices you made.'

'It didn't seem like making sacrifices at the time.'

'How come you never married Dean?' Vincent asked curiously. 'He was always round. Still is.'

'Because I don't love him,' she said patiently. 'I love Michael and I always will.'

'Then why didn't you and Michael get married?'

'You *know* why, Vincent. I don't have to explain.'

'Yeah, yeah, I know. He has a wife and daughter in New York.'

'That's right,' Dani said, reluctant to discuss it.

'So why the hell doesn't he divorce her?' Vincent demanded.

'I'm not complaining,' she said quietly.

'Perhaps if you complained he'd do it.'

'I'm not sure if it's what I want any more. Lately we've been drifting apart. Michael doesn't come here as much as he used to. I'd like him to see more of Sofia, but what can I do? I can't force him to spend time with her.'

'Don't worry about Sofia,' Vincent said. 'She's a tough little cookie.'

'I realize that,' Dani said. 'Both of you have lots of your father in you.'

'We're not alike at all,' Vincent said quickly. 'I'd never string a woman along the way he's done with you.'

'Well, you *look* alike. And I might point out that Michael has never strung me along. We have an arrangement, and I'm perfectly happy the way things are.'

'Yeah?'

'Yes, Vincent,' she said firmly. 'I've never wanted for a thing. Michael pays all my bills, he bought me a lovely house, I get a new car every year. What more could any woman ask for?'

'How about a man beside you to protect you? You deserve that, Mom.'

She turned away so that he couldn't see the tears that suddenly filled her eyes. Vincent meant well, but his words had upset her.

'I'm very excited about your hotel,' she said, gazing out of the car window. 'And I'm sure your father is too.'

The following week Michael flew in. 'I can only stay for a couple of days,' were the first words out of his mouth.

'Then you'd better spend all your time with Sofia and Vincent,' Dani said. 'They both miss you.'

'I miss them, too.'

'Vincent is dying to show you his hotel. It's almost finished.'

He gave her a quizzical look. 'Are you trying to make me feel guilty?'

'Take it any way you want,' she said, tossing back her long blonde hair.

He obviously took it to heart, because he spent every minute with his two children, and when he departed, Dani realized it was the first time he'd come to Vegas and they had not made love.

After he left she was depressed. Perhaps Dean had been right all these years. Was it possible that Michael *was* using her?

She decided it was time to make some changes. Sofia was growing up fast, Vincent was long gone from the house, living in his own apartment, and it was prudent to start thinking about her future. She needed a career, something to do with her time. She could hardly go back to being a showgirl; she was too old – and besides, the idea did not appeal to her.

Vincent had asked her to help with the design concept of the hotel, and that was interesting and fun. Maybe when that job was completed she could get into the PR side. She knew plenty about publicity and how to present things.

Yes, that was it. She decided she'd ask Vincent and Nando if she could handle special events at the hotel.

At least it would take her mind off Michael.

Chapter Fifty-two

Michael and Madison: 2000

One day Michael came home and discovered that Stella was gone. Just like that. The house in Connecticut was empty. Her clothes were gone. She'd emptied the safe of her jewellery. And that was it. No note. Nothing.

He was not surprised, although when he discovered she'd run off with a twenty-six-year-old struggling artist, his ego was slightly deflated. Only slightly, because what really pissed him off was that she obviously didn't give a shit about Madison's reaction. Which meant that she didn't care if Madison discovered the truth.

Now he'd have to tell Madison. Whether he liked it or not, the time had come.

First he'd have to summon the courage, and that was not going to be easy. It might take a while.

A few days later, sitting round in Vito Giovanni's old brownstone drinking Jack Daniel's on the rocks, Michael felt as if he was a kid again. He felt melancholy, too, because Vito was in extremely bad shape. The old man had lost about fifty pounds and was a skeletal figure. It was upsetting to see him that way. His jaw seemed to have caved in, his eyes were hollow, and his paper-white hands shook uncontrollably. Now his favourite armchair completely enveloped him.

'You're lookin' good, Vito,' Michael lied, knowing how vain Vito was.

'You always was a lousy liar,' Vito replied, indulging in a vigorous coughing fit. 'I'm a sick old man. I ain't got much longer.'

He'd been suffering from prostate cancer for the last three years. Chemotherapy and radiation treatments had completely debilitated him, but he still knew how to bitch. And bitch he did – about his treatments, his doctors, the hospitals and the nurses. The only person he had a good word for was his wife, the former stripper Western Pussy, now officially Western Giovanni.

Western was a cheery soul who obviously made him very happy. Unlike Vito's former wife Mamie, Western did not have a bitter bone in her body. Oblivious to criticism, she sailed through life with her 46D boobs and her cheery smile.

'How's my baby boy?' she said, sweeping into the room, smelling of cheap scent and pizza. Western never *had* learned to spend Vito's money: she still preferred the small pleasures in life.

'Didya say hello to Michael?' Vito asked, coughing again.

'I *always* say hello to your handsome friend. How's it shakin', Michael?'

'I'm good, Western. How about you?'

'Can't complain.' She turned to her ailing husband. 'Look what I bought you in the sale at Bloomingdale's, honeybunch,' she said, digging into her shopping bag and producing a most unsuitable pink V-neck sweater. She waved it in front of him. 'It's cashmere,' she said reverently. '*So* soft and cuddly.'

'That's nice, babe,' Vito said. 'Now run along. Me an' Michael got business to discuss.'

'Business at your age,' she scolded. 'You gotta give it up, Vito.'

'Scram,' he said affectionately.

She blew him a kiss and left the room.

Vito turned to his nurse who was sitting in the corner. 'Wait outside,' he commanded.

'But Mr Giovanni—'

'Go!' The woman went. 'They try to keep me in bed,' Vito confided. 'I ain't havin' that shit. I'm no fuckin' invalid. I got prostate cancer. Big fuckin' deal.'

'I guess they feel you should get plenty of rest,' Michael offered.

'Rest for what?' Vito demanded. 'My fuckin' grave?'

'Look, Vito, I'm glad you saw me today. We've got to discuss what you want me to do with your money.'

'Oh, yeah. My money,' he said vaguely. 'How much is it now?'

'About three times as much as you gave me.'

'You always was good at makin' dough.' The old man guffawed. Then he frowned. 'I sure as shit don't want the taxman gettin' it.'

'Then *what*?'

'Here's what you do. Western can't manage nothin', so it's no good givin' it to her. Once I'm gone, you arrange a monthly income for her. Somethin' that goes straight into her bank.'

'Okay.'

'Then I want ya t'take a coupla million an' give it to Mamie.'

He said it so casually that Michael didn't register what he was saying for a moment. When it hit him, he was outraged. '*What?*'

'Mamie – remember her, my ex-wife?'

'What the fuck would you want to do that for?'

'I promised her that when I went she'd get it.'

'From what I hear, she's doing okay with her porno empire.'

'She was with me a lotta years, Mike,' Vito said. 'I think she deserves it.'

'You do, huh?'

'Yes, I do,' Vito said, his gruff voice hardening. 'So Mike, I can trust you, right?'

Michael nodded. He had no intention of giving one dime to Mamie Giovanni. By withholding the money, he could finally exact a very small revenge.

And that's exactly what he planned on doing.

Fresh back from L.A. and an exciting assignment interviewing a powerful super-agent, Madison lunched with Jamie in a Manhattan restaurant.

She was at the top of her game now. *Profiles in Power by Madison Castelli* was a big deal. Publicists were clamouring for her to sit down with their clients. In the magazine-publishing world she was a star.

Jamie leaned across the table. 'What's the best sex you ever had?' she asked.

'Huh?' Madison said.

'You know,' Jamie said. 'Mind-blowing, down and dirty sex. The kind where you never want to see the guy again, but at the exact moment you're doing it, anything goes. And I *do* mean anything.'

'Well . . .' Madison wondered where Jamie was heading with this. 'Miami,' she said at last. 'Remember that weekend I spent with my dad when I was sixteen? Well, I met this guy, a forty-something major playboy with all the toys – penthouse, Porsche, and an oversized waterbed covered in rose petals. Also . . .' she paused for effect '. . . an extraordinarily talented tongue.'

'Damn!' Jamie exclaimed. 'You never told me.'

'It was my secret,' Madison said, laughing. 'His name was Frankie Medina. I'll never forget him. He taught me plenty.'

'You *sly* one,' Jamie said. 'I didn't know we kept secrets from each other.'

'Just one.'

'Ha!'

'What's with all this sex talk anyway?' Madison asked.

'I think Peter might be having an affair,' Jamie blurted, mentioning her husband.

'You've only been married a few years,' Madison pointed out. 'Give the guy a *chance* to get bored.'

'Thanks a lot,' Jamie said huffily. 'What makes you think he'd *ever* get bored?'

'Anyway, don't talk to *me* about unfaithful men,' Madison said. 'They're all dogs.'

Recently she'd broken up with her live-in boyfriend of two years, David, a TV producer. She suspected that he had got uptight because he'd discovered she made more money than him. One day he'd informed her he was going out for cigarettes, and failed to return. A few weeks after his abrupt departure, she'd heard he'd married his childhood sweetheart, a vapid blonde with fake boobs and an annoying overbite. So much for good taste.

David had been her longest relationship – she wasn't looking for another, although she'd recently met Jake Sica in L.A., and he was very attractive. Unfortunately he was hooked up with someone else.

'Ever since David took a runner you've turned into a real cynic,' Jamie remarked.

'For your information, I'm glad he's gone,' Madison said. 'I've discovered that work is more important than a man any day.'

Later that night they met up at a dinner party at Anton

Couch's house. Anton – a gay and extremely social man – was Jamie's partner in her design business. During the course of dinner, Anton mentioned that Madison's mother had called him.

'My mother?' she said, surprised.

'You do *have* a mother, don't you?' Anton said crisply. 'You didn't just spring from the streets of New York with a pen in your hand?'

'Why would she call *you?*'

'To enquire about a design concept for their new apartment.'

'*What* new apartment?' Madison said, puzzled. 'My parents live in Connecticut now.'

'Apparently they're moving back to the city.'

The moment she got home, she called Michael. He sounded half asleep. She didn't care.

'I do not appreciate hearing from Anton Couch that you guys are getting an apartment in New York,' she said.

'Hey, sweetie,' he mumbled. 'I'm asleep. Can we talk about this tomorrow?'

'Sure,' she said, slamming the phone down. She couldn't stand it when Michael didn't give her his full attention.

The next morning he was on the phone bright and early. 'If you're available I'll drive into the city and we can go for brunch.'

'You *and* Stella?' she said, stifling a yawn.

'No,' he said shortly. 'Stella can't make it.'

An hour later he picked her up and they went to the Plaza where, after talking about a dozen other things, he finally told her that Stella had left him for another man.

'*What?*' she said, totally shocked. 'You and Mom have always been so close.'

'That's what *I* thought.'

'How did it happen?'

'Who knows?' he said evenly. 'I'm merely the guy who got left. Came home one day and she was gone. I haven't spoken to her since.'

'So it's her who's getting the apartment?'

'I guess so.'

They sat in silence for a few minutes, until Madison suddenly blurted out, 'How can you let her do this to me?'

He laughed drily. 'No one's doing anything to *you*.'

'You're my *parents*,' she said accusingly, knowing she sounded unreasonable, but unable to stop herself. 'I don't *want* divorced parents.'

'What are you? Eight?'

'No,' she said heatedly. 'But I've always looked up to you both as an example.'

'Everything isn't always what it seems,' he said mysteriously.

'Why hasn't Stella called me?'

'You were never exactly close.'

'She *is* my mother. Don't you think I should have heard it from her?'

He sighed. 'The truth is that you didn't always get the attention from either of us that you deserved, and that bothers me.' He paused for a long moment. Was now the time to tell her the truth? Yes. He couldn't procrastinate any longer. 'Listen, sweetheart,' he said, hesitating slightly, 'there's something else I have to tell you. Something that might help you understand things better.'

She felt queasy. What could be worse than them getting a divorce? Obviously it was something she didn't want to hear.

'Here's the thing,' he said, his eyes fixed firmly on hers. 'Stella . . . She's uh . . . well . . . she's not your real mother.'

Her world began spinning out of control. Stella wasn't her real mother? How could that be? It didn't make sense. *What the hell was he talking about?*

Michael was still speaking, telling her a long, involved story about when he was single, and a girlfriend had his baby, then his girlfriend got shot because business people he was dealing with decided they had to punish him.

What kind of insane story *was* this? She felt as if she was in the middle of some crazy soap opera as she listened to him speak.

When he was finally finished there was another long silence.

Suddenly she had a blinding headache. For God's sake, was this her life? Everything had suddenly changed. She was no longer the person she'd thought she was. 'I – I have to go home and . . . digest this,' she managed, standing up.

'Don't run away from me,' Michael implored, grabbing her hand. 'I need you, sweetheart. I've always needed you.'

'Maybe you do,' she said, feeling a sharp pain burning within her, 'but this is too much of a shock, and I have to deal with it on my own.' Pulling her hand away from his, she stood up and hurried from the restaurant.

Outside on the street everything seemed different. She felt dizzy and faint, and she didn't know what to do or where to turn. All she really wanted to do was burst out crying.

Why do you want to cry? her inner voice asked.

Because I don't know who I am any more.

Watching his daughter bolt from the restaurant, Michael felt a sense of relief – not because Madison had gone, but because he'd finally told her. And by telling her, he'd freed himself from the guilt he'd been living with for all these years.

Madison was upset now, but she was a sensible girl, she'd get over it. Especially when he explained it to her in more detail. It was a lot for her to absorb in one sitting. Too much.

He couldn't wait to phone Dani, although he wasn't ready to tell her about Stella. He'd sit on that information for a few more weeks.

Right now he wasn't in the mood to make any life-changing decisions.

Dani would always be there. Waiting.

One day she might get a nice surprise.

Chapter Fifty-three

Dani and Vincent: 2000

'Everything's set, Mrs Castle,' the caterer said.

'You're sure? I don't want any mistakes,' Dani responded.

'Mrs Castle,' the caterer replied, 'I never make mistakes.'

She nodded. 'Just checking.' Then she smiled.

The man smiled back. He loved dealing with this beautiful woman. She was an exquisite creature. And yet, like all his other clients, she was extremely fussy. And so she should be: it was her son's wedding, and who could blame her?

When she was finished with the caterer, Dani took the elevator to her suite in the Castle Hotel. Vincent was finally getting married, and Michael was late. Although, since it was out of his control, she had to forgive him. She'd called the airport a couple of times and found out that his flight had been delayed leaving New York. The plane had finally taken off and he should be arriving at any minute.

She'd told him to come directly to the hotel. She no longer had a house, she'd sold it and moved into an elegant apartment shortly after Sofia had dropped out of school at fifteen, and run off to Europe. She blamed Michael for

Sofia's defection. He'd had a massive fight with his daughter, who'd accused him of never being there for her. A few weeks later she'd taken off.

Dani had been a wreck about it, until Sofia had called from England and said, cavalierly, 'Don't worry about me, Mom. I'm with friends and I'll check in occasionally.'

Dani had appealed to Michael. He'd been his usual stubborn self. 'She can look after herself,' he'd said. 'Sofia's okay, she's just like me.'

Michael's favourite description of his children was that they were just like him, when in fact the only resemblance was physical.

Did he think he was so perfect?

She had news for him. He wasn't. Although that didn't stop her from loving him. She always would. Michael Castelli was her incurable addiction.

The Castle Hotel and Casino had turned out to be a big success. Nando and Vincent had managed to build and operate a boutique hotel that appealed to the younger crowd. The hotel was always fully booked, and the casino always packed. Business was excellent.

Today was a special day. Vincent's wedding day. He was marrying Jenna Crane, the very pretty, honey blonde daughter of a local lawyer.

Naturally Vincent had gone for looks. Jenna was not the girl Dani would have picked for her son. Yes, Jenna was very pretty. Yes, she appeared to be quite innocent. However, she didn't seem too bright. Dani would have preferred to see Vincent marry a more intelligent woman.

At least he was getting married. Nando had done the deed a year earlier. His wife, Jolie, was quite gorgeous. A former dancer, Jolie was beautiful *and* smart. A winning combination.

As Dani put on her mother-of-the-groom outfit, it occurred to her that this was the first time that Michael would meet Dean. When she'd told Michael that Dean would be at the wedding, he'd been livid. 'Why do I have to look at *that* asshole?' he'd complained.

'He's not an asshole,' she'd answered firmly. There was no way she was *not* inviting Dean to her son's big day, so Michael would just have to get over it. 'I've told you many times, Dean's my best friend.'

'Fuck the prick,' Michael had said, put out. '*I* should be your best friend.'

'Well, you're not. You're my lover.'

Her words had pissed Michael off even more.

She was putting the finishing touches to her hair when Michael arrived. He entered the suite, put his arms round her from behind, nuzzled her neck, and said, 'Guess what?'

She spun round. 'What?'

'I told Madison.'

'About us?'

'No . . . No, I, uh, told her that Stella isn't her real mother.'

'Oh, my God,' Dani gasped, realizing what a big deal this was for him. 'You did?'

'Yeah.'

'How did she take it?'

'She ran out on me. She's angry.'

'Of course she is. That's understandable.'

'You know what, Dani? I'm glad I did it. Now that I've told her, I'll give her a couple of months to digest it, then slowly I'll tell her about you and the kids.'

'You will?'

'It's time.'

'Good.'

'I love you, Dani,' he said, nuzzling her neck again. 'Now that I've told Madison, things will be different. You'll see.'

*

Instead of calming him, Nando was making Vincent into a nervous wreck. As it was, he had a hangover from hell. The night before, Nando had insisted on throwing him a bachelor party. It had turned out to be the bachelor night to beat all bachelor nights. Strippers, contortionists, mud wrestlers – all of them naked, all of them female, and all of them on his case.

His last memory was of tequila being poured down his throat at three-thirty a.m. and a beautiful Eurasian girl thrusting her breasts into his mouth and begging him to fuck her – an offer he'd turned down. He groaned at the memory.

He'd had two hours' sleep and now he felt like shit.

Nando was grinning as they both got dressed. 'You gotta go out in style,' Nando explained. 'It's the only way.'

'Thanks,' Vincent said grimly. 'I doubt if I'll be able to get it up tonight. You've ruined my wedding night.'

'Once you're married you don't *have* to get it up,' Nando said, still grinning. 'Sex takes on a whole new meaning.'

'Jesus Christ!' Vincent exclaimed. 'Why don't you just stay quiet for once?'

Vincent and Jenna were married in the grounds of the hotel. The flowers, the music, the food – everything was perfect.

At the reception Michael stayed by Dani's side, shooting dark looks at Dean, who was sitting at another table.

'Will you *stop*,' Dani said, noticing what was going on.

'Who – me? What'm *I* doing?' Michael said innocently.

Earlier, when she'd introduced them, Michael had barely managed a surly hello. 'I hate that asshole,' he'd muttered. 'He's the prick who kept us apart for seven years.'

'He was doing what he thought was best for me.'

'No, Dani,' Michael had corrected her. 'He was doing what he thought was best for *him*.'

Vincent's bride looked stunning, in a white lace Vera Wang gown. She was surrounded by all her girlfriends, dressed in pink.

'Man, if I wasn't married, I'd fuck every one of 'em,' Nando confided to Vincent, nudging him in the ribs.

'What else is new?' Vincent said, shaking his head.

Dani watched her son with love and pride. Her only disappointment was that Sofia was not here to share in this happy family day. It was a source of great sadness to Dani that her wild daughter was roaming round Europe somewhere when she should be at her brother's wedding.

She observed Michael as he danced with the bride. Still so tall, dark and handsome. A heartbreaker. *Her* heartbreaker. How she loved him.

What would her life have been like if she'd never met him?

She had no regrets. If they'd never met, she wouldn't have Vincent and Sofia, so somehow things had worked out for the best.

Chapter Fifty-four

Tuesday, 10 July 2001

'Where are we going?' Madison asked.

'Christ!' the gunman said. 'Don't you ever shut up?'

Loud rap music was blasting, and she was stuck in the back of a strange car with this maniacal asshole. Two other men were in the front. It was too dark to get a good look at them.

It struck her as odd that she'd been singled out. Why? And where had this vehicle come from? Had the gunman been in contact by cellphone with people to come get him?

What about the other two gunmen and the hostages? Something weird was going on, and she couldn't figure it out.

'What'll happen to the people we left behind?' she asked.

'That ain't your concern,' he said roughly.

'Will they be freed?'

'For crissakes!'

She tried to get a better look at the two men in the front. The driver was a big man, with a totally shaved head. His bare arms were festooned with intricate tattoos.

The man sitting beside him had long, greasy hair, and

studs in his nose and ears. That's all she could see.

I'm not frightened, she told herself. *I'm not scared. I'm my father's daughter, and he'd expect me to be strong. So fuck 'em!*

But inside she was filled with trepidation.

As far as Jolie was concerned the situation was heading from bad to worse. Not only did she have Darren eyeballing her with a lecherous twist to his thin Snoop Doggy Dogg lips, but now the two men had set out several lines of coke on a glass-top table, and a couple of topless girls had wandered in to join the party.

Jolie was offended. She didn't want to be here, this was not her scene.

She kept on looking over at Nando to see if he'd got the message that she wanted to get the hell out of there. He took no notice of her, he was too busy laughing and bullshitting with the guys. The next thing she knew he was doing a line of coke.

Determined to act with dignity, she stood up. 'Will you excuse me for a moment?' she said, tight-lipped.

'Sure, babe,' Nando answered, half eyeballing one of the topless babes.

'The pisser's on your right,' Darren offered with a sly smirk. 'Want me t'take you?'

'I'm sure I'll find it,' she said icily.

She walked out of the room and back into the club, practically bumping into a huge bouncer who was in the process of dragging some hapless drunk towards the door.

Now she was really angry. How *dare* Nando bring her to such a place? He should have more respect for her. After all, she was his *wife*.

She glanced up at the stage. It was Open-leg City, girls spreading them like there was no tomorrow.

Shaking her head, she walked to the front entrance. The

parking valet who'd taken care of Nando's car was standing there smoking a cigarette.

She fished in her purse and took out money. 'Here's that other twenty my husband promised you,' she said, handing him a twenty-dollar bill. 'Can you please bring the car?'

'Sure,' the guy said, giving her an appraising once-over as he flicked his cigarette on the ground. 'The Ferrari, right?'

Tapping her foot impatiently, she watched as a fat man rolled out of the club chortling with amusement. He was holding on to his friend, who staggered over to the side of the kerb and proceeded to puke.

Nice. Very, very nice.

The valet brought the car round and she got in. 'Oh, by the way, tell my husband when he comes out that he can take a cab.'

And before the parking valet could say a word, she shot off.

The plane made a smooth landing. Michael disembarked quickly. He'd always kept in touch with Gus, his former prison mate and co-worker in crime. Gus had moved to L.A. fifteen years ago to run the West Coast operation for Lucchese.

Gus was there to greet him. They shook hands, walked out of the airport, and got into a black limo with tinted dark windows that was waiting at the kerb-side. 'Good to see you, Michael,' Gus said, looking very L.A. in a silk T-shirt worn under a lightweight cream suit.

'Shame it has to be under these circumstances,' Michael replied.

'Don't worry about it,' Gus said. 'I done what you asked. Everything's set.'

'Those morons,' Michael said, his eyes filled with an unholy anger. 'I think they might've taken my daughter.'

'What?' Gus said, squinting at him.

'You been following that hostage situation on TV?'

'You mean the one from the restaurant on Beverly Boulevard?'

'Yeah.'

'What about it?'

'It's not a hostage situation,' Michael said grimly. 'I think they could've snatched Madison.'

'I suppose,' Sofia said, as she sat on Gianni's private jet, sipping iced tea, 'that you're expecting an explanation about last night.'

'I've forgotten about last night,' Gianni said.

'No, really,' she insisted. 'I want to explain.'

'You don't have to.'

'Why don't you want to hear it?' she said, fidgeting in her seat.

'I'm not interested. I'm prepared to forget it ever happened.'

'Oh, that's great, isn't it?' she said sulkily. 'Make me feel like a piece of shit.'

'Sofia, if a gentleman gives you an opportunity to forget something that is embarrassing to you, then you should take that opportunity.'

'Why are you always lecturing me?' she demanded.

'I'm not. I'm merely trying to tell you that it is more prudent to listen to good advice.'

'You're very smug, Gianni.'

'I'm sorry you feel that way.'

She leaned back and stretched. 'I called my mother this morning.'

'You did?'

'Yeah – I figured, y'know, she'd like to hear from me. I didn't tell her about jumping into a swimming pool from eight storeys up!'

'No, I'm quite sure she wouldn't have appreciated *that*.'

'Anyway, she wants me to come home.'

'And do you wish to do that?'

'Well, she kind of, like, said there was an emergency with my father.'

'Is he sick?'

'No, she just said it was like, um, a situation.'

'What *kind* of situation?'

'How would I know? My mom's mysterious. You'd probably fall madly in love with her. She's a gorgeous blonde.'

'What makes you imagine I would fall madly in love with a gorgeous blonde?'

'Men fall in love with Dani all the time,' Sofia said, stating a fact. 'She used to be a showgirl in Vegas. She was like a *real* hot number.'

'Your mother was?'

'Yeah. She's only, like, y'know, fifty-something.'

'When we get to Rome, you'll do the audition photos, and after that I'll arrange for you to fly home. Is that a plan?'

'Yeah, 'cause if the photos work out and you want me to do the campaign, I can always come back.'

'Excellent.'

'So, you'll buy me a ticket home, and my dad'll pay you. He's rich, y'know. Probably as rich as you.'

'Does he have his own plane?'

'Oh,' she said, staring him down, 'I guess you're mega rich, huh?'

'What does your father do?'

'That's a good question,' she answered vaguely. 'Investments and crap, real estate, shopping centres, things like that.'

'Is he like Donald Trump?'

She giggled. 'Donald Trump *wishes*.'

*

Purposefully Vincent set off to collect his erstwhile wife, and maybe beat the shit out of Andy Dale. He'd warned him. Hadn't the cretin got it the first time?

Probably not. Andy Dale was a movie star. The dumbest of the dumb.

He'd dragged Jenna home once tonight, and now he had to do it a second time. This was ridiculous. He didn't need these kind of headaches.

He'd rescue her, and that was it.

After this little experience, Jenna was on her own. She'd no longer have him to protect her.

Chapter Fifty-five

Michael and Madison: 2001

Michael got the call in the middle of the night. He had been alone in Connecticut, since Stella had moved out to live with her boyfriend. He didn't care. Things between him and Stella had cooled down long before she left. A divorce was inevitable.

He was trying to get things straight in his own head before he started thinking about the future. Madison wasn't talking to him: she was still upset about his revelations concerning Stella. He hadn't called Dani in a while because, quite frankly, he wasn't sure where he wanted their relationship to go, and once he had told her about Stella leaving, it would definitely be decision time. Sofia was wandering around somewhere in Europe. Vincent was the only one who was doing great. He had a new wife, a successful hotel, and seemed all set.

The call informed him that Vito Giovanni had passed away. Michael was heavy-hearted to hear the news. It didn't seem possible that Vito was gone, a man who'd always been such a strong presence in his life.

He got into his car, drove into town, and checked into a hotel. The next morning he got up early and went directly to the Giovanni house.

Western greeted him with red, puffy eyes. 'He was such a sweet old guy,' she said mournfully. 'My Vito was real good to me.'

'He loved you very much,' Michael assured her.

'I don't know what to do,' she worried, twisting her diamond wedding ring. 'Who am I supposed to call?'

'Don't worry,' Michael said. 'I'll take care of everything.'

And he did.

The day of the funeral, two surprise guests turned up. Mamie and Bone. Almost seventy, Mamie was still trying to look like a teenager. She wore a bright blue suit with a skirt way above her bony knees, her bleached-blonde hair was ratted and brittle, her makeup was caked all over her face, and she was festooned in diamond jewellery.

A scowling Bone had dyed his hair boot-polish black and swooped it across his head to hide his receding hairline. He'd also applied some kind of fake suntan, which gave his face a sickly orange tint. He looked ridiculous.

The two of them made quite a bizarre sight.

The turn-out for the funeral was enormous. Vito had had an endless stream of friends, business associates and acquaintances, all of whom were anxious to pay their respects.

Michael immediately spotted Mamie and Bone, and did his best to avoid them.

Mamie was having none of it: she accosted him on his way out of church. 'Mikey,' she said, spiky black eyelashes dominating over-made-up eyes. 'My little Mikey.'

Did she not remember their past history? Had she forgotten that she was directly responsible for his mother's murder and, God knows, probably Beth's too?

He tried to turn in the other direction.

She placed her bony hand on his arm. Long fingers,

every one beringed. 'Don't walk away when I'm talking to you.'

'What is it?' he said, keeping his voice low and even because he did not wish to cause a scene.

'We came to New York to pay respects to my ex-husband,' she said. 'Vito would've wanted that.' Michael nodded silently. 'And also,' she said, leaning confidentially towards him, 'to work out how we're gonna get the money he promised me.'

Now was his moment of triumph. 'What money?' he said blankly.

'The money you've been looking after for him,' she said, fixing him with a malevolent glare.

'I have no idea what you're talking about.'

'Don't screw with me, Mikey,' she said, talking to him as if he were still the teenage kid she'd known way back.

He brushed her hand off his arm and, in a very low voice so nobody else could hear, said, 'Go fuck yourself, Mamie.'

Then he walked away.

Bone came up to him at the reception. 'I understand you and Mamie had a talk,' Bone said flatly, fingering the long, thin scar on his cheek.

Michael stared at him and didn't say a word. How he hated the man who'd shot his mother. A mother he'd never known because of Bone.

'Take this as a warning,' Bone said with a great deal of malice in his voice. 'You get her the money or you're gonna regret it.'

'I'll tell you the same as I told Mamie,' Michael said, holding back his anger. 'I don't know what you're talking about.'

Bone shook his head in wonderment. 'You're still the same dumb bastard.' His voice rose. 'You get Mamie her money or you'll see what'll happen.'

'Jeez!' Michael said, taunting him. 'Threats. What're you going to do to me now?'

Bone's eyes were cold and dead. 'You'd be surprised,' he said. 'You'd be *very* surprised.'

Once more Michael walked away. There was *nothing* they could do to him. There was no way they could prove that Vito had entrusted him with any money. Besides, he was a legitimate businessman now; he was way out of their reach.

Over the next few days he made arrangements for Western to receive a princely income for the rest of her life. He didn't feel bad about keeping the rest of Vito's secret stash. He considered it Bone and Mamie's punishment, a punishment that was not nearly harsh enough. Eventually he'd give every dollar of it to some deserving charity. Now, *that* was justice.

As the years had passed he'd begun to realize that seeking endless revenge could poison a person's soul. Another thought: did revenge ever satisfy?

This particular time it did.

Later that night he spoke to Warner Carlysle. She was still close to Stella, and with her help he planned to move on.

'I want a divorce,' he told her. 'Can you talk to Stella for me?'

'I don't know why you two can't speak to each other,' Warner grumbled.

'She refuses to talk to me,' he said, 'so I'd appreciate it if you'd step in and tell her that either she proceeds with a divorce or I will. I won't fight her. She can have anything she wants – including the house.'

'Very well.' Warner sighed, reluctant to get involved.

'Thanks.'

'Michael,' Warner added curiously, 'aren't you interested in knowing why she ran off with another man?'

'I couldn't care less.'

'Well,' Warner said, 'you have to admit that you were hardly ever there for her. And Stella felt you still loved Beth, and that you always put Madison before her.'

'What're you – her shrink?' he said coldly.

He had no interest in Stella any more. She'd left him, and the truth was that he was relieved. He wished she'd done it years earlier.

'I'll talk to her, Michael,' Warner promised. 'It's better for both of you to end it.'

A few days later, he was in his office when the phone rang. It was Warner.

'Do you have news for me?' he asked.

Her voice sounded tired and strained, unlike her usual spirited tone. 'Yes, Michael,' she said slowly, 'I do.'

'So tell me, is she willing to start divorce proceedings?'

'It won't be necessary,' Warner said haltingly. 'Stella and Lucien are both dead.'

'*What?*'

'They were shot in the back of the head, execution-style.'

'Jesus!' he said, almost dropping the phone.

'Michael, I have to ask you this.' A long, silent beat. 'Did you do it?'

'Are you out of your fucking mind?' he screamed.

And then he knew.

Bone and Mamie had struck again.

Madison was confused, angry and upset. She'd been that way for a while. And it was all because of Michael and his bullshit lies.

When he'd revealed that Stella wasn't her mother, and then made up some story about her real mother getting shot, she'd failed to believe him. Somehow his story didn't make sense. So she'd hired a private detective to find out the real truth. The detective, Kimm Florian, had come up with plenty of information. She'd presented Madison with a stack of press clippings about a man called Michael Castellino who, of course, was Michael Castelli. Almost thirty years ago Michael Castellino had been accused of killing the woman he was living with, and that woman was Madison's mother, Beth.

According to the newspapers he'd been acquitted.

So what? She'd spent her entire life loving a stranger. It was glaringly obvious that she didn't know Michael at all. And she realized that was why Stella had always been so cold towards her. Growing up she'd thought it was just the way her mother was, but obviously Stella had never loved her.

It made her so sad. She felt disoriented, like an orphan with nowhere to go.

And then, like a light in the darkness, Jake Sica, the guy she'd met in L.A., had come into town. And this time he was free, with no romantic entanglements.

They'd spent an incredible week together holed up in her apartment, until he had to take off for an assignment in Europe.

Being involved with Jake had made her feel good again. She needed someone who cared about her, because Michael sure as hell didn't.

A few days after Jake left, Michael phoned her. She really didn't want to talk to him. Not yet. She had too much information to process.

'I have something important to tell you,' he said.

'What?' she answered coldly.

'It's about Stella,' he said.

Like she could care about Stella, although she *was* planning on going to see her when she could summon the mental strength to do so.

'Go ahead,' she said wearily.

'Stella's dead,' Michael said. A long beat. 'The funeral's tomorrow. I'd like you to be there.'

Stella's funeral was a sombre affair. Jamie and Peter drove Madison to Connecticut, and stayed by her side, looking out for her.

As soon as she arrived at the house, she attempted to comfort Michael – not that he deserved it – but she felt she should make an effort in view of the tragic circumstances.

He seemed quite calm and collected, not in need of her comfort at all.

At the reception she spoke to Stella's best friend, Warner, a woman she'd known since she was a child. When she told Warner that Michael had revealed the truth about her relationship to Stella, Warner was shocked. 'I never thought he'd tell you.'

'He did, and I was hoping Stella could explain. Only now that she's gone . . .'

'It's such a tragedy.' Warner sighed, tears in her eyes. 'Stella was my best friend for over thirty years.'

'I know,' Madison said. 'Can I call you? I have so many unanswered questions I was hoping Stella could help me with. Maybe you can answer some of them for me.'

Warner nodded. 'Call me anytime.'

Back in New York, Kimm Florian was waiting with more news. She informed Madison that she'd discovered that her real mother, Beth, had had a twin sister, Catherine. And she'd tracked Catherine down to Miami.

Madison decided to fly to Miami and see what she could find out.

The detectives working on the murder of Stella and her boyfriend came to question Michael several times. Unfortunately he had no alibi for the night the murders had taken place. He'd been home alone.

They questioned him endlessly until he finally called in his lawyer, which he realized he should've done immediately. He had an uneasy feeling about what was taking place – especially when he discovered that one of his guns was missing.

He had no doubt that the murders were Bone and Mamie's work. But why? If they were planning on implicating him, why hadn't they set a trap like they had when they killed Beth?

He had to do something about Bone and Mamie. The time had come.

He called his old pal Gus, in L.A., and began making plans.

An eye for an eye.

A tooth for a tooth.

A fucking bullet for a fucking bullet.

Then, a few days later, he got the call he'd been expecting. Mamie. Angry and vengeful.

'Mikey,' she said sweetly, 'it's me, Mamie. I thought you should know that it was *your* gun that killed your wife and her boyfriend. Isn't that interesting? So get me my money, or the cops get your gun. Do it soon, Mikey, or you'll be lookin' at the rest of your miserable life behind bars.'

Michael got early word of his imminent arrest. It paid to have friends in the right places.

By the time the police arrived at his house he was long gone.

Destination Los Angeles.

But first he had to make a side trip to Las Vegas. Dani was his main priority. He'd neglected her, and right now he needed to be with her, if only for a few hours.

He knew she was probably mad at him for being on the missing list, but very soon he would make up for everything.

Chapter Fifty-six

Wednesday, 11 July 2001, 1 a.m.

'Y ou got somethin' for me?' the gunman said, leaning forward to talk to the man in the front passenger seat of the Cadillac.

'Sure, dude,' the man said, groping in his pocket.

Madison sat in silence as the gunman reached over, grabbed a handful of pills and crammed them into his mouth.

Nice. Like he isn't stoned enough, she thought. 'Is this a ransom deal?' she asked wearily. ''Cause if it is, my magazine will pay.'

'What you talkin' about?' the gunman snapped.

'You wanted *me*, didn't you?' she said, watching him carefully for a reaction. 'This was all about *me*.'

'Shut the fuck up, *bitch*.'

She knew she was right. This was no random hold-up. They'd targeted her right from the beginning.

Why? Was it something she'd written?

Maybe it had to do with the exposé she'd had published on L.A. call-girls a few months back, an explosive, raw piece that had been bought by an independent producer to develop as a movie.

Could *that* be it? Unlikely. But anything was possible.

She took a long, deep, life-affirming breath, trying to ignore the fact that she was tired, hungry and thirsty, and that the unbearably loud rap music was assaulting her ears. *Stay alert. Stay alive.*

She hoped Cole, Natalie, and the other two hostages were okay.

The horror of the night was beginning to get to her. Three people possibly dead.

God! This was more than a nightmare, this was devastating.

Over the years Michael had not forgotten his friends. Gus was one of them. He'd helped Gus with his investments, and in return Gus was ready to do anything he wanted. Loyalty counted.

He'd filled Gus in on the situation. Gus had a long-standing feud with Bone himself – something to do with stepping on each other's territory. 'The prick's an amateur,' Gus informed Michael in the car as they rode to his house. 'Him an' his rinky-dink porno empire. It'll be my pleasure to put an end to the dumb fuck.'

'I should've done it a long time ago,' Michael said, thinking that surprise was on his side. Bone and Mamie would never imagine he'd fly to L.A. They probably thought he'd be hiding from the cops in New York, shivering and shaking because of their dumb-ass threats.

Gus was right. They were amateurs. Did they honestly think they could get away with a carbon copy of Beth's murder? Any competent lawyer would be able to prove he'd been set up, gun or no gun.

'How many men we using?' he asked.

'Enough to get the job done,' Gus replied. 'Mamie and Bone got this estate in Bel Air with shit security. They won't know what hit 'em.'

'I want them awake,' Michael said grimly. 'I *want* them to know when I come calling.'

'Whatever you want, you got. Now, what we gonna do about your daughter?'

'Can you find out what's going on?'

'Done,' Gus said. 'I'll call my connection, get an update on the situation.'

'Thanks, Gus. I appreciate it.'

'Big freakin' deal. You made me a coupla mill last year. Somehow I got a feelin' I owe you.'

As Jolie drove along the Strip behind the wheel of Nando's Ferrari, she noticed a slew of police cars racing in the opposite direction. It crossed her mind that they might be heading to the Manray. Then she thought, *why would they be going there*? Payoffs were rife in the city. She was sure Darren and Leroy had things well under control.

She was still mad at Nando. He shouldn't have exposed her to a place like that. Vincent was right, it was not the kind of business they should even consider getting into. The Castle Hotel and Casino were both doing great, money was plentiful, so jumping into the sleazy side of things was simply being greedy.

She thought about discussing it with Vincent. It seemed like a good idea, because with Vincent to back her, perhaps the two of them could talk some sense into Nando.

On impulse she turned the Ferrari round and, instead of driving home, headed for the hotel.

Dani couldn't sleep: her mind was in turmoil. Michael and his problems. The story of her life.

And she was always there, forever available, ready to comfort, advise, and pick up the pieces whenever *he* felt like seeing her. Because there was never a set plan. Michael came and went as he pleased.

Using her.

Vincent's words.

The most upsetting thing of all was that when Stella had left him, he'd never told her. She'd only found out after Stella's brutal murder.

Why *hadn't* he told her?

Why *hadn't* he asked her to marry him so they could finally be together?

Damn! He made love to her and she melted. Was that the basis for a future together?

Marry Dean.

Vincent's words.

If she married Dean, who genuinely loved her, she'd *have* to be free of Michael, for she would never cheat on a man she was married to.

It was a momentous decision, and one she probably shouldn't make while Michael was in trouble. But how else could she expect to be happy?

Mrs Dean King. It was the only way to guarantee a smooth and happy future.

She'd tell Dean in the morning.

Waiting impatiently for his car outside the hotel, Vincent was surprised to see Jolie drive up in Nando's Ferrari.

'What are you doing in Nando's car?' he asked. 'You know he doesn't let *anybody* drive it.'

'Too bad,' she said, getting out and tossing the keys to a valet. 'You won't believe where I'm coming from.'

'Where?'

'The Manray.'

He knew this was not good news. 'Want to tell me about it?'

'I will.' She looked round. 'Where's Jenna?'

'Over at the Mirage, trapped in a suite with that movie asshole.'

'You mean Andy Dale?'

'Is there another movie asshole on the prowl tonight?'

'I'm so sorry,' she said, placing a sympathetic hand on his arm.

'Don't be,' he said edgily. 'I've recently come to the conclusion that I made a big mistake marrying Jenna.'

'Really?'

'She's way too young.'

'I never thought I'd say this,' Jolie ventured, 'but you're right. Jenna is *very* immature.'

'Don't you think I know that?'

'Listen,' Jolie said, 'I can tell that you're pissed off. I am too. So why don't we go inside and have a drink at the bar?'

'I don't know,' he said. 'Jenna was crying on the phone. I'm supposed to be getting her.'

'What you *should* be doing, Vincent,' Jolie said firmly, 'is teaching her that she cannot behave like this. If she's dumb enough to go to his suite, then she should be ready to accept the consequences.'

'This is the second time tonight,' he complained. 'The first time I dragged her out of a Jacuzzi half naked.'

Jolie shook her head as if she couldn't believe what she was hearing. 'That is *not* good behaviour.'

'I know,' he agreed, mesmerized by her cat-like amber eyes.

'Come on,' she said briskly. 'You and I are getting a drink. We both need it.'

Why hadn't he married a woman like Jolie, instead of a kid like Jenna? She was certainly more his style.

Madison realized that the Cadillac was heading away from downtown and back in the direction of Santa Monica. She could just about make out the street signs.

The gunman, totally chilled out on E, was now singing along with Ja Rule. He seemed perfectly content and happy.

Stoned, of course. Not as angry as before.

'Who are you working for?' she asked, trying again for any kind of information.

'Man,' he muttered, 'I'll be glad to dump your sorry mothafuckin' ass.'

'So you're the errand boy?' she said, refusing to shut up. 'Somebody wanted to snatch me, and they used you? Only I bet they didn't count on people getting killed along the way.'

'Hey, *bitch*, what makes you think they wanted *you*?' he asked belligerently.

'It's obvious,' she replied. 'Why dump the other hostages and just take me?'

'Maybe 'cause I was thinkin' of *fuckin'* you,' he said, with a lecherous leer.

The young guy in the front, with the long greasy hair and the sharp pointed nose, craned his neck to see how she was taking that piece of information.

She rewarded him with a stony glare.

'Tell you one thing,' the gunman in the back chortled, 'the bitch got herself a set of balls.'

'Well,' she said evenly, 'that's more than I can say for you.'

Gus lived in a big, modern house in the Hollywood Hills. It resembled the house that Mel Gibson had managed to destroy in one of the *Lethal Weapon* movies. Very stark, very white, with large abstract paintings on the walls. The L.A. life obviously suited Gus.

Michael sat on a high bar stool in the all chrome and black kitchen and clicked on the TV. The pretty blonde newscaster on Channel Two was still talking about the hostage situation. 'Three of the hostages abducted from Mario's were recently found outside an abandoned building in the industrial area downtown. Well-known radio and TV personality Natalie De Barge was one of them. The hostages were able to give police an accurate description of the three wanted gunmen.'

Christ! Michael thought. *Natalie was one of the hostages too.*

He picked up the phone and tried her number. She wasn't there, probably still with the cops. He left his cellphone number on her voicemail.

The newscaster continued her report. 'Journalist Madison Castelli is still missing. Lila Hartford, the young woman thrown from the van on the freeway, was rushed to the hospital and is currently undergoing surgery. To sum up, two dead, one seriously injured and one missing. The rest of the hostages are apparently safe.'

When Gus returned to the kitchen with the same story, Michael said sharply, 'This changes things. I'm not finished with Bone until I know where Madison is.'

'You sure he's responsible?' Gus asked.

'I'm sure,' Michael said grimly.

'Okay, so what d'you wanna do?'

'Go ahead with the plan.'

'You got it,' Gus said. 'The guys are ready. How soon you wanna roll?'

'Now,' Michael said. 'Let's get this done.'

Chapter Fifty-seven

Wednesday, 11 July 2001, 1.30 a.m.

Mamie and Bone had created a monument to bad taste. They called it home. Home was an over-built, overdecorated, neo-classical disaster in the hills of Bel Air. A porno empire translated into mega-bucks. Mamie had finally come into her own. The once impoverished hairdresser from Queens now considered herself the lady of the manor and, as such, had surrounded herself with rooms full of ornate, gilded furniture, elaborate chandeliers, baroque mirrors on every wall, nude paintings of men *and* women, and a lifesize nude bronze sculpture of herself in the grand foyer. She considered her home to be her palace. Two security guards working eight-hour shifts guarded it along with two ferocious Dobermans.

In spite of all her riches, Mamie still wanted more. Which is why she'd been so peeved when Michael had refused to acknowledge the money Vito had promised her upon his demise. Not that she cared much about the money – she was richer than she'd ever dreamed – but how dare Michael think he could get away with keeping it?

Mamie did not appreciate being crossed, especially by a piece of shit like little Mikey Castellino. Oh, yes, he might strut round calling himself Michael Castelli, big businessman with his investments and estate and shopping centres. But she knew the real truth about his humble beginnings. And she knew how to punish him too.

Years ago he'd narrowly escaped getting convicted for that Cuban slut's murder. Let's see him squirm his way out of *this* mess. It was common knowledge that his wife had left him for a younger man. So who would doubt that a man with such a murky past was not responsible for the murder of his wife and her young lover? No question at all when it became known they had both been shot with *his* gun.

And this time there was no Vito with his powerful connections to help out.

Mamie cackled at the thought.

Then, just to torture him further, she'd arranged to have his daughter snatched. He'd hear his precious Madison was gone while sitting in his jail cell, and there was absolutely nothing he could do about it. Mamie had plans for Madison. As soon as Serge, her guard, alerted her that Madison was on the premises, the girl would be drugged, and tomorrow she'd be shipped off to a brothel in Pakistan. They paid top dollar for white girls.

Finally she'd got Michael back for shooting her beloved cousin Roy. *And* for being the son of that Italian tramp Vinny had chosen over her. Beth's murder had not punished him enough. Vengeance, all these years later, was very sweet.

To celebrate, Mamie had ordered up two exquisite call girls for the night, paying them three thousand bucks each for the pleasure of their company.

It was one of the advantages of living in L.A.: every year a new batch of ambitious young would-be actresses came to the city – hence a better-looking class of hookers.

Mamie was into girls.

Bone was into watching.

Theirs was the perfect marriage.

The two call-girls, Heather and Tawny, went about their business with taut, toned bodies, matching capped teeth and practised smirks. Their sexual activities seemed almost choreographed.

Bone, sitting on a chair in a red silk robe with his fake orange suntan and dyed black hair, watched every move like a snake about to pounce.

Mamie hovered round the two girls with their silicone-enhanced breasts and smooth, tanned bodies, waiting for an opportunity to join in. Liposuction, daily massages, collagen, Botox, and once-a-month high colonics kept her from falling totally apart, although she was still a pretty scary sight with her crêpey skin, predatory eyes, and bottle-blonde hair.

Both Mamie and Bone popped Viagra, claiming it kept them young and vital, instead of just plain horny and disgusting.

Effortlessly Heather raised her long, suntanned legs above her shoulders. Her tiny strip of pubic hair matched the blonde hair on her head.

This was Mamie's cue to dive in. And dive in she did, sucking out the juices of a woman who was at least fifty years her junior, while Bone continued to watch.

The Cadillac took a sharp turn off the Santa Monica freeway and headed up to Sunset. The three men in the car were happy. Stoned, actually. They saw an end to their job and payment in their pockets.

Madison's mind was running on overdrive. She had to figure out some kind of escape move. But what? Throw herself out of the car and risk being killed? Put up a fight? Or . . . talk herself out of it? She'd always been good at that.

'How much are you getting paid?' she asked.

'To kill people?' her gunman singsonged. 'We do that for nothin' – it's sweet, y'know.'

'I'll double whatever you're getting paid if you let me go.'

'Why'd we do that?'

'Why do you do anything? For money, of course.'

'How much money?'

'You tell me.'

'Fifty thou'.'

'Okay.'

'Where you gonna get money like that?'

'Let me go and I'll get it.'

'*Sheeit!*' he sneered. 'You think I'm stupid?'

'No,' she said quickly. 'Actually, I think you're quite smart.'

'Forget it, lady. We're almost there.'

Serge Gorban checked his watch. It was an old one he'd bought in Moscow many years ago, and sometimes it ran slow.

Not *that* slow. His idiot nephew should have been here hours ago. He'd given him a simple task to perform, and somehow Zaroff had managed to screw it up, just as he managed to screw up most things.

Serge realized that he should never have listened to his pathetic, whining sister, who had begged him to give Zaroff another chance after the boy's last disaster.

But listen he had, and now where *was* the fool?

Never send a boy to do a man's job.

Any second now, when the whores left the estate, Bone or Mamie would be calling him in the guardhouse, making sure that everything was taken care of.

Why had he trusted that no-good nephew of his? The out-of-work loser was nothing but trouble.

They were in his penthouse, still in the living room, but soon heading for the bedroom. Jolie was coming on to him big-time, and Vincent wasn't in the mood to resist.

'I like you, Vincent, I always have,' she murmured.

His problems with Jenna tonight were all Nando's fault: if Nando hadn't insisted on Andy Dale joining them, none of this would have happened. Now, on top of everything else, Nando was meeting with Leroy Fortuno and Darren Simmons behind his back. Yes, Nando had definitely gone too far this time.

'I always felt it should've been you and me,' Jolie purred, all soft skin and glowing, catlike, amber eyes.

'Nando's my brother,' Vincent said, his resolve weakening slowly. Resisting Jolie was getting harder by the minute. He'd always had an eye for her. She was smooth and sexy and sophisticated. Plus she was a woman, unlike Jenna, who was still a girl.

'I know,' Jolie murmured softly. 'Only sometimes brothers have to part ways. And maybe the time has come . . .'

He was still mesmerized by her lips. Such soft, pouting, inviting lips.

Was one kiss such a bad thing? After all, Jenna had run out on him, and Nando was busy making deals elsewhere.

One kiss . . .

His cellphone rang.

'Don't answer it,' Jolie said, her voice a silky whisper. 'We have more important things to do.'

Gus's black limousine with its dark, tinted windows, followed by a large black Suburban, headed up into the hills. Michael felt as if he was part of a funeral procession. And, in a way, that's exactly what it was. *Welcome to the funeral of Mamie and Bone.*

Gus did not do things on a small scale. He was from the old school of how to get things done. There were quite a few men packed into the Suburban. Men ready to deal with anything or anyone who got in their way. Among them was a dog wrangler, who would take care of the Dobermans.

Michael's only worry was Madison. He knew Vincent could take care of Dani and himself. Sofia was in Europe. So it was only Madison he was concerned about.

Madison. His beautiful, smart daughter who was barely speaking to him, and he didn't blame her. He'd allowed her to live a lie, and that wasn't fair.

He made a solemn vow that in the future he would make it up to her. And he'd make it up to Dani, too, the woman who'd stood by him through everything.

But first he had to take care of these two maggots. Because if he didn't . . .

The Cadillac turned off Sunset and sped up into Bel Air, the road twisting and turning all the way to the top.

Madison didn't know what to think. Bel Air of all places. What were they doing there?

She went to look at her watch, realized they'd stolen it, and tried to figure out what time it was. One a.m? Two? She had no clue.

Suddenly the car slowed down and came to a stop in front of a pair of ornate wrought-iron gates.

'What I do?' the driver asked.

'Ring the fuckin' buzzer. Tell Serge we're here.'

They were all so stoned now that no one seemed to notice names were flying. Madison made a mental note of all of them. Ace, from earlier. Now Serge. And finally a name for her gunman, her psycho killer. Zar– short for? She'd find out.

'Zarren?' she said to him, as if she were about to ask a question.

'Zaroff,' he slurred.

'Press the fuckin' buzzer,' the one in the front passenger seat said, leaning across the driver to do it for him.

She wondered if this was the time to make a run for it. The car was stationary, the music too loud for clear thought. Besides, the three of them were so out of it they probably wouldn't even notice.

She decided to do it. Take a risk and go.

She glanced quickly at Zaroff. The Uzi was on the floor of the car between his feet. His other gun was stuffed into the belt of his pants.

Goodbye, suckers. I'm out of here.

And she lunged at the door, wrenched it open, threw herself out and began running.

Chapter Fifty-eight

Wednesday, 11 July 2001, 1.45 a.m.

D ani still couldn't sleep. Now that she'd made such an important decision about her future, she was nervous that she might change her mind.

Only one way to solve *that* little problem. Dean was staying at the Mirage.

She picked up the phone and called him.

The front-gate buzzer rang. Serge checked out the security monitor in the guardhouse. He was relieved to see the old Cadillac he'd lent to Zaroff waiting outside.

Finally, he thought, pressing the entry button to activate the heavy gates.

He continued watching the monitor as the gates rolled open. The Cadillac stayed put.

'Come on,' Serge muttered under his breath. 'Drive in, you fool.'

Then he saw his idiot nephew jump out of the car and take off.

What was happening?

Serge didn't know, but he'd soon find out. Making sure his gun was secure in the underarm holster, he set off to investigate.

*

The limousine slid to a stop a short distance from the entry gates to the Bel Air mansion.

'What's the deal?' Gus asked, leaning forward to ask his driver.

'We're checkin' it out,' the driver said. 'Seems there's a car blockin' the gate.'

'Going in, or out?' Gus asked.

'Stationary.'

Michael took himself back many years to the night in Central Park when he'd shot Roy. The waiting was the worst. Not knowing what would happen. Hoping everything would go down smoothly. Never sure.

Then the moment when it happened. The act of vengeance executed. *Bang bang – you're dead*. It was almost like playing a game.

Was he capable of doing it again?

Yes. They'd been capable of murdering Stella and her boyfriend in cold blood.

Mamie and Bone deserved the ultimate punishment.

Madison had always fancied herself an athlete. At school she'd excelled at sports, and living in New York, she'd always made sure to work out at the gym at least a couple of times a week.

Thank God! Because she was now in a life-or-death situation, and only her speed and agility could save her.

She was faster than her captors and a lot smarter. If she could outrun them she could possibly hide in the heavy underbrush at the top of Bel Air until it was safe to emerge.

The house they'd been taking her to stood alone. No neighbouring houses, only steep hills and brush and trees. Not that she could see much of anything as she stumbled into the bushes. It was pitch black. There were not even any streetlights because they weren't on a proper street.

Her heart was pounding like a sledgehammer. It felt as if it might burst out of her chest and explode. She could hear her captors somewhere behind her, cursing and threatening as they chased her up the hillside.

A branch hit her in the face, almost knocking her down. Dizzily she moved on, clawing her way through the thick brush.

She stopped for a moment to catch her breath, bent over, stood up, and kept going. Climbing, climbing, one foot in front of the other. *Don't look back. Keep going. Mustn't weaken.*

And then suddenly, as she put her right foot forward, she lost her balance and began falling, tumbling downwards over the side of a precipice.

'You moron!' Serge exclaimed, slapping his nephew hard across the face with the back of his hand. 'Your shit could cost me my job.'

'Didn't know she was gonna run,' Zaroff said sullenly, not such a big man now that his uncle had hold of him. Serge was notorious in the Gorban family. A tough, scowling man with a vicious attitude, he'd arrived from Moscow via Switzerland several years ago. Rumour had it that he'd been involved with the Russian Mafia and had been forced to flee because of a 'misunderstanding' about some missing money.

He'd soon landed a job working as chief security adviser for Mr and Mrs Porno – a title Zaroff had bestowed on them when he'd done a few maintenance jobs round their house. Zaroff hated the way his uncle kissed their big, fat American asses. They were a couple of freaks – especially the hateful woman, who'd tried to come on to him.

'You arrive here hours late,' Serge scolded, 'with no girl. And you bring those other losers with you. What the fuck is the matter with you?'

'I had some problems,' Zaroff mumbled. 'Needed help.'

'You needed *help* to get one girl from the airport?' Serge demanded.

'Couldn't work it there,' Zaroff muttered. 'Hadda follow her to a restaurant. There were complications . . .'

'You're *shit*!' Serge spat in disgust. 'Dog shit. No,' he said, changing his mind, 'dog shit's too good for you. You're fuckin' *pig* shit, that's what you are. Now take my flashlight and your useless friends, an' go find the girl.'

'I don't do S and M,' Tawny said, all teeth and perfect tits.

'Nor do I,' Heather chimed in. She was fairly new to the game and followed everything Tawny did and said.

'Putting on rubber masks is not S and M, you moronic cunts,' Bone snapped. 'Put on the fuckin' masks an' stop your bitchin'.'

'I'm out of here,' Tawny said, getting off the bed.

'Me, too,' Heather agreed.

Mamie was in the bathroom, otherwise the argument would not have happened. She was as fond of the rubber masks as he was, but she knew that special girls had to be booked for such activities, and tonight she'd requested pretty ones. Pretty did not come cheap. And pretty hardly ever wanted to do anything unusual.

Bone's fury escalated. Were these two pieces of trash actually telling him *no*?

He stood up, his red silk robe flapping open, revealing a poor excuse for a cock.

Heather made the unforgivable error of tittering. Bone moved faster than a man half his age, and whacked her so hard that she fell like a log, hitting her head on a side table.

Tawny began to scream. Mamie ran out of the bathroom wearing a man's suit and flourishing a riding crop. 'What have you *done?*' she yelled at Bone.

'Cunts,' he muttered.

'Jesus!' Mamie exclaimed, turning on a still screaming Tawny. 'Shut your mouth!'

Tawny shut up and began dressing feverishly, while Heather remained motionless on the floor.

Mamie assessed the situation. It was bound to cost money, and if there was one thing Mamie hated, it was spending unnecessary money.

'I'm calling Serge,' she said, buzzing the guardhouse. 'He'll take care of it.'

Serge got behind the wheel of the Cadillac and moved it to the side of the driveway, muttering to himself all the while. As he was doing so, a black limo slid into view.

Serge marched over to it. 'Yes?' he said to the driver, thinking that the limo probably contained more hookers. The two people he worked for were insatiable. Sex parties sometimes went on all through the night.

'Guests for the house,' the driver said.

Serge could feel the comforting bulge of his gun tucked snugly into his shoulder holster. He wished he had the security of the gate between him and this unknown limo, but unfortunately he'd been caught unaware.

'Who do you want to see?' he asked.

Before he could say any more, the Suburban rolled up behind the limo, and two men with automatic weapons jumped out.

Serge had no chance to pull his gun. He was wrestled to the ground and overpowered, while the limo headed up the driveway, the Suburban right behind it.

As the car approached the house, two huge Dobermans came racing over, growling ferociously. The dog wrangler jumped out of the Suburban waving large, raw juicy steaks under the dogs' noses.

Once the dogs were taken care of, several other men sprang into action, sealing off the servants' quarters and making sure no one else was round.

As soon as everything was secure, the driver opened the door for Gus and Michael, and they got out of the limo outside the house.

'Showtime,' Gus said calmly. 'I hope you remember the tune. It's been a while, hasn't it?'

Michael nodded. 'Some things you never forget.' And the two of them entered the house.

'Where the hell is Serge?' Mamie screamed. 'When I buzz, he'd better get on the fuckin' line pronto, or he's *fired*!'

'He's probably taking a piss,' Bone muttered.

'Jesus Christ!' Mamie said.

Tawny was now dressed and sitting on a chair. 'I'd like to leave,' she said.

'I'm sure you would, dear,' Mamie replied, 'now that you've ruined our evening.'

'What did *I* do?' Tawny asked.

'You're hookers,' Mamie reminded her. 'Don't you understand that hookers are supposed to do anything the client wants? And if my husband wants something, you shouldn't argue. This is all your fault.'

'It is not,' Tawny said, thinking that it was better if she didn't argue any further. Obviously this couple were totally insane. She couldn't wait to get back to her madam and complain about them.

The worrying thing was that Heather had not moved. She was still lying on the floor.

'Don't you think we should call a doctor?' Tawny suggested.

'Oh yes, let's announce it to the world,' Mamie said sarcastically.

'We can't just leave her lying there.'

'Why do you think I'm trying to get my guard?' Mamie said. 'He'll drive her to the hospital. You don't have to worry about her.'

'But I *am* worried about her.'

'Don't, dear,' Mamie said, fixing her with a cruel smile. 'It's in your best interest not to remember anything about tonight. Do you understand?'

'You're sure?' Dean said, holding the phone to his ear.

'Absolutely sure,' Dani replied, determined to go through with it.

'What made you change your mind?'

'I was thinking about how you always said that we'd be so happy together. And, Dean,' she added softly, 'I finally realized that you're the only person who really cares about me.'

'You're worth it,' he said.

'Let's not wait,' she said quickly.

'Fine with me. We can do it tonight if you like.' He glanced at his watch. 'It's morning. Nothing unusual about a three a.m. wedding in Vegas. I can pick you up in half an hour.'

'Tonight's a little *too* soon,' she said, laughing nervously. 'How about noon tomorrow?'

'Are we telling anyone?'

'Maybe Vincent.'

'Dani, was Michael with you tonight?'

'Why are you asking me that?'

'Because when we had dinner earlier, none of these thoughts were in your head, so *something* must have happened.'

'Yes,' she admitted. 'He was here, and something *did*

happen. We spent time together, and after he left I knew that you are the man I want to spend the rest of my life with.'

'You'll never regret it,' Dean said.

'I know,' she whispered.

Chapter Fifty-nine

Wednesday, 11 July 2001, 2.00 a.m.

Zaroff was seething. All night long he'd been the man in charge, the one with the balls. Now his fat uncle was telling him what to do. Didn't he realize that Zaroff was the man?

He'd taken over that fucking restaurant with the help of his uncle's Uzi, and he'd kicked ass good. Serge should be proud of him instead of calling him names.

Serge was pig shit. *Serge* was a Russian fucking peasant. *Serge* had no idea how exciting it was to have total control and to kill people.

Tonight everybody had been scared of him. He could've made them do anything. He could've taken any of those hostages and fucked the ass off them. Now he was at this fancy house in the hills, and his uncle was treating him like crap as usual.

Russian Mafia my ass, Zaroff thought. *I can take him any day.*

His two cohorts were busy searching the hillside for the girl. His friends always did what he told them. Ever since he'd stopped a car one night and shot the driver just for kicks they'd been in awe of him. He was the man. No question. They were all scared of him. And he liked that.

Now his fat uncle was dissing him. The same uncle who'd go running to his mother. And she was a hard-assed bitch – she'd come down on him big-time.

A thought entered his head. What would happen if when they found the girl, *he* kept her, hid her somewhere, and demanded a ransom?

The bitch had mentioned fifty thousand dollars. Fifty thousand fucking dollars!

If he blew Serge away, nobody would know it was him who'd done it.

Zaroff began to laugh. He was so clever. He'd just come up with the perfect plan.

'Can you believe this freakin' place?' Gus said, as he and Michael climbed the ornate staircase.

Michael shook his head. His palms were sweating and he felt short of breath. This wasn't the kind of thing he knew how to do any more. As bad as they were, was he honestly going to be able to take out his gun and shoot Mamie and Bone?

Gus had told him that, if he wanted, he could have people do it for him.

Could he stand there and watch?

Was he the same Michael Castellino who'd shot Roy in the park so long ago? Or was he a different person now?

He didn't know. He'd soon find out.

Vincent and Jolie headed into the bedroom. There was no chance of Jenna walking in on them. She was trapped at the Mirage. There was no chance of Nando finding them either, he was with his two new business partners.

'I've *always* felt this way about you,' Jolie said, putting her arms round him and kissing him on the mouth with her soft, provocative lips.

'We shouldn't be doing this.'

'Stop it, Vincent,' she scolded softly. 'We're both beyond the point of saying no any more. This thing has been building between us for years.'

She was right. He was hard and she was ready.

So why was he suddenly developing a conscience?

Pig shit. Yeah, that's what his uncle had called him. He'd show him who was pig shit.

How many men had Uncle Serge killed? One? Two? None? Fuck him! It was time Zaroff took control of the Gorban family.

He told his two cohorts to keep looking for the girl. 'When you find her, tie her up and shove her in the trunk of the car,' he said. 'We're taking her.'

'Where?' asked the driver.

'We'll take her to the warehouse. The one Ace lives at.'

'Where *you* goin'?' they asked.

'I'm collectin' the fuckin' money Serge owes me. Then we're outta here. Go find the girl,' he said, reaching into his pocket and taking out a small glass vial of coke. There was still some left. He shook the white powder on to the back of his hand and snorted it. Jesus, he'd done a lot of drugs tonight.

So what? He could handle it. He could handle anything and anyone.

He ran back towards the house. The big gates were still open, the Cadillac parked nearby.

He knew where the guardhouse was on account of the maintenance work he'd done at the house, helping Uncle Serge like a good little boy, getting ten bucks an hour if he was fucking lucky.

The guardhouse was empty. Nobody around.

As he headed up the driveway, a man stepped out of the bushes. 'Stop!' the man said.

Zaroff lifted his Uzi and sprayed him.

Christ! The feeling of power that surged through his body gave him such a high. Or was it the drugs?

He kept walking. There were two dogs lying out in front of the house. It looked like they were asleep because they didn't move. Lucky for them, he would have shot them too.

The front door was open. He walked through it and stepped into the foyer.

Michael and Gus, followed by three of Gus's men, entered the master bedroom. The sight that greeted them was not a pretty one.

Standing there in his red silk robe, his dick hanging out, was Bone. Mamie was across the room from him – a sorry sight in a man's suit, a riding whip in her hand. A young blonde girl was sitting on a chair fully dressed, while another, totally naked, was lying sprawled on the floor.

'Nice,' Michael said.

Mamie's face registered pure shock. 'How did you get into my house?' she screamed. 'What are you doing here, you murderer?'

Tawny shrank back in her chair.

'Retribution,' Michael said. 'Isn't that what your husband taught me? Isn't that what *you* always wanted, Mamie? Revenge?'

'You'd better get out of here now, or I'm calling the police,' she threatened.

'Lines are dead. But go ahead.'

'You no good scum-sucking *bastard*,' she screamed, her face contorted with rage. 'You're just like your stinkin' father, Vinny. I hate you. I FUCKIN' HATE YOU!'

Zaroff burst into the bedroom, murder in his crazed eyes.

He was flying on coke, grass and Ecstasy. He was filled with power, sure that he could conquer the world.

What kind of game was going on in here with Mr and

Mrs Porno? He barely noticed Michael and Gus as he focused on the naked girl on the floor. And in spite of his drugged-out haze, he felt the stirrings of a hard-on. He hadn't got laid in twenty-four hours, and Zaroff needed sex. He needed it more than he needed food and his mother's bitching and his dumb uncle telling him what he could and could not do.

He was The Man. He could do whatever he wanted.

Michael took a step back. The boy, who couldn't have been more than seventeen or eighteen, had an Uzi and a trace of white powder under his nose. Not a healthy combination. He was the wild card that nobody had taken into account. There was always a wild card.

Mamie stopped screaming at Michael, turning her attention to the boy.

'Who the—' she began to say.

'Mothafuckers!' Zaroff yelled, raising the Uzi. 'Rich mothafuckers!' And he began spraying the room.

After that everything seemed to take place in slow motion, like some carefully choreographed intricate dance. Zaroff spraying the room. Two of Gus's men bursting in and tackling him from behind. The Uzi flying out of his hands. Too late for Mamie and Bone. They were both hit. Mamie in the face and heart. Bone in the stomach.

It was a fitting end for the two of them.

Michael turned and walked away.

It was over, and he hadn't had to do a thing.

Epilogue

Zaroff Gorban was arrested for multiple murders, including the killings of Mamie and Bone. His Uncle Serge was also arrested for possession of an unlicensed weapon – the Uzi. And for assisting a minor in a kidnapping plot.

Zaroff couldn't remember any of it.

Michael's lawyer in New York provided the police with enough evidence to prove that Michael had had nothing to do with the murder of Stella and her boyfriend. One of the most pertinent pieces of evidence was the tape of Mamie's phone call to Michael, boasting of how she'd set him up. Rule one in business: *always* tape important calls. Michael did.

Vincent, with temptation staring him in the face, had resisted Jolie's considerable charms and decided to give Jenna one last chance.

Jenna, a wiser girl because of her experiences with Andy Dale, matured overnight, and became the daughter-in-law that Dani had always wanted.

Vincent decided that he'd better knock her up soon, if only to keep her out of trouble.

*

Sofia did a photo session for Gianni in Rome. And then, as promised, he bought her a ticket home to America.

Two days later he phoned to inform her that the camera loved her, and that she was to become the new Gianni Jeans spokesmodel.

Sofia kind of got off on the idea. It sure beat bumming around Europe.

Jolie talked Nando out of the strip-club business. This was after Nando had been involved in a drug bust at the Manray, along with Darren Simmons and Leroy Fortuno. Once that had taken place it was an easy task to put a bad vibe on the whole idea.

She was grateful that Vincent had not fallen for her charms. After all, Nando was the man she'd married. And the truth was that Nando was the man she loved.

Madison suffered a mild concussion, many cuts and bruises, and a broken wrist. How surprised she was when the fire-rescue team hauled her up from the bottom of the cliff to find Michael there.

'Daddy!' she'd gasped. 'I knew you'd come riding up on your white horse.'

'It was a black limo actually,' he'd said, grinning. 'And how come you're calling me "Daddy"?'

''Cause I kind of like it. Do you mind?'

'No, sweetheart, I don't mind at all.'

'How did you know where I was?'

'It's a long story.'

A musclebound paramedic helped her into the ambulance. 'Not *another* long story?' she groaned. 'I don't know how much more I can take.'

'Well,' he'd said, grinning again, 'I *do* have a couple more surprises . . .'

*

Michael flew back to Vegas immediately after the shootings. To Dean's chagrin, he was just in time to stop Dani marrying him.

And so Dani and Michael had a June wedding at their son's hotel.

Dani, exquisite in a pale cream Valentino wedding gown, gazed at her husband-to-be. Michael was more good-looking than ever in an Armani tuxedo. Tall, dark, and handsome. He never changed.

Everyone they loved was present at the wedding, including old friends like Tina and Max with their kids. And Charlie with his wife. And, of course, Warner and Karl.

Sofia sat next to her brother, Vincent.

Madison was surrounded by her best friends, Natalie, Jamie and Cole.

She watched as her father married the beautiful blonde woman. They weren't exactly a family yet. But one day they would be.

Michael and Dani couldn't wait.

Now read an exclusive extract from
her next scorching bestseller

HOLLYWOOD
DIVORCES

by

JACKIE COLLINS

Coming to a bookshop near you
this September!

Chapter One

S helby Cheney took a long deep breath and prepared to make her entrance. Head up. Shoulders back. Superwatt smile. Artfully windswept, shoulder-length, raven hair. Dazzling Badgely & Mishka lace gown cut down to Cuba. Diamonds at her throat and ears. Movie star husband by her side.

Shelby Cheney had it all. Or did she?

Tonight she was at the Cannes Film Festival with her husband, Linc Blackwood. Each had a movie to promote.

Hers, an edgy drama about a woman on the brink of a total collapse – a thirty-something sex addict who reveals more than her mental breakdown on screen – with nobody around to help her. And, of course, one blistering sex scene, because Shelby had the attributes and since this movie smelled of an Oscar nomination she hadn't minded showing them.

His, a tough-guy superhero movie. Hard-boiled cop, sexy, sardonic. A sequel to his two previous blockbuster hits playing the same character. Linc Blackwood, once one of the highest paid box office stars in the world, was still up there.

Tonight Linc wore a midnight blue Armani tuxedo with a dark blue silk shirt. No tie. Muscular body. Murky green

eyes. Longish dark hair. Stubbled chin. Crooked nose –
broken in a fight or two before he was famous and powerful
enough to demand a double for his more dangerous stunts.

Shelby and Linc. A movie star couple set to thrill the
throngs of fans who eagerly watched them as they made
their way – flanked by various publicity people and assorted
flacks – into the Palais des Festivals, where Shelby's movie,
Rapture, was about to be shown.

'Shit,' Linc mumbled under his breath, waving at the
paparazzi while flashing his trademark grin. 'I need a
fuckin' drink.'

'No you don't,' Shelby managed to reply, as she smiled
for the assorted cameras and TV crews lined up three deep,
all shoving and struggling for the best shots.

Linc's drinking was a big bone of contention between
them. He'd been in rehab twice, and it hadn't done him
much good, he was still a hard boozer whenever the mood
took him. And tonight the mood was *definitely* taking him.

Shelby knew he'd had a couple of shots at the hotel, and
now he was muttering that he wanted more. This was not a
good sign. She'd hoped to relax and enjoy the night, but if
Linc was on the prowl, she'd have to spend the evening
watching him to make sure he didn't embarrass them –
something he was quite capable of doing. When Linc got
drunk it was disaster time. He either became belligerent and
ready to pick a fight, or amorous, flirting outrageously with
every woman in sight. Both were equally unappealing traits.

Damn! Why couldn't she simply revel in her triumph?
Because everyone had assured her that her performance in
Rapture was a triumph – everyone except Linc, who'd seen
her movie at a private screening and immediately commented that she looked tired and drawn and that the
cinematographer hadn't lit her well.

Didn't he *get* it? She was playing a woman on the verge,
she wasn't supposed to look her usual gorgeous self.

The truth was that even though he'd never admit it, Linc was jealous, eaten up with envy that she was starring in a movie that was destined to receive critical acclaim *and* box office success. A combination he'd never managed to achieve.

The one thing Linc craved was respect and acknowledgement for his acting talent, not merely his physical antics. His movies still made mega-millions, but his reviews were abysmal. This drove him slightly crazy – especially now that Shelby was about to make a major impact as a serious actress. She had no doubt he loved her, but things were about to change for her career-wise, and she wasn't sure how Linc would take it.

Sometimes Shelby worried that maybe she should give it all up, stay home and do nothing but look after Linc, because even after four years of a somewhat turbulent marriage she still loved him, in spite of his drinking and womanizing and going off on binges with his gang of asshole buddies whom she'd never been able to persuade him to get rid of. Lurking within the macho movie star was a lost little boy, and the little boy was always there – sweet and needy and most important – all here. Especially at night when they were in bed together and she snuggled up behind him and fell asleep breathing his smell, feeling his warmth, loving every inch of him. It wasn't all about sex, and Shelby liked that. Linc was her man, and she desperately hoped that he always would be.

Nobody knew the real Linc except her. Nobody had any clue about his abusive childhood with a father who'd beaten him daily when the old man wasn't busy battering Linc's mother, a gentle woman who was simply not capable of protecting her only son.

Linc had one sister, Connie, who, at forty-eight, was six years older than her brother. They shared a tough family history. When Linc was twelve his dad had beaten his mom to death, then turned a gun on himself, blowing his brains out all over the kitchen walls, leaving Connie and Linc to fend for themselves.

To her credit, Connie had never let her brother down. She'd taken a job as a waitress, managing to keep him out of foster homes, until at the age of seventeen he ran off to L.A. and started on the long and sometimes treacherous road to success. Connie was a dedicated lesbian who refused to have anything to do with men. She lived with her girlfriend, Suki, on a ranch in Montana – bought for her by Linc, and the two of them rarely left it.

On his own, Linc had achieved phenomenal success, and Shelby loved and admired him for it. On the other hand, Linc Blackwood was a handful and Shelby wasn't sure how long she could continue putting up with all his games.

She wanted a baby.

He didn't.

She wanted to lead a less public life.

He didn't.

She wanted him not to cheat on her with every woman who gave him the 'available' signal. And they *all* did. Linc was a movie star, he might as well have FUCK ME emblazoned on his forehead.

Shelby, however, was completely loyal to him. It wasn't part of her moral code to even contemplate having an affair. Her parents had been together forty years, and they *still* held hands, exchanged loving looks and indulged in secret conversations. She often dreamed of a marriage as good as theirs.

'Shelby!' screamed the photographers. 'Over here! Look over here! Shelby! SHELBY! SHELBY!'

As their pleas grew more frantic, Shelby obliged, turning her head this way and that, holding everything in, making sure she didn't fall out of her daringly low-cut gown. She tossed back her mane of raven hair, her hazel eyes wide and appealing. Image was incredibly important, and even though Shelby was only thirty-two, she was well aware of the hordes of up and coming actresses rabid for their chance at stardom. They all wanted to be her. They all wanted to have her career, be married to a movie star and live in a magnificent Beverly Hills mansion.

Tough luck, girls, she thought, smile fixed firmly in place. *Linc Blackwood is mine. All mine. And in spite of his many shortcomings I definitely intend to hold on to him. So back off, Linc Blackwood is taken.*

'I want Linc Blackwood,' Lola Sanchez said in her low-down husky voice, not looking at Elliott Finerman, the producer of her upcoming movie, who sat in the back of the limo next to her. Her second husband, Matt Seel, a former tennis coach, perched opposite them, sitting beside her publicist, Faye Margolis.

'We've gone over this a dozen times,' Elliott said, barely able to contain his annoyance. 'I was thinking Ben Affleck or Matthew Mc—'

'No!' Lola interrupted sharply. 'I *want* Linc Blackwood. And if you *can't* or *won't* get him, then I suggest you find yourself another leading lady.'

Bitch! Elliott thought. *Who do you think you are? Four years ago you were a waitress at Denny's, now you're telling me what to do. Me! Elliott Finerman, producer of over thirty successful movies.*

'Well?' Lola demanded imperiously, tilting her pointed chin.

'If you insist, sweetie,' Elliott said, forcing himself to sound calm. 'But I think—'

'Good,' she said, cutting him off again. 'Then if Linc says yes, we're all set.'

Elliott stared out of the window. It was glaringly obvious that the bitch couldn't care less *what* he thought.

He considered it all Anna Cameron's fault. Anna, head honcho at Live Studios, had only agreed to greenlight his latest movie if he signed Lola Sanchez. And Lola had only agreed to sign if she had final say on who her leading man would be.

'Give it to her,' Anna had said. 'We'll steer her in the right direction.'

Sure, Elliott thought bitterly. *Some right direction*.

From the word go Lola had started mentioning Linc Blackwood. He'd thought he could sweet-talk her out of it. But no, Lola wanted Linc, and she was one determined, spoiled, full-of-her-own-importance movie star.

Elliott couldn't understand why she was so insistent, she didn't even *know* Linc, and when she did get to meet him she'd be sorry. Linc was trouble, making outrageous demands on the set, and screwing other men's wives when he thought he could get away with it. Elliott had personal experience with the way Linc operated. He used some of the oldest lines going, and yet women still fell for them. Not that they needed much pushing, when it came to movie stars, women were open-leg city, ready to give it up for a glance, a smile. Elliott should know, his ex had been no exception. Lynsey Fraser, a pretty but easily influenced young actress. Three months after marrying her he'd foolishly given her a minor role in one of his movies, a movie that starred Linc Blackwood. A week of location later he'd caught her servicing Linc with a blow job in his trailer.

That had been ten years and one divorce ago. Needless to say, Elliott had chosen not to work with Linc since.

Elliott felt sorry for Shelby. She was a talented actress and a desirable woman, although obviously not too smart, because apparently she was completely unaware of what a cheating piece of crap her husband really was.

'If you're absolutely sure –' Elliott began in an uptight voice.

'Yes!' Lola snapped, hardly giving him time to finish his sentence. 'I'm sure.'

Elliott fumed. *Diva cunt!* America thought she was such a sweet and sexy piece, when in fact she was a twenty-four-year-old killer bitch who happened to have been blessed with long legs, big breasts, full sensual lips, glowing skin and a stone-cold heart. America was in love with her legs and her lips, and her wide appealing smile. They were unaware of her failings as a human being.

On second thought, Elliott mused, maybe Lola and Linc deserved each other. Between the two of them they could self-destruct their way out of the business. As long as his upcoming movie was a box office smash what did he care? Let them create chaos, garner major publicity, and after the movie was launched they could ruin each other's miserable lives.

Movie stars! A bunch of over-inflated assholes with a short shelf life. Five years down the line people would be saying 'Lola who?'

Unfortunately, Linc Blackwood would probably always be around. Like Stallone, Willis and Schwarzenegger, he was a survivor in a tough business. Plus his movies still made money, especially in foreign video sales.

'We're almost there,' Faye Margolis said. She was a thin, formidable woman in her late forties, with a stern, iron-grey, bobbed hairstyle and an unbeatable knowledge of the P.R. business. Any celebrity in Faye's care was guaranteed maximum exposure *and* copy approval. Faye protected her clients with a fierce loyalty.

'How do I look?' Lola asked, exhibiting a rare insecurity.

'Hot!' enthused Matt, who was quite hot himself with an athlete's body, long dirty blond hair and a small Van Dyke beard.

Lola ignored him. 'Faye?' she asked tentatively.

'Make sure you stand up straight,' Faye ordered in her

smoke-enhanced voice. 'That dress is a walking hazard, and don't you forget it or your breast'll fall out.'

Lola giggled. Only Faye could get away with speaking to her in such a fashion. Now that she was a big star she demanded respect from all who came in contact with her.

'If her tits fall out she'll make every front page in France,' Matt sniggered.

'Don't you mean *the world?*' Lola corrected, throwing him a withering glance.

'Yeah, honey,' Matt agreed, suitably abashed.

They'd been married for five months. As far as Lola was concerned the honeymoon phase was way over, although Matt had yet to realize it.

They'd got married on a billionaire's Malibu estate in a blaze of publicity, with helicopters hovering overhead, paparazzi hanging out of trees, and a star-studded guest list of people they hardly knew. An English magazine paid two million dollars for exclusive pictures of the happy couple, and Faye had made sure that everything happened exactly the way she planned it. *No mistakes* was Faye's motto. Anyone who made them was permanently off Faye's quite extensive payroll.

Lola wasn't quite so thrilled anymore. She got bored easily, and apart from beach boy looks and a buff body, Matt did not bring a lot to the party. He'd given up coaching, preferring to leech off her. When she'd complained about his lack of activity, he'd informed her he wished to be an actor and was planning on taking classes.

Great! Why hadn't he confided *that* little piece of information *before* she'd married him.

Here's what *he* didn't know. She'd only married him to preserve her public image as *the* sexy superstar of the new millennium. Forget about Halle Berry, Jennifer Lopez and Angelina Jolie. Lola Sanchez was *it*, and she had to keep her credibility level right up there. Before her marriage to Matt, she'd been indulging in a high profile romance with Tony Alvarez, a brilliant young Latino movie director who some considered the Pedro Almodovar of his generation, except Tony was a product of the Bronx, so the three movies he'd directed were pure Americana with an edge.

Tony's problem was that he had an ongoing drug habit, and in spite of a couple of well publicized arrests for possession, and a lengthy probation, he still managed to get into trouble. Once his bad boy ways began reflecting negatively on Lola's image, her advisors had warned her that she'd better distance herself from him, as it was becoming increasingly possible that he might have to serve a few months in jail for supposedly dealing – which everyone knew was bullshit, but since Tony was a celebrity, the authorities had to look like they were doing *something*.

Lola, ever mindful of her public image, had reluctantly broken up with him and hurriedly married Matt, who could not believe his luck and had willingly signed an iron-clad pre-nuptial agreement.

Now she was stuck with Matt. But not for long. Lola had plans, and those plans included Linc Blackwood.

Cat Harrison was not happy to be at the Cannes Film Festival. Celebrity events were so boring, full of stars with enormous egos. Not that she'd been to that many, but ever since she'd written and directed her first movie, *Wild Child*, a film loosely based on her own somewhat unconventional life, she'd been forced to work the circuit. And ever since her low budget (try non-existent budget) movie had become a cult hit, Cat was flavour of the month.

Big freaking deal. She hated being the center of attention. She loathed having to get dressed up and play nice to the money men and movie big shots who were hot to finance her next project.

'Ya gotta do it, luv,' advised her English musician husband, Jump Jagger, no relation to Mick – although he wished.

'Why?' she'd argued.

''Cause it'll be good karma for us both. An' I could do with a bit of karma.'

Trust Jump to put himself in the mix. He had an annoying habit of always putting himself first. It didn't matter because she was crazy about him. They'd been together since school and knew everything about each other.

The child of divorce, Cat had an eccentric English mother and a totally crazy American father, which meant that she'd spent most of her childhood drifting between the two countries, until at seventeen she decided she needed her own space and her own career (Daddy was a hugely successful sculptor and Mummy an award winning photographer). So she and Jump had done the conventional thing, got married and settled in New York, where in between various gigs as a nanny, dog walker and personal assistant to a sullen but extremely creative theater director, she'd started shooting her own movie on an old Sony handy-cam she'd found in her father's basement. She'd written the script herself, using their weird and wonderful assortment of friends as actors, while Jump had worked on putting together an edge and interesting soundtrack. *Voila!* Instant movie.

A small distributor had picked up her film, and from the first screen – like *The Blair Witch Project* before it – the buzz began. First there was a website, then two, then three. Within weeks there were twenty-one websites devoted to discussing her movie.

Cat could hardly believe it, she was beyond excited, until reluctantly she was thrust into the limelight. The media loved her. It helped that she was now nineteen, tall and agile, with short blond hair (natural), olive green eyes and a challenging face with fine cheekbones. She could have easily been a model or an actress, but neither profession interested her. She got her kicks being on the other side of the camera, the side where she was able to maintain a certain degree of control.

Merrill Zandack, head of Zandack Films, had taken over distribution of *Wild Child*, and now he was offering to finance her next project, a quirky film she'd written about a womanizing con-man, and a duplicitous female undercover cop, hence her visit to the Cannes Film Festival.

'Be nice to everyone, kitten,' he'd told her when she arrived. 'You're on the fast track.'

'*I'll* be nice if *you* stop calling me kitten,' she'd responded a tad irritably.

Merrill, a plump, bald man who spent most of his time sweating profusely while sucking on a large Cuban cigar, found Cat to be a refreshing presence. He admired the way she didn't kow-tow to anyone and he enjoyed her non-conformist attitude. Merrill had a gut instinct for talent, and if Cat kept her head and didn't piss off too many people, he knew she was destined to soar.

Shelby did the dance and she did it well. Linc did it better. Linc was an expert at making everyone feel they were his best friend. He had charm and then some. Shelby watched him as he flirted with a very svelte looking Sharon Stone. She got a kick out of watching him when he didn't know she was looking. He was *so* damn sexy.

'You're a beauty, sweetie,' Merrill Zandack puffed, lumbering up behind her. 'Can't wait to see your movie.'

'Thanks, Merrill,' she said, turning towards the powerful producer as he planted a sweaty kiss on her cheek, leaving an irritating wet spot that she was dying to wipe off.

'You an' me gotta work together,' Merrill continued,

blowing a stream of expensive cigar smoke directly into her face. 'I hear tell you're dynamite in tonight's flick.'

'Really?' she said, surreptitiously attempting to wipe her cheek dry with the back of her hand.

'I was supposed to give it a private screenin',' he wheezed. 'Only I never had time.'

'Sorry to hear that.'

'Naw. This way's better,' he said, puffing more cigar smoke in her face as he managed a not-so-discreet peek down her cleavage.

She took a step back and smiled politely at Merrill's date, a statuesque Angelica Huston clone. Since his wife had died several years ago Merrill had never been seen with the same woman twice. He appeared to favour a long line of interchangeable brunettes, women he never saw fit to introduce.

'Well . . . I do hope you enjoy it, Merrill,' Shelby said, once more glancing over at Linc, who was now in an intense conversation with Woody Allen. No rescue there.

'Ya look beautiful, sweetie,' Merrill repeated.

'Thanks,' she murmured, and to her relief, Merrill spotted Lola Sanchez making a much admired entrance, and immediately headed in her direction, his brunette date trailing regally behind him.

Shelby's appointed P.R., a young French woman with her hair worn in a tight bun, and a sulky, turned down mouth, hovered nearby. 'Do you wish to meet with the reporter from *Paris Match* now?' the woman asked.

Shelby shook her head, the last thing she wanted to do was speak with a journalist. 'Tomorrow, at the press conference,' she said softly.

The woman's thin lips tightened. 'He has to leave for Paris early in the morning. He will not be able to attend the press conference.'

A couple of years ago Shelby would've said yes to

anything. Two years of therapy and she'd learned to say no.

'If he's so anxious to speak with me,' she suggested, 'then perhaps he should stay over.'

Before the P.R. woman could reply, Linc reappeared and took her arm. 'C'mon, sweetheart,' he said warmly, winking at the P.R. woman. 'Let's go take our seats.'

Shelby nodded, her stomach fluttering. This was her big night and she was determined to enjoy it.

**POCKET
BOOKS**

LETHAL SEDUCTION

Jackie Collins

'Decadence, luxury and film-land plotlines make Collins
one of the bestselling authors of our time'
LA Times

Madison Castelli is back! The beautiful and street-smart
heroine of L.A. CONNECTIONS is having problems:
her ex-lover who walked out on her is trying to walk
back in; her new lover is giving her a hard time; and her
father turns out to be a man with deadly secrets.

Set between the high-powered world of New York and
the manic excitement of Las Vegas, here is a deliciously
uninhibited tale of cover-ups, deception and mob
involvement. Packed with intrigue, glamour and an
irresistible cast of characters, LETHAL SEDUCTION
will seduce you all the way…

'Jackie, we salute you!' *Cosmopolitan*

ISBN 0 7434 3003 4

PRICE £5.99

**POCKET
BOOKS**

HOLLYWOOD WIVES
The New Generation

Jackie Collins

**Power! Sex! Money! Fame! – the new Hollywood wives
are back with a vengeance.**

Ambitious, young, smart and lethal, whatever they
don't have, they want – and whatever these women
want, they get.

You will meet Lissa Roman, mega movie and singing
star, her wild daughter Nicci, Michael Scorsinni,
the handsome private investigator with an edge, and
Taylor Singer, a sometime actress married to
the Hollywood mogul.

Into their lives comes Eric Vernon, a dangerous
psychopath with kidnapping on his mind…

'Cancel all engagements, take the phone off the hook
and indulge yourself' *Daily Mirror*

ISBN 0 7434 0383 5

PRICE £6.99

POCKET BOOKS

Don't miss these books!

These books and other titles are available from your bookshop or can be ordered direct from the publisher.

☐ 0 7434 3003 4 **Lethal Seduction**   £5.99

☐ 0 7434 0383 5 **Hollywood Wives** – The New Generation £6.99

☐ 0 7434 0406 8 **Deadly Embrace**   £6.99

Please send cheque or postal order for the value of the book; free postage and packing within the UK; OVERSEAS including Republic of Ireland £1 per book.

OR: Please debit this amount from my:

VISA/ACCESS/MASTERCARD ....

CARD NO ....

EXPIRY DATE...

AMOUNT £ ....

NAME...

ADDRESS..

....

SIGNATURE...

www.simonsays.co.uk

Send orders to: SIMON & SCHUSTER CASH SALES
PO Box 29, Douglas, Isle of Man, IM99 1BQ
Tel: 01624 83600, Fax 01624 670923
www.bookpost.co.uk
Please allow 14 days for delivery.
Prices and availability subject to change without notice.